Published by ECW Press
665 Gerrard Street East
Toronto, Ontario, Canada, M4M 1Y2
416-694-3348 / info@ecwpress.com



Editor: Jen Hale
Paper texture © Kamyshko/Shutterstock
Honeycomb © sauletas/Shutterstock



LIBRARY AND ARCHIVES CANADA CATALOGUING IN PUBLICATION

Masson, Cynthea, 1965–, author
The Alchemists' Council / Cynthea Masson.

Issued in print and electronic formats.
ISBN 978-1-77041-271-2
also issued as: 978-1-77090-845-1 (pdf); 978-1-77090-846-8 (epub)

I. Title.

PS8626.A7993A43 2016 C813'.6
C2015-907283-2 C2015-907284-0

The publication of *The Alchemists' Council* has been generously supported by the Canada Council for the Arts, which last year invested $153 million to bring the arts to Canadians throughout the country, and by the Government of Canada through the Canada Book Fund. *Nous remercions le Conseil des arts du Canada de son soutien. L'an dernier, le Conseil a investi 153 millions de dollars pour mettre de l'art dans la vie des Canadiennes et des Canadiens de tout le pays. Ce livre est financé en partie par le gouvernement du Canada.* We also acknowledge the Ontario Arts Council (OAC), an agency of the Government of Ontario, which last year funded 1,709 individual artists and 1,078 organizations in 204 communities across Ontario, for a total of $52.1 million, and the contribution of the Government of Ontario through the Ontario Book Publishing Tax Credit and the Ontario Media Development Corporation.

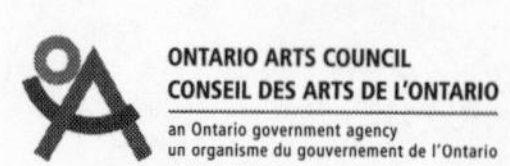

Canada Council for the Arts   Conseil des Arts du Canada   Canada

PRINTED AND BOUND IN CANADA   PRINTING: FRIESENS 5 4 3 2 1

# THE ALCHEMISTS' COUNCIL

CYNTHEA MASSON

For the Initiates

Jessica, Jayde, and Sarah.

And for Jen/Nikki,

whose conjunction brought

this book to the outside world.

The Alchemists' Council
forbids you to read this book.

## prima materia

Long ago — so very long ago that the truth of the matter now exists only as a primordial myth — the Lapis and the Flaw were co-equivalents known in their conjunction as the *Calculus Macula*. Quintessence — the fifth and most sublime element, the very breath of life and life everlasting — flowed between the two in a harmony of such congruence that everything, above and below, naturally maintained perfect elemental balance. The sapphire Lapis and the ruby Flaw entwined to illuminate in deepest amethyst the concurrence of all. No Council existed. No Council needed to exist. Everything simply and absolutely *existed* without intention. Without intention, conflict remained unknown.

But one day — so the story goes — a being named Aralia spontaneously gained intention and thought itself to be better than all other beings. Aralia stood beside the *Calculus Macula* and proclaimed possession thereof. In response to Aralia's new-found intention, another being — this one named Osmanthus — disagreed, claiming itself to be better than all other beings, including Aralia, and demanding possession of the *Calculus Macula* for itself. Thus individual intention bred conflict between one and the other, and the harmony among all beings began to dissolve. At first the Dissolution, as it became known, progressed slowly. But within what is now considered a mere fragment of time, the progress hastened. Before long, other beings, of their own volition, intentionally chose sides, and the Crystalline Wars began.

For the first several years of the Crystalline Wars, the *Calculus Macula* remained virtually unchanged. On rare occasion, a vigilant observer noticed a slight fluctuation — a movement of colours, a purple hue along the border between cobalt and crimson. These observations were initially dismissed — a trick of the light, many said. But one day, the truth could no longer be denied. On that day, the deep blue, which had until that point mutually co-existed with the blood-red in the *Calculus Macula*, spread itself to well over half the total area. Thereafter, even the most casual observer understood that victories by Aralia increased the blue of the *Calculus Macula*, whereas victories by Osmanthus increased the red. For many years thereafter the blue and the red increased or receded in accordance to the battles waged between Aralia and Osmanthus.

Angry and saddened by the slaughter, Aralia and Osmanthus finally agreed to end the Wars. They proclaimed a truce and arranged to divide the *Calculus Macula* equally between them. Though their decision was both admirable and honourable, their proclamation came too late. By the time a truce had been called, no one other than Aralia and Osmanthus was willing to relinquish being an individual with intention, to return to being unified as One.

Recognizing the chaos they had created, and realizing that the battle for supremacy would never cease among the beings of their world, Aralia and Osmanthus stood atop the *Calculus Macula* and embraced. This action was more than a mere symbolic gesture of their desired return to congruence. Having fought for years over the *Calculus Macula*, they had come to understand its power. Combining its influence over the elements with their pure intention for congruence, Aralia and Osmanthus conjoined as One.

The surge in elemental energy created by the First Conjunction was so extraordinarily powerful that the Prima Materia — the very world in which Aralia, Osmanthus, and all other beings existed — fractured into three dimensions, only two of which maintained access to the *Calculus Macula*. One of these two was claimed by the Aralians, the other by the Osmanthians. The third dimension ultimately and of necessity became the responsibility of whoever controlled the *Calculus Macula*. The beings of this third dimension, in their lack of proximity to the *Calculus Macula*, never again understood the truth of their existence.

From the end of the Crystalline Wars through the thousands of years leading to the current era of Eirenaeus, only those alchemists initiated to the Council ever become true masters of alchemy. For the uninitiated, alchemy remains shrouded — a mystery both arcane and exquisitely beautiful, visible yet hidden amidst the pages of ancient manuscripts, inscribed with meticulously inked calligraphy, illuminated with the vibrancy of gemstones and gold. Only the privileged few of the outside world lay hand to such manuscripts — scholars in pursuit of knowledge and unique theories — but even these few are so far removed from the truth of alchemy that not a single alchemist has ever taken an alchemical scholar seriously. One or two of the privileged may glimpse a fragment of truth if, for example, such a scholar were to observe *British Library MS Additional 5025* at precisely the right moment on the right day. But even then such a scholar would most likely attribute the apparent movement of the silver dragon to a fatigue-induced illusion rather than to ceremonial rites of the Alchemists' Council.

But for the Initiate, an alternative world awaits.

They walk among you, Initiate potentials, moving through life measured by successes and failures, by bus tickets and coffee cups and outdated technology. They walk among you until they are read, until the Council seeks and finds and interprets in its manuscripts one of the chosen few, until a member of the Council touches this one, stone to skin, with a Lapidarian pendant strung on a silver cord. Once touched, the Initiate is forever altered, and Council dimension thereafter unfolds. From the intricately carved turrets of the border walls to the resin-imbued trees of the Amber Garden, from the silver-inlaid floor of Council Chambers to the crimson velvet and mahogany chairs of the North Library, the Initiate takes preliminary steps along the well-trodden paths of the Elders.

From the youngest of the Initiates to the eldest of the Elders, *true* alchemists — those of the Alchemists' Council — have worked together through the centuries not, as is the common misperception, to produce the Philosopher's Stone. One cannot replicate *the* Stone. It has always already existed as the Lapis — the heart, the foundation, the divine manifestation responsible for the very fabric of Council dimension. Nor do true alchemists work to turn lead into gold. Though this feat of elemental transformation has long been misunderstood by outside practitioners as a foundational goal of alchemy, for the true alchemist such transmutation is mere child's play, an exercise readily mastered by each Initiate within a few months of arrival in Council dimension.

No, a true alchemist works to maintain elemental balance, without which the outside world would collapse, without which life as we know it — life as *you* know it — would transform from the quintessential gold of existence to the elemental lead of decay. A true alchemist is master of both word and icon, inscribing and interpreting alchemical manuscripts through the ages. A true alchemist is both mystic and chemist, both magician and scientist. A true alchemist has genetic and elemental encoding that enables interaction with Quintessence — the transcendent fifth element, the metaphorical soul of the Lapis. This Quintessence, this ineffable force, is the very substance of life itself — the essence that allows for all and nothing, for (as the mystics would say) the divine nothing that is all.

Initiates of the Alchemists' Council originate from all corners and cultures of the outside world; they speak with one another through *Musurgia Universalis*, the sacred language of the alchemists, the universal phonology intuited by all Initiates and facilitated by proximity to the Lapis. Once attuned to its rhythms, alchemists can communicate unhindered for extended periods even when — on official business or otherwise — they find themselves outside Council dimension. Thereafter, even the smallest fragment of — the tiniest drop of essence from — the Lapis enables communication not only among alchemists but also between alchemists and the people of the outside world, no matter their native tongues. Together the alchemists of the Alchemists' Council transmute Quintessence into life-enhancing Elixir and Lapidarian ink — an immeasurably powerful substance that, when used to inscribe *Musurgia Universalis* by an alchemist equipped with pen and Lapis-forged nib, can construct or deconstruct the elemental foundation — the eco-systems, the environment — of the outside world.

Unlike the outside world, Council dimension is made manifest, perfected, and maintained by the Lapis itself. This alchemically sustained dimension is primeval yet pristine. The grounds are vast and lush and tinged with blue mist at dawn, the gardens abundant with cerulean flora. The courtyard fountain flows with essence-laden waters of the deepest wells, trickling through copper channels amidst the stone buildings — from the main Council Chambers to the edge of the redwood forest. Murals, in ruby and emerald, in citrine and sapphire, as vivid today as a thousand years ago, span the walls of the ritual chambers. The Initiate classroom, with its rosewood desks and terracotta floor, elicits awe in even the most reluctant of students who cross its threshold. Classroom walls are shelved from floor to ceiling with alchemical vessels and powders and liquors and crystals ground finer than the most precious of salts, with parchments and pens and inks so potent that they can change the world in a single point bled from pen to parchment. Such inks, in the hands of the alchemists, manipulate all that is and all that will be.

The intricacies of Council dimension are visible only to those graced with the gift to see what is and what is not, to recognize both the ink and the page, to comprehend with and without words, to perceive beyond thought the message inscribed herein. Brush with your fingertips these letters extolled by the alchemists, and you will know with a certainty you have never before attained whether you are worthy to turn the page.

## ORDERS OF THE ALCHEMISTS' COUNCIL

AZOTH MAGEN (ONE) Guardian of the Council and Head of the Elder Council, the Magen rules supreme throughout Council dimension, proffers the gift of *projection*, of returning matured Quintessence to the Lapis through Final Ascension, of sacrificing life for life everlasting, of ushering in the dawn of each new Council.

AZOTHS (TWO) Guardians of the Lapis and members of the Elder Council, Azoths proffer the gift of *multiplication*, of nourishing the Lapis, of ensuring the continued purity and potency of Quintessence.

ROWANS (TWO) Uniters of Opposites and members of the Elder Council, Rowans proffer the gift of *conjunction*, of shepherding two bodies into one, and of sealing the promise of each new Initiate to the Council.

NOVILLIAN SCRIBES (FOUR) Interpreters of Providence, Distillers of Ink, and members of the Elder Council, Novillian Scribes proffer the gift of *dissolution*, of extracting Quintessential visions from the Lapis, of transforming the Lapis's essence into Lapidarian ink, of reviewing and revising the work of Lapidarian Scribes.

LAPIDARIAN SCRIBES (TWELVE) Masters of Inscription, Lapidarian Scribes proffer the gift of *calcination*, of inscribing Novillian visions onto parchment and into manuscripts, of preparing manuscripts for Novillian review and for interpretation by Readers through the generations.

READERS (TWENTY-EIGHT) Interpreters of Word and Image, Readers proffer the gift of *exultation*, of interpreting the text and icons on the page and, thereby, of advising the Elder Council on all matters affected by the manuscripts.

SENIOR MAGISTRATES (SIXTEEN) Professors of the Great Work, Senior Magistrates proffer the gift of *crystallization*, of transmitting their knowledge of the Great Work to the Junior Magistrates and Initiates.

**JUNIOR MAGISTRATES (TWENTY)** Graduates of the Great Work, Junior Magistrates proffer the gift of *rectification*, of maintaining purification, of ever increasing their knowledge of the Great Work, and transmitting their knowledge to all Initiates.

**SENIOR INITIATES (TWELVE)** Senior Apprentices of the Great Work, Senior Initiates proffer the gift of *purification*, of purifying the body to receive Quintessence, of continuing engagement with the Lessons of the Great Work.

**JUNIOR INITIATES (FOUR)** Junior Apprentices of the Great Work, Junior Initiates proffer the gift of *purgation*, of emptying the self, of releasing outside world influences, of initiating engagement with the Lessons of the Great Work.

Drink of this, the Elixir.
Read of this, the Word Eternal.
From the Lapis to the Scribe;
From the Scribe to the Reader.
Long live the Quintessence.
Long live the Alchemists' Council.

# Prologue
## five years ago

Dark trees and dark mountains. Dark clouds, waiting. She waited in an even darker place, against the flat rock of the cliff face, letting the wind shower her with drops of water pulled from the trees or sky. She would die today.

Amidst the ritual chanting of the Elder Council, she thought of her failures. She thought, in particular, of the one that had set her on a path she would not have otherwise imagined herself taking. She should have known better than to make such a mistake. But she had been selfish and believed it mattered — believed conjunction would be more meaningful with passion and attraction. Pride had decisively turned her away from Council protocol. And for what? Now she was alone and vulnerable to those who had witnessed her mistake. Now the one who came to her today, the one with whom she must finally conjoin, would be the one to know sacrifice. Two bodies conjoined in sacramental service to the Council. She needed to understand herself as such — as a means to an end. One body alone could no longer contain her ambitions. No attraction. No love. Conjunction in and of itself. Victory.

"Thus two shall be one," the Elders declared.

The chanting slowed, transformed momentarily into a cacophony of individual voices, and then progressed to the harmonious yet nearly inaudible intonation of the "Sol und Luna."

A figure emerged from the trees and moved past the Elders towards her. She turned, placed her palms against the cold rock face. She could feel warm breath against her neck. She could no longer hear the chanting. Then, sudden and harsh, she felt the other's essence inside her before her body had time to prepare. She gasped in struggle until the darkness of the cliff turned to the light of conjunction — sulphur and mercury, red and white. Her cry — one piercing note of anguish — rang through the forest as the ineffable presence of self rushed out, purified in its escape. She was no longer the one she had been. She was dead. She was life everlasting.

"I am Cedar, Novillian Scribe of the Alchemists' Council. I have carried my pendant three hundred and six years. On the final day of the Donum Dei of the 18th Council, I conjoined with Saule."

Cedar stood in Azothian Chambers in a private meeting with Azoth Magen Ailanthus. He looked down at her from the dais, the emeralds and rubies of its high back glittering above Ailanthus's head in the light of the kiln fire. Cedar had always admired this room, its low ceilings painted in silver and gold, creating an intimacy not found in the vaulted spaciousness of the main Council Chambers.

"What is your current mission?" Ailanthus asked.

"The recruitment of Jaden."

"Where does Jade reside?"

"Jad*en*. According to the Readers, the manuscripts indicate a variant pronunciation. As to her whereabouts, I have all the Readers attempting to narrow the field. A rather extensive lacuna on the fifth folio of the *Summum Bonum* has caused delay."

"And what is your plan to ensure success?"

"I thought perhaps you could help."

Ailanthus smiled — a response that surprised Cedar.

"You are rare, Cedar. Your status is well earned."

"Thank you."

He walked to her, bowed his head, and extended a hand, palm up — waiting.

"Why?"

"You question me?"

"An innocent question, Azoth Magen. Forgive me."

He needed to read her, she realized. And she had hesitated.

She withdrew the silver cord and pendant from beneath her robes, suddenly aware of the pendant's weight — metal and stone resting momentarily in her hand. He accepted it as if she had offered it willingly.

"You are bound to her, though you have not yet met."

"Yes, Azoth." She paused, focusing her thoughts. "Jaden may be the one."

"Jaden may be the one," he repeated calmly, moving Cedar's pendant from his palm to his forehead. "So you believe, and so we all must hope. But when you are as old as I am — when you have officiated at as many initiations as I have — little hope remains that the next Initiate will be *the one*."

"Then I will maintain that hope for you, Azoth."

Ailanthus smiled once again, lowering the pendant from his forehead. A few seconds passed before he returned it to her, his fingers momentarily brushing her palm. Here, in that brief exchange, in that rare moment of touch between Azoth Magen and Scribe, Cedar understood his intention in reading her. He needed to be certain that when the time was right, when the one for whom they had been waiting was ready, Cedar would graciously accept his decision to enact Final Ascension.

"Long live the Quintessence," he said, his ancient fingers trembling slightly as he held them in traditional steepled position — the first position of the sacred gesture of the Ab Uno.

"Long live the Alchemists' Council," she responded. Along with him, she folded her steepled fingers into two mirrored fists, holding the second position slightly longer than usual as she contemplated her hands poised in symbolic gesture of the Lapis.

The next day, Cedar woke before dawn, dressed quickly, and walked silently through the muted light of the hallways to the Scriptorium. By the time she arrived, four Lapidarian Scribes were already at work, presumably inscribing onto parchment the Novillian visions dictated by Obeche a few days earlier. One of them — Katsura — smiled, head slightly bowed, to acknowledge the arrival of a Novillian Scribe and then, unabashedly, held up a bottle of ink, shaking it slightly, indicating to Cedar that it was almost empty. Cedar nodded, wondering if Katsura could sense her annoyance at being hurried. She would replenish the ink as soon as possible; surely, as a Lapidarian Scribe, Katsura understood that Cedar could not begin her work before the first ray of sun entered the Scriptorium. She knelt on a blue velvet cushion beside the Lapis closest to the spot where, based on the astrological principles of Council dimension, the sun's light would first illuminate the Quintessence on this particular day. Her timing could not have been more perfect; the moment she had finished reciting the "Cauda Pavonis" — the ritual chant used to prime the Lapis for the scraping of its essence — a patch of light appeared precisely where Cedar had calculated. With a ruby-bladed knife, Cedar began to scrape the Lapis methodically, allowing the dust of its essence to fall into the small emerald bowl she held in her other hand. The Lapis itself controls the amount of dust it releases on any given day. Today Cedar had scraped for only two minutes before the Lapis would yield no further. She pressed her fingers into the temporary abrasion she had created, silently expressing her gratitude to the Lapis for its perpetual abundance. One of the Azoths would ensure the healing of the abrasion later that day.

Cedar walked to the desk where Katsura worked.

"What colour do you require?" she asked.

"Indigo," replied Katsura.

*Indigo*, thought Cedar. *What are the chances that today's dust will manifest indigo?*

She moved to the corner of the Scriptorium that housed a slate table and small fountain. Using one of the dedicated horsehair brushes and a glass funnel, she carefully moved the dust from the emerald bowl into an ink bottle. She then added channel water from the fountain and carefully stirred the mixture with a thin gold rod before corking the bottle. She held the newly minted mixture up to the light and awaited the revelation of its colour.

"Azure," she called out to Katsura. "Will azure do?"

"No," replied Katsura. "I will go check the storehouse for indigo."

"I will take the azure," said Ela.

Cedar passed the bottle to Ela on her way out of the Scriptorium. As she walked from the main Council building to her office, Cedar thought about Sadira. *Would she forgive me if she knew the truth of my conjunction with Saule? Can forgiveness ever displace betrayal?*

Cedar waited in a window bay of the Council Chambers. For now, she was alone, thankful that the other Council members were, she presumed, sleeping soundly in the residence across the courtyard. She dared herself to move from her window seat to the throne. Surely the Azoth Magen would not mind. Yet even in the knowledge that no one would discover or punish such an indiscretion, Cedar could not bring herself to break protocol. She remained seated, momentarily transfixed by the icons of Sol and Luna glistening above the throne in the light of the Dragon's Breath. The flames were so radiant that the murals of the *Mutus*

*Liber* on the north wall seemed to glow. Such was the custom on each of the three nights leading to a Meeting of Decision: *the Dragon's Breath will illumine both Sol and Luna for three and three, before and after, above and below*. And such was Cedar's custom to contemplate the icons and murals of the room on the night before any significant event, Meeting of Decision or otherwise. Contemplation encouraged her to clear her mind of all but necessity.

"Are you thinking of me?" he said.

"Ruis!"

"I startled you."

"I was—"

"Contemplating the icons. Just like before your conjunction. Perhaps it's true, what they say — only your colour has changed," he said.

"Do not joke, Ruis. I cannot bear it. Not tonight."

He moved towards her.

"Cedar, you have nothing to fear. I predict this particular Meeting of Decision will result in the preservation of the status quo. The bees will remain safely ensconced in the apiary."

"*That* is what I fear! We do not agree on this matter, Ruis. If Council decides not to release the bees — *all* the bees — the outside world could fail beyond measure."

"And if Council were to release all the bees, Council dimension could fail beyond measure. And where would that leave either dimension in years to come? Besides, we are at least a decade away from imminent crisis in the outside world."

"A decade away! Ruis! The Council should have worked to resolve the crisis permanently decades ago. Too much independence has been given to the people of the outside world. Ever since the Vulknut Eclipse—"

"Not the Vulknut Eclipse again, Cedar! Enough! As you well know, if not for Rebel Branch interference, we would all — alchemists, rebels, and people alike — be living happily ever after right now, free eternally from Meetings of Decision!"

Cedar stopped arguing. She knew better than to try to convince Ruis that making a bad decision was better than having no decision to make at all. With that realization, she was grateful she at least still maintained the ability to choose.

"All this talk of bees," said Ruis, taking advantage of Cedar's silence. "Remember our days in the lavender fields of the apiary?" He stepped closer and reached for her pendant, holding it gently in his right hand. She could feel the Elixir respond.

"Ruis. Don't."

"Come back to my room with me."

"No. Not tonight." Cedar moved away from him, towards the main entrance, and adjusted her hair under the hood of her robes.

"Nothing has changed."

"Everything has changed," she replied.

"'I think it mercy, if thou wilt forget.'"

She shook her head and smiled.

"'Death,'" she quoted, for this was the literary game they had played long ago when they had fallen in love, "'thou shalt die!'"

"That's the plan," he said. He turned and walked slowly out of the room.

## I

## cũrrent day

"The bees are disappearing."

"Protocol, Cedar. I am Azoth," replied Ruis.

He looked down at her from his position on the library platform. He held a manuscript against his chest. Several others lay open on the desk below. The light from the east window shone on the illuminations.

"Even the Azoth Magen permits me to call him Ailanthus," she responded.

"But you don't," he reminded her. He walked down the steps from the platform and stood beside her. "You never know who might be listening — an impressionable Initiate might well be seated within hearing distance." He paused briefly before quietly adding, "Besides, as you well know, Scribe Cedar, you and I no longer share the level of intimacy we once did."

"Forgive me, your Eminence." She waited until he had taken his seat at the desk and nodded his permission for her to speak. "Azoth Ruis," she began, "Junior Magistrate Linden has reported that the bees are disappearing."

"If this news is leading to another request to release more Lapidarian bees into the outside world, the answer is *no*. The bees must be left to mature as scheduled prior to discharge. Contrary to rebellious sentiments, Cedar, the Council is not responsible for the earth's destruction. Our very doctrine ensures its preservation. And we will do so *on schedule* as Council protocols dictate."

"Not those bees, your Eminence. Though the Council should—"

"The Council *should* . . . ?"

"Apologies, Azoth. I do not mean to suggest . . ." Cedar paused here, reading Ruis's expression. Though she did question Council's more recent decisions regarding elemental dissolution and preservation, now was not the time to broach the matter. "Azoth, I refer to the bees of certain Lapidarian manuscripts, not to the bees of the apiary or of the outside world — though, of course, the manuscript anomalies may well lead to unforeseeable effects."

"The point, Cedar."

"Yes, Azoth. During his current assignment, Linden was conducting manuscript transcription in the library of the Vienna protectorate when he witnessed bees disappearing from an illumination."

"Which manuscript?"

"*Ruach 2103*, folio 51 verso. He was transcribing the icons to use in a Senior Initiate lesson. He counted five bees amidst the roses — suddenly he saw them vibrating and then three disappeared. Then, only minutes later, he witnessed the same phenomenon in *Viridarium Chymicum 3204*, folio 43 recto."

"What are you suggesting, Cedar — that they flew away?"

"I do not know, your Eminence."

"Perhaps Linden was fatigued. Perhaps his Elixir fluctuated. Perhaps the Senior Initiates are up to their pranks again."

"Linden was observing the bees, and they vanished." Cedar waited for Ruis to reply, but he moved his attention to one of the manuscripts before him. "Azoth, Linden believes this is a sign. He requests Council intervention."

"A sign of what?" He stood up, turned, and walked to a manuscript cabinet set into an alcove behind the desk.

"Should this determination not be left to the Elders?" asked Cedar.

"A sign of what, according to Linden? Surely manuscript speculation is not beyond the skills of a Junior Magistrate."

Cedar waited until Ruis had taken his seat once

again. The dark green velvet of his robes made him appear even paler than usual.

"A sign, according to Linden, of the Rebel Branch. A sign of an impending rebellion. A sign of an attempt to disrupt elemental balance and increase negative space."

Ruis sighed. "I hardly think the Rebel Branch would trouble itself with removing bees from manuscripts — unless, of course, its members are hoping to distract the lesser Magistrates from appropriate Council business."

"With all due respect, Azoth, bees do not simply disappear without reason. Aside from the potential of rebel involvement, this situation requires investigation."

"Very well, Cedar. Investigate. First, rule out Initiate pranks; then, bring me additional evidence. Find out if more manuscripts have been affected."

"Yes, Azoth," Cedar replied. "However, if the bees have already disappeared, finding evidence will be difficult. The cross-referencing alone could take years."

"Then I suggest you begin immediately."

"Is later tonight immediate enough? Linden is due to return to Council dimension by sundown. Or would you prefer I join him for lunch in the Vienna protectorate?"

"Perhaps you should consider where you might gather the sweetest honey." Ruis smirked, retrieved one of the smaller manuscripts from the desk, and left the room.

Cedar did not follow. Instead, she walked to a window on the library's west wall and peered out into the main courtyard. Sadira sat near the fountain where she was writing in a small notebook. Her long golden hair shimmered in the light. She appeared as beautiful and serene today as she had all those years ago when Cedar was first drawn to her. She glanced up and noticed Cedar at the window. Cedar nodded, held up her pendant briefly, and then retreated from the window into the depths of the library's myriad stacks of manuscripts. Though her choice might have appeared random and sudden to an outside observer, Cedar knew precisely which manuscript to remove from precisely which shelf. Thus, with one to be compared with others, her work began.

Cedar sat in the lower levels of the Council archives reading through yellowed but well-preserved notes she herself had taken years ago as part of a Senior Initiate assignment.

*Sursum Deorsum* 5055, folio 63 verso

*Under the two attached vessels is another such vessel diagram accompanied by Latin text describing the Rebis. Near the bottom of first panel is a dragon with its head tilted back; lunar images fill its mouth — three crescents in three colours — with a sun, shining beams of three colours both inside and expanding beyond the sun itself, in the centre of which is the following image —*

Following several obscurely worded and poorly scripted sentences, Cedar had depicted what she now assumed to be a barely recognizable replica of the original image: three conjoined circles surrounding a bee. Serendipitous, she thought, that a nearly forgotten task performed on her road out of the Initiate towards the Magistrate would prove useful now. She opened the original manuscript, attained earlier from the library, to folio 63 and examined the pristine Lapidarian illumination thereon. Her own ancient description proved both accurate and useful: the three conjoined circles within the manuscript no longer housed a bee. Could these lacunae indeed be rebel activity of which she remained unaware? Perhaps she should not have spoken to Ruis before seeking answers for herself. Doing so may have been imprudent, all circumstances considered. On the other hand, *not* doing so may have been equally imprudent. Regardless, with additional evidence now in her hands, she would undoubtedly need to convene the Elders.

In the meantime, she would need to leave Council dimension to investigate in the outside world as soon as possible, with or without the Azoth's approval. Novillian status afforded her some license. Leaving Council dimension without giving notice or receiving permission was a privilege in which she had indulged since becoming an Elder; she could come and go as she pleased, whether or not engaged in official Council business. Another trip to Vienna, regardless of her stated intention, could prove useful.

Amur walked into the room, stopped in front of the first cabinet, and motioned to Cedar. She returned the archival material to its case, replaced the case on the shelf, collected her current notes, and followed Amur into the hall.

"We have a meeting," he said.

"I have nothing to report."

"Nothing to create. Nothing to destroy. All to transform," he reminded her.

"I prefer the version without the sentence fragments," Cedar responded and walked towards the stairs.

"Meet me in the Scriptorium at six," he said and walked the other way.

Cedar could see it if she gazed to the left, as the angle of light fell onto the Lapis from the northwest window of the Scriptorium just before dusk: the Flaw in the Stone, the fleck of absence within alchemical perfection that prevented absolute, permanent union. Yet they all yearned — or professed to yearn — to be united forever as One in the ultimate Final Ascension. Official records of the 17th

Council indicate the achievement of such perfection for a period of three days during the Vulknut Eclipse. If not for the Rebel Branch, the Lapis would have remained perfected until this very day. But the rebels had successfully wounded its core once again, an ultimate act of treason during the Third Rebellion. Ruis's desire, as Azoth of the 18th Council, was to re-establish perfection of the Lapis. "One day, when you have ascended to Azoth yourself, we will work on this task together," he had all but decreed to her. Of course, his assertion assumed not only that she aspired to Azoth but also that she desired to help him, two assumptions that were contrary to her current will. Surviving conjunction had been challenging enough to her ethics. As for Ruis, she had loved him once, had welcomed his power, but had more recently observed his abuses.

"It's time," Amur said. He was standing in the southern archway, oblivious to the part he would play in Cedar's plan. She glanced at him with affection. He did not deserve to be the sacrificial lamb. Still, when the time came, she would bear no guilt or remorse.

"I'll follow you," she replied, holding her pendant against the Lapis to enjoy a momentary surge of Quintessence before joining him.

"It's your fault, you know," Amur whispered as they walked towards Council Chambers.

"My fault?"

"The agenda has been lengthened yet again — an item about bees."

"So, his Eminence has taken me seriously after all."

"It would be best not to let Azoth Ruis hear the sarcasm."

"The wise Amur."

Knowing that Amur had long harboured an attraction to her that could prove useful to her someday, Cedar brushed against his back as she moved past him and into her Council seat.

Jaden, from her hard wooden seat in the Initiate sector, watched Cedar and Amur enter Council Chambers and assume their positions on the ornate chairs among the other Novillian Scribes. She expected Amur's conjunction would be on the agenda. *Perhaps he will be the one*, someone would say. *Perhaps he will enact* sine macula. *Perhaps he will remove the Flaw from the Stone.* Perhaps. But Jaden did not care about conjunctive outcome as much as she cared about conjunctive partnership. A rumour had reached the Junior Initiates this week that Senior Magistrate Sadira had been selected as Amur's partner. To Jaden, Amur's fate was of little consequence; Sadira's was not. Sadira was the only Magistrate whose classes Jaden could tolerate. What if she conjoined with Amur and they kept *his* position in the Order? What if Sadira's days as a Magistrate were hurtling towards their end?

Though she had disliked having to sit through this morning's classes with Magistrate Tesu as tutor, Jaden was pleased Sadira had left Council dimension on assignment for the day. Surely an official announcement of her conjunction could not be made in her absence. At this very moment, Sadira was enjoying the freedom of the outside world — in London or Paris or New York or wherever she had been sent to meet the new Initiate. Perhaps she was sitting in a café, sipping espresso, contemplating how best to approach the Initiate. These imagined scenarios proved a far more satisfying pastime than official Council business and its interminable deliberations. Apparently bees were on today's agenda. The previous time bees were an agenda item a lengthy debate ensued; more than two hours later, the dilemma had remained unresolved. *To release or not to release?* Jaden cared little about the question. If they all disappeared, she thought cynically, the debates would be moot.

Jaden thought back to her first meeting with Cedar, over a year ago now at the café in the Vancouver Art Gallery. She had just finished her coffee and was preparing to leave for an exhibit when a tall imposing woman with brilliant blue eyes and long dark hair — similar in colour and texture to Jaden's own — approached her table and asked if she could sit down. Jaden initially thought the woman simply wanted the only remaining available seat in the crowded café, but that possibility was swiftly replaced by her theory that she was a cult member in search of a new recruit. This wasn't too far from the truth, Jaden had gradually come to realize after the excitement of being initiated had vanished and her lack of freedom had been firmly established.

Only a few moments into their pleasantries at the café, the woman had announced, with a formality that implied importance, "I am Cedar, Novillian Scribe of the Alchemists' Council, and I am here to escort you to Council dimension."

Jaden made a move to depart, but Cedar reached out and touched her hand.

"How long have you had that scar?"

Jaden did not respond.

From beneath multiple layers of fabric — scarf, coat, sweater — Cedar pulled out a pendant on a long silver cord and held it against Jaden's hand. Moments later, the scar Jaden had had for many years disappeared.

"It makes no sense right now, but it will soon," Cedar assured her. "The manuscripts have foretold your existence. According to the Nazhin Prophecies — sacred manuscripts inscribed by ancient alchemists — you are Jaden."

"What? No. My name is—"

"You are Jaden, Junior Initiate of the Alchemists' Council. The Scribes have named you. The Readers have read you. The Word of the Book is the Word Eternal."

And thus it had begun. Her life as she had known

it — as she had envisaged it progressing before she was Jaden — ended. For much of her first year with the Council, despite her admiration for the dimension's exquisite beauty, with its ancient architecture and lush gardens and abundance of decorative gemstones, she had felt like a prisoner. Even though both the alchemically induced vapours — meant to ease Initiate transition to Council dimension — and the passing of time ensured she no longer missed people the way she had when she first arrived, she still occasionally wondered whether or not anyone in the outside world continued to look for her. Of course, like all Initiates, she did not have much, if any, family to mourn her loss. Her parents had died five years ago — drowned in a boating accident that Jaden preferred not to bring to mind — and she had no siblings. She had never been close with her extended family. In that sense, she had been a perfect candidate for forced relocation. But she had enjoyed her two years in Vancouver, and she had especially enjoyed the friends she made at university. So she remained unconvinced that the promise of eternal life was worth the sacrifice of everything and everyone she had known.

Yes, as an alchemist, she now had privileges she could never have imagined in the outside world, but here in Council dimension she remained a lowly Initiate. Her questions to the Elders — especially those inquiries regarding the Council practice of virtually kidnapping Initiates from the outside world — were typically met with reference to the manuscripts as "the Word Eternal." *From the Lapis to the Scribe; from the Scribe to the Reader*, Cedar would recite, thus bringing a temporary end to Jaden's questioning.

Now Jaden longed to revise the manuscripts, to change the eternal words — to edit them, improve them where necessary. Years from now, when she had ascended to Scribal status and thus attained Scribal power, she would amend the manuscripts. She would inscribe her own destiny regarding ascension and conjunction. Cedar had told her on numerous occasions that by the time Jaden became a Lapidarian Scribe, she would have learned, instinctively, to honour the manuscripts and the Law Code proscriptions against self-interested amendments. But Jaden doubted Cedar's conviction on this particular point. Someday she would control her own destiny, regardless of any Law Codes dictating otherwise.

For now, Jaden could only hope Sadira would return with an acceptable candidate as the fourth of the Junior Initiate quarto. Jaden barely tolerated Laurel and Cercis. They were obnoxious and intelligent. Even worse, they were beautiful — almost eerily so with their matching pale complexions and shiny, spiky auburn hair. If she did not know better, Jaden would have assumed they were siblings rather than lovers. Whenever possible and with little discretion, Laurel and Cercis flirted with one another during tutorial lessons, even composing what Jaden believed to be the occasional love poem — or so Laurel had claimed on the day Jaden discovered her inscribing practice parchment with an unrecognizable alphabet. Their flirting drove Jaden to retreat even further into her escape plans or, on a good day, into the text under discussion. Every now and then during joint sessions, when the presence of twelve additional students from the Senior Initiate afforded Laurel and Cercis space to ignore the lesson temporarily, one or the other suddenly would be selected by an observant tutor to answer a question. In such circumstances, in the silence that followed the question, Jaden would volunteer an answer and win praise from the Magistrate. Such a rare occurrence was especially welcomed when Sadira was the lesson's tutor.

"Have you seen Laurel?" Cercis asked, taking the seat beside Jaden. He removed a notebook and pen from his satchel.

"Have you secretarial aspirations?"

"Very funny, Jaden. You may not care to excel, but I aspire to a seat among the Elders. Initiate exams commence in less than two months."

"We're bound to the Council for eternity. I can begin to aspire next year."

"We're not *bound*. And eternity is by no means assured."

She looked away, feigning a search for Laurel. "Is that her?"

"Where?" Cercis looked at the person to whom

Jaden pointed. "No. That's Rowan Kai. Honestly, Jaden, if you can't tell a Rowan from a Junior Initiate by this point you're clearly en route to being held back from ascension for decades! I plan to ascend in the next rotation."

"The next rotation?"

"Even you must have heard the rumours about Amur and Sadira. Their conjunction, assuming Amur is victorious, will open a Senior Magistrate position vacated by Sadira, which will be filled by a Junior Magistrate, which will be filled by a Senior Initiate, which will be filled by me."

"I'm surprised you take notice of rumours."

"My source is trustworthy," he replied, ignoring her sarcasm. He scanned the room once again for Laurel.

"Even if the rumours are true, no one can predict who will be victorious."

"True, but either way, a place in the Orders of Council will be vacated, and a place in the Senior Initiate will need to be filled."

"Unless the conjunction fails."

"Do you always dwell on the negative?"

"Unlike the rumours, the *fact* is failure can occur."

"If you are referring to Cedar and Ruis, their conjunction was the first to fail in hundreds of years. And it failed because they were in love."

"Perhaps Amur and Sadira are in love."

"Right. Amur and Sadira are in love," he responded sarcastically. "Don't be naïve."

"You're naïve if you think alliances can't shift after hundreds of years living with the same people. Just wait. Several decades from now, you may be seeking some handsome young man instead of Laurel."

He glared but then responded calmly. "Perhaps. But Laurel and I will have conjoined by then, so I wouldn't be looking for her anyhow."

"Conjoined? So you don't love her then? Or you *won't* love her by then?"

"You need to learn your Council history, Jaden. In rare circumstances, it is indeed possible for a couple to conjoin out of love. Such a conjunction occurred during the 17th Council with Ilex and Melia."

"So, you and Laurel are planning to be the Ilex and Melia of the 18th Council?"

"Or 19th or 20th. I'd want to wait until Laurel had caught up with my status. That might take a while."

For the first time since she had met her, Jaden felt sympathy for Laurel.

"You'll lose her," she said to Cercis.

"No. We'll conjoin, as one, forever after."

"No. You'll lose her."

"No, Jaden. We will conjoin. And together we will ascend to Azoth."

"Good luck with that, your Eminence."

Jaden turned away from Cercis and towards Azoths Ruis and Ravenea, who were about to call the meeting to order.

Sadira sat on a bench in the park near the Blue Mosque of Tabriz. She glanced at her watch, adjusted her scarf, tucked back a wayward section of hair, and then glanced at her watch again. According to *Razhi 8621*, folio 45 recto, the next Initiate would stop at this bench in approximately eight minutes. Specifically, according to the Nazhin Prophecies, she awaited Arjan. Arjan, of course, not yet knowing that he was Arjan, did not know that Sadira expected him. Perhaps he was at prayer or chatting with a friend or reading a newspaper or doing any number of things one could do within eight minutes travel of this bench. As she had anticipated, Sadira was the most anxious in these ten minutes or so leading up to the crossing point. What if the Initiate refused to listen or, if he listened, refused to return with her to Council dimension? What if an ancient Scribe had misrepresented the prophecy? What if a current Reader had misinterpreted the text? Or what if the Rebel Branch, in an act of heresy years ago, had inscribed an undetectable palimpsest? Such occurrences, though rare, must befall even a skilled Senior Magistrate on occasion. She should have asked Wu Tong to accompany her — or, better yet, one of the Scribes. Readers and Scribes had far more experience recognizing Initiates both in text and in life than did Magistrates. But the decision of the Readers, once confirmed by the Elders, must be accepted; they had read and interpreted the text and illuminations inscribed by the ancients and had chosen her — Sadira, a Senior Magistrate — to meet the new Initiate in this place at this time. If they were correct, if he appeared in the predicted place at the predicted time, if he agreed to accompany her to Council dimension, she would be forever linked with him on the alchemical tree. He would be hers to teach and to protect. And, in that sense, he could well be just what she needed — a distraction from Cedar's demands and the impending conjunction.

Sadira thought about Council dimension. Ruis and Ravenea would have called the meeting to order by now. Would Sadira herself be a matter for discussion? She had been careful to express no interest beyond duty to the cause over the intended conjunction with Amur. She certainly did not, as a less modest Magistrate might, exude undue pride in being paired with a Novillian Scribe. If anything, that particular aspect of the situation frightened her — Amur's essence could well be stronger than hers, despite the precautions she had taken at Cedar's insistance. Although official doctrine emphasized that Council status did not affect the outcome of conjunctive pairings, Council history suggested otherwise. Of all the conjunctions Sadira had witnessed in her two centuries as an alchemist, the majority confirmed her suspicions that mature essence exerts dominance. Of course, depending on the outcome, she may never discover the truth.

She glanced at her watch again. Only one minute remained, and no one in the park appeared to be moving towards her. Though an uncommon occurence, it was possible that the Readers had indeed misinterpreted the texts. Sadira stood to improve her sightlines. A small group of women were chatting under a tree to her left, and an older man stood looking at a map just beyond the statue. She walked in the direction of the man, satisfying her assumption that no one was waiting out of sight behind the statue. When she turned back to face the bench, she flinched. Arjan — or so she presumed — sat precisely where she had been sitting only moments earlier. Where had he been? Why had she not seen him?

He wore a long black jacket — of obvious and exquisite quality — and a bright red scarf. He held a leather-bound book, opened, in his left hand and a pen in his right. The pen was poised above the book as if he were about to edit or highlight a passage. Or perhaps the book was a journal and he was about to record the particulars of his day thus far. Perhaps he was a Scribe in the making. She moved towards him, pendant in hand.

"You are Arjan," she stated, extending her pendant on its silver cord to touch Lapis to skin.

"Yes."

She paused. Had she heard him correctly?

"Yes, I am Arjan," he said.

"You know who you are?"

He laughed. "Do you know who you are?"

She paused again. Of the various scenarios she had envisioned in the days and hours leading up to the meeting, this was not one of them.

"I am Sadira, Senior Magistrate of the Alchemists' Council. I am here to escort you to Council dimension."

"I am pleased to meet you, Magistrate Sadira."

She assessed him silently for a moment before asking the most obvious of questions: "How did you know you were Arjan before you were told?"

"I heard the name as a child. Many years later, I came across it in an alchemical manuscript featuring the most exquisite illuminations of trees. I knew that day, reading of the elemental qualities of *Terminalia arjuna*, that I was to be Arjan."

She tilted her head slightly as if hoping for a better angle to view and thus comprehend this strange young man. Never had Sadira heard of an Initiate discovering his own name in a manuscript.

"How are you able to read alchemical manuscripts?"

"My grandparents introduced me to alchemy when I was very young. I have studied for many years, helping them with their alchemical experiments."

"You and your grandparents have studied the alchemy of the outside world. You will find that true alchemy — the alchemy of Council dimension — requires centuries to master."

Arjan shrugged. "Perhaps I will prove myself a prodigy."

If not for his amiable smile, which suggested his comment was offered in jest, Sadira would have balked at his arrogance.

Arjan closed his book, put it and the pen inside a satchel, adjusted his scarf across his neck and over his shoulders, and stood up. "Shall we go?" he asked.

"Do you want to say goodbye? You may not be back for a while." She gestured towards the mosque behind them and then out towards the city.

"I have said my goodbyes."

She looked at him.

"Well then. Let's go. A temporary portal has been opened nearby," she explained, pointing to the statue.

Moments later, standing beside the statue, Sadira took Arjan's hand, clasped her pendant, and recited the key. The women chatting under the tree in the park adjusted their scarves against the breeze, and the man with the map continued his slow pace along the path, undisturbed.

Sadira found Cedar sitting alone at a table in the lower archives. A few manuscripts were opened in front of her. Several others lay closed and stacked on a nearby bench. The reading lights available throughout the room had been extinguished in favour of a single

Lapidarian candle. Cedar held a magnifying glass to a section of an illumination in one of the manuscripts. She did not appear to notice Sadira until she was standing directly beside the table.

"I've returned with the new Initiate."

"Uneventful?" Cedar asked.

"Interesting, to say the least."

"I'm intrigued," she motioned for Sadira to sit in the chair on the other side of the table.

"He knew his name before my arrival. He claims to have read it in a manuscript."

Cedar sat up, eyes widened.

"I couldn't believe it either. I'm still not sure if I do. I mean, I'm not sure if I believe the *truth* of it. I suspect Azothian interference. Perhaps this is yet another attempt by Ruis to unnerve me, just when I thought he had abandoned his mission."

"Ruis may have paid our young Initiate a preemptive visit to ensure Azothian first contact. Under different circumstances, I certainly would not put such a covert move past him. But in this particular case, I have my doubts. If Ruis intends to drive us apart, providing you with a reason to confide in me would do nothing other than defeat his objective."

"True enough," replied Sadira. She reached out her hand to Cedar. "I've missed you."

Cedar lingered in the touch momentarily before moving her hand away.

"Tell me more about the new Initiate."

"He's handsome — beautiful even — and extraordinarily well spoken. His hair is long and dark with a slight wave. He looks good in red."

"Should I be jealous?"

"Alas," she said in mock disappointment, "he is far too young for me. At least for now."

"Continue."

"He was completely content to leave the outside world — no resistance or regrets. He liked his residence chambers. He said he is most looking forward to beginning classes tomorrow. More specifically, he eagerly anticipates continuing his study of alchemy, which he proudly admits to having begun several years ago. And after inquiring about the inherent powers of my pendant, he asked when he'll be able to earn his own."

"Was he sorely disappointed with the answer?"

"Indeed."

"Other than knowing his name, did he do or say anything that would lead you to suspect he had been contacted prior to today — whether by an Azoth or otherwise?"

"Otherwise?"

"Did he do or say anything that would lead you to suspect rebel involvement?"

"Rebel involvement?"

"Stop echoing me, Sadira. In light of the manuscript lacunae, I am obligated to ask."

"Well, given the sorts of questions he asked me

throughout the day, he does appear to know quite a bit of alchemical terminology, apparently gleaned from the outside world."

"One would not necessarily require Azothian or rebel instruction to attain basic knowledge of alchemical terms. Thanks to certain libraries housing certain manuscripts, the outside world does offer up a diluted — albeit perplexing — version of alchemical principles. Still, you should take your observations — especially regarding his apparent foreknowledge — to Azothian Chambers. I suggest you first approach Ravenea rather than Ruis."

"And what about tonight? Shall I visit your chambers?"

Cedar smiled. "No. I have work. As Ruis so ardently reiterated at today's Council session, he requires additional proof before he will take Linden's disappearing bees seriously." She looked down at the open manuscript. "I thought I saw a trace of one amidst the flowers here, but even by candlelight I cannot be certain. Ironic, I think — to be searching for bees in the light of a candle made from Lapidarian beeswax." She reached for a light switch, turned it on, and blew out the candle.

Sadira closed her eyes against the sudden brightness.

"Take this," Cedar said, holding out a tiny brown packet to Sadira. Sadira knew better than to ask Cedar where she had procured the Sephrim. She had done so on a few occasions, only to be told not to concern herself with the details, that it was safer for her not to know. But such reassurances only increased Sadira's concern. She could not help but worry about Cedar's source of procurement — who was, for all intents and purposes, a drug dealer. Where would Cedar meet such a disreputable character? Did she go to the source or did the source come to her? Surely such an illicit meeting would not take place in Council dimension itself.

"Stop worrying, Sadira. All will be well."

"Yes. All will be well," Sadira responded, not wanting to start an unwinnable debate.

Cedar reached for another manuscript.

"Goodnight Sadira."

Frustrated with Cedar, Sadira shook her head slowly, stood, and moved towards the door. Before leaving the room, she turned back to face Cedar and said, "By the way, Amur was looking for you. Shall I send him to you?"

Cedar glared in feigned annoyance and then returned her attention to the manuscripts.

The next day, after Arjan attended the orientation session with the Elders, Sadira escorted him into a Junior Initiate class already in progress. When they arrived, unheard, at the back of the classroom, Linden was at the board drawing a stick-figure version of the Rebis — defining it as he progressed as "the iconographic union of male and female principles conjoined as one body, often referred to as the alchemical hermaphrodite." Jaden was doodling a rather more graphically explicit version of the same concept in her notebook. Cercis was composing an encoded poem for Laurel. And Laurel was gazing out the window at a bloom in the magnolia tree. When Sadira spoke, she startled everyone.

"Linden, Cercis, Laurel, and Jaden — I introduce to you Junior Initiate Arjan."

Arjan smiled and bowed his head slightly in Linden's direction. He was dressed in robes of dark amethyst — so dark they seemed black, the purple sheen revealed only when he moved. He wore a long silver chain around his neck, which Jaden assumed, out of habit, was a pendant cord. But as he approached her to take a seat at the table, Jaden saw that the chain was merely decorative, a piece of jewellery brought to Council dimension from the outside world. Of course it would be, she realized, almost reprimanding herself for the error. Arjan would have received neither Elixir nor pendant yet, and thus would have no need for a pendant cord. He was only a Junior Initiate, most likely in his early twenties. Like the others of his cohort, he would not receive a pendant or cord until he had reached Senior Initiate status. Still, the chain was beautiful — thick and braided of four or five separate strands of silver with a level of intricacy absent in even the most elaborate pendant cord.

"Do you like it?" Arjan asked her, holding the chain away from his robes and towards her.

"Yes. I've never seen anything like it."

"It's very old — a gift of inheritance from my grandfather."

"Will it hold your pendant?" she asked him.

"If all goes well," he replied.

"When you—" she began, but Linden drew their attention back to the board, and the lesson continued.

"Welcome, Arjan. You have joined us amidst a fourth-level lesson of Rebisian theory. I have been informed that you have studied alchemy in the outside world. What are your thoughts on conjunction? Do you know of the Rebis?"

"I have no thoughts on the matter, Magistrate."

"No worries, Arjan. I will ask you again next day. By then you will have had time to read chapter six of *Elemental Theory*." He held up a textbook to emphasize his point.

"I apologize, Magistrate, for my poorly executed pun."

"Your pun?"

"My understanding is that conjunction requires no thought. Thus, when you asked for my thoughts on the matter, I said I had none."

Cercis laughed aloud.

Linden glanced momentarily at Cercis and then returned his attention to Arjan. "I see," said Linden. "Well, then, it is I who must apologize. Far be it from me to stand in the way of a well-placed turn of phrase."

Arjan smiled and, as he had done earlier, bowed his head slightly towards Linden. Only this time, Jaden was not sure if the gesture was one of respect or condescension. Linden turned to jot a few terms on the board and then proceeded with his lecture on the Rebis. Jaden shifted her attention between Linden and each of her classmates. While watching Linden and feigning interest in Rebisian theory, she thought she detected a slight blush of discomfort in him. While watching Arjan, in sidelong glances and with polite smiles, she detected nothing beyond keenly focused attention of the sort expected of a new Initiate. Arjan appeared to be taking meticulous notes, writing at a speed that surpassed even Laurel at her most focused. Cercis sat back in his chair, arms crossed, ignoring Linden entirely and watching Arjan with no effort to disguise his scrutiny. Laurel, having slipped a note to Cercis when Linden had turned away, became more visibly agitated with each passing minute that Cercis ignored both the note and her.

And Jaden, for the first time since her arrival in Council dimension, completely forgot her desire to flee from a lesson taught by Linden.

When she entered the Great Hall that evening for dinner, Jaden purposely walked past her generally preferred place at the small table near the south entrance and made her way to the large central table occupied by her fellow Initiates. If Cercis or Laurel were surprised by this decision, neither of them gave Jaden more than a passing glance before returning their focus to Arjan. Arjan, on the other hand, stood to greet Jaden and motioned to the seat next to his.

"Good evening," he said.

Jaden smiled and nodded. "What's on tonight's menu?"

"Curried halibut stew," replied Cercis. "I'll get some for you." Cercis stood up and headed towards the end of the table where a large serving bowl rested. Jaden would have questioned Cercis's new-found courteousness if not for Arjan. She did not want Arjan to think her ungracious this early in his Council experience.

"It's quite delicious," Arjan said.

"It should be," said Laurel. "Most of the cooks have well over a hundred years of practice. They're hired from the outside world and paid with Lapidarian honey."

"Lapidarian honey?"

"Honey made by the Lapidarian bees in the apiary. Its effect on non-alchemists is similar to the effect of the Elixir on alchemists."

"So in return for their services, the cooks receive good health and extended life?"

"The cooks, the groundskeepers, the librarians, the stonemasons, the artisans — everyone you see in Council dimension who is not a member of the Alchemists' Council," explained Laurel. "They are approached in the outside world, chosen specifically because they are weary of life and seeking a way out, an alternative. Once here, the vapours and honey transform their minds and bodies fundamentally, enabling them to live out their extended lives free of despair and with a sense of purpose."

"Fascinating," responded Arjan. He looked amused, smiling and shaking his head.

Cercis set a bowl of stew in front of Jaden.

"Thank you," she said.

Cercis returned to his seat, finished the last few spoonfuls of stew from his own bowl, wiped the bowl clean with a piece of bread, bit into the bread, and then said with his mouth full, "So, Arjan, what would you like to know about the Council that Sadira hasn't already told you?"

"Sadira has not yet told me a fraction of what I would like to know. We are supposed to have a series of meetings next week. I will question her then."

"Question us now," said Laurel.

"Yes, ask away!" insisted Cercis.

Arjan paused momentarily, ate a spoonful of stew, and then asked, "Why do you eat?"

"What do you mean?" asked Laurel.

"Why do you eat when the Elixir could sustain you indefinitely?"

"Oh. Well, first of all, none of us is thirty yet," said Laurel. "Elixir is granted on your thirtieth birthday. It slows the natural aging process and provides an antidote to any disease you may contract while on assignment outside Council dimension. But it doesn't *feed* you."

"So alchemists over thirty never fall ill?"

"They do, but not for long. An alchemist afflicted with a disease or injury deemed life-threatening or not healed within a few days by Elixir is sent to the catacombs."

"So alchemists die and are laid to rest in the catacombs?"

Cercis and Laurel laughed, but Jaden understood. She had made the same assumption herself before her Council lesson on the catacombs.

"No, they are sent to the catacombs for healing within the catacomb alembics."

"Catacomb alembics?"

"Natural stone vessels filled with mineral waters whose extraordinary powers can heal the most severe illnesses and the most grevious of wounds — waters that flow directly from the source of the deepest wells that feed the channels throughout Council dimension," explained Laurel.

"So alchemists do not die?" asked Arjan.

"Generally, no. Alchemists do not die. They age slowly and leave Council dimension only through conjunction or Final Ascension — an alchemical process that returns mature Quintessence to the Lapis."

Arjan nodded, pondering what he had been told before continuing his inquiry.

"At what ratio does Elixir slow one's aging?"

"Depends on the person," Cercis replied. "But according to an Azothian report I read last year, the current average is eighteen-to-one. After age thirty, it takes approximately eighteen Elixir-infused years to age one biological year. The ratio changes with age — the more Quintessence one acquires, the slower the aging process. According to Magistrate Linden, it currently takes Azoth Magen Ailanthus twenty-five years to physically age one year." He reached for a slice of cake from the dessert tray. "But, of course, for all orders, Elixir's power to slow aging is limited to Council dimension and proximity to the Lapis. Time progresses at the same rate both in Council dimension and in the outside world. In other words, if you leave for a day, you age by a day. If you leave for a year, you age by a year. Elixir requires proximity to the Lapis."

"I thought the pendant contains a portion of the Lapis?"

"Yes, but only a fragment," explained Cercis.

"Which is inlaid," interrupted Laurel. "You can see it only if you look closely at the right angle. Linden's fragment, for example, looks like a tiny dark teardrop hovering in the midst of the aquamarine. And Sadira's is a fleck of gold against black onyx."

"I like Cedar's best," said Jaden. "A speck of red — like a drop of blood — in citrine."

"Upon ascension to the Senior Initiate or upon your twenty-ninth birthday," explained Laurel, "you get to choose your own base pendant — gemstone and silver usually — from anywhere in the outside world. When you turn thirty, it's inlaid with a Lapidarian fragment and presented to you at a ceremony called the Night of Albedo."

"The Lapidarian fragment maintains your connection to the Lapis," continued Cercis. "Without it, you would not be able to return to Council dimension from the outside world without accompaniment."

"I understand." Arjan nodded.

"May I pass you a piece of cake, Jaden?" Cercis asked, turning the dessert tray around in contemplation.

"No, thank you."

"This must be boring for you," Arjan said to Jaden.

"No," replied Jaden. "I remember what it was like being new here. I used to spend hours with Ritha — before she ascended to Senior Initiate — barraging her with questions."

"You will not mind, then, if I ask you my questions as they occur to me?"

"Not at all," said Laurel, who had neglected to notice that Arjan had addressed this particular question to Jaden.

Jaden had noticed, and she smiled at Arjan when Laurel responded. Arjan nodded.

Jaden was not sure what to make of this situation. She already felt more familiar with Arjan than with either Cercis or Laurel. She realized the connection might be only an illusion based more on her dislike of the other Initiates than a bond with Arjan. Or perhaps she was merely curious about the newcomer. That night, as she lay in bed contemplating the day, she realized she had spent more time thinking of Arjan since his arrival than of anyone else in or out of Council dimension. Finally — potentially — she had found an ally.

For the entire month following Arjan's arrival, nothing seemed quite the same to Jaden. Both Linden and Sadira repeatedly stumbled in the classroom, apparently fatigued, forgetting pertinent points and referring more often than usual to lecture notes. Elders moved swiftly along corridors from room to room, from the lower archives to Council Chambers, in a rush of movement that Jaden had not witnessed outside the final minutes leading up to Council meetings. On this very morning, Azoth Ravenea crashed directly into Laurel, who, accompanied by Arjan, was carrying a tray of cups and spiced milk to the courtyard for a Junior Initiate study session. The milk spilled down the front of Laurel's robes; the cups and tray clattered against the stone floor. Though Ravenea's robes sustained only minor splatters and the accident was clearly not Laurel's fault, the Azoth confined Laurel to her residence chambers for the rest of the day. Laurel dashed to her room in tears, leaving Arjan to clean up the mess. Jaden and Cercis had, by then, run into the corridor from the courtyard to determine the cause of commotion. Jaden regretted not being able to drink the spiced milk that Arjan had prepared.

"Another time," said Arjan.

In the classroom that afternoon, Jaden expected Cercis to be in a foul mood thanks to Laurel's temporary banishment. Instead, he seemed perfectly content, joking with Arjan about Laurel crying over spilt milk.

Jaden had to admit a change in her own behaviour too. Though Sadira, again appearing fatigued and anxious, required Jaden and the others to pay attention to the session's lesson, Jaden could think of only one thing: Arjan is *my* friend. *You already have Laurel.* She imagined that if Cercis were older and wore his pendant, she would reach for it, press it firmly against her forehead, and learn his intentions regarding Arjan. Cercis would resist, of course, pull himself and his pendant away, but not before Jaden could ascertain something useful — some half-hidden whisper of desire he harboured for Arjan that she could report to Laurel. *Have you forgotten your conjunctive plans with her already?*

"What about Ilex and Melia?" she said aloud.

Arjan jolted slightly, apparently startled by Jaden's enthusiastic volume.

"Ilex and Melia?" repeated Sadira. "You mean

their story? Well — certainly its iconography, if not its specific details and related controversies, are recorded in Lapidarian ink within several manuscripts accessible to the Initiate orders. Perhaps we could investigate a few of them during next week's practicum in the archives. Thank you, Jaden. Good idea."

Jaden had, it appeared, missed the better part of the lesson's introduction during her jealous reverie. She had no idea why Sadira thought her idea worthy. Seemingly aware of Jaden's plight, Arjan discretely pointed to a section of the textbook that lay open in front of Jaden. Thus she learned that the session involved distinguishing the subtle differences between Lapidarian ink and other inks used to inscribe manuscripts, such as those compiled by medieval monks. Thanks to events of the Second Rebellion, thousands of alchemical manuscripts had been removed from Council dimension into the outside world. Though many had been accidentally destroyed or purposely hidden, several thousand had made their way into protectorate or other libraries around the world. Council members — Magistrates and Readers in particular — were continually engaged in locating these manuscripts and transcribing the Lapidarian sections for the Council archives. Thus, Initiates must learn to recognize Lapidarian ink within manuscripts to fulfill future Council duties.

"Cercis," said Sadira, "based on your previous

lessons on the subject matter, please explain to Jaden and Arjan how Lapidarian ink is made and what purpose it serves."

Though Jaden would have balked at such a request, Cercis seemed to relish the opportunity. He sat up even straighter in his chair and looked directly at Arjan. Jaden rolled her eyes, though she knew no one was watching her.

"Lapidarian ink is gleaned from the Lapis by the Novillian Scribes. Novillians are granted this alchemical skill by the Azoth Magen through a ritual known as the Blood of the Green Lion. Once sanctified through this ritual, a Novillian Scribe has the power to *bleed* the Lapis, a process that involves physically scraping the Lapis to collect a fine dust. The dust is then transferred to a crystal bottle and mixed with channel water. Stirring the mixture with a rod of pure gold transforms the dust and water into Lapidarian ink, whose colour then emerges. The colours vary and cannot be predetermined by the Scribe. Novillians are also granted the power of *Sapientia* or mystical wisdom. With one hand on the Lapis and the other on a slate tablet, the Novillian Scribe acts as a conduit. Messages from the Lapis emerge on the tablet in the form of both text and icons. The material on the slate is then fixed into manuscripts by the Lapidarian Scribes using Lapidarian ink."

"Why?" asked Arjan. "Why not just archive the slate tablets?"

"See for yourself," said Sadira, retrieving from her desk a thin but relatively large tablet of slate and setting it on the desk between Arjan and Jaden.

"Touch it," said Sadira to Jaden. "Run your fingers over one of the icons."

Jaden followed Sadira's instructions. She ran two fingers over an icon of a butterfly; the image smudged as if written in chalk. Arjan nodded.

"The material on the slate is impermanent. Not to worry — this one has already been transcribed. To become permanent, to become an enduring record of Novillian visions, the material on each tablet must be fixed with Lapidarian ink onto parchment made from fibres of the trees of the redwood forest. Once fixed by the Lapidarian Scribes, so too are the prophecies potentially affecting both the outside world and Council dimension — prophecies to be read and interpreted by the Readers. Once interpreted, the prophecies can be adjusted by Lapidarian or Novillian Scribes at the command of the Elders."

"Adjusted?" asked Jaden.

"Reinscribed to remedy elemental imbalances of the outside world, in particular. But that is a lesson for another day," responded Sadira. "Today you are to concern yourselves with recognizing the qualities of Lapidarian ink. If you aspire to be a Reader, you must first learn to *recognize*."

Sadira set several small bottles of ink in front of each Initiate. She also laid two manuscripts on the table — one between Arjan and Jaden, the other between Arjan and Cercis.

"Compare the inks in the bottles to the inks on the pages," Sadira instructed. "Determine which bottles contain Lapidarian ink and which folios are inscribed with Lapidarian ink. You may refer to the chart of common characteristics in your text for assistance."

At that moment, Cedar appeared at the doorway and beckoned to Sadira.

"I'll be back momentarily," Sadira said as she walked to the door. "Keep working."

Jaden began with the bottles — peering at the ink through the thick, clear glass, one bottle at a time. She thought she saw a bluish-green sheen in the black ink, but the flash of colour, if it had existed at all, vanished as quickly as it had appeared. She had no better luck with the manuscript — though she admired the azure blue of a highly stylized flower depicted in the margin of one illumination.

"Does such a flower actually exist?" she asked Arjan.

Arjan turned away from the manuscript he shared with Cercis and leaned towards the image of Jaden's inquiry.

"How beautiful! Yet I am not—" he began, but Cercis interrupted him to ask for his opinion on the scent of an ink. Arjan reached for the bottle, moved it gently under his nose as if evaluating the bouquet of a glass of wine, and handed it to Jaden. "What do you think?"

And then it happened. Just as she reached for the bottle, just as her fingertips touched his, the bottle dropped between them, spilling its ink onto the manuscript.

All three of them leapt to their feet.

"Jaden!" cried Cercis.

"I—"

"No! It was my fault!" Arjan insisted.

"Get a cloth!" shouted Jaden.

Cercis ran to the front of the room and grabbed the chamois from the blackboard ledge. He dabbed the cloth against the ink on the manuscript, then ran it across the desk and other papers onto which the ink had spilled.

"The manuscript is ruined, Jaden!"

"We're in so much trouble," moaned Jaden.

"*We*? You mean *you*!" said Cercis.

"No," said Arjan, "it was my fault. I thought you had hold of the bottle."

"So did I!" replied Jaden.

"Okay, stop! This is pointless! Let's think! We have to—" Cercis stopped suddenly. "Where did it go?" he asked.

"Where did what go?"

"The ink I wiped up." Cercis held out the chamois.

The ink had vanished from the chamois. Indeed, all evidence of the spilled ink had vanished except for a few splotches that remained blackened on the manuscript.

"I don't understand," said Jaden.

"Maybe it is a distinguishing feature of Lapidarian ink," suggested Arjan. "Maybe it remains permanent only on manuscript pages."

"Is that in the chart?" she asked.

They all reached for their textbooks.

"No," said Cercis. "But the chart refers only to the differences in ink already inscribed in the manuscripts."

They spent the next few minutes reading over the chart and flipping through the textbook, unsuccessfully trying to determine if Arjan's theory was correct.

"We should clean everything up," suggested Arjan. "We'll ask Sadira about this when she returns."

They tidied up the books and papers on the table, placed the chamois back on the ledge, fit the ink bottles back into the box, set the remaining pristine manuscript on Sadira's desk, and, finally, sat calmly with the ink-stained manuscript open in front of them, waiting for Sadira.

"We could try to look on the bright side," said Arjan.

At first unable to think of a bright side, neither Cercis nor Jaden responded.

"Well," Cercis finally said, "at least Laurel will not be punished for this."

"And the three of us will never forget this day," mused Arjan.

"True," said Jaden. "In the grand scheme of things, decades from now, would you rather be remembered as the Initiate who spilled spiced milk on the stone floor or Lapidarian ink on an alchemical manuscript?"

Thus, upon her return, Sadira found her three Junior Initiates laughing rather than working, heads flung back with apparent abandon.

Ritha, a Senior Initiate with whom Jaden had spent much of her time in the months after her arrival, ushered Jaden into Cedar's office and instructed her to make herself comfortable.

"What could possibly be comfortable about this situation?" Jaden asked, anxiously anticipating Cedar's reprimand.

"If you don't want to be summoned to the inner offices, Jaden, don't do anything that warrants a summons."

Before Jaden could respond to the palpable condescension, Ritha lowered her voice to a whisper and asked, "What did you do?"

Jaden then realized that the disdain in Ritha's tone had been for the benefit of anyone nearby who might have been listening. Perhaps Ritha would remain a friend after all.

"I spilled some ink on a manuscript."

"On purpose?!"

"Of course not. But according to the Council Elders, I've . . ." She removed the summons from her satchel and quoted directly, "'rendered illegible approximately nine square centimetres of *Elementa Chemicae 5663*, folio 26 recto.'"

Ritha brought both hands up to her mouth. "What if they erase you?"

"Erase me?"

"You'll never come back. Jaden! You have to do something! You must apologize profusely."

"Never come back? What do you mean?" Jaden asked, but just then someone called to Ritha from another office.

"Good luck," Ritha said as she closed the door behind her.

Jaden sat on the red velvet sofa in the corner of Cedar's office. She had not been here in months, not since her early Initiate lessons with Cedar had ended. She liked the office — it felt luxurious with all the silk and velvet and crystal and gold. But her interest in the particulars of Cedar's decor was superseded by nervousness, which was gradually replaced by annoyance and impatience as the minutes passed. Laughter filtering in through one of the windows distracted Jaden enough to tempt her from the sofa to a spot just in front of the curtains on the north wall. She moved one curtain back far enough to allow her a view of the courtyard below. She could see Arjan, Cercis, and Laurel chatting near the fountain. Resisting the urge to call out and wave, she watched the group and tried to interpret the conversation. Arjan had read something from his notebook that seemed of particular interest to the other two. Laurel's laughter, in response, was so grating that Jaden contemplated closing the window — if only she could do so without being noticed.

"Good morning, Jaden." Cedar entered her office and moved to stand beside her desk near the opposite wall. "Enjoying the view?"

"Yes, it's beautiful — with the trees and the fountain."

Cedar nodded. "Have a seat, Jaden."

Jaden sat upright, hands clenched around the carved wooden arms of the chair.

"Did you or did you not purposely pour ink onto *Elementa Chemicae 5663*?"

"I did not. It was an accident."

"Are you generally careless in the presence of manuscripts?"

Jaden thought for a moment. "I don't know. I've only just begun—"

"Are you generally careless?"

"No."

"Why did you have a bottle of ink open in the presence of a manuscript?"

"Sadira, our tutor that d—"

"Magistrate Sadira."

"Yes. Magistrate Sadira had been giving us a lesson on Lapidarian ink. She said if we aspire to become Readers, the first step is to distinguish the inks — to recognize Lapidarian ink among other inks. So, she placed a few bottles of ink on our tables, and left us to determine which bottles were Lapidarian. I couldn't see any difference just looking through the glass, so I smelled one of the open bottles."

"And?"

"And then I dropped it."

"You dropped it? Just like that, out of the blue, you dropped an open bottle of Lapidarian ink."

"So it *was* Lapidarian ink?"

Cedar sighed loudly. "Do you realize the seriousness of this incident?"

"I know that the Readers may never again be able to read a nine-centimetre section of *Elementa Chemicae*."

"Fortunately, for your sake, that particular manuscript — as with all manuscripts taken into Initiate classes — had already been transcribed years ago, the records of which are stored in the Council archives. As a consequence, the other Novillian Scribes and I have managed to restore most of the damage. Amur is still in the Scriptorium working on the final transposition."

Cedar paused, momentarily bringing her hands and her pendant to her forehead.

"Jaden, I need to impress upon you the seriousness of this matter. You destroyed a Lapidarian section of an original manuscript — one, I might add, that dates back to the 17th Council. Such a transgression, whether an accident or not, can affect us all through the generations. What if this manuscript had not been part of a lesson or had not already been fully transcribed? You could have changed Council history. You could have erased a primary icon or a critical fragment of information — the location, for example, of a potential Initiate who, as a consequence of your carelessness, might never be found. Even more devastating in its effect, you could have erased a reference to — and thus affected the readings of — a member of the current Council."

"But it was only nine centimetres. There are thousands — hundreds of thousands — of manuscripts. How could nine centimetres of accidental spillage possibly erase anything or anyone?"

Cedar shifted in her chair, and Jaden couldn't tell whether Cedar's expression was one of frustration or affection.

"Certainly permanent or *complete* erasure is a complicated procedure that involves several Scribes and numerous manuscripts rather than accidental spillage. But all modifications to Lapidarian manuscripts — even miniscule ones — leave scars, whether an irreparable lacuna that remains empty for eternity or an unintentional palimpsest that confounds Readers for generations. Theoretically, with the right ink accidentally spilled or purposely inscribed in the wrong place at the wrong time, you could erase or obscure a reference to anyone, including me."

Jaden, with as much respect and humility as she could manage, with the knowledge of Cedar's possible affection, asked, "Even if I had erased — *could* have erased — someone completely, what would it matter? I mean . . . in the end, wouldn't the Council still exist? Wouldn't a single rotation fill the place of the one erased?"

"Again, theoretically, yes. But you need to think through the implications. If *you* were erased, the rotation to the new Initiate would occur with relative ease since you have not yet been granted a pendant. But if *I* were erased — a Novillian Scribe who has carried her pendant for hundreds of years — the implications for the Council would be dire. An alchemist's pendant is an extension of the alchemist and, through its connection with the Lapis, of the entire Alchemists' Council. Its essence strengthens over time, through ascension and conjunction until, ultimately, its potent Quintessence is returned to the Lapis at Azothian Final Ascension. Thus is the Lapis replenished; thus is the Flaw in the Stone diminished. However, when an alchemist is erased, his or her pendant is confiscated and gradually rendered inert. Its Quintessence neither matures nor returns to the Lapis. Thus the Flaw in the Stone increases, and the power of the Lapis is weakened, as is every alchemist on the branch of the one erased."

"What branch?"

"Picture a tree, Jaden — a trunk, large branches, smaller branches, smaller branches than that. Now picture yourself as a small branch — a very small branch — whose Quintessence depends on a larger branch. If you break the smaller branch, little else is affected. But if you break the larger branch on which you subsist, you too will be broken."

Jaden felt the sting of this apparent threat.

"I am the larger branch upon which you thrive. Erase me and you temporarily erase the Quintessential power — the alchemical power — of everyone directly associated with me: all my Initiates through all rotations including you and Sadira and some of her cohorts, and all *their* Initiates, including your friend Arjan. Should Arjan not have a chance to thrive in Council work without enduring the anguish of Quintessential absence? Replenishment of the branch can take weeks. In the meantime, dozens of alchemists can suffer debilitating weakness and, in certain cases, excruciating pain."

"But they heal, don't they? They're alchemists, after all."

"Of course they heal, Jaden. But while the healing process is underway, balance within Council dimension is disrupted. All four primary elements must remain balanced in cooperative equivalency for these same elements to remain balanced in the outside world. Surely you have learned this much in your lessons?"

Jaden recited her response by rote: "Of the one hundred and one members of the Alchemists' Council, twenty-five maintain earth, twenty-five maintain air, twenty-five maintain water, and twenty-five maintain fire. The four primary elements are bound together by the fifth element — the Quintessence within the Lapis enacted by the Azoth Magen."

"Precisely," Cedar responded. "However, this definition suggests simplicity where complexity reigns. The alchemical process is complicated and requires the Council to work as one to perform the sacraments according to the alchemical calendar: the rituals of the Lapis, the creation of the inks, the inscriptions of the manuscripts. All our work contributes to maintaining elemental balance. When alchemists fail, even temporarily, the sacraments are necessarily neglected, and the stability of both Council dimension and the outside world is threatened until replenishment is complete and balance restored."

Cedar rose, walked around the desk, and stood at Jaden's side. From beneath her garnet robes, she withdrew her pendant on its long silver cord. She held it towards the light streaming through the east window, manipulating its angle so the pendant-filtered light fell upon Jaden.

"The Council works as one, Jaden. Quintessence flows from the Azoth Magen to all the orders on all the branches: from the Azoths to the Rowans, from the Rowans to the Scribes, from the Scribes to the Readers, from the Readers to Magistrates, and from the Magistrates to the Initiates. The Council is Eternal Life, Jaden. As one, we are responsible not only for one another, but for the world outside Council dimension. In Council time, you have only just been born into the Alchemical Tree. Thus *you* could be erased without incident, despite being foretold and sealed in the manuscripts."

Though unexpectedly aroused by the sensuous infusion of Quintessence streaming from Cedar's pendant, Jaden found the words to respond. "Do you mean I would die?"

Cedar retracted her pendant and looked directly at Jaden. Jaden could no longer read her expression.

"No. You would be erased from Council dimension and returned to the outside world."

"So erasure is a form of escape? I could see my friends again."

"Escape? Council dimension is a privilege, not a prison. Surely after a year of breathing in the vapours of the channel waters you no longer *miss* anyone from the outside world."

"No, I don't," Jaden admitted. "But I still think about them occasionally."

"If erasure is your preference, I can arrange it for you." Cedar's tone was calm and her pace steady as she walked back to the other side of her desk. "Alternatively, you can accept your place on the Council and remain alive and well for centuries, potentially for an eternity, through ascension and conjunction. Outside Council dimension, you must face your mortality. The choice is yours to make."

Jaden said nothing. Finally, instead of choosing, she challenged Cedar. "Why has the Council not initiated everyone? Why is every man, woman, and child not on your Tree, not privileged to Eternal Life?"

"We are the elite, Jaden. We are the Alchemists' Council. And our responsibility to the world is unfathomable to the uninitiated."

"Expand the Tree. Save the world."

"The Council is all the Tree can sustain. One hundred and one is constant. That is all. When one is erased, we add another by necessity. But the Tree is best renewed through alchemical conjunction or by the Final Ascension of the Azoth Magen, not by erasure. When two alchemists conjoin, we sustain the Tree with one new life, a new Initiate. The enhanced Quintessence of our conjoined pendants infuses the Council with power, coursing through the Tree to and from the Lapis like Elixir itself. A space is created both physically and alchemically for an Initiate, whose longing for Quintessence is satisfied by the abundance created through conjunction."

Jaden sensed a trace of regret in Cedar's tone.

"You're conjoined," Jaden said. "Who were you before?"

"I have always been Cedar in Council dimension. I conjoined with Saule."

"So why aren't you Saule or Cedar-Saule or whatever?"

"I remain, now and eternally, Cedar."

"Do you look like Saule?"

"My skin is a slightly darker complexion and my eyes are a slightly brighter shade of blue than before the conjunction, but overall I appear as I have always appeared."

"Why?"

"My essence was stronger than Saule's. The conjunction is alchemical. During the ritual of conjunction, each essence struggles for dominance. My essence was stronger. Saule's essence was dissolved in the process."

"But the Rebis . . . Linden taught us . . . I don't understand. You're supposed to be conjoined *together as one*."

"We are conjoined as one — *alchemically*. The Rebis — every hermaphroditic image in the manuscripts — is merely a figurative representation of an alchemical process. In conjunction, the stronger essence dissolves the weaker essence and, in the process, becomes even stronger. To put it in terms of a simple analogy, if you were to eat an apple, you would, on some level, conjoin with that apple; but when the process ends, you would remain you, and the apple would have dissolved."

"Saule wasn't an apple. She was a human being!"

"Conjunction is a sacrament. Do not forget that, Jaden."

"One person dies. It's barbaric. Why haven't I learned this before today?"

Cedar stood and walked to the other side of the

room to close the door, not replying to Jaden's outburst until she was seated again.

"You were not ready to hear this before today. What you learned before today is what you need to remember now: Conjunction is the Path to Azoth; the Eternity of the Lapis; the Sacrifice of the Alchemist; the Endurance of the Earth."

"You're reciting the Law Codes, Cedar — word for word — to justify murder!"

"The Law Codes are sacred. Conjunction is a sacrament. The Words are Eternal."

"Stop! Stop quoting! It's all just words. You murdered Saule to gain eternal youth. How can you live with yourself?"

Cedar reached for her pendant, ran her thumb over the stone, and took a breath.

"I could have been the one dissolved, Jaden. I was willing to take that risk, to make that sacrifice for the sake of the Council and, through the Council, for the sake of the world. Conjunction is a necessity to sustain Lapidarian essence within Council dimension and, through the Council, to maintain the elemental balance of the outside world. The Alchemists' Council strives for Eternal Life through Final Ascension and thrives on the Return of Azothian Quintessence to the Lapis. The cost of maintaining life is life itself. One body eternally lives; another eternally dies. This is the quality and the quantity — the *Conjunctio Oppositorum.* When an alchemist fulfills the Sacrament of Conjunction, that alchemist offers death in order to save life. As above, so below."

"Then the alchemists are playing God."

"We are not divine — not in Council dimension, certainly. We are on the path to divine conjunction through Azothian Final Ascension. The alchemical sacrament of conjunction is a step along that path."

"So how do you choose? *Whom* do you choose? Why Saule?"

"On the recommendation of the Readers, Elders choose conjunctive partners whose essences mirror one another. Each alchemist has a unique elemental essence — an alchemical fingerprint, so to speak — that matures in proximity to the Lapis. Through a single drop of blood or strand of hair, each alchemist's essence is mapped; then, based on the map, the Elders match essence types — think of the process like matching blood types, only on the level of essential particles and with infinitely more varieties. Once a match is confirmed, the pairing is then officially sealed by a Rowan. I was paired for conjunction with Saule only because her essence mirrored my own — a conjunction of opposites, as the hermaphroditic image suggests."

"And what about her soul? Was her soul destroyed?"

"We are not in the business of creating or destroying souls, Jaden. We're in the business of extending lives. In conjunction, one life is offered and another life is saved. That is all."

"It's an act of manipulation. It's evil and imposed!"

"You must be careful, Jaden, to whom you utter such heresy."

"Is that a threat? I don't care! Erase me! I don't want to be part of this."

Cedar stood once again beside Jaden, this time running a hand over the length of her hair. Jaden did not flinch at the touch.

"It is not a threat, Jaden. Why would I threaten one of my own? And why would I betray Saule of my own accord?"

"Betray her? How would erasing me betray Saule?"

Cedar threw back her head, releasing something between a sigh and a laugh.

"She was your saviour."

"What do you mean?"

"Saule conjoined with me so that you could live and renew the Council. Her death gave you the potential for eternal life as the new Initiate. If Saule had been victorious, you would have died on the day Saule and I conjoined."

Jaden sat transfixed as she thought through the implications of this alchemical logic. Finally, she asked, "If Saule had lived and you had dissolved and I had died, who would have become the new Initiate?"

"Her name was Taimi. In the weeks leading to conjunction, the Readers determine two potential Initiates as foretold in the manuscripts. In the weeks or, on occasion, months following the conjunction, the surviving Initiate is confirmed by the Readers and sealed by the Rowans."

"Both Saule *and* Taimi died?"

"Yes, Jaden, both Saule and Taimi died. Saule died in the sacrament of conjunction, and Taimi died of natural causes when you were chosen as the Initiate. If she had been granted an extended life as an alchemist, you would have been the one to die."

"I didn't ask for this! I didn't know!"

"Now you do, and now you have a choice. If you choose to leave us, if you choose to be erased from the Council, you will betray us all, and the deaths of Saule and Taimi will have been in vain. Once erased and returned to the outside world, you will live out your natural life — granted only a temporary reprieve from death, which in your case will be rather swift given you have not yet received Elixir. Within Council dimension, on the day you receive Elixir, you will be granted Eternal Life until the day of your own conjunction. So choose carefully, Jaden, and watch your step. And don't spill ink on the manuscripts."

"It . . . it was an accident." Jaden lowered her head and gripped the wooden arms of the chair even tighter. "I'm sorry. I made a mistake."

"No one is perfect, Jaden. We all make mistakes. Let's just hope you're not mine."

## II
## cūrrent day

Jaden had promised Cercis and Arjan that she would meet them in the Initiate common room and report on every detail of her meeting with Cedar. But as she headed across the courtyard and towards the residence, Jaden realized she could not possibly express to either Cercis or Arjan her current furor. Her life and her place on the Council were the result of two deaths. Taimi had died in her stead, and Saule had purposely sacrificed herself. How could she live with this knowledge? How had she lived here for over a year ignorant of what conjunction truly meant? How could she have been so naïve?

She stopped midway across the courtyard. Laurel would probably be with Cercis and Arjan. Jaden could not face them — not without a story sufficiently different from the actual meeting with

Cedar. She moved to the eastern corner of the courtyard and sat on a small stone bench under a willow tree, thankful for the strands of leafy branches that formed a curtain between her and the rest of the Council dimension.

If only she could speak with Arjan alone. She could tell him the truth. She felt certain that he would understand, that he would be concerned not only for Saule and Taimi but for the people who had been sacrificed for *his* place on the Council. She imagined his reaction — sympathy and outrage — at learning the truth. She realized she did not know who had been sacrificed for Arjan. Or for Cercis. Or for Laurel. Perhaps she should have paid more attention in Council history classes. Cercis and Laurel had arrived several years before Jaden, so she understood why she did not know who had conjoined prior to her own arrival. But she was dismayed — disgraced even — that she could not remember which alchemists had most recently conjoined and, of the two, who had consumed whom. Had this matter come up during one of the many Council meetings when she'd been daydreaming?

She moved quickly from the bench, across the courtyard, and through the north corridor to the staircase of the lower-level archives. She slowed her pace on the staircase, its stone steps slick and steep. Most of the rooms were empty, but she noticed Obeche alone in Archival Room 4 comparing images in two manuscripts.

"Excuse me, Scribe Obeche?"

"Yes, Jaden."

"Could you tell me where the Council minutes are filed?"

"From which century?"

Though she was not certain whether he was joking, Jaden replied, "This one, sir."

"Archival Room 8," he said. She had just turned to leave when Obeche added, "Is there something particular you need to know? I am reputed as an archival mastermind."

For a moment, Jaden wondered if she should keep her queries about conjunction to herself. But Obeche raised an eyebrow and gave her a look that she could not ignore. Not telling him could make her request for archival material look suspicious — and the last thing she needed was a return trip to Cedar's office. "I was just wondering which two Council members were the most recent to conjoin." She paused. "Homework. For history."

Obeche looked towards the ceiling as if pondering the issue. Surely an archival mastermind — indeed any member of the Elder Council — should know such details without a second thought. Perhaps Obeche's prolonged pause was for dramatic effect.

"That would be," he said and then paused again. "Let's see . . . Cedar and Saule, I believe."

"No, after them. Before Arjan."

"Arjan?"

"The new Initiate."

"Oh, yes . . . Arjan. How could I forget?"

"Forget, sir?"

"I have been informed of his arrival, of course." He paused, as if considering what to say next. "However, Jaden, no one conjoined prior to Arjan's arrival. The most recent Council seat — that is, Arjan's place on the Council — was created by erasure, not conjunction."

"Erasure?"

"Yes. The Elders decided to erase a certain, shall we say, *wayward* member of the Council. However, as I'm sure you are already aware, such decisions are not made during regular Council meetings."

Jaden did not respond. She was not by any means *aware* of the decision-making process, but she did not want to appear completely ignorant of lessons that had undoubtedly been covered by one tutor or another.

Obeche continued, "Therefore, such decisions are not recorded in the general minutes. Searching through the records of Archival Room 8 would have been a waste of your time. It is your good fortune that you came to me instead."

"But I didn't. I mean, I did, but . . . but I didn't ask about erasure. Why did you tell me? I mean, why did you *have* to tell me? Why don't I already know about the erasure? Was I here or did it occur before my arrival?"

"When did you arrive?" This too, Jaden surmised, was yet another moment of Elder posturing.

"Last April."

"Last April. So, fourteen months ago. Then, yes, you were here. It occurred only — let's see now — just about a year ago. For some of us, the event was memorable indeed, given its rarity. However, erasure affects not only the person erased but all non-Elders within Council dimension."

"Yes, Cedar explained this to me — the branches."

"Yes, erasure does affect the entire branch, if a branch exists. But it also affects Council memory. If you knew the person whom we, as Elders, chose to erase, you would not remember him — or *her* as the case may be. And, therefore, you would not remember the erasure."

"But *you* remember."

"Yes. All the Elders remember, of necessity."

"But who was he?"

"Or *she*," he said. He paused again and sighed before explaining. "That information is Elder knowledge only. You will be informed only if circumstances necessitate such a transfer of knowledge."

"But what if I knew him or her? What if we were friends?"

"What if you were? It matters little now. It would be in your best interest as a Council member to disassociate. Erasure is for the safety of the entire Council, including you."

Jaden refrained from asking, *According to whom*? Instead, after taking a few seconds to think about the implications of Obeche's revelation, she asked, "Would the person remember me?"

"Unfortunately, yes."

"Unfortunately?"

"Elders have control over alchemical memory only through Lapidarian proximity. Once the pendant is confiscated and the alchemist — the *former* alchemist — is removed from the dimension, he or she retains all memories of time spent with the Council. However, one who has been erased, one whose pendant has been confiscated, no longer has access to Council dimension or the power of the Lapis. His or her memories — along with the knowledge that immortality will never again be within reach — are haunting, like nightmares. This is sufficient punishment, would you not say?"

Jaden remained silent, wondering whether Obeche's question was rhetorical.

"Nonetheless," he continued, with a tone that Jaden read as regretful, "total erasure of such knowledge would be in the Council's best interest if it were possible."

"But — what if we were friends?" she asked again.

"Elder decisions are always for the best. I know this knowledge is difficult for Initiates to understand at first. The Alchemists' Council, including you, has the duty to maintain the elemental balance of the world. We cannot fulfill that duty if we are misaligned within Council dimension itself. We work for the higher good. You may have lost a friend, but you have saved the world for now and — provided our continuation — for eternity."

"Provided our continuation?"

"If the Rebel Branch were ever fully to succeed in their mission, the entire Council — as we currently know it — would be destroyed."

"Is that possible?"

"Theoretically, yes. On a practical level, no. The Rebel Branch has been trying to infiltrate and dismantle the Council for generations with little success."

"With their *wayward* behaviour?"

Obeche laughed. "Precisely."

"Why are you telling me this?"

"It appears to be your time to know."

Zelkova entered the room with a message for Obeche. As Zelkova related the details involving a meeting called by Azoth Ravenea, Jaden bowed her head to Obeche as a sign of gratitude for his time and swiftly departed.

Though she had often felt overwhelmed during her year with the Council, the knowledge Jaden had gained on this day was proving particularly difficult to bear. Everything she had learned in her classes, everything she had observed at meetings, everything she had experienced in Council dimension, seemed a mere façade hiding the truth. She walked away in fear — not of her own erasure, but of the erasure of others. How many wayward alchemists would she know over the years? How many would she forget? Whom had she already forgotten?

Within half an hour of her meeting with Jaden, Cedar received word that Azoth Ravenea required the immediate presence of all Novillian Scribes, two Lapidarian Scribes, and two Readers in the North Library. Though she had left her office immediately, Cedar was the last to arrive. She took a seat amidst the other Novillian Scribes — Amur, Tera, and Obeche — who had opted for the long plush sofa under the great stained glass window of the east wall. The Lapidarian Scribes — Katsura and Ela — were seated to Cedar's left on a smaller sofa. The Readers — Olivia and Wu Tong — sat across from Cedar on wooden chairs retrieved from one of the nearby reading tables. Ravenea, in extraordinarily bright golden robes, stood near the main entrance, as if waiting for someone — perhaps Ruis. Finally, apparently satisfied that no one else was approaching, she took a seat in the large burgundy wingback chair to the right of the long sofa.

"It appears Azoth Ruis is otherwise occupied. We will proceed without him."

Everyone nodded his or her agreement.

"Frankly," said Ravenea, "I disagree with Ruis's apparent apathy regarding the matter raised weeks ago by Cedar and Linden. Manuscript images — bees included — do not simply disappear before one's eyes. These lacunae may be a sign of rebel activity, as Cedar has already suggested. I request your input and suggestions towards resolution."

She crossed her arms and sat back in her chair.

After an initial awkward silence, Katsura spoke. "Azoth, I too share your concerns. The matter received scant attention at the Council meeting — a mere footnote, if you will — despite its presence on the agenda, and little has been done since then. I would advise all Scribes and Readers begin immediate investigation to determine a definitive cause."

"With all due respect," Obeche nodded first to Azoth Ravenea and then to Katsura, "and regardless of my general sentiments regarding Lapidarian bees, we cannot devote all Scribes and Readers to a virtually impossible, not to mention *mundane*, task. Searching for bees *appearing* in the manuscripts would be difficult enough. Finding bees that have *disappeared* would require months of cross-referencing work. We cannot simply abandon our regular duties, thus risking the elemental balance of Council dimension itself."

"On the other hand, we cannot continue to ignore a potential rebel threat!" rebuked Ravenea. Before Obeche could offer a response, Ravenea gestured to Cedar for her input.

"Even if we were to dedicate only half the Scribes and Readers to focus exclusively on locating the bees, or *lack* of bees, we face a potential problem," began Cedar, thus receiving a rare nod of approval from Obeche.

"Continue," said Ravenea.

"Linden's observation occurred in the Vienna protectorate, not within Council dimension. Of course, we would be amiss to assume the manuscript anomalies are limited to Vienna, but I would advise we prioritize the protectorate libraries. As the Third Rebellion taught us, protectorate manuscripts are not immune to rebel manipulation despite our vigilance. To determine the extent to which the protectorate libraries have been affected, we must conduct some of our research outside Council dimension. Of course, we must also bear in mind that sending too many members of the upper orders to the outside world could upset elemental balance and leave Council dimension vulnerable."

"Surely, Cedar, you are not recommending we dedicate members of the lower orders to this task?" asked Ravenea. "If we are witnessing the early days of a potential rebellion, caution is paramount."

"Yes, Azoth, caution is paramount," replied Cedar. "Thus we must consider not only the risks but also the benefits. We must maintain balance within Council dimension, yet we must simultaneously carry out research within the protectorates."

"What then do you suggest, Cedar?"

"I suggest we form a rotating coalition of two

members per Order — from Novillian Scribes to Senior Initiates — to conduct research outside Council dimension. This will give us twelve members who can work in shifts of six and six, while still maintaining dimensional cohesion of the upper orders." She paused here, assessing the reaction.

"You appear to have given this some thought already," Obeche mused, with the slightest tinge of condescension.

"Of course I have. I brought the matter to Ruis weeks ago, and I have since noticed a bee missing from the *Sursum Deorsum 5055*."

"So the problem is not limited to the protectorates?" said Obeche.

"Neither is the problem limited to Council dimension," replied Cedar.

"Who do you propose should make up this coalition?" asked Azoth Ravenea.

"I propose myself, of course, and Novillian Amur; Lapidarians Katsura and Ela; Readers Wu Tong and Terek; Senior Magistrates Nunnera and Tesu; Junior Magistrates Linden and Xiang Chun; and Senior Initiates Ritha and Zelkova."

Ravenea raised her pendant to her forehead as she considered Cedar's proposal.

"I agree. However, before commencing the plan, we must first acquire consent from both the Azoth Magen and Azoth Ruis. Objections?"

"Yes, I object!" Obeche said. "If the manuscript

lacunae are signs of rebel activity and if the protectorate libraries have indeed become vulnerable, then Amur must remain in Council dimension. Given his impending conjunction, his safety and well-being must be a priority."

"Obeche, are you volunteering yourself as a replacement for Amur?" asked Ravenea.

"Yes, I most certainly am."

Amur nodded, amenable as always.

"Fine. Further objections?" asked Ravenea.

No one spoke.

"The matter—"

"One moment, Azoth," said Cedar. "I apologize for the interruption, but I have one further proposal. I suggest all four Junior Initiates also assist with protectorate research."

Cedar was not certain who objected first. Several members spoke at once, until Azoth Ravenea raised her hand in request for order.

"Preposterous!" exclaimed Obeche. "At most they have attained only the basics of training. Not *even* the most basic in certain areas! Are you suggesting we trust them with matters far beyond their scope of understanding?"

"I am suggesting we aim to curtail a repeat of our most recent debacle. What better way to further Initiate training and allegiance to the Council than practical fieldwork against a potential rebel attack?"

"Fieldwork? What would you have them do?" Obeche asked.

"I would have them cross-reference bees within protectorate library manuscripts and archival records. Such a straightforward — one might even say *mundane* — task is certainly within the scope of Initiate abilities."

"And outside time won't affect their aging," Amur added, "since they've not yet received Elixir. They can remain outside Council dimension to complete basic cross-referencing work that would drain our essences unnecessarily."

"I recommend the Initiates work in pairs, with each pair assigned to a different protectorate library," continued Cedar. "Each Initiate would be paired with a Scribe for transport to and around the outside world. Howeover, once ensconsed in their respective protectorates and provided with instructions, the Initiates could be left to work without assistance, thus freeing the Scribes for other business until the time comes for the Initiates to be escorted back to Council dimension."

"Employment of Initiates for the occasional outside task certainly has precedent," said Katsura, "but this situation is different. In light of the potential rebel threat, Initiates could be vulnerable. Without pendants, how would Lapidarian proximity be ensured?"

"Yes, what of that?" echoed Obeche. "You seem to forget that the very *debacle* so recently erased from Initiate memory is most likely to be recalled outside Lapidarian proximity. Surely, you are not planning to grant pendants to the Junior Initiates."

"Actually, I am," replied Cedar. Again, the room erupted into a chorus of dissent.

"Outrageous!" Obeche stood up and gestured emphatically to Ravenea. "Reprimand her!"

"Silence!" Ravenea ordered. "We require further explanation, Cedar."

"We would grant them interim pendants, until the potential rebel threat has passed. The pendant will be infused with Lapidarian essence only, not inlaid with a Lapidarian fragment. Turquoise works well to absorb such an infusion, and choosing the pendants should require no more than a few hours outside Council dimension. Thereafter, the essence-imbued pendants will provide Lapidarian proximity, albeit weakened, for a limited time — the time frame determined, of course, by the proportion of essence to turquoise. The Initiates can be scheduled to return to Council dimension from the protectorate libraries when essence renewal is required."

"Who has heard of such a thing?" objected Obeche.

"Interim pendants were sanctioned under the war measures during the Second Rebellion," replied Cedar. She had come prepared.

The debate continued for more than two hours, with every member in attendance asking for — or, in some cases, demanding — explanations for any number of scenarios. Cedar remained calm and, as she would describe the situation to Sadira later, informative throughout the meeting. In the end, she managed to convince everyone, with the exception of Obeche, that including the Junior Initiates was not only practical but necessary. Thus, when taken to a vote, the motion to grant interim pendants to the Junior Initiates and, thereafter, to include them in manuscript cross-referencing both within and outside Council dimension passed, despite Obeche's objections.

"As Azoth Ravenea mentioned earlier, you still need approval from both Azoth Magen Ailanthus and Azoth Ruis," Obeche reminded the others.

"I leave that to you, Cedar," said Ravenea.

"Good luck," Obeche offered sarcastically. He left the room in one final act of defiance.

Cedar nodded respectfully to Azoth Ravenea before leaving, content with this small but necessary accomplishment.

As traumatic as the knowledge of Saule's death had been, and as guilty as Jaden felt for having been the one to benefit from the sacrifice, Obeche's revelation was the one that haunted her. Now, rather than wanting to hide from Arjan and the others, Jaden sought them out anxiously, her panic increasing with every passing minute. She felt sickened by the idea that at any moment, without warning or consultation, without a full Council meeting or deliberation, someone she knew could disappear not only from

Council dimension but from her memory. She could lose Sadira. She could lose Arjan. Or they could lose her — forever, despite their potentially eternal lives.

She found Arjan in the Initiate common room. He was chatting with Ritha and Zelkova. The room was full of Senior Initiates. She looked around for Laurel and Cercis.

"Jaden!" said Ritha. "What happened at the meeting?"

"The meeting?"

"With Cedar."

"Oh. Nothing. She warned me to be more careful in the future. You know — in that serious voice she uses when she's annoyed."

"Yes, that voice," said Zelkova. "I know it well." Ritha laughed. Clearly they shared some sort of privileged Senior Initiate information about Cedar — yet another aspect of the Council of which Jaden was ignorant.

Arjan reached across one of the tables and gathered up a few books into his satchel. "Laurel and Cercis said to meet them in the South Library," he said to Jaden.

"Have fun," Ritha said, rolling her eyes. She too disliked Laurel.

When Arjan and Jaden had walked far enough down the corridor to be out of hearing range, Arjan admitted he had no idea where Laurel and Cercis were. He had wanted to extricate himself from the common room with a reasonable excuse. He wanted

Jaden to tell him about her meeting with Cedar — particularly the parts she was not willing to share with the others.

"Did you tell her," he asked, "that the spillage was my fault and not yours?"

"Of course not."

"Why? You should have done so. If I had not—"

"It doesn't matter, Arjan. Besides, she barely spoke with me about the manuscript. There's something else."

"What?" He stopped walking and waited for her response.

"It's about conjunction. Did you know that only one person survives?"

"Yes, one made from two."

"No — not like we've been taught, not like in Initiate textbooks. One person's essence consumes the other person's. Only one survives."

"Cedar told you this?"

"Yes. She said that when she and Saule conjoined, she survived and Saule died. And that Saule died for me, since I was the next Initiate brought to the Council after Cedar's conjunction. And I would have died if she had not. And another potential Initiate — Taimi — died *because* I did not."

Arjan sat on a window seat and ran his hands through his hair, thinking. Jaden leaned against the wall beside him. Neither he nor Jaden said anything.

"These deaths are an unfortunate necessity for the continuation of the Alchemists' Council and, through Council work, of millions of citizens of the outside world," said Arjan finally. "Taimi is gone. But as for Saule, perhaps Cedar only *thinks* she completely consumed her. Perhaps Saule is still present in ways that Cedar cannot acknowledge consciously, since they are one now."

Jaden exhaled. "Maybe. But I didn't get that impression."

"Or perhaps the result is different for different partnerships."

"I don't know."

"Conjunction is sacred," said Arjan, "regardless of outcome."

"You sound like Cedar!"

"Is that a compliment?"

Jaden smiled half-heartedly and sat beside him. "Obeche told me something even more disturbing."

"Yes?"

"He said that . . ." She paused, not sure how Arjan would take the news.

Arjan raised his eyebrows slightly, waiting. Now he reminded her of Obeche.

"He said that *your* place on the Council was opened by erasure, not conjunction."

"Yes, I know."

"You know?"

"Sadira told me during one of our initial meetings."

"And it doesn't bother you?"

"No. No more than Saule's conjunction should bother you."

"I thought you would understand!" Jaden regretted that she had sought Arjan as her confidant.

"I do understand," he said. "But I did not know the person. And you did not know Saule. We have to trust the wisdom of the Elders, the knowledge of the Council."

"But I may have known him — or her."

"Whom might you have known?"

"The one erased. I may have known the one erased. Obeche said only the Elders retain memories of the person after the erasure; everyone else forgets."

"Yes. Through Lapidarian proximity, Elders control our ability to remember — or, more accurately, to forget — the one erased within Council dimension. The one erased is banished from Council dimension and thus physically removed from proximity to the Lapis. Thus, he or she will be the only one, other than the Elders, to remember what happened."

Both Arjan and Jaden sat in silence momentarily.

"So," said Jaden, "if memory is controlled by proximity to the Lapis, what happens when someone leaves Council dimension?"

Arjan furrowed his brow. "I would guess that one's pendant extends the Lapidarian laws of proximity. A Council member would not dare abandon a pendant in the outside world — such a move could prove hazardous to both self and Council."

"But we haven't earned our pendants, so if we were to leave Council dimension, we would remember the one erased."

Arjan smiled. "Theoretically. However, we cannot leave *because* we do not have pendants. We have no means to activate a portal."

"But hypothetically, if we *could* leave without pendants, what would happen?"

"Based on my understanding of Lapidarian law, an extended stay in the outside world without a Lapidarian pendant could potentially allow us to regain our erased memories. Of course, if I am correct about this aspect of the law, then the regained memories would be erased again immediately upon return to Council dimension and, thus, to Lapidarian proximity." He then added, as if anticipating another objection from Jaden, "According to what I have read, all attempts to counteract Lapidarian law have proven futile."

Though awed by Arjan's grasp of Lapidarian law, Jaden was dejected. She felt trapped. Arjan was knowledgeable but not helpful.

"If they erased *me*," Jaden said, "you would never know because you wouldn't remember me. Or don't you care?"

"Of course I care. You are my colleague and friend."

"Then will you help me? Please. I may have cared about the one erased."

Arjan ran his hands through his hair again. "Yes, Jaden, I will help you."

Jaden jumped up and pulled Arjan with her. "Where do we begin?"

"We begin outside Council dimension," he said emphatically.

"Outside? But how?"

"Have faith."

"Faith?"

"Not everything is written in stone. An opportunity will present itself."

Though Jaden did not understand Arjan in that moment, she believed him.

"Until then," she said.

"Until then," he replied.

Sadira waited anxiously. She wrapped herself in her green silk shawl, mildly comforted by its texture and warmth. Images both past and present streamed through her thoughts. Most present was Arjan. She wondered if his adjustment to Council life was progressing as effortlessly as his first contact with her. The Elders concurred he was unusual, certainly, but none of them had negatively remarked on Sadira's account of her initial contact with him. Indeed, after interviewing Arjan — a process to which Sadira had not been privy — the Elder Council concluded that his pre-Initiate ability to read alchemical manuscripts was another sign of his importance to the Council. They added this detail to the extensive manuscript evidence pointing to Arjan's significance, evidence provided by various Readers over the months leading up to initiation. During their discussion with Sadira, Rowan Esche even cited a 7th Council manuscript tale of a prophet who had foreseen her alchemical destiny. She had joined the Council with knowledge of her destiny and, years later, singlehandedly undermined the Breach of the Yggdrasil — a rebel influx of the First Rebellion that could have ended Council control of the outside world. And, as Obeche had reminded Sadira in his post-interrogation meeting with her, if Arjan did prove to be a liability, an erasure could easily be arranged. "He is *only* an Initiate, after all — no one else would be affected," Obeche had said. "Just keep an eye on him." But she had known from their first meeting that he was not *only* an Initiate; he was different. She would do more than merely observe him; she would learn what the Elders had learned and, more importantly, what they had failed to uncover. He was, after all, her charge, just as she was Cedar's.

Occasionally, over the years, Sadira had questioned her devotion to Cedar — especially last year before Cedar had once again swayed her back into trust and alliance. Recently, Sadira found such moments of hesitation were rare and fleeting. Nonetheless, she had had such a moment just a few hours ago; thus she languished now in a once-familiar state of apprehension over her decision to trust Cedar, to trust that she would be victorious in her own conjunction with Amur. She knew she need only see Cedar again for an instant to realize their alliance was both potent and necessary. Without Cedar's influence, Sadira would have remained in a state of lonely desperation, mired in the restless discomfort that had plagued her for the months preceding and following the conjunction of Cedar and Saule.

Beforehand, Sadira had desperately feared losing Saule; in the aftermath, Sadira agonized over her loss. Gradually, with gentle persistence in the years following the conjunction, Cedar had managed to secure not only Sadira's trust but also her love. Indeed, Sadira had become so emotionally connected and comfortable with Cedar that it had been Sadira herself who had made the first gesture towards their physical intimacy. With the exception of her occasional bouts of jealousy over Ruis, Sadira had never doubted that Cedar genuinely loved her or that her long-term plans took Sadira's best interests into account. Thus it was not her relationship with Cedar that Sadira questioned of late, but her future role within the Alchemists' Council — questions she had not asked since her early years as an Initiate.

Unlike Arjan, Sadira initially had fought against Council indoctrination. In her first months in Council dimension, she had routinely sought escape. She all but devoured everything she could find on dimensional space, including ancient designs, sketched into vellum, for the Council buildings and grounds. She had convinced herself that the tunnels under the Council grounds led to the outside — that she need only find the proper route through the labyrinthine paths. Even the eldest of the Elder Council would require a conventional means of escape in times of crisis. What of the rebellions? What of necessary retreat from threat? What of the historical rebel breaches into Council dimension? But no matter what path Sadira took, no matter how many hours she spent in the tunnels, she inevitably ended up in the same place. She would emerge, tired and frustrated, into the Scriptorium so late into the night that on occasion dawn was mere minutes away. Yet despite numerous nighttime adventures, she had never been caught. Even amidst the predawn haze of that day she had met Cedar unexpectedly in the main courtyard, she had managed a credible excuse for her presence. *I am contemplating the light through the trees*, she had said. Cedar had smiled and touched Sadira's shoulder before wandering away towards the western archway. She thought now of those tunnels. Perhaps they would prove useful to her yet.

She paced the room to no avail. Her restlessness — her clichéd pit-of-the-stomach nervousness — could not be quelled by conventional coping mechanisms. So Sadira reached for a leather-bound book, third from the left on the lowest shelf of her bookcase. From its hollowed-out core, she extracted a small red vial. And from this, she removed one tiny essence-laden tablet that she placed under her tongue. The effects were instantaneous. Both she and her pendant responded in tandem — softly ascending in vibration to match the room, the air, the light, the objects, the fabrics. She moved to her bed, where she lay down and laughed quietly. Though she continued to question the ethics of ingesting Sephrim, she nonetheless enjoyed the immediacy of its pleasure-inducing side effects. All would be well again long before Cedar arrived.

Immediately after her successes at the meeting, Cedar had returned to her office to consult a few files. A few hours later, she made her way carefully down the steep staircase to the lower-level archives. The antechamber was dimly lit — most of the light emanated from the dozen or so archival rooms currently occupied by Readers. She noticed Linden working in one of the rooms but did not stop to talk with him. She was too concerned about her own progress with the manuscripts and her impending trip outside Council dimension to spend time with a Junior Magistrate, especially one who would regale her with his suspicions about rebel activity. She needed to find Amur, to ensure he would continue to support her decisions and be where she needed him to be.

She found him in the penultimate room on the left of the antechamber. From the doorway, she watched him momentarily. He sat at a desk under a reading lamp, peering at a section of a manuscript through a magnifying glass. At the next table, Obeche casually flipped through a magazine — one of many spread across his desk.

"Obeche! In light of recent events, I hardly think it prudent to waste time."

Amur looked up at Cedar and gestured towards Obeche. "He disagrees."

"Do not fret, Cedar," said Obeche. "Contrary to your assumption, I am not wasting time. I am doing my part to aid the cause by skimming these outside world magazines for an article I recall."

"Why?"

"I thought it might help."

Cedar sighed in frustration. "Again . . . *why*?"

"It outlines the history of the honeybee in North America."

"Fine. You read magazines. Amur and I will attend to Council business."

"*As above, so below*," Obeche quoted.

Cedar shook her head and reached for a box of archival material she had placed on the reserve shelf. She began to spread it out on the room's central table. Further discussion with Obeche would do little more than vex her.

"I suspect the process is reversing," said Obeche.

"What process?" asked Amur.

"What if the bees of the outside world — or, more accurately, the disappearing bees of the outside world — are negatively affecting the bees of the manuscripts?"

"It doesn't work that way," said Amur.

"So we have always assumed," replied Obeche.

"So we have always known," said Cedar. "For legions of generations, the Scribes—"

"Cedar, I am over four hundred years old. I know the power and abilities of the Scribes. And I know the power of manuscripts. As you know, I have been advocating for years that we release additional Lapidarian bees into the outside world to help repair environmental damage. Now bees have begun to disappear from Lapidarian manuscripts. None of us knows whether the disappearance is an isolated incident or the start of an epidemic. I do not use that word lightly. You know perfectly well the disaster that could occur if the manuscript lacunae affect the apiary, if negative space negatively affects the *actual* Lapidarian bees. The manuscript manipulation *may* well be merely a malicious prank by a juvenile rebel. But I have an alternative theory."

"Yes?" responded both Amur and Cedar.

"I suspect an elemental breach in the structure — another *flaw* in the Stone, if you will."

"A flaw in the Stone . . ." echoed Amur.

"Figuratively speaking. Not the literal Flaw in the Lapis, nor its effect on Final Ascension. I refer to a fissure, a tear in dimensional coherence that would allow the outside world — or someone within the outside world — to affect anything within Council dimension or its protectorates, including Lapidarian manuscripts."

"Has this ever happened?" Cedar asked.

"No, not to my knowledge. But as our interminable debates on the problem indicate, the balance of the outside world is faltering. Repercussions are inevitable. To put it bluntly, in recent years, the outside world has changed drastically. We cannot ignore the possibility of an interdimensional event we have not previously encountered. Thus, I have concluded that we might find a place to begin the next stage of our investigation where we least expect it — or, where *you* least expect it."

"If your theory is valid — and I am not suggesting it is — wouldn't a book or two on the subject of bees of the outside world prove more helpful than an article in a magazine?"

"Good point, Cedar. In fact, I had just been thinking that on your trip to the outside world with your chosen few, you could do some research and find me a book or two."

"Find them yourself!"

"Delegate the task! You have requested the assistance of the Junior Initiates. Once they have attained their pendants, set them up in a coffee shop with a computer. You have heard of the Internet?"

Cedar glared at Obeche.

"Perhaps, Cedar, your time would be better spent

preparing the Initiates for their upcoming tasks rather than rummaging through archival material looking for the proverbial needle."

"What do you think, Amur?"

"He has a point," Amur admitted.

Cedar gathered the items she had placed on the table, returned them to the box, and returned the box to the shelf.

"May your work here be productive, Amur. See you tomorrow."

"Yes, see you then."

"Good day, Obeche."

"Always a pleasure, Cedar."

Cedar walked calmly out of the room, retracing her steps until she reached the main courtyard and could veer determinedly yet casually towards residence chambers. *All will be well*, she reminded herself. *All will be well.*

Moments later, she stood in Sadira's room contemplating which details to reveal.

"I was unable to discuss the conjunction with Amur. Obeche was with him working on his new theory."

"He has a theory?"

"He suspects that outside world events have caused a fissure in dimensional structure and, consequently, the manuscripts are being affected."

"Has he any proof?"

"Not yet."

"Has he told the Azoths?"

"He surely will. And if even one of them gives credence to it, if an investigation were to begin, your conjunction may be delayed for months — *years* even."

Sadira sat on her bed, allowing her silk shawl to slip slightly away from her shoulders. She motioned for Cedar to join her.

"Nothing you can do about it now. So, you might as well keep me warm instead. You would be much more effective than this shawl."

"Obeche has advised me to meet with the Junior Initiates," Cedar replied.

"And whether or not to follow his advice is up to you."

Cedar smiled. She moved to Sadira's side and ran a hand over her hair. As Cedar leaned towards her, Sadira took Cedar's pendant in her hand and held it against her lips. The sensation of Sadira's breath against the pendant weakened Cedar's resolve beyond what she could have anticipated. A flash of emerald-coloured silk fell quietly to the floor.

The following week, as Jaden walked towards the North Library in hopes of finding additional information on erasure, she noticed Laurel and Sadira sitting near the fountain in the main courtyard. Laurel was laughing and applauding. Cercis stood against the wall across from them; he was speaking excitedly to Arjan through a corridor window.

"Jaden!" Arjan called. He waved, and everyone turned to look at her. Arjan disappeared from the window, presumably to make his way outside. Cercis took a seat beside Laurel, and Jaden stood nearby, directly in front of Sadira.

"Guess what?" Laurel asked Jaden.

"What?"

"We're going to lunch outside Council dimension."

"We who?" Jaden asked.

"All of us — the Junior Initiates — with Cedar."

"Where?" asked Jaden.

"Really now, Jaden," said Cercis, "does it matter? It's a day of freedom."

Arjan arrived and stood beside Jaden. "From what I understand," he said, "we are en route to Santa Fe."

"Why?"

"It's an Initiate test," said Sadira. "If you pass, you will progress to the next stage of the venture."

"What venture?"

"Jaden! Enough questions already!" demanded Laurel. "Sadira said that Cedar will explain everything later."

Sadira stood up, put her hand briefly on Jaden's left shoulder, and said, "You will meet Cedar in the portal chamber in one hour. Since our journey will take us to North America, we will use the Salix portal rather than the Quercus. Bring layers. You'll be in Santa Fe from mid-morning to early evening, and the temperature is likely to drop. I'll see you all when you return." She headed across the courtyard towards the Magistrate offices.

Jaden stood silently for a moment and then risked another question.

"Did Sadira say what type of test?"

"No," responded Arjan.

Laurel rolled her eyes. "What difference does it make, Jaden? They are always testing us! Every step we take within Council dimension is potentially a test! The point is, test or not, we're getting out for several hours to a place we've never seen."

"I have seen it," said Arjan.

"What's it like?"

"Clay coloured," Arjan began, and then continued as if reciting a poem, "dry and beautiful in the evening light, landscapes lined with juniper and cottonwood, strands of bright red chili peppers hanging from wooden beams."

Laurel applauded and laughed. "Sounds beautiful! Lucky us! I'll see you later — I'm going to get ready." She jumped up and moved in the direction of the residence building. Cercis followed her.

"And what about you?" Arjan said to Jaden. "Have you been to Santa Fe?"

"No. And I think this is strange. Initiates rarely have outings — let alone an outing with a test. What if we fail?"

"What if we pass?" Arjan mused.

Jaden sighed. She had assumed being summoned to Cedar's office for questioning had been trying enough. Now she faced a test in a place she had never seen.

"Why Santa Fe?" she asked. "Do you think we will learn the basics of reshelving manuscripts in the protectorate library?"

"Given the protectorate, we can presume Santa Fe has various historical connections to the Council. Perhaps we are indeed headed to the library — but for a lesson on Lapidarian ink recognition in Santa Fe manuscripts rather than a lesson on shelving techniques," laughed Arjan. "That would be my guess." He took a few steps away and then turned back to say, "If we are put in teams for this test, I want to be with you."

Jaden smiled. "Should I be honoured?"

She watched him until he disappeared through the western archway. Then she sat by the fountain for a few minutes wondering why she felt so nervous about this turn of events. Isn't this what she had wanted — a chance to remember the one erased? Had Cedar, inadvertently, just handed Jaden the very thing for which she hoped? She should be happy. What's the worst that could happen? But on her walk back to her chambers to prepare for the journey, she imagined several worst-case scenarios — her own erasure among them. *Have faith*, she recalled Arjan telling her. *Have faith.*

Jaden stood near the corner of the Old Santa Fe Trail and East Water Street, watching the various passersby in hopes of seeing one of the other Junior Initiates. With no other alchemist assisting that day, Cedar had to transport each Initiate separately through the portal on the power of her pendant. Jaden had been told to wait at this spot for the others to arrive. But she had been waiting for twenty minutes, walking slowly back and forth in front of a small courtyard near the Loretto Chapel. In doing so, she reached the conclusion that Cedar should have asked her to wait somewhere with more shade and a place to sit down. By the half-hour point, Jaden began to worry about what she would do if Cedar never returned. Here she was, abandoned on a street corner in a foreign city, without the ability to return to Council dimension. She did not have a pendant of her own. What would she do? She realized that she could return home to Vancouver. Would anyone remember her? Did they believe she had died? It then occurred to her that she had no money or passport. Her fear grew as the minutes passed. Finally, Cedar and Arjan appeared beside her.

"What happened?" Jaden demanded. "You said you'd be only a few minutes!"

"I was delayed by an impromptu meeting with Obeche," Cedar said. "All is well now. I'll bring Laurel next."

"Wait!" said Jaden. "I don't want to stay here on the street. I want to sit down somewhere."

Cedar paused. "Fine. Go into La Fonda and wait in the coffee shop." She pointed towards the hotel. "We will eat in the restaurant later as a group." She disappeared immediately thereafter.

"Where did . . . Don't people notice?" asked Jaden, looking around anxiously.

"Apparently not," Arjan replied in his calm voice. "Come. I will buy us coffee."

"You have money?"

"Of course. I never commence a journey without money."

"You have a secret stash of American money?"

"Yes," he replied and began to cross the street. "Come this way," he said. Jaden decided not to question him further. Instead, she silently followed him along the side of the hotel and through an entrance.

They found themselves a table in the small Parisian-themed café and placed an order for coffee and croissants. Arjan's silver chain stood out against his bright red scarf draped around his neck and over his shoulders. Once again Jaden contemplated how different he was from the other Initiates. Yet because of this difference, she trusted him.

"Have you had time between homework assignments to learn more about erasure?" she asked.

"I have questioned Sadira on the matter. She reiterated what I have read. The Council member is stripped of the pendant — if a pendant has been earned — and physically removed from Council dimension. The Council provides the member with basic survival needs — identification, a place to live, money. After that, all ties are severed, and the one erased will live out the remainder of his or her life. The length of that life is relative to the amount of Elixir previously ingested while an alchemist — an Elder would survive far longer than a Senior Initiate, for example. Meanwhile, Scribes manually and alchemically erase all known references to the member from Lapidarian manuscripts."

"All *known* references. So there could be others — *unknown*?"

"If a reference is unknown to the Council, I doubt we could find it."

"Still — it's a possibility." Jaden paused, taking a sip of her coffee. She closed her eyes and lowered her head to concentrate. After a few seconds, she asked, "Why don't I remember anything yet? I'm outside Council dimension, and I'm not wearing a pendant. I *must* have known the person."

"When did the erasure happen?"

"Obeche said it occurred last year. So why can't I remember?"

"You have not been outside and away from Lapidarian proximity for long. The process of regaining erased memories is usually gradual."

"Usually?"

"Last night, I read of a 15th Council alchemist

who lost his pendant during an outside journey and within an hour began to have flashes of someone who had been erased during the previous rotation. He became confused and disoriented. Finally he was rescued by a Rowan who returned him to Council dimension. I assume the story was intended as a warning to those attempting to regain erased memories — the swift timing exaggerated as a fear tactic. In most circumstances, a person would have to be outside Council dimension for several days to regain erased memories completely. Perhaps I should not say *completely* — after all, memories are rarely complete, regardless of Lapidarian effect."

"But I want to remember. I *need* to remember," said Jaden.

"You are probably better off not remembering. Erasure is an extreme measure. It occurs only if the person is posing some sort of threat to the Council and — through the Council — to humanity."

"But it isn't fair."

Arjan laughed. "You might not think that if you knew the circumstances."

"Exactly! Then that's the reason I *need* to remember! Maybe if we're here long enough today, I will remember something."

"Maybe. But you'll forget again as soon as you return to Council dimension. And then, were you to leave again, you may not have the same memory or set of memories you had previously. Memory changes with each remembrance — theoretically."

Jaden made a grunt of annoyance. "Did you learn all this from your books?"

"I have asked Sadira many questions about many subjects over the weeks. Each time she tells me one thing, I ask something else. On the topic of erasure, I asked for details. And then I consulted the books. I have found the third floor, eighth case of the North Library to be particularly useful regarding Lapidarian law."

Jaden slumped down in her chair and crossed her arms in frustration. As Arjan sipped his coffee, Jaden stared at hers. After a minute or so of silence, her eyes widened.

"I could write it down and take it back with me."

"Write what down?"

"Whatever I remember today. I could write it down and take it back with me. Then, if I don't remember after I return to Council dimension, I would still have the record." Jaden looked around the café. "I need some paper. I should have brought my journal."

"You keep a journal?"

"Well, I *have* a journal. I haven't written in it for a while."

"Have you consulted it?"

Jaden looked puzzled.

"Perhaps you wrote about the one erased — before the erasure."

The possibility that she had written something of the one erased — the possibility that she had a way to outmanoeuvre Obeche and the other Elders — startled Jaden to such an extent that her sudden, swift movement sent her coffee cup crashing to the floor.

"Really, Jaden, the coffee can't be that bad," said Laurel, who was approaching their table. A young woman who worked in the café came over to aid in the clean-up. Arjan gathered the fragments of cup and tossed them into a bag the waitress held open. Jaden repeatedly apologized. Once everything was cleaned up, Laurel pulled up a chair to the table and ordered an espresso. She then began a rapidly paced monologue on the plans she and Cercis had for their afternoon in Santa Fe. Jaden barely listened. She no longer wanted to be in Santa Fe. She wanted to return to her residence chambers and search her journal for references to the one erased. If she had known the person well enough to care about him or her, she most certainly would have made some reference in an entire year's journal, even if her entries were infrequent.

"I think Cedar has plans for us," Arjan was saying to Laurel when Jaden refocused on the conversation.

"She'll give us some free time, won't she?" protested Laurel. "What's the point otherwise?"

For several minutes, the conversation moved along these argumentative lines, with a continual contrast between Arjan's logic and sense of Council duty, and Laurel's hopes for a romantic getaway with Cercis. Just as Jaden was thinking she would rather be back pacing the street corner than sitting in the café with Laurel, Cedar and Cercis appeared.

"Finally!" exclaimed Laurel. She reached for Cercis's hand.

"All right, everyone, finish up here and meet me in La Plazuela," Cedar instructed, handing Jaden some money. "I will arrange a table."

Jaden looked at Arjan and shrugged. He need not spend his secret stash of money. Laurel finished her espresso while Jaden paid the bill.

As the group walked through the lobby, Arjan pulled Jaden aside and into a small shop. "Go ahead," he said to the Laurel and Cercis. "We'll be right there."

"What are you doing?" Jaden asked, startled.

"Paper," he said. He picked up a small spiral notebook and a pen from a display case. "Will these do?"

"Yes," Jaden responded. "Thanks for thinking of it . . . and for paying for it."

Arjan laughed. "You know, as an alchemist, you really should learn to create some wealth for yourself."

"You didn't—" She began but then stopped herself when she noticed the cashier's puzzled look.

As they walked down the hall towards the restaurant, Jaden put the notebook and pen into her coat pocket. Thus far, no erased memories had reappeared, but at least now she was prepared if they did. Cedar, Laurel, and Cercis were seated at a table near the middle of the restaurant. Cedar, to Jaden's surprise, was drinking what appeared to be a margarita. Laurel and Cercis were discussing the menu. The room was large and colourful. A stylized but majestic double-headed eagle graced the beam above the table. Jaden liked this place. She wondered why Cedar had chosen it, whether she had history with this hotel in particular. *Cedar has a history*, Jaden realized. At one time, hundreds of years ago, she too had been a Junior Initiate. Perhaps Santa Fe had meant something to her, back in the day.

When the Initiates had placed an order for lunch and all the drinks had arrived, Cedar raised hers and made a toast. "Welcome to Santa Fe," she said. "May you find here all that you seek."

*I seek the one erased*, Jaden thought. But Cedar had something else in mind altogether.

"This afternoon, after lunch, you are to find your pendants," Cedar announced.

"Pendants!" Laurel exclaimed.

"Today, you are being given the opportunity to attain interim pendants."

Laurel and Cercis stared at Cedar in disbelief. Arjan twisted his silver chain as if anticipating its pendant. Jaden wondered about the implications this unexpected task could have on her search for the one erased. Finally, Laurel ventured, "Why?"

"You will wear your pendants in order to help the Council research the phenomenon of the disappearing bees within the protectorate libraries of the outside world."

"Here? In Santa Fe?" asked Jaden.

"Not necessarily. Council maintains protectorate libraries throughout the world. Together, they house thousands of Lapidarian manuscripts we have recovered over the centuries in the aftermath of their theft and dispersion during the Second Rebellion. Elder Council will determine in which library you would be of most value."

"Why not bring the manuscripts back to Council dimension?"

"The Elders maintain that the manuscripts are safer if secreted in numerous locations rather than one. The protectorates also act as safe houses for Council members as well as training facilities for our allies in the outside world."

"William Butler Yeats studied alchemy in both the Dublin and London protectorates," Cercis chimed in, seemingly proud to offer up this fact to Arjan.

"Really?" replied Arjan, noticeably impressed.

"But that," said Cedar, "is a story for another day. Over the next few weeks, you will be given details of the mission and your duties as necessary. The interim pendants will be infused with Lapidarian essence of a potency strong enough to last twenty-four hours per infusion. The pendant will ensure you remain connected to Council. Under accompaniment, you may come and go from Council dimension as required and as warranted for the duration of your term of duty."

As Jaden processed the explanation of the libraries and news about the interim pendants, she realized that the one erased might well have been an Initiate. After all, as Cedar herself had implied in their conversation over the ink spillage, Initiates would be the easiest Council members to erase. They had the least history with the Council and had not themselves added any new Initiates to their branch. As far as Jaden could recall, no Council branch had become weakened or ill since her arrival. Even if she could not remember the one erased, she would surely remember bouts of illness and pain throughout the orders. She realized then with growing discomfort that Junior Initiates, especially those without pendants, were certainly the most expendable members of the Alchemists' Council.

"What about the test?" Jaden asked. "Is this trip not about a test?"

"Yes, it is," replied Cedar. "The test is to locate a pendant that can withstand Lapidarian infusion. Turquoise works best, no matter its shade. Other than that, you are on your own. Choose wisely." Cedar then stood up. "Enjoy your lunch. Divide this money among you," she said as she placed an envelope on the table. "Meet me at the San Miguel Mission at five." She turned and walked away, leaving Jaden, Arjan, Cercis, and Laurel to discuss the turn of events.

"Can you believe this?" asked Laurel.

"I am astonished," said Arjan. "But the granting

of interim pendants is not without precedent. I read about a similar situation in one of our history textbooks."

"Really?" said Cercis. He wanted to know more, but Laurel interrupted.

"Well, a history book is one thing, but can you believe this is happening to *us* right here and now?" Laurel threw her head back and her arms up as if making a victory cheer. "This is the best thing that has happened to me since that spa day in Vienna with Kalina."

"Before you joined the Council?" asked Cercis.

"No — last year, with Kalina. You know, the Senior Initiate. Remember, when Obeche sent us to that spa as a reward for our exam scores?"

"I don't remember anyone named Kalina."

"What happened to her?" asked Laurel. "I haven't seen . . . Wait . . . I don't remember . . . Who is she? I don't remember her except . . . This is . . . weird."

Jaden, who had been sipping her drink and only half-listening, suddenly sat straight up. She ran through the names of all twelve Senior Initiates.

"I don't know Kalina." She looked at Arjan. "Do you?"

"No. No one on the Council is named Kalina."

"She's the one," gasped Jaden. "Kalina is the one."

"Which one?" asked Cercis.

Jaden pulled her notebook and pen out of her pocket. "The one erased!"

"What?" said Laurel.

"My seat on the Council opened as a result of erasure," explained Arjan. "Kalina may be the one who was erased."

"I can picture her at the spa with me, but I don't *remember* her," said Laurel.

"And even this memory may be temporary," said Arjan.

"You have to tell me everything you remember about her before we return to Council dimension," Jaden said.

Laurel looked puzzled. She squinted and then glanced up towards the ceiling.

"I just . . ." Laurel paused. "I don't know. I just . . . I have . . . fragments. It's like I suddenly saw us at the spa, and I knew the spa was in Vienna. But then when I try to think about the details, I can't remember anything except that I'd had the memory. I mean — *now* I remember the memory but not the actual event." Laurel shook her head in frustration.

"Okay, then, describe the memory of the memory before it vanishes too," said Jaden. "Describe anything — everything."

"Why?" asked Cercis. "Are you hoping to resurrect her? If she's erased, she's erased. We're not supposed to remember. Dredging up fragments is futile."

"She was erased for a reason, Cercis. Don't you want to know the reason?"

"No, I don't care to know the reason. If we were meant to know, we'd know."

Cercis stood up and reached out a hand for

Laurel. "Come on. Let's go. Finding our pendants is the current priority."

Laurel pushed back her chair and gathered her belongings. She took Cercis's hand and smiled. "Our pendants await!" she exclaimed, in what Jaden read as forced enthusiasm.

Jaden thought about pleading for Laurel to stay, but she knew it would only aggravate Cercis further and, consequently, have no effect on Laurel. She smiled weakly at Laurel who, to Jaden's surprise, maintained eye contact for a few seconds longer than usual. Perhaps Laurel remembered something after all. Perhaps she would tell Jaden as soon as the opportunity arose. As she and Cercis walked away, Jaden pulled out her notebook and wrote the following words, which she then showed to Arjan: *The one erased may be a former Senior Initiate named Kalina. Laurel recalls spending time with Kalina at a spa in Vienna last year.* Arjan nodded his approval.

"You could look through Council archives for evidence of travel to Vienna last year. I believe all travel to and from Council dimension must be recorded."

"No doubt our journey to Santa Fe has been duly noted."

"Yes, I suppose it has. Shall we go then?"

"I don't want a pendant. Its Lapidarian essence will make me forget."

"You have not yet remembered anything. Besides, the pendant will remain essence-free until the Night of Albedo. And you must also keep in mind that the advantages of possessing a pendant outweigh the disadvantages."

"Time will tell," said Jaden.

They walked from La Fonda to the Palace of the Governors, where vendors from local pueblos displayed their wares. Arjan said he was not interested in searching the stores of Santa Fe: he would find his pendant along the palace walkway or nowhere. At first Jaden thought his decision was limiting, but she soon found herself immersed in searching for her own pendant among myriad possibilities of varying shapes, sizes, and colours. Indeed, Jaden lost track of Arjan completely at one point, presuming he had wandered amidst the crowds to the other end of the palace. Eventually, she found herself comfortably seated beside the display of jewellery offered by a woman named Florence. Jaden held one, then another, then another of Florence's pendants until finally she narrowed her choices to three. She stared and stared at the pendants. She felt their weight and texture. She looked at the silver casing and at the specks of colour within the turquoise. Finally, after long deliberation, she chose one of blue turquoise flecked with black. *The Flaw in the Stone*, she thought to herself. Florence smiled, nodded, took Jaden's money, and rummaged for change. "Thank you," Jaden said before walking away in search of Arjan.

Arjan had chosen a large pendant of green turquoise, crisscrossed with seams of brown. It hung elegantly from his chain against the black of his shirt. Jaden removed her chosen pendant from its little plastic bag and showed him. She did not yet have a chain on which the pendant would find its home.

"That will look beautiful against your robes," Arjan offered.

Their pendant search completed with almost two hours to spare before the appointed time of return to Council dimension, Arjan and Jaden wandered the streets of Santa Fe. They talked of Kalina and of Laurel and of Cercis. They interjected comments on the exquisite or gaudy or shocking or elegant objects displayed in the windows of various shops. They stood near the sculpture of the burro on Burro Alley and read over the sentences in Jaden's notebook. "I wonder which spa," said Jaden, leaning against the burro.

With only a few minutes to spare before the rendezvous, Jaden found a chain for her pendant in an exquisite boutique on West San Francisco Street. The chain, in both length and flexibility, would not be suitable for a permanent pendant — that would require an official pendant cord — but Jaden decided it would work for her temporary pendant. Thus she, like Arjan, donned her pendant as they returned to the Old Santa Fe Trail and made their way towards the rendezvous point.

Cedar accompanied each of the Junior Initiates back to Council dimension, one by one in the order she had brought them to Santa Fe. Thus Jaden was the first to return. She sat in the main courtyard by the fountain and waited for Arjan. She would ask him for tea — spiced perhaps — before she settled in for an evening of lesson review. She recalled that Arjan had suggested she search the archives upon return, but she couldn't remember the reason. Perhaps he needed her help for an assignment. Or perhaps it had something to do with the one erased — but what? Perhaps she had forgotten the details now that she had returned to Lapidarian proximity. She would ask him when he arrived. She opened the notebook that Arjan had bought for her to search its pages for any memories she may have recorded and subsequently forgotten. But it was blank. *Today's journey must not have been long enough for the outside world to offer up any of its secrets*, she thought.

A few days later, Cedar crossed the threshold to the Inner Chamber and knelt on one of the smooth granite inlays. She lowered her head, in gesture to the Azoth Magen, who sat high on the alembic ladder, his back turned to the Elders. The Ritual of Restoration would soon begin. A full restoration — used to repair elemental damage throughout Council dimension — would take the better part of the day. Since Cedar could think of little other than her plans for the upcoming week, she was thankful that today's ritual would be limited to chanting only the fifth portion of the text — the section concerned with protecting Lapidarian manuscripts. She needed to focus on the ritual, not on the Junior Initiates. Obeche's acknowledgement of Cedar, made in the form of a brief nod from his position on another inlay across the room, was taken by Cedar as a patronizing sign. He still believed he was right, and he would ensure that the interim pendants for the Initiates would be swiftly revoked upon the restoration of the bees.

The Azoth Magen himself had called the Elder Council together for the ritual. His research and Azothian consultations with Ruis and Ravenea led him to conclude that invoking restoration could well be the Council's best defence against the possibility of manuscript sabotage by the Rebel Branch. Certainly, another rebellion could not be allowed under any circumstances. Above all, the Earth itself could fail to recover from such an outright attack on elemental balance. He raised his arms, inviting the Elders to do the same, and within moments the blue light of transmutation filled the Inner Chamber. Pendants glowed against the surrounding blue — beacons identifying each of the Council members and the Azoth himself.

"We call on the Earth. We call on the Wind. We call on the Sea. We call on the Ember," Azoth Ravenea began.

"From the Stone to the Scribe; from the Scribe to the Reader," continued Azoth Ruis.

"We, the Elders of the Alchemists' Council,

hereby restore the balance," commanded the Azoth Magen. His voice rang out against the growing resonance of the elements. He had written the invocation for this restoration in particular. He called out to the arboreal essence, to the vines on the ground and on the cliffs, to the flowers on the earth and in the mountains. He invoked the Lapidarian promise of *Ruach 2103*, folio 51 verso — the manuscript leaf from which Linden had first witnessed the bees disappearing. He called upon the apiarian memory from this and other manuscripts inscribed with Lapidarian ink. He intoned the ancient Council chants, to which Cedar and the others responded in sequence when called upon.

Over an hour had passed with chanting before the Azoth himself knelt at the base of the alembic ladder and began dissolution of the restoration formula. Obeche's voice could be heard above the others. *Thus commands the Alchemists' Council. Thus commands the One over the Others.* Cedar too spoke and sang and chanted the ritual elements to return the bees to the manuscripts. At the height of the ritual, her attention remained astutely set on the task — her focus sharp, her intention clear. She was indeed so intently focused that she failed at first to notice the alchemical blue light fading prematurely. Unlike Cedar, several of the Elders had already stopped chanting. Not until the Azoth Magen roared for silence did Cedar understand the gravity of the problem.

In this silence, as the blue light continued to fade, a red light began to grow. Obeche bellowed, "No!" But the light took only moments to change completely. The air dripped with crimson-red moisture. Amur struggled for breath. Ravenea raised an Azothian sceptre, shining its light across the room. Cedar stood and moved towards the alembic. Though the red haze itself remained in the room no longer than five minutes, the sudden and strident laughter that accompanied the vanishing haze echoed in Cedar's mind for several hours after the ritual. She recognized the disembodied voice immediately, as did several of the others. But no one dared speak before the Azoth Magen. Even Obeche had adopted a posture of submission, awaiting instructions.

"The sanctuary has been breached!" cried the Azoth Magen. "The Rebel Branch mocks us with laughter to which we will respond with battle cries. Long live the Quintessence!"

"Long live the Alchemists' Council!"

The Ritual of Restoration having failed, the Elders moved from the Inner Chamber to Azothian Chambers for instruction and consultation. Obeche and Amur worked with Azoth Ruis and Rowan Esche to determine whether the erasure itself had failed at the elemental level. Azoth Ravenea and Rowan Kai, along with Cedar and Tera, scanned dozens of manuscripts for signs of a Lapidarian breach or lacuna. Yet after hours of labour, well into the night, no one had located a single piece of evidence suggesting an imminent rebellion beyond a single voice. And the voice itself was an impossibility. It had been banished forever from Council dimension through official erasure; yet it had been heard within the Inner Chamber by the entire Elder Council.

"She kept her promise," Obeche reminded the others at the first sign of dawn.

"She did indeed," replied Cedar.

Thus they finally acknowledged aloud the name that had remained unspoken through the night.

"Kalina."

## III
## one year ago

Jaden arrived early to the Elixir Chamber of the Initiate classroom. She wanted a chance to choose her supplies and equipment before the others arrived so she would be ready to begin before Magistrate Sadira appeared. Despite her status as the newest Initiate, Jaden wanted to appear *impressive* in Sadira's eyes. Not only was Sadira Jaden's favourite tutor, but today was the day the Initiates would be reproducing with physical ingredients the alchemical formula that Linden and Tesu had been discussing over the previous four lessons. Finally her first day of laboratory work had arrived. Jaden was about to participate in an *actual* alchemical experiment. She would not have to listen to Linden droning on and reiterating what she could have read for herself in the textbook; instead she would measure and combine and stir and heat the requisite liquids and powders and minerals and metals to turn a pellet of lead into a nugget of gold. Yes, Jaden understood that such basic transmutation was the most stereotypical alchemical practice of all. Yes, she knew that Azoth Ailanthus — indeed, all the Elders — could transform any compound to gold with a mere touch of a Lapidarian pendant and the recitation of a few key words: no ingredients required. And, yes, Jaden knew that for most alchemists of the Alchemists' Council, alchemical practice comprised official Council duties — making ink, transcribing visions, inscribing manuscripts, reading icons, and participating in various works and rituals aimed at the Council's main purpose: to maintain elemental balance of the dimensions. But an Initiate had to begin at the beginning, and today Jaden would begin. Today she would become an alchemist. Perhaps, as a result of this new beginning, she could put an end to (or at least give herself a reprieve from) her desire to escape Council dimension.

Jaden had decided, after only her first few weeks, that Sadira's lessons were preferable to those of both Linden and Tesu. Today, a few months later, she hoped Sadira would arrive before her fellow Initiates and take note of Jaden's enthusiasm for laboratory work. Though Jaden knew that practical and written exams were the ultimate measure of one's alchemical competency, she hoped that punctuality and organization would give her a slight edge over Laurel, Cercis, and Ritha in Sadira's moral assessment of the Junior Initiates. What other advantage could Jaden have, given that she was the most recent arrival and, thus, the most naïve when it came to alchemical knowledge and protocols? The other three of her quarto had been here substantially longer than Jaden, and Laurel appeared particularly grateful to relinquish the role of newest Initiate. Of course, she surpassed Jaden in all arenas — including physical attractiveness, with her short and spiked hair. Jaden's own long, wavy hair looked to be a tangled mess in comparison. Cercis, with only a few more years of experience than Laurel, acted as if he had both seniority and superiority over not only the other Juniors but the Senior Initiates as well. During joint Initiate classes, Cercis did indeed surpass most of the Seniors in his ability to solve theoretical dilemmas posed by the tutors. Another person may have gained respect from fellow students in such circumstances, but Cercis appeared to annoy everyone other than Laurel. Ritha had been a Council member the longest. Thus, she regularly asserted her hope that a conjunction in the upper orders would open a space for her own ascension out of the Junior Initiate. A week ago, Cercis had overheard Ritha expressing such a hope, at which point he adamantly reminded everyone that assessment for Initiate Ascension — like ascension to any Order — was made by Elder Council recommendation, not by seniority. "Exactly," Ritha had responded, thus securing Jaden's admiration.

"I've heard a rumour," Ritha whispered as she took her place at the table beside Jaden.

"Yes?" said Jaden, mildly disappointed that Ritha had arrived before Sadira.

"Tesu has been cleared for conjunction by the Elders. So, my days in the Junior Initiate may soon come to an end."

Jaden, not sure how to respond to such news, muttered, "I'll miss you." Ritha was the only person with whom Jaden had bonded here. Without Ritha's presence in the Junior Initiate, Jaden's desire to leave Council dimension would heighten exponentially.

Ritha laughed. "It's not immediate. But I can see the light — so to speak. Apparently he discovered his own conjunctive destiny in the manuscripts last month. Can you imagine? Of course, all the Elders had to verify his findings, which they finally completed yesterday. Well, that's the rumour — *unofficially*. The Azoths should make the official Announcement of Concurrence next week." Ritha paused, looked behind her towards the door, as if checking for eavesdroppers, and then grabbed Jaden's arm. "Who do you think his partner will be?"

"I have no idea," said Jaden.

"I predict a Reader — maybe Terek or Wu Tong — which means someone from the Junior Magistrate will ascend to Senior Magistrate, and someone from the Senior Initiate will ascend to Junior Magistrate."

Jaden nodded, trying to follow Ritha's hierarchy of the Orders of Council.

"So," Ritha continued elatedly, "a few months from now, *yours truly* will ascend from the Junior to Senior Initiate and wave to you from on high. Just kidding . . . about the on high part." Though she remained in her spot beside the table, Ritha performed a short but enthusiastic dance of joy. "Can you believe it?" she asked. "I thought I'd have to wait years."

"So this isn't the usual time frame between conjunctions?"

"There's no standard. Timing depends on the manuscripts, so you never know for sure. Linden once told us, in one of his otherwise boring lessons, that the longest stretch between conjunctions was fifteen years. Imagine! Someone — I think it was Ela — remained a Junior Initiate for thirty-two years. And, of course, at the higher orders, the waiting can be interminable. Imagine being an Azoth for hundreds of years waiting for the Azoth Magen's Final Ascension!" She laughed. "Zelkova was lucky getting out of the Junior Initiate when she did — she ascended thanks to Cedar and Saule's conjunction. And then we waited almost four *years* for you to arrive. Usually a new Initiate is found within a few months of the conjunction, which will be lucky for you."

"Lucky for me?"

"You won't have to be the newest Initiate for more than a few months. Really it would be perfect timing for everyone."

Once again, Jaden was unsure how to respond.

She had no idea whether this was perfect timing or not. Time, more than anything else in Council dimension, seemed relative. She merely hoped she would like whoever replaced her as the newest Initiate.

Sadira entered the classroom, thus bringing Ritha's aspirations for ascension to a temporary end. A few minutes later, after Laurel and Cercis had taken their seats, Sadira instructed everyone to choose appropriate vessels and heating implements before collecting the ingredient list. Having prepared her materials in advance, Jaden stood quietly and waited for further instructions.

"The primary vessel must be made of dark glass," Sadira said as Laurel carried one of light green to her table. "Is that *dark*, Laurel?"

"It's not clear," responded Laurel.

"It's also not dark."

When everyone was prepared, when vessels had been heated to precisely the correct temperature, Sadira directed everyone in the mixture of a chemical solution that was then poured slowly into the primary vessel.

"Position your lead pellet directly over the vessel. Allow it to be moistened by the vapours before letting it drop into the liquid."

Jaden followed each step with care. Every minute of the first two hours was spent on a specific aspect of the transmutation. After the liquid came the mineral powder, then the salt block, then the silver infusion, and after that came the recitation of four particular alchemical chants — one of which had to be said in a specific 4th Council dialect. Jaden had rehearsed the chants repeatedly the night before. If she did not manage to turn her lead into gold, mispronunciation would be the most likely culprit. Step by step, Jaden followed Sadira's instructions. Finally, the penultimate stage arrived: settling. The Initiates must wait to let the alchemical transmutation complete itself. Sadira said they could take a break as they waited, which Laurel, Cercis, and Ritha immediately did. But Jaden stayed put, peering into the dark vessel, hoping to observe the movement and colour shift that would indicate completion. Perhaps someday, after several years in the Initiate, after several years of repeating this same experiment, she would become lackadaisical, as the other Initiates seemed to be today.

"You seem anxious," said Sadira, who was now standing on the other side of the table from Jaden.

Jaden smiled and nodded.

"As was I," continued Sadira, "all those years ago."

"Was your first transmutation successful?" asked Jaden.

Sadira laughed. "Not exactly. Be patient, Jaden. A hundred years or so from now when you are teaching this class, you may well find yourself nostalgic for these Initiate days, for a time when everything was something new to be discovered."

And thus Jaden waited as patiently as she could.

Twenty minutes later, she poured the contents of her vessel into the drying solution, moving what felt like a hard pebble around with her fingertips through blue-tinged sand. Finally, she extracted the pebble and took it to the small fountain to be rinsed. The water felt soothing against her hand.

"Congratulations," commended Sadira, as each of the four Initiates held up a small but perfect piece of gold.

The rumour of Tesu's conjunction was confirmed the following week at a Council meeting. Azoth Ravenea made the Announcement of Concurrence, which was met by enthusiastic applause from the Council followed by the recitation of the "announcement" portion of the Law Codes of Conjunction, which Jaden had not yet memorized. Thus, instead of reciting, she stood silently and listened, trying to determine from the codes the precise meaning and outcome of conjunction. As she had done on countless occasions since her arrival, she found herself wishing that alchemical texts and icons were not as utterly incomprehensible as she found them to be. *Reading alchemical manuscripts requires you to move beyond language. You will learn to do so soon enough*, Cedar had told her. Jaden wondered how many decades comprised *soon enough* and how many times through those decades she would fail to believe Cedar.

Rowan Esche escorted a young woman to the dais. Cries of astonishment and whispers erupted. The woman, Jaden assumed, had been chosen as Tesu's partner for conjunction. The Elders nodded solemnly, but the other Council members were visibly and audibly shocked at the Elders' decision. Even Tesu himself appeared taken aback, though Jaden knew little of him and nothing of the woman who, shortly thereafter, stood on the Azothian dais face to face with Tesu, holding his hands. Cercis, who had fallen back into his seat beside Jaden, was shaking his head in apparent disbelief.

"It could have been me!" he whispered to Laurel, loud enough to be overheard by both Jaden and Ritha.

"You!" exclaimed Ritha. "It could have been *me*!"

"What do you mean?" Jaden asked.

"Tesu's partner — she's from the Senior Initiate. If I had ascended to Senior Initiate instead of Zelkova, I could have been among the candidates," said Ritha.

"It doesn't work that way," insisted Laurel. Her annoyance was clear by her tone, but Jaden did not know whether she was annoyed at the ignorance of her fellow Junior Initiates or at the choice of the Senior Initiate for conjunction.

Jaden turned towards the woman standing beside Tesu. She wore garnet-coloured robes. Her long blonde hair fell loosely over her shoulders. She stood calmly, seemingly unabashed despite the Council members' ongoing whispers. Though Jaden had not noticed during the initial flurry preceding the announcement, she saw now that the woman looked significantly younger than Tesu. Jaden did not recall having seen her elsewhere in Council dimension. How could she have missed noticing someone so utterly serene and captivating? The woman smiled and clasped her pendant in her left hand, holding it against her chest. Bowing towards the Initiates, her eyes briefly met Jaden's, and Jaden turned swiftly away, aware of the heat of her sudden blushing.

"Who is she?" Jaden asked Ritha.

Ritha, Cercis, and Laurel answered simultaneously: "Kalina."

Though she did not recall having seen Kalina prior to the Council meeting, Jaden began seeing her continually thereafter. She would turn a corner in the North Library and notice Kalina pulling a book from a shelf. She would cut across the courtyard in search of Ritha and glimpse Kalina sitting under the willow tree writing in a journal. She would wander into a room of the Council archives looking for material to complete a lesson assignment and find Kalina studying documents by candlelight. Once she literally bumped into her while turning a corner on her way to the dining hall. To Jaden's surprise and, gradually, bafflement, Kalina did not speak a word to her during any of these chance encounters. Even when Jaden attempted to engage in conversation by saying hello, Kalina merely nodded quickly. On one occasion, in the hazy light of the deepest archives, Jaden dared to comment on the beauty of Kalina's pendant — a dark green stone encased in silver repoussé. In response, Kalina caught Jaden's eyes for longer than usual and smiled. She then returned to her archival work, leaving Jaden to wonder whether Kalina thought herself too good to speak with a Junior Initiate thanks to her pre-conjunction status.

This, of course, led Jaden not to give up on Kalina but to persevere. One morning, having been jolted awake by two birds fighting outside her window, Jaden serendipitously spotted Kalina — hair and garnet robes flowing — heading away from the residence building along the stone path that led to the backwoods. Jaden quickly threw her robes on over her nightclothes and hurried from her chambers, moving swiftly out the back door of the residence and down towards the woods. She followed the stone walkway until it reached the edge of the forest and then proceeded along a dirt path through the trees. After a few minutes, with no sign of Kalina, Jaden reached a point along the path that required a decision: should she continue moving forward or make a sharp turn to the right? As she stood contemplating the situation, she suddenly heard voices: a man and a woman arguing. She could not make out most of the words, but the voices most certainly came from farther ahead; thus Jaden progressed forward quietly and slowly, holding her robes as close to her as she could so as not to accidentally rustle the bushes along the path. When she glimpsed a shot of colour through the trees — presumably the robe of one of the two speakers — Jaden moved off the path into the bushes and positioned herself low to the ground.

From her crouched and concealed position she could make out only one of the two figures. He — or perhaps she — wore blue alchemical robes, their sheen distinctly visible against the dark grey background of the cliff face. She crept forward slowly, moving cautiously from gap to gap within the bushes, attempting to catch a glimpse of a face. But the leaves and branches, even with her improved proximity, continued to hinder her view. Nonetheless, from her new position a few feet closer to the pair, she could clearly hear their conversation.

"Are you certain Tesu did not see us?" asked the man.

"I am certain," responded the woman. "All is well."

"Still, we cannot continue to take such unnecessary risks alone."

"No. We must request assistance."

The figure Jaden could see pulled out a large red stone from beneath the folds of the blue robes. Then, in a language Jaden did not recognize, the man recited what sounded from its rhythm and intonation to be an incantation of some sort. For a few moments, both the man and the woman were silent, the blue-robed figure facing the cliff face. Then, suddenly, the figure became shrouded by a swirling mist and disappeared. Jaden gasped. She stood up and moved cautiously towards the cliff face. Faint footprints were the only remaining trace of the strangers on the dusty ground.

Jaden ran her hand against the rock of the cliff face. She bowed her head and waited silently. Nothing happened. If the spot was a portal to the outside world, Jaden had no means of activating it or replicating the events she had witnessed. Nonetheless, given this newly discovered possibility of escape, her life in Council dimension unexpectedly became vastly more interesting. For now, though, she decided she should return to her chambers, before anyone noticed her absence.

"What are you doing here?"

Jaden jolted and turned. Adrenaline flooded through her, burning the tips of her fingers and toes. She stood perfectly still, staring at the person who had startled her.

Sadira had not spoken with Cedar for over a week — not since Cedar had reprimanded her in front of the other Magistrates for neglecting to secure a Lapidarian manuscript in the archival vaults. Now, sitting at her desk in the calligraphy classroom, supervising an early morning session for a few Senior Initiates who required additional scribal practice, Sadira could barely remain focused. She had dreamed of Saule the night before and now longed for her. She questioned, as she had so many times since Cedar's revelation about her victory in her conjunction with Saule, whether the outcome could be justified — and, with the now familiar and persistently nagging anxiousness, whether she would defend the outcome if ever questioned by the Elder Council. *I was coerced to agree*, she imagined herself pleading at the trial. *I heeded my Elders.*

But even if she managed to convince the Council of her innocence, she was unlikely to convince herself. In her love for Cedar, she had betrayed Saule. How could her action be called anything other than betrayal when she had become lovers with the person who, for all intents and purposes, had murdered the love of her life? No rhetorical manoeuvring could persuade her otherwise. And for what? For the good of the Council? For the good of humanity? *Ha!* She accidentally released an audible interjection of sarcasm, which caused every one of her would-be Scribes to look up from their work. She coughed, as a belated disguise, and motioned for the students to continue their work. Perhaps one of them, someday, hundreds of years from now, would inscribe Sadira's final ascension. Perhaps one of these Initiates would, indeed, inscribe the ultimate Final Ascension, and all her work would be for naught.

"Excuse me, Magistrate Sadira," said Zelkova loudly, pulling Sadira from her reverie.

"Yes, Zelkova."

"My *m*s and *n*s are indistinguishable when I use a number two Lapidarian nib on vellum. If this were a real manuscript, chaos would ensue."

"Chaos is underrated," she responded, without thinking.

She immediately regretted her words and their implication. But the students laughed.

"I'll keep that in mind for theory class," joked Li, one of Sadira's current favourites.

"I'm serious!" protested Zelkova. "I need some help."

Sadira refrained from uttering a sarcastic verbal agreement. Instead, she walked over to Zelkova's table and examined both the transcript and the pen. "The nib is cracked," she said. "Come and get another." She escorted Zelkova to the implement cabinet, helped her fit the new nib onto her pen, and then said to the class, "Remember, inspect all your pens and nibs before engaging the ink. Save yourself from inscribing something you regret."

"Regrets need not be permanent," said Li. "Mistakes can be corrected, right?"

"A manuscript can be adjusted on the advice of the Readers and permission of the Elders. However, such a discrepancy between Novillian visions and Lapidarian inscription may not be noticed immediately. Indeed, depending on the extent of the error and the subject matter of the inscription, it may never be noticed. Even an astute Reader may miss one jagged stroke caused by a broken nib, yet that same jagged stroke could lead to a minor imbalance in the outside world. Would you want to be responsible for an earthquake? A tornado? A flood? A forest fire? Earth, air, water, and fire — all must remain balanced. Maintaining elemental balance is the responsibility of the Scribes and the Readers working together *not* making mistakes."

"I don't want to do this," said Zelkova.

"You don't want to do what?" asked Sadira.

"I don't want to make a mistake. I don't want such responsibility."

"You do not have the choice," replied Sadira. "You are duty-bound. Your fear will dissipate. You have many years of study ahead of you — indeed, most likely hundreds of years ahead of you — before you will achieve Lapidarian status. By then you will no longer be making Initiate mistakes. For now, you need only pay attention to the lessons we attempt to impart."

"Yes, Magistrate," said Zelkova. She dipped her pen and newly replaced nib into the ink and recommenced her attempts at *m*s and *n*s.

"What are you doing here?" Kalina asked again.

"I . . . I followed someone," said Jaden.

"Whom?"

Jaden did not know how much of the truth to reveal.

"Whom did you follow?" Kalina repeated.

"At first, you. But then I came across two people talking, so I hid and listened."

Kalina raised an eyebrow and waited for further explanation.

"I couldn't see their faces. I don't know who they were."

"But you overheard their conversation?"

"I heard part of it — a few sentences. One was a man and the other a woman, but I didn't recognize their voices. I was hiding over there." Jaden pointed to the shrubbery behind Kalina.

"And what did they say?"

"First something about Tesu and then something about requesting an assistant."

"And then?"

"And then they disappeared through the rocks — here." She turned around and ran a hand over a small area of the cliff face.

Kalina did not seem surprised by this revelation. She leaned back against the cliff face and crossed her arms.

"And why did you follow me here in the first place?"

Jaden, having recovered slightly from the sequence of events, decided she had no reason to continue being interrogated.

"Why are you asking me so many questions?"

Kalina seemed not to have expected Jaden to be so brazen. She moved away from the cliff and walked towards her. Stopping close enough to her that their robes brushed against one another, Kalina touched Jaden's arm.

"Do you trust me?" she asked.

"Trust you? I barely know you!" Jaden replied. She pulled away from Kalina.

"Not yet," she said.

"I don't trust you yet?"

"You don't *know* me yet. And there may come a time that you don't know me again."

"What?"

"I can't explain right now. I have to go. You will understand soon."

Kalina turned swiftly away from Jaden, put both her hands on the cliff face, and, like the other two, vanished instantaneously. Jaden, shocked, took a step too quickly backward and tripped over her robes. She sat on the dusty ground waiting for her racing heart rate to slow. Though she understood virtually nothing of this morning's events, she had already witnessed enough to regret her choices. Kalina and the others were clearly engaged in something so far removed from Council protocols that Jaden now feared for her safety. She had been in Council dimension only a few months and had already managed to invite peril into her new life.

Not knowing what to do, she remained seated

for several minutes until she finally stood up, dusted herself off, and moved once again to the cliff face to investigate further. Surely the apparently impenetrable surface would offer up some clue to its permeability. But it did not. After a while, frustrated in her failed attempts, Jaden headed back towards Council grounds. Not wanting to lose her footing again, she walked slowly and carefully along the path. By the time she reached the main courtyard, she realized she could not keep this information to herself. She needed to talk to someone. But whom could she tell? Whom could she trust? Whom did she know enough to trust?

She would find Sadira.

Sadira, Linden, and the six other tutors sat at a large table in the mid-morning light of the majestic stained-glass window of the North Library. They were planning the lesson rotation and timetable for the summer quarter. All Magistrates, as part of their own ongoing training and Council business, regularly worked on assignments prescribed by the Readers and Scribes. Thus all twenty Junior Magistrates and all sixteen Senior Magistrates participated daily, directly or indirectly, in maintaining elemental balance both within and outside Council dimension. Additionally, eight Magistrates — four from each Order for four-year terms each — were assigned as tutors for the Junior and Senior Initiate classes. Of these eight tutors, two were renewed after their initial four-year terms for an additional four years to act as supervisors for the tutors and classes. Currently Sadira and Linden were in the midst of fulfilling these supervisory duties. Both would rather have more time to hone their alchemical skills with the Scribes and Readers, but they knew their tutorial terms would fare them well during Elder Council ascension decisions. So, on this day, they explained the process to the new tutors; divided Junior and Senior courses based on tutor strengths and aptitudes; provided course materials and lesson plans; outlined techniques for adapting official lesson plans to suit the varying proficiency levels of the Initiates — no small task, given that each quarto comprises Initiates with vastly differing years of Council experience — answered myriad questions; and finally sent them on their way, classroom keys in hand.

"This part is inevitably tiring," said Sadira, reorganizing the various papers and folders she had brought to the meeting.

"I don't mind," said Linden. "I always find the beginning of a new course rotation to be invigorating."

His enthusiasm exasperated Sadira. Was he putting on a show for her sake? Did he believe that her Senior status afforded her influence when it came to Junior ascension? Even if it did, he would do better to admit his weaknesses to her rather than play up his confidence. She frequently wondered whether most men — even here, in a dimension where gender lines were blurred over the millennia through conjunction — were like this in their displays of self-assurance. Among the men on the Council, she did not mind Linden — indeed, she was rather fond of him at times — but she refused to believe that he never felt overworked, and she wished he would just be honest with her.

The double doors of the library swung open swiftly, crashing loudly against the pillars framing the doorway. Both Sadira and Linden were startled enough to jump. Jaden rushed across the room to the table. She was out of breath and agitated.

"Sadira, I've been looking for you everywhere. I need your help."

"What is it?"

"May I speak with you in private?"

"Is this a personal matter or a matter of Council business?" Sadira asked.

"I believe it's a matter of importance to the Council," said Jaden.

"Then you may tell both Sadira and me," insisted Linden.

Jaden did not speak. She stood, breathing heavily, still out of breath from her long trek through various Council buildings.

"Go ahead, Jaden," said Sadira.

"Can I trust you?"

"Are you suggesting that certain members of the Alchemists' Council are not to be trusted?" asked Linden.

"I don't know. I just saw people disappear through solid rock."

Sadira and Linden briefly looked at one another before inviting Jaden to sit down.

"Explain everything from the beginning," said Sadira.

Linden took out a notepad and pen. Sadira nodded to Jaden to begin. Jaden sat with the two Magistrates for almost an hour, reviewing the details of her morning adventure, and thereafter answering numerous questions asked by both Sadira and Linden. *Was the woman's voice high-pitched? What colour were the man's robes? Was the woman wearing a ring? What time — exactly — did the disappearance occur? Would you recognize the precise location of their disappearance? You are certain that the only alchemist mentioned by the strangers was Tesu? Was his conjunction with Kalina mentioned? Was Kalina mentioned?* Jaden answered as completely as she was able, but some details had escaped her observation.

With regard to Kalina, she did not lie — not exactly. She had described, to the best of her ability, the words and actions of the two strangers, and neither had mentioned Kalina. But she purposely chose not to mention her encounter with Kalina. She had not originally planned to edit the details. Her decision to do so resulted — abruptly and unexpectedly — from a distrust of Linden. At the moment he had asked her whether certain members of the Council could not be trusted, Jaden realized that she had no particular grounds to trust him or any Council member more than she had reason to trust Kalina. She had, after all, been virtually abducted into the Council, her mind altered with its alchemically enhanced vapours. If the strangers at the cliff face were a danger to Jaden herself or to the Council, Jaden had done her duty by reporting the incident. The Elder Council could investigate further if they so chose. In the meantime, she saw no reason to implicate Kalina before she had the opportunity to speak with her again. At the very least, she now had something she did not have a few hours ago: a secret that could prove useful.

"Jaden," said Sadira, after the questions had ceased, "we need to impress upon you the seriousness of this matter. You did well to come to us. Please do not discuss anything you witnessed today with anyone else on the Council — including the other Initiates. Linden and I will take the matter to the Elders."

"What's going on?" Jaden asked.

Sadira and Linden glanced at one another but neither answered.

"Please," said Jaden. "I need to know. I trusted you."

"I'm not certain," said Sadira. "The people you

saw could be Council members on official Council business of which I am simply unaware."

"Alternatively, in a worst-case scenario," added Linden, "the incident could be Rebel Branch activity, complete with a breach into Council dimension."

"The Rebel Branch," repeated Jaden. "What's the Rebel Branch?"

"Vigilantes," said Linden. "A self-sustaining branch of the Alchemical Tree as old as the Council itself. For thousands of years, legions of generations, the Council has maintained control over the Tree, its Rebel Branch, and the outside world, but not without losses and irreparable damage. Congratulations, Jaden, you may have thwarted a rebel plot — quite the feat for a new Initiate."

"Are we in danger?" Jaden asked. The fear she had managed to suppress earlier now invaded both mind and body.

"Not for long," replied Linden. "We will consult with the Elders. Until told otherwise, do not venture beyond the main courtyard and surrounding buildings. We will call you if we need you to appear before the Elder Council."

Sadira and Linden left the library, leaving Jaden to contemplate her circumstances. Though Sadira had praised her decision to report the incident to the Magistrates, Jaden questioned whether she had indeed made the right choice. Perhaps she should not have said anything at all. Perhaps she should have gone directly to the Elder Council instead of coming to Sadira. She could not help wondering if the comfort of familiarity with Sadira had caused her to act impulsively, without justification. What if the two strangers were completely innocent? She could have waited to learn more information, waited at least to talk to Kalina again. She questioned what the Elder Council would do with the strangers and, worse, with Kalina if they were determined to be members of the Rebel Branch. Of course, this made her wonder what precisely the rebels were rebelling against. She stood up, but instead of returning to her room, she ventured farther into the library.

Sadira and Linden had almost reached Azothian Chambers when Sadira stopped and pulled Linden aside into a small alcove.

"What are you doing?" Linden said loudly.

"Quiet! The Azoths might hear you."

"Isn't that the point?"

Sadira glanced up and down the corridor to make certain they were alone. "I have been thinking that perhaps this is not the best course of action." She paused, attempting to anticipate Linden's response. "Perhaps we should not go directly to the Azoths."

"An Initiate has witnessed a potential breach!"

said Linden. "The Elders must be consulted immediately."

"Yes, of course, but do you think it wise to disturb the Azoths directly? What if these so-called strangers were, in fact, Council members on assignment for the Scribes? You know as well as I that the cliff face can be used as a portal to eastern hemisphere destinations. Perhaps they were en route to the Qingdao protectorate on official Council business. I believe it would be prudent to consult Amur or Cedar or one of the other Novillian Scribes. If the activity is cause for concern, the Scribes can inform the Azoths. On the other hand, if Jaden misunderstood the situation, we could be saving ourselves potential embarrassment by going to the Scribes rather than the Azoths." Sadira again glanced along the corridor. "Think about ascension," she added.

Linden glowered at Sadira. "What is going on?" he asked. "Do you know who they were?"

"Who?"

"The strangers!"

"Of course not! I am simply . . . thinking about our future."

Just then the door to the Azothian Chambers opened. Linden stepped out of the alcove, prepared to address whichever Azoth appeared before him. To Sadira's relief, the Council member who entered the corridor was not an Azoth, but a Novillian Scribe: Obeche.

"Where's Cedar?" asked Sadira before Linden had a chance to speak.

"Still in Azothian Chambers," responded Obeche, "with Ruis. She requested private council with him." Obeche looked specifically at Sadira as he said this. "I would not disturb them, if I were you."

"Then may we hold council with you, Scribe Obeche? Sadira and I have a matter of potential urgency to discuss with," Linden paused momentarily, "a member of the Elder Council."

"*Potential* urgency?"

"We require an Elder's judgment on the matter, sir," said Linden.

Sadira nodded her agreement. Privately, she hoped Cedar would emerge before Linden revealed anything else to Obeche, but it appeared to be too late. Obeche was intrigued and, it seemed to Sadira, pleased at the happenstance that ensured him a place of privilege on a matter of urgency. *Potential*, for Obeche, had already dissipated.

"Come to my office," Obeche instructed.

Both Linden and Sadira followed. What choice did they have now? Cedar had not arrived. Sadira would have to update her later and could now hope only that Obeche would not overreact to the news. From what Sadira understood and had, on occasion, observed, Obeche tended towards the dramatic.

After they had settled into Obeche's office and ordered tea from the kitchen, Linden recited Jaden's account of events with admirable accuracy.

Occasionally he consulted his notebook and provided a direct quotation. Obeche punctuated his reaction with a periodic grunt of surprise or echo of Linden's words intoned as a question. *Two people? At the cliff face? One held a large red stone?* When Linden had reached the end of his account, Obeche asked Sadira if she had anything to add. She did not. Obeche held his pendant to his forehead and breathed deeply and audibly. After a few moments, he released the pendant and announced his plan to consult the Azoths and convene the Elder Council.

After Sadira and Linden had left the office and were rounding the corner of the corridor en route to their own offices, Linden admitted that Sadira had been wise to suggest they not go directly to the Azoths. Sadira then realized that Linden must believe he had won approval, or at least recognition, from Obeche — a rare feat for a Junior Magistrate. Sadira, meanwhile, barely managed to hide her concern. She could not help but worry that the strangers were associated with Cedar's recent procurement of Sephrim. What if the Elder Council meeting led to an investigation? What if the investigation revealed the identities of Jaden's two strangers? What if the strangers identified their Council dimension accomplice? What if Cedar were implicated or, worse, erased? Sadira shook her head against the encroaching anxiety, took her leave of Linden, made her way past the classrooms, through the kitchen garden, over the back grounds, and into the forest. If evidence remained, she needed to be the first to find it.

Jaden did not see Kalina in the dining hall at lunch. More surprisingly, she did not see her during afternoon lessons. Linden, who was the tutor for the joint Initiate session on minerals and metals that day, did not remark on her absence. Jaden wondered if he simply had not noticed Kalina was missing, given the presence of both Junior and Senior Initiates in the classroom. But this theory dissolved when, just before the mid-afternoon break, he called attendance from a registry list and purposely (or so Jaden assumed) skipped Kalina's name. Linden must have received advanced notice of her absence, and he most likely knew her whereabouts.

Kalina must have returned to Council dimension. Surely classes would not continue as if all were well if an Initiate had disappeared and not returned. During break, Jaden stayed close to various pairs or groups of Senior Initiates in hopes of overhearing a snippet of conversation about Kalina, but no one mentioned her — at least not within Jaden's hearing. Finally she asked Zelkova, as casually as she could manage, if Kalina would be joining the class after the break. Zelkova shrugged, looked around, and claimed she had not realized Kalina was missing. Jaden found that difficult to believe given that Zelkova and Kalina were in the same quarto. Further inquiries about a Senior from a Junior Initiate would seem odd at best and suspicious at worst, so Jaden kept her concerns to herself for the rest of the day.

After the dinner hour, Jaden sat in the window seat of her residence chambers and stared out across the Council grounds. The evening light was such that the greens of the lawn and trees appeared unnaturally bright. She wondered if the landscape was influenced by an alchemical process. She could not determine whether she liked the effect or not.

A red light suddenly flashed amidst the branches of the large willow tree near the edge of the Amber Garden. She had been looking directly at the tree when she saw a flicker of light, barely noticeable at first but then distinct and, finally, rhythmic — like a code. She opened the balcony door and walked outside. She breathed the cool evening air. If the flashes were indeed a message, it must be meant for someone in this wing of the residence chambers. She leaned with her back against the balcony railing and looked up towards the other balconies and windows. She could see no one — not at the windows and not on the grounds. Yet the flashes continued.

Jaden moved swiftly through the halls and across the courtyard. Just before she reached the tree, she turned to look at the residence-wing windows and balconies. As far as she could tell, no one was watching her. She ducked through the hanging branches and leaves and then stood upright under the tree's canopy. Kalina, holding a portable lantern and dressed in dark robes, appeared relieved to see her.

"Come with me," she insisted. "We don't have much time."

"Wait! How did you know I would be the one to respond to your signals? What if someone else had seen the lights and come to investigate?"

"The light frequencies were alchemically synced to your elemental essence; no one else could have seen them. Come with me."

She brushed aside the willow branches and moved swiftly across the courtyard. Jaden, her curiosity piqued enough to acquiesce, followed closely behind. As on the earlier occasion when Jaden had followed Kalina across Council grounds and into the woods, the cliff face was her destination. Jaden was startled to see a robed figure awaiting them.

"This is Dracaen," Kalina said.

Jaden stared, attempting to determine if Dracaen was the man she had witnessed disappear through the cliff face. In the light of Kalina's lantern, she could see his robes were a brilliant blue — brighter, perhaps, than the robes worn by the stranger.

"You must trust us," Dracaen asserted.

"How can I trust you? I have no idea what's happening."

"You must trust us. Otherwise we will repeat this perpetually."

"Repeat what perpetually?"

"We've met before," said Dracaen. "You don't remember. But we have met before."

"When?"

"We have met in the past and we will meet in the future, but you will know me only in the present. I exist here. Elsewhere, I am erased."

"Erased?"

"Come with us," said Kalina. "We will explain. It isn't safe here."

"You mean through the cliff face?" Jaden looked apprehensively at what appeared to be solid rock.

"Take my hand," said Dracaen. He held out a dark red gemstone in his left hand.

Jaden hesitated.

"What do you have to lose?" asked Kalina.

Jaden stepped forward, reached out, and touched the stone. For several seconds, she moved effortlessly through darkness. When the movement stopped, she stood in a cave, illuminated by small, glowing protrusions around the walls. Wind chimes made of wood hung at intervals, filling the cave with light, hollow notes. Dracaen and Kalina motioned for her to have a seat at a table. Dracaen poured a dark, red liquid into a clay cup and handed it to Jaden.

"Drink this," he said. "It will help you remember."

"What is it?"

"Dragon's Blood," Dracaen responded. "Not literally, of course."

Jaden peered cautiously into the cup. She accepted it and drew it cautiously towards her nose. It smelled fragrant, like cinnamon and cardamom.

"It is a tonic of spiced wine infused with the essence of the Dragonblood Stone," said Kalina. "Do you know of the Dragonblood Stone?"

"No," replied Jaden.

Kalina gestured towards a large alcove on the other side of the cave.

"Observe for yourself," said Dracaen.

Jaden walked to the alcove and peered over an intricately cast, wrought-iron structure that formed a barrier between the place where she stood and a deep, open chamber. In the midst of the chamber was what appeared to be a much larger version of the stone Dracaen had earlier held out to her by the cliff face.

"Do you recognize it?" Kalina asked. She now stood beside Jaden.

"No. Should I?"

"It's the Flaw in the Stone. It exists simultaneously here and there."

"But the Flaw is so small — just a fraction of the Lapis."

"From your perspective. Time and space are relative in Council dimension."

"But I remember. Cedar showed me. She said the light must fall onto the Lapis at a certain angle in order for the Flaw to be seen at all."

"Yet here," said Dracaen, "it is all you can see."

"If not for the Flaw in the Stone," explained Kalina, "Council dimension would cease to exist as you know it. The Flaw permits free will both within Council dimension and here. Without it, we would all be One — a goal of the Council in its quest for unified perfection, but one with severe implications to those who prioritize individual intention."

"I don't understand," said Jaden. She watched ribbons of mist move slowly across the surface of the Dragonblood Stone.

"Drink the Dragon's Blood tonic, Jaden. It will allow you to remember what we have discussed before and to retain, at least temporarily, what we discuss now."

"Have I drunk it before?"

"No," said Dracaen. "But you will drink it again. Each time, as long as you are here, you will remember what you have forgotten. But the effects will last only a few hours once you return to Lapidarian proximity. The Dragonblood Stone and Lapis vie for supremacy, even over alchemists themselves, let alone Council dimension. Here, in the presence of the Flaw in the Stone, you are freed from the Lapidarian effect to which you are bound in Council dimension."

Jaden held the cup to her lips; she took only a sip first and then drank the entire portion of tonic. Within seconds of setting the cup on a nearby table, she noticed the effects of the Dragon's Blood. She recalled images — as if from a dream — that gradually progressed out of the realm of her imagination into the seeming solidity of memory and reality.

She had indeed met Dracaen previously — not in Council dimension, as she would have predicted, but outside, a few days before her first meeting with Cedar. She had been standing in the rain at a bus stop. Several people had also been waiting, huddled under the nearby shelter of a storefront awning. A man had stood beside her, sheltering both of them with his large umbrella. She had smiled at him, grateful rather than discomforted. *Keep this with you at all times*, he had said to her. She had assumed he was offering her his umbrella. Instead, he had held out to her a small red gemstone. *For good luck*, the man had said. Though she had found the offer perplexing, she had nonetheless accepted the stone. Perhaps it would bring her luck, she had thought at the time. She had placed it in the right pocket of her jacket — the same jacket she had been wearing when Cedar approached her. Upon her arrival in Council dimension, the clothes she brought with her from outside had been abandoned in favour of Council robes. She had completely forgotten about both Dracaen and the stone until now.

"The stone you gave me at the bus stop — was it a fragment of the Dragonblood Stone?" Jaden asked.

"Yes. We knew you were to be the next Initiate. We hoped you would indeed keep the fragment with you and thus transport it into Council dimension. Even the smallest fragment of the Dragonblood Stone inside Council dimension — existing independently, outside the containment of the Lapis — provides a means for its bearer to counter Lapidarian memory loss after consumption of Dragon's Blood tonic. You, of course, having lost immediate proximity to the Dragonblood fragment and having gained proximity to the Lapis upon your arrival in Council dimension, forgot both the fragment and me. Not that memory of either would have done you much good before today. After all, to you I was merely a stranger at a bus stop offering you a good luck charm."

"I left it in my jacket pocket."

"Yes. I know. We know the location of every Dragonblood fragment. Upon your return, you must retrieve it. As I advised then, I will insist now: keep it with you at all times," said Dracaen. "Otherwise, you will have no means of remembering me once the effects of the Dragon's Blood tonic have worn off. Of course, ultimately, you must choose whether or not to accept proximity to the Dragonblood Stone. Its power cannot be forced upon you."

"Be careful," warned Kalina. "If you are caught with the fragment, you will be suspected — perhaps accused, with dire consequences — of rebel activity."

"Rebel activity? You're rebels?"

Dracaen gestured towards a chair and asked Jaden to sit down.

"Tell me who you are right now!" insisted Jaden.

Dracaen moved slowly towards Jaden, stopping directly in front of her.

"I am Dracaen, High Azoth of the Rebel Branch of the Alchemists' Council. I have carried my Dragonblood pendant for four hundred and forty-three years. I restored the Flaw in the Lapis on the third night of the Third Rebellion of the 17th Council."

"And what is your current mission?" asked Kalina.

"The recruitment of Jaden."

Cedar walked along the corridor towards Azothian Chambers for the second time that day. The Azoths had called the Elders to an evening meeting. Based on what she had gleaned from Sadira, Cedar assumed Obeche to have been the meeting's instigator. If only she had emerged from Azothian Chambers before Obeche earlier that day. She could, at the very least, have delayed an Elder Council meeting until the next day, suggesting to the Azoths that a few Novillian Scribes investigate the situation thoroughly beforehand. She saw no reason for yet another meeting of little consequence. Obeche seemed always too willing to suspect the worst. His paranoia regarding Rebel Branch activity had all too often led to accusations, followed swiftly by meetings, investigations, and trials that proved, in all but a few cases, to be completely unnecessary. Still, even Cedar could not deny that today's events, as witnessed by Jaden and reported to her by Sadira, were cause for concern.

Obeche sat beside Azoths Ruis and Ravenea near the head of the Council table. The self-importance he garnered from reporting potential rebel activity to the Azoths was abundantly clear. When the last of the nine members of the Elder Council to arrive finally took a seat, Ailanthus called the meeting to order. Obeche's news of a potential rebel breach of Council dimension caused the predictable eruption of response. Of the various countermeasures proposed as the discussion progressed later and later into the night, the one that gained unanimous support was offered by Amur: around-the-clock monitoring of the cliff face for portal activity by appointed members of the Senior Magistrate. The Readers, from whose ranks delegates for such an assignment might otherwise have been chosen, were occupied in the task of locating the next Initiate in anticipation of Tesu and Kalina's conjunction. At the mention of this conjunctive pair, Obeche stood to protest, once again — as he had done when the pairing had initially been suggested.

"Obeche," said Azoth Ravenea, "you have previously graced us with your opinion on this matter. I ask you to refrain from repetition. Have you anything new to add?"

"Yes, Azoth, I do. Though I respect majority

opinion on this conjunction as conferred by the Elders as sacred, I cannot help but question the coincidence of occurrence. According to the witness, Tesu was named specifically by the intruders who, I suspect, are members of the Rebel Branch with intentions to prevent — or, alternatively, *encourage* — the upcoming conjunction. As such, I propose that both Tesu *and* Kalina be monitored for the continued well-being of all."

"Do you suspect Tesu or Kalina of involvement with the Rebel Branch?"

"I suspect nothing in particular. I merely propose caution. From what I understand, Kalina took ill today. *Today*, the day of a potential rebel breach. This is not a coincidence to be ignored."

"I would have to agree with Obeche in this case," said Ruis.

"Thank you, your Eminence," replied Obeche.

"I can think of no one better than you, Obeche, to monitor both Tesu and Kalina," said Ailanthus. "You may choose an assistant for the task if you require one. Report back to us any suspicious activity."

"Certainly, Azoth Magen," said Obeche.

"I will assist you," offered Cedar. "Conjunction is too great a sacrament to place at risk."

Obeche seemed momentarily surprised by Cedar's proposal, but he thanked her graciously and suggested they meet the next morning to discuss the practicalities.

When the meeting ended and the Elders dispersed, Cedar made her way quietly to Sadira's residence chambers. From the doorway, Cedar watched Sadira as she sat by the fire, staring into its flames.

"Whom do you suspect?" Cedar asked.

Sadira turned towards her.

"Whom do you suspect Jaden saw at the cliff face?"

"She said that one of them wore blue robes."

"Well, that narrows the field," responded Cedar sarcastically, closing the door and moving to Sadira's side.

"Tell me the truth, Cedar."

"What truth?"

"The truth about the strangers."

"If you are suggesting that I know their identities, you can rest assured I do not."

"So they are not your source?"

"My source?"

"For the Sephrim!"

Cedar paused, attempting to calm herself before she responded.

"Do you honestly think that I would risk not only our supply of Sephrim but also our reputations by inviting my source for an illicit drug — a drug, need I remind you, that will assure victory at your conjunction — into Council dimension?"

Sadira begrudgingly admitted, "I suppose not."

"Good. Then the matter is closed."

*Not for me*, thought Sadira.

"Obeche and I have agreed to monitor both Tesu and Kalina," said Cedar, purposely shifting the subject to one on which they could both agree.

"I suspect Obeche's intentions differ from yours," said Sadira.

"I suspect they always will."

"My recruitment?"

"According to our Dragonian interpretation of the Lapidarian manuscripts, your destiny belongs with the Rebel Branch."

"Dragonian interpretation?"

"Interpretation by the rebel Elders."

"If I have been inscribed as a rebel, why would the Council have initiated me?"

"The Council does not have access to the Dragonian Coda," replied Dracaen. "We too have our Scribes and Readers. Our Readers found you. And rebel Scribes are virtuosos of palimpsest revision and the occasional well-placed lacuna."

"Provided, of course, they are able to gain access to Lapidarian manuscripts," added Kalina.

"How?" asked Jaden. "How do the rebels access Lapidarian manuscripts?"

"We have our methods. We always have."

"You yourself, Jaden, have benefitted from a lacuna — on the fifth folio of the *Summum Bonum*," said Dracaen. "If not for the work of an adept Dragonian Scribe, the Elder Council may well have blocked your initiation."

"You have no right to manipulate destiny," said Jaden.

Dracaen and Kalina laughed.

"What the average person ascribes to the heavens is little more than alchemical manipulation," declared Dracaen.

"Despite our efforts," explained Kalina, "the people of the outside world are currently at risk because of archaic Council protocols and abuse of Azothian power."

"In your opinion," said Jaden.

"In our *expert* opinion," replied Dracaen.

Jaden moved to the edge of the wrought-iron barrier. She stared at the Dragonblood Stone. Whom should she believe? Her knowledge of the Council was sparse at best, and her understanding of the Rebel Branch insufficient to judge its validity. If destiny can be written and rewritten, then her destiny could be changed.

"We do not expect you to make a decision right now," said Dracaen. "We simply offer you an alternative to consider along your journey through the ranks of the Alchemists' Council. As long as the Rebel Branch exists, you will always have a choice."

Jaden turned back towards Dracaen and Kalina. "What is the Council doing to endanger the outside world?"

"Human beings, with their pervasive pollution and obsession with technological advancements, are destroying the elemental balance of the Earth beyond basic alchemical repair. To repair the world, the Council may opt to eradicate the free will of the people of the outside world."

"How?" asked Jaden, astounded.

"By releasing more Lapidarian bees into the outside world than ever before. To briefly summarize a complex alchemical process, the wings of Lapidarian bees vibrate at a frequency that will, when enhanced through sheer numbers, interfere with the ability of people to make decisions contrary to those influenced by Council. The more bees, the stronger the vibration, the weaker the will. We solicit your support, your critical influence in matters of Council protocols and decisions."

"I'm a Junior Initiate. I have no influence over Council protocols."

"Not yet. But you will in the future."

"What do you hope to achieve in the end?"

"Our current and future intention, as has always been our intention, is to maintain the Flaw in the Stone and thereby assure, within Council and Flaw dimensions, the continued existence of free will — of individuality, of debate, and of varying opinions, rather than absolute orthodoxy. We likewise support free will for the people of the outside world."

Kalina pulled her silver cord from beneath her robes and held her pendant against her forehead.

"We must go," she said. "The Elder Council meeting will have ended, and our absence may be noted if we do not return."

"Remember, Jaden, you must retrieve the Dragonblood Stone immediately upon return, and keep it with you at all times. Otherwise after a few hours you will forget all that you have experienced and learned here."

"What if I am delayed? Why don't you give me another fragment to take with me now?"

"Pure Dragonblood Stone cannot be directly transported from negative space — that is, from *here* — into the positive space of Council dimension. The fragments of stone and drops of tonic that have found their way into Council dimension have been brought over the dimensional border from neutral space — from the outside world. And the tonic you drank, like any food or liquid you ingest, will quickly dissipate thanks to human digestion, no matter in what dimension you reside. Only a Lapidarian pendant inlaid with a fragment of the Dragonblood Stone can successfully cross between dimensions. You have not yet earned your pendant; therefore, you must rely on the Dragonblood fragment that I gave to you in the outside world."

Kalina placed a hand on Jaden's left shoulder. "We must go now. We will continue this conversation later. Good night, Dracaen." Together Kalina and Jaden moved through the darkness until they stood once again beside the cliff face.

"Good night, Jaden," said Kalina. "You must hurry."

Jaden nodded and moved swiftly along the moonlit paths and cautiously across the grounds, back to her residence chambers.

Later that night, desiring uninterrupted sleep, Cedar made her way from Sadira's company through the dimly lit corridors of the residence building towards her own chambers. En route, she passed through the Initiate wing, where all seemed quiet. She stopped momentarily outside Jaden's door, where light streamed through the space between the wooden door and the stone floor. She thought of knocking, of inquiring whether her latest Initiate was coping effectively with her role in the Council, but decided her queries could wait.

As Cedar reached the corridor leading to the Novillian wing, she found Obeche blocking her path.

"I would have expected you to be in your chambers at this hour."

"Yet once again I defy expectations," she replied.

He did not respond to her rebuttal but instead nodded towards a door in the Initiate wing.

"Kalina is gone," he said.

Cedar said nothing.

"After the meeting, I made my way here. I

knocked — several times. She did not answer. I opened the door . . ."

"What! You have no right!"

"I most certainly have the right! As you well know, Azoth Ruis himself requested I monitor both Kalina and Tesu. And I suspect Kalina may be in danger."

"No — you suspect *her* of endangering us."

"Either way, as a member of the Elder Council, I most certainly have the right to open her chambers when I suspect her safety *or our own* may be compromised."

Cedar shook her head and took a step to move past him.

"You cannot retire now, Cedar. You must assist me in locating Kalina. After all, you did volunteer your services before the entire Elder Council."

Cedar turned away from Obeche. "Have you checked the libraries?"

"No, I have been waiting here in anticipation that Kalina will eventually return, at which point I will question her regarding her nighttime adventures."

"She is most likely at a desk in one of the libraries catching up on the lessons she missed today. You yourself said she had taken ill."

"Or so she claimed."

"Your suspicions are tiresome, Obeche."

"As is your apathy, Cedar."

Just then, a door opened at the end of the Initiate corridor. A tall, enrobed figure moved steadily towards them. Soon both Obeche and Cedar recognized Kalina.

"Where have you been?" asked Obeche.

Kalina flinched. She had not noticed the others standing in the shadows of the corridor.

"Obeche asked you a question," said Cedar. Kalina briefly caught Cedar's eye and then turned to address Obeche.

"Scribe Obeche, I didn't realize you wanted to see me. I was in the annex of the South Library reviewing lessons I had missed earlier today."

"Which subject specifically?" asked Obeche.

"Alchemical manuscripts of the outside world."

"Very good. Which century?"

"Sixteenth."

"Which manuscript?"

"*British Library Additional 5025.*"

"Ah, yes! *Additional 5025*," replied Obeche. "That too was one of my favourites as an Initiate. Perhaps, given your extraordinary dedication to its review, you could remind me what image illuminates the final folio."

"The fourth segment includes multiple images," Kalina answered without hesitation. "Would you like me to list them all?"

"One will suffice."

"A silver dragon grasping a crescent moon in its mouth."

Cedar did not respond. Obeche hesitated, regarding Kalina with a new intensity.

"Is something wrong?" asked Kalina.

"We have reason to suspect that a rebel breach has occurred," explained Obeche. "We are, of course, concerned about your safety given your impending conjunction with Tesu."

"Am I in danger?"

"We are merely taking precautions," responded Cedar.

"We trust you will stay in your chambers for the remainder of the night," said Obeche.

"Of course," replied Kalina. "Good night." She nodded to the Scribes and then retreated to her room.

"You know, Obeche," said Cedar, "your undercover skills require refinement. If Kalina is aligned with the Rebel Branch — as you so clearly suspect — you have now warned her to be cautious in her rebellious activities."

"Alternatively, I have prevented the Fourth Rebellion."

"You cannot prevent the Fourth Rebellion, Obeche. You can merely delay it."

Cedar brushed past him and walked decisively to her chambers.

From the right pocket of her jacket, which had remained in the depths of the wardrobe since her arrival in Council dimension, Jaden retrieved her fragment of the Dragonblood Stone. She placed it into a small leather pouch, which she had used to hold coins in the outside world. She then slipped the pouch into a deep pocket of her robes, where she believed it to be both safe and readily accessible. Though she tried to sleep, she tossed and turned until dawn.

She did not sit with Kalina at breakfast. Indeed, she purposely avoided the possibility of contact with her. During the morning's joint Initiate lesson on the rhetoric of conjunction, she sat at a desk one row behind and one aisle over from Kalina, which meant they would be able to exchange glances on occasion during the discussion period. Jaden wanted Kalina to understand that she had indeed retrieved the fragment and thus recalled everything from the previous night. An hour or so into the lesson, Obeche entered the classroom and spoke briefly with Sadira. He then stood at the front of the classroom and addressed the Initiates.

"I am here to announce the winners of the winter quarter reward for outstanding academic achievement."

Of course Jaden, having joined the Council during the spring quarter, had no previous knowledge of such procedures and thus was surprised when Obeche informed the Initiates that Junior Initiate Laurel and Senior Initiate Kalina would be treated to three days at a Viennese spa.

"You will depart this afternoon," said Obeche. He then congratulated all the Junior and Senior Initiates on their overall performance during the previous quarter and expressed his hopes for the current quarter before formally bidding everyone good day.

Jaden could barely focus on the remainder of the morning's lesson. Though she knew her fear to be irrational, she nonetheless worried that Kalina would not return from Vienna. At the mid-morning break, as Jaden sat on a bench in the Amber Garden sipping lavender tea, Kalina stood with a couple of her fellow Senior Initiates a few feet away. The trip to the spa was, of course, the topic of conversation. When the time approached to return to the classroom, Kalina told the others to go ahead without her, claiming that she needed to find Laurel and prepare for the trip. Thus, walking behind and out of immediate sight of her fellow Initiates, Kalina let fall from her parchment folder one small sheet, which landed at Jaden's feet. Inscribed in dark red ink were the words *Sapientiae Aeternae 1818*, folio 16. Jaden placed the sheet among those of her own folder and returned, as if nothing was amiss, to Sadira's lesson.

Seated on a small red sofa in an ornately decorated lounge of the Hotel Sacher in Vienna, Cedar waited for Laurel and Kalina. The young Initiates had spent several hours at the spa, enjoying chocolate massages among other luxuries. Now, on the evening of the third day in Vienna, Cedar had been dispatched by Obeche to accompany them back to Council dimension. Though Kalina had already earned her pendant and could thus travel on its power between dimensions, she was still required by Council law to be accompanied until she graduated to Magistrate. Obeche had to meet with Ruis that evening, otherwise he would have retrieved the pair himself — or so he had claimed when convincing Cedar to follow through on her duty. Cedar wondered whether Obeche had been suspicious enough of Kalina to warrant tracking her every move. Depending on one's constitution, the residual effects of Lapidarian Amrita could be debilitating to the unsuspecting consumer. If Obeche had managed to feed her the Amrita, Kalina could be quite disoriented upon her return to Council dimension.

Laurel was visibly more excited than Kalina — recounting the various details of her Viennese experience to Cedar as they wove their way through the streets to the Council's Vienna archives, housed in a Lapidarian protectorate, twenty minutes on foot from the Hotel Sacher. Once there, Cedar consulted briefly with Linden, who was sitting at a table poring over manuscripts. She then escorted both Initiates to a portal near the Vienna protectorate, from which she accompanied first Laurel and then Kalina back to Council dimension. Upon her arrival back at the Quercus portal, Laurel thanked

Cedar and then rushed away to find Cercis. A few minutes later, when Cedar arrived with Kalina, Obeche emerged from the anteroom accompanied by Rowans Esche and Kai.

Obeche stepped forward and grasped Kalina's right arm.

"By the order of the Alchemists' Council," he pronounced, "you are hereby accused of high treason."

Kalina said nothing. She was led immediately and forcefully through a variety of back corridors to Azothian Chambers, where the entire Elder Council was assembled. Cedar, the last to enter the room, took her seat at the Council table among the others. As she had suspected, Obeche had indeed managed to feed Kalina Lapidarian Amrita, apparently infused in a pastry that Kalina had ordered on the afternoon of her arrival in Vienna. Obeche had thus been able to trace not only her movements within the hotel and spa but also those of one particular late night meeting with Rebel Branch High Azoth, Dracaen. Obeche had thus been able to produce for the Elder Council photographic proof of the illicit meeting. He also had photographs of her pre-dawn visit, which took place a few hours after the meeting with Dracaen, to the Vienna archives where she had succeeded at bypassing security protocols and gaining unaccompanied access to both Lapidarian ink and the southeast sector manuscripts.

During the entire recounting of events, Kalina sat still and silent, showing no emotion. Indeed, the only moment during the proceedings when Cedar noticed even a flicker of concern pass over her face came the split second after Ravenea demanded that Kalina surrender her pendant. She detached the pendant from its cord and held it out to Ravenea. Ravenea held the pendant to her forehead.

"The pendant's memory has been wiped," she announced. "Such treachery is surely the result of manipulation by one skilled with Dragon's Blood tonic."

"Recommendation?" asked Ailanthus.

"Complete erasure," replied Ravenea. "Once a rebel, always a rebel."

"As Azoth Magen, I concur. Erasure shall commence immediately. Obeche and Cedar, you will accompany the traitor to the outside world. All other Scribes, you will gather the manuscripts related to Kalina and commence the protocols of erasure immediately."

When the procedural meeting finally reached its end, Obeche and Cedar stood on either side of Kalina, awaiting instructions for departure.

"You betrayed me — your own Initiate," Kalina said to Cedar.

"No, Kalina, you have betrayed yourself."

"As all rebels eventually do," asserted Obeche, standing proudly in his apparent victory.

Jaden had chosen a shortcut to the North Library, where she planned to examine for the third time in as many days *Sapientiae Aeternae 1818*, folio 16. Thus she crossed paths with Obeche, Cedar, and Kalina in the hallway outside the portal chamber.

"What are you doing here?" demanded Obeche immediately.

"Heading to the library," responded Jaden. She then turned to Kalina, "How was your time in Vienna?"

"Delightful," replied Kalina flatly.

"Will you be busy later?" Jaden asked Kalina. "I could use some help with my lesson review."

"Yes, she is busy," answered Obeche. "She is headed to the outside world."

"Again?"

"No worries, Jaden. I will return."

Obeche slapped Kalina across the face. "You will not return!"

Jaden, stunned by Obeche's hostility, reached out to Kalina instinctively.

"Let go!" Obeche commanded. He grabbed Jaden by the collar of her robes and harshly wrenched her away from Kalina.

"Obeche! Restrain yourself!" said Cedar.

Jaden fell back against the wall, landing directly beside one of the heavy ornate benches that punctuated the corridors throughout the main Council building. As she fell, her robes became snagged on a section of the bench's wrought-iron embellishment.

Both Cedar and Kalina helped her, pulling Jaden up from the ground and releasing the torn fabric of her robes from the bench. Only then did Obeche move towards Jaden again and only to restrain Kalina.

As she adjusted her robes, smoothed the fabric, and inspected the damage, Jaden realized with a physical rush of utter dread that the pouch containing the fragment of the Dragonblood Stone was gone. She scanned the stone floor desperately but could see nothing.

"Unless you desire an official reprimand for Elder Council interference, I advise you to leave this area immediately," Obeche warned Jaden.

Jaden gave one desperate glance at Kalina and then rushed down the hall. She planned to go no farther than the next corridor, where she would wait until it was safe to return to search the hallway thoroughly. Perhaps the pouch had fallen under the bench.

But the power of the Dragonblood Stone is intense, both in its presence and in its absence. Thus, as quickly as her memories of Dracaen had returned when she drank the cup of Dragon's Blood tonic, as quickly they disappeared when she abandoned the fragment of the Dragonblood Stone in the corridor outside the portal chamber. By the time Jaden reached the next corridor, she had forgotten her desire to return. By the time she reached the library, she had forgotten about *Sapientiae Aeternae 1818*. And by the next day, she had forgotten Kalina.

## IV
## cũrrent Day

Jaden stood on the balcony of her residence chambers and looked out over the Council grounds. In the distance, she could see the glow of the lanterns hanging on the gates of the outbuildings. She wondered if the groundskeepers were asleep and, briefly, how many decades — centuries even — they had worked in Council dimension. Did they not tire of their duties? Did they not tire of their extended lives? Would she tire of hers? She listened to the soothing trickles of water running through the channels below. Just last week, Linden had provided an impromptu lesson on the healing properties of Council dimension water in response to Arjan's inquiry on the matter. Now Jaden questioned how it was possible that a place so ancient and beautiful and peaceful could perpetrate the atrocities of sacrificial conjunction and erasure. Jaden could not reconcile the inconsistencies. Perhaps the Elders were correct. Perhaps she still had a lot to learn, a lot she would someday come to appreciate. If only she could convince herself of this prospect.

She ran her new pendant back and forth along its chain, wondering how long she and the others would have to wait for the infusions of Lapidarian essence. She had discussed the matter at length over breakfast, lunch, and dinner with the other Junior Initiates. Laurel was convinced that the notable absence of Cedar and the other Novillian Scribes from the head table at dinner meant they were busy developing new protocols for the interim pendants and an itinerary for another journey to the outside world. But Jaden suspected a problem beyond the Initiate. Much earlier that day, as she was making her way through the ground-level corridors before breakfast, she had overheard part of an argument between Cedar and Sadira. She had taken a detour from her usual route in order to ask one of the kitchen staff if she could borrow a silver polishing cloth — if such a thing existed in Council dimension — for her new pendant and chain. As she approached the corridor that ran behind the kitchen, her vision momentarily obscured by the bright sunlight radiating through the ceiling-high windows that lined the hall, she heard Sadira say vehemently, "You could show some compassion even if you already have everything you want!"

"You are naïve to think I have everything I want," Cedar responded.

Jaden ducked into a window alcove to avoid being seen.

"The entire Alchemists' Council may be in jeopardy, Cedar!"

"Including you, if that's the case."

The sweeping rustle of robes followed. Jaden remained in the alcove until she was certain both Cedar and Sadira had left the corridor. She abandoned her quest for the polishing cloth and moved quickly towards the Great Hall, where she hoped to find Arjan and tell him what she had overheard. But Laurel and Cercis had already garnered Arjan's attention. The three Junior Initiates were huddled together admiring one another's pendants yet again, and, as was her usual practice of late, Jaden had no intention of telling anyone other than Arjan her most recent news, even if the entire Council was in jeopardy. Consequently, the day had passed without an opportunity to speak privately with Arjan. And the evening was filled with mandatory Initiate exam review with several Junior Magistrates as tutors.

Now, as she stood in the moonlight, she contemplated whether she should visit Arjan tonight or wait until morning. From her position on the balcony, she could see that his chamber lights, one floor above, still shone through his open windows. He would likely hear her if she yelled out to him, but so would several other people. So she left the balcony, randomly collected a few notebooks and texts from her bookcase — in order to feign a late-night study session if any of the Elders questioned her — and made her way towards Arjan's chambers. The fourth floor corridor was empty and dimly lit, punctuated with light escaping from under the doors of individual chambers. But by the time she arrived at Arjan's door, the space between his door and the stone floor was completely dark, so Jaden assumed he had turned out the light to sleep or had left the room in the few minutes it had taken her to move from her balcony to his door. Thus she continued along the corridor and made her way to the North Library, where she planned to continue her research on erasure without Arjan.

Though she had, in her recent trips to the library, read relatively little of the available material on the subject, she had learned that erasure, in rare circumstances, was vulnerable to error — a phenomenon referred to as the Error of the Unknown. Over the past few days, in two different texts, she had found references to such an error having occurred during the 17th Council. From what Jaden could determine, a certain erased individual had participated in the Third Rebellion, thus breaching Council dimension several years after the erasure. In both texts, the description of the incident was brief and obscure — neither passage indicating the name or gender of the one erased. But Jaden reasoned that if an error could occur once, an error could occur again, and that such an error might help her find the most recent one erased.

On this particular night, while turning the fragile leaves of a small leather-bound manuscript outlining Scribal Protocols of Erasure, she came across yet another brief reference to the incident. The passage itself offered no additional information beyond the Latin name of the error. However, to Jaden's surprise and satisfaction, someone had inscribed by hand a marginal gloss citing another manuscript title directly beside the Latin words *erratum imperceptus*: *Serpens Chymicum 1414*, folio 44 verso. The manuscript title was encircled with an image of a dragon sketched with brilliant green ink.

Moments later, she stood in front of the North Library's alchemical equivalent of a card catalogue: a large rectangular piece of jade, named the Emerald Tablet. Months ago at a library orientation, Jaden had mistakenly assumed the catalogue was *the* Emerald Tablet — the mythical *Tabula Smaragdina* revered as the origin of alchemical texts by would-be and actual alchemists alike. But when she expressed this thought, the Keeper of the Book laughed, assuring her that this Emerald Tablet was a mere tool. "Mere" relative to the *Tabula Smaragdina* perhaps, but it held the location data for every manuscript known to the Council, a supercomputer of sorts, powered by the Lapis rather than lithium. She placed her hands on its surface, palms down with her index fingers and thumbs touching to form a flattened version of the Ab Uno gesture.

"*Serpens Chymicum 1414*," she said aloud three times.

Within seconds, a code glowed in gold on the jade screen: MS 50.2.7.9.4.NL. Jaden knew from her library training that this referred to "fiftieth position, second shelf, seventh case, ninth division, fourth floor, North Library." She jotted the code in a notebook and moved quickly to the stairs. Though still unfamiliar with the library compared to most alchemists, within ten minutes she had managed to locate the manuscript.

*Serpens Chymicum 1414* was excessively large, so large that she could not pull it from its high shelf unaided. As quietly as possible, she moved one of the library's ladders along its track, climbed three rungs until she was within arms' reach of the manuscript, removed it with two hands, set it on an arm-level ladder rung, then descended the ladder, moving the manuscript rung by rung along with her. Like the smaller manuscript containing the marginal gloss, *Serpens Chymicum 1414* was leather-bound. Its cover piece comprised both a decorative metal plate detailing a serpent entwined in a tree and the upper portion of an elaborate lock that sealed the manuscript shut. To her dismay, the lock required a key, which meant she must request the assistance of a librarian. As she soon discovered, at this late hour, the Keeper of the Book himself was on duty, rather than one of the Council Magistrates.

"Excuse me, sir. I need a manuscript key."

The Keeper of the Book glanced at Jaden over the top of his glasses. She wondered why his vision had not been restored. Had no alchemist offered to heal his eyes with Lapidarian essence or Elixir? In that moment, Jaden realized yet again that she had so much more to learn of life in Council dimension.

"You are a Junior Initiate."

"Yes, sir."

"Why does a Junior Initiate require a manuscript key?"

"It seems preferable to picking the lock."

The Keeper of the Book smiled. He moved, with some difficulty, from his desk to a cabinet set against a nearby wall. He removed a key from under his robes, then unlocked and opened the cabinet. Jaden's eyes widened. The cabinet, far larger inside than it appeared on the outside, was filled with hundreds, perhaps thousands of keys of various shapes and sizes and metals. The Keeper of the Book reached a hand amidst the keys and, a few seconds later, retrieved a large silver key inlaid with jade. He handed the key to Jaden.

"Upon completion of your work, please return the key through this slot," he pointed to a small opening in the cabinet door.

"How did you know which key I needed?"

"I am the Keeper of the Book," he responded.

He then turned, locked the cabinet, and shuffled back to his desk.

*Strange*, Jaden thought. *He is old — such a rarity within Council dimension.* Someday Jaden would learn more about his role and that of the other Keepers within the protectorates, but for now she had work to do. Jaden returned to her table and positioned the key in the lock. She soon realized that the manuscript comprised illuminations of serpents and dragons representing assorted alchemical practices. Jaden turned the leaves slowly, reviewing as many details as she could of each image as she made her way through the folios. Folio 44 verso struck her in its vibrancy: an emerald green dragon positioned above a ruby circle. Inexplicably drawn to the image, she brushed her fingers across the word *cruentus*, which was inscribed in blood-red ink below the circle. She opened one of her notebooks, wrote *cruentus* at the top of a blank page, and then walked to the dictionary alcove on the east side of the library. The word was Latin. She listed its variant meanings in her notebook: *bloody*, *blood-thirsty*, *blood-red*. And suddenly, in this moment, as she wrote the final "d" of *blood-red*, she remembered something as if from a dream — a small sheet of parchment inscribed in the same blood-red ink as *cruentus*. She then understood, beyond all doubt, that she needed to find the parchment.

Despite what she had been told, officially, regarding Arjan and his destiny with the Council, Sadira had grown increasingly curious about him. Everyone knew that he knew too much — far more than the average Initiate, both Junior and Senior. Even if he had studied his prescribed course texts and a variety of library manuscripts for hours more than all the other Initiates every day and night since his arrival, this alone could not explain certain aspects of his knowledge. An interest in alchemical lore before his initiation — especially with access to the oldest alchemical manuscripts in the libraries he could well have frequented in the outside world — could certainly account for some familiarity with alchemical terms and language. But he had, on occasion, outshone even the Magistrate during classes. Linden had spoken of such an incident just last week. To no avail, Sadira had broached the topic on a few occasions with Cedar. But Cedar repeatedly assured her that the Elders were satisfied by Arjan's responses to their questions regarding his pre-Council history. As with the Sephrim, Cedar insisted that Sadira no longer concern herself further with the matter but instead focus on her impending conjunction, which did little to mitigate Sadira's curiosity. Indeed, she was becoming increasingly impatient with Cedar's requests that Sadira *not concern herself.* She could not *not* concern herself with Arjan. For reasons she could not yet understand, but instinctively knew she would someday, she felt the need to protect him.

She knew from Cedar that the Inner Chamber had been breached last night and that Rebel Branch activity was suspected. Cedar had claimed to have no knowledge of rebel involvement to offer Sadira beyond that detail. The Senior Elders intended to conduct a Trance of the Nine that very evening. As with all Elder Council rituals, Sadira had only read about it rather than witnessed it. She longed to participate, but only Elders were granted the privilege. For years, she had been fascinated by the prospect, wondering what it would be like to enter a trance so deep that one could physically sense — could actually *see* — the very fabric of Council dimension. Cedar had described the sensation to Sadira once, saying that though her body remained in the Scriptorium during the trance, her mind allowed her to wander the Council buildings and grounds virtually looking for tears in the fabric. Each of the Elders was responsible for investigating one-ninth of Council dimension space, reporting back if anything seemed amiss — a tear, a fissure, a disturbance in the elemental grid.

But even if everyone, including Cedar, reported nothing, would the Elders not suspect that Arjan, as both the most recent and the most knowledgeable of the Initiates, may have been recruited by the Rebel Branch prior to his arrival at the Council? If they knew he was a rebel — if Cedar knew he was a rebel — and did not inform Sadira, she would consider this withholding of knowledge a betrayal.

Even the Magistrates, not privy to erased memories, knew that the most recent one erased had been a rebel. Across the higher orders, rumours abounded regarding the possibility of rebel contact with pre-Initiates, despite countermeasures the Elder Council had instigated in the aftermath of the most recent erasure. Before last night's breach, the Elders may well have been satisfied that these measures were effective. But in light of the breach, Sadira could not believe that Arjan would remain completely beyond suspicion.

The knock at her office door startled her, even though she had been expecting his arrival. Arjan nodded respectfully and waited for Sadira to invite him to sit. She gestured towards a chair across the table from her own and offered him a cup of tea, which he accepted graciously.

"Your tea set is exquisite. I have never seen anything like it."

"No, you wouldn't have. It was handcrafted for me by a Neidan of the 17th Council."

"A Neidan?"

"A Neidan is an artisan of the outside world hired by the Elders to work on Council dimension artifacts, such as the Lapidarian tapestries or Azadirian shawls."

"Which Neidan is represented here?" Arjan asked, gesturing towards the tea set.

"Arjan, I did not summon you here to discuss alchemical teaware." She transferred a silver spoonful of Lapidarian honey into each cup; it looked like liquid gold as she stirred it gently into the tea. After taking two sips, she asked, "What do you know of the Rebel Branch?"

Arjan recited his response by rote: "The Rebel Branch maintains and seeks to increase the Flaw in the Stone. Its ultimate goal is to prevent Final Ascension with the One, which, if attained by Council, would simultaneously eradicate the Rebel Branch."

Sadira paused before responding. "As your tutor, I am pleased to know you have effectively grasped — indeed, memorized — the definition of the Rebel Branch from the *Avicennian Codex*. However, as your Senior Magistrate and, thus, your elder, I require you to tell me what you know of the Rebel Branch beyond textbook definitions and recorded historical accounts."

"Nothing, Magistrate."

Sadira took a sip of tea. "The Elders suspect Council dimension was breached last night by a member of the Rebel Branch. I expect a full lockdown — the usual procedure. Imbuing your recently attained pendant with Lapidarian essence will, in all likelihood, be delayed."

"Do the Elders suspect I am a rebel?"

"No one is beyond suspicion in the aftermath of a breach, Arjan."

"Including you?"

Sadira clenched her hands beneath the fabric of

her robes. "*No one*. A complete lockdown is likely, in which case the Wardens will be vigilant in their observations. Rebel or not, I suggest you refrain from engaging in activities that could draw suspicion upon you. Once suspected, you will be monitored closely, most likely without your knowledge, day and night."

"From what sorts of activities should I disengage?"

"I will leave that to your discretion."

"I understand, Magistrate."

"That will be all, Arjan."

"Good evening, Magistrate."

Arjan left the room, leaving his honey-laden tea untouched in its handcrafted cup.

Cedar stood alone in the Scriptorium. As if mocking the Council itself, the Flaw in the Stone appeared radiant in the candlelight. This Flaw — this tiny imperfection — was all that had barred generations of alchemists from eternal union with the One. On this night, the Flaw shone as a glowing ember amidst the searing blue of the Lapis. All light in Council dimension was an illusion of sorts — the light of the sun, the light of the Eternal Flame, the light reflected off the channel waters.

She awaited the Azoths, the Rowans, and her fellow Novillians. In particular, she anticipated Obeche, apprehensive of his inevitable rage. He would find some means to blame Cedar herself for Kalina's audible breach of the Inner Chamber during last night's ritual. He would comb the manuscripts for evidence of error — for a fragment of Kalina that had not been effectively erased last year. And if he found one, he would surely point the finger at Cedar before requesting lockdown and preparation for battle. Thus Cedar's plans to escort the Junior Initiates outside Council dimension to help cross-reference bees would be all but forgotten in the commotion of an impending fray. Of course, she would attempt to convince the Azoths that lockdown was unwise and that outside ventures must be undertaken as part of the strategic plan against Rebel Branch activity. But even if she did manage to convince the Elder Council of this necessity, she had little reason to believe that the Elders would permit the departure of even one Junior Initiate under the circumstances. For now, the pendants that Jaden, Arjan, Laurel, and Cercis donned would remain mere pieces of jewellery awaiting Lapidarian essence.

Ruis and Amur arrived simultaneously from the north and east entrances respectively. Ruis climbed the steps to the marble platform above the Lapis and knelt, head bowed and hands poised in mirrored fists — the second position of the sacred gesture of Ab Uno. Cedar and Amur likewise bowed their heads in respect. Moments later, when Obeche arrived, he had no choice but to follow suit and remain silent under Azothian protocols. Thus any expression of anger that he might have otherwise uttered was temporarily quelled. He waited, silently, on a Scribal chair to the right of the Lapis, his hands clasped firmly against the gold-sheathed edges of the armrests. After Azoth Magen Ailanthus and Azoth Ravenea had taken their positions, after Rowans Esche and Kai had taken their seats on the lower dais, and after Tera had assumed her position in the remaining Scribal chair amidst the other Novillians, the nine Elders spent over an hour immersed in elemental contemplation. Pendants in hand, within the Lapis-induced Trance of the Nine, they projected their minds to their respective segments of Council dimension, walking the hallways or grounds or forest, seeking any sort of disturbance in the grid. Cedar enjoyed the trance; she found it relaxing, and she felt particularly pleased when she noticed a glimmer of crimson against the indigo of the grid fabric. *You are far too pretty to be considered a disturbance*, she thought to herself and said nothing. Neither she nor any of the eight others reported an abnormality of any sort beyond the Flaw in the Stone.

Finally Ailanthus released his pendant, thus breaking the trance.

"We have found nothing," he affirmed, pulling his robes tightly around him as if to ward off the chill. For the first time in the hundreds of years she had known Ailanthus, Cedar noticed the greyness of age along the shadows on his face.

"If she did not breach the Inner Chamber through a newly inscribed fissure, she must have found a means to unlock a portal from the outside world," said Obeche. "Let us not forget the incident at the cliff face last year."

"We have not forgotten, Obeche," responded Ravenea. "Each of the three portals — Salix, Quercus, and the cliff face — has been scanned, and the Senior Magistrates have been monitoring them since before dawn this morning in a scheduled rotation of two-hour shifts. Though we have not yet discovered Kalina's means of breaching Council dimension last night, we can rest assured that all possible avenues of further breach are now under surveillance."

"All *known* avenues, your Eminence," ventured Tera. "Let us not forget that the breach was aural, not, as far as any of us witnessed or experienced, physical. The portals, given their function for physical transport, may be irrelevant."

"Of course, we have considered the possibility that Kalina may have breached Council dimension by means hitherto unknown. Thus we urge each of you to take precaution and make rigorous observation during all activities — both within and outside Council dimension."

"Outside, your Eminence?" questioned Obeche.

"Though I am loathe to accept this possibility," said Ravenea, "Kalina's breach may be linked to the manuscript abnormalities. Indeed, Obeche, your own theory necessitates observation in the outside world."

"My theory, your Eminence?"

"Was it not you who, regarding the disappearance of bees from the manuscripts, presented in Azothian Chambers the possibility of an elemental breach in the dimensional structure?"

"Yes, your Eminence."

"Then I congratulate you for presenting us with a hitherto unknown possibility. Cedar will arrange a schedule of delgates, including Junior Initiates, for assignment to the outside world as previously determined."

"But, your Eminence, the security risks have dramatically altered!" protested Obeche.

"Then," said Ailanthus, "I congratulate you on your new position as head of security."

"I cannot be held responsible for the irresponsibility of youth! The Junior Initiates have not yet built sufficient mistrust of the outside world. They are vulnerable to corruption by the Rebel Branch. You know as well as I the means by which the rebels hunt their prey. We had might as well dangle the forbidden fruit before the Initiates' eyes and tell them not to eat."

"It worked the first time," responded Ailanthus, effectively silencing Obeche yet again.

Through the debate that followed, Cedar remained calm and relatively quiet — nodding agreement or contributing her opinion only when necessary. Otherwise, she kept her focus on the emerald eyes of the Green Lion depicted in the mural directly across from her Scribal chair. Though she did not relish the idea of following the innumerable security protocols that Obeche would inevitably proffer, she nonetheless granted her unreserved agreement to the Azoths on the matter of an outside excursion with the Junior Initiates. And Obeche was, most certainly, not about to stand in her way.

Jaden arrived back at her residence chambers to find Arjan standing outside her door.

"Where have you been?" he asked her.

"Researching erasure. Where have you been?"

"Speaking with Magistrate Sadira. I learned something I thought might interest you."

"We should go inside," said Jaden. She opened her chamber door and ushered him in. She drew shut the heavy tapestry curtains and gestured for Arjan to sit on the small corner sofa.

"Sadira told me that the Elders suspect that there was a breach of Council dimension by the Rebel Branch last night."

So many thoughts traversed Jaden's mind that she could not speak for several seconds.

"I heard her today — with Cedar. She said the entire Council was in jeopardy."

"According to Sadira, complete lockdown is the usual procedure."

"The usual procedure? How often does a breach occur?"

"I neglected to inquire."

"It can't be a coincidence."

"Cedar's meeting with Sadira?"

"No, that I remembered something. I mean — I found something in the library. And then I remembered something about the one erased."

"But a memory of the one erased is impossible."

"No. I'm not explaining this properly. I don't remember the *one* explicitly, but I remember something related to the one — a piece of parchment. And it can't be a coincidence that I found the gloss and remembered the parchment in the wake of a rebel breach."

She handed Arjan her notebook and then began pulling each of her textbooks and notebooks from her bookcase. As she leafed through one after the other, she explained, in detail, her discovery of *Serpens Chymicum 1414*.

"The gloss could have been inscribed hundreds of years ago," said Arjan. "It may have nothing whatsoever to do with the rebels or erasure or the most recent one erased."

"But I *know* that it does. I don't know how I know. I just know. I know without knowing. I know that the parchment will lead us to the one erased."

Jaden stood on a worn ottoman and reached for the neglected materials she had stored on the uppermost shelf of her bookcase. From the pile of loosely stitched Initiate exercise booklets in which she had inexpertly traced her imitations of calligraphic inscriptions, she pulled a worn parchment folder. She remembered this folder. She had used it in the first month or so of her arrival before Cedar presented her with an official leather folder, seared with her full Council name: *Crassula argentea*. The folder contained several pieces of used parchment, inscribed with lines from calligraphy practice.

"You have improved," observed Arjan, having retrieved from the floor a few sheets of parchment that Jaden had tossed aside.

She sat on the ottoman across from Arjan, riffling through the various pages in the folder. "Here it is," she finally said, almost inaudibly. She held out to Arjan a small piece of parchment from the folder whose calligraphy did not match that inscribed on any of the other sheets. "You see. I didn't inscribe these words. This is a message from the one erased."

"*Sapientiae Aeternae 1818*, folio 16," read Arjan. "Do you know this manuscript?"

"No. Do you?"

"No."

"We need to find it." Jaden stood up, put a notebook and pen in her satchel, and moved towards the door.

"Now?" asked Arjan. "It is after midnight."

"Though we may live for an eternity, I don't think we have time to spare," said Jaden.

Mere minutes later, she and Arjan stood in front of the North Library's Emerald Tablet.

"*Sapientiae Aeternae 1818*," she said three times.

"MS 20.6.1.5.3.NL," Arjan read aloud as he recorded the code in a notebook. Together they raced to the third floor.

*Sapientiae Aeternae 1818* contained illuminations and descriptions of innumerable trees, shrubs, and plants — their properties and their names, which were inscribed in several languages. They admired the illustrious beauty of Arjan's sacred namesake, the Arjun Tree, *Terminalia arjuna*. Jaden was particularly satisfied to learn that one of its medicinal uses involves healing ailments of the heart. But the sixteenth folio contained only the illuminations of an unnamed specimen — a tree or tree-like shrub with no descriptive properties whatsoever. The image on 16 recto appeared to depict the height of summer, whereas 16 verso appeared to depict the depths of winter. The illuminations were exquisitely lifelike, but the only distinguishing feature of the tree from most of the others in the book was its large red berries, which looked like ice-laden red snowballs in the winter version.

"We need to compare this manuscript with other botanical manuscripts or textbooks," said Jaden. "I can continue on my own if you're tired."

"I am tired. But I am also intrigued."

Thus they spent the remainder of the night, making their way through volume after volume, image after image of plants and trees, distracted periodically by the namesakes of their colleagues. Jaden declared rather enthusiastically to Arjan that the *Cercis siliquastrum* was far too beautiful at full bloom with its cascading magenta flowers to resemble their fellow Initiate whatsoever. Arjan laughed but quickly regained his usual dignified composure and reminded her that physical appearance had little if anything to do with moral character. At regular intervals, the Keeper of the Book passed by, shaking his head as if dismayed at the growing number of volumes piled haphazardly on the table and surrounding chairs. Perhaps he was calculating the time and labour it would take him to return each of the copious volumes to its assigned shelf and location. Of course, under no circumstances were Initiates permitted to reshelve manuscripts.

Several images of trees with red berries led to lengthy discussions on their resemblance or lack thereof to the two depicted in *Sapientiae Aeternae 1818*. Not until minutes before dawn did Jaden and Arjan find one that they both agreed could indeed be *the* tree: *Viburnum opulus*, also known as Snowball Tree, European Cranberrybush, Water Elder, Guelder Rose, Kalina.

"I have completed and sealed the revisions," said Cedar. She stood by the fire, the sheen of her garnet robes causing, from Sadira's perspective, the illusion that Cedar herself was on fire.

Sadira could focus neither adequately or efficiently. The effects of the latest essence-laden infusion lingered. She wanted to fall back onto the pillows and into her dreams — as dark and unsettling as they had become of late. She shook her head. If ever she needed clarity, now was the time. Had she heard Cedar correctly? Was her life about to end?

"Kalina's breach necessitates immediate action. To retain choice in the future, we have only one choice now." Though she faced the fire, Cedar watched Sadira's reaction in the golden mirror above the mantel. Sadira opened and closed her silver robe clasp repeatedly, readjusting her robes and repositioning herself. Even in the gilded light of the mirror, she appeared agitated.

"Do not worry," Cedar assured her. "I have made the arrangements."

"Amur is Novillian," said Sadira. "Elixir has been granted to him for generations. His essence will not waver. The conjunctive power will be his. You will lose me."

"Is that truly what you fear, Sadira? That I will lose you? Or do you fear that you will lose yourself?" Cedar turned from the fire and walked towards Sadira.

"I lost myself long ago," replied Sadira. She submitted to her desire to rest her head on the silk cushions of the chaise.

"The Essence of Sephrim will ensure your victory."

"You cannot be certain!"

"Have you forgotten Saule?"

"Of course not! I take Saule as evidence of my point! She was of a lower Order than you, and *you* were victorious. Amur is a Novillian Scribe, and I am only a Senior Magistrate. The Sephrim may not be enough. If anything, it has weakened me. The nightmares—"

"The Sephrim may have weakened you physically. But such negative effects are temporary."

"As are its effects on conjunction! You know this as well as I! Despite your influence with the Elders, you cannot guarantee what date the Council will choose for the event itself."

"No, I cannot *guarantee* a specific date, but I can certainly suggest one. And I can present arguments against a delay if need be. The Sephrim has enhanced your essence, and it will continue to do so for the foreseeable future."

"So you can see the future now, Cedar? Are your alchemical powers more advanced even than those of the Azoth Magen himself?"

"Sadira, I will do all that I can to ensure that the day of your conjunction occurs within the time frame of the Sephrim's effectiveness. You will have victory. You must *believe* in this outcome. The timing will work. Your status as Magistrate will be of no consequence at the time of conjunction. Your essence will be stronger than Amur's, regardless of status. Do you believe this?"

Sadira closed her eyes. Unbidden and seemingly random images of her Council life moved through her thoughts in rapid sequence: watching her reflection on the pond in the Amber Garden as she laughed with Saule; grinding a cinnabar ink cake against a lotus stone under the window well of the Lower Scriptorium; imprinting her official seal on the Scroll of Ascension to mark her graduation into the Magistrate.

In four swift steps, Cedar moved from the fire to Sadira. She reached for Sadira's pendant and clasped it tightly in her left hand. "Sadira, answer me! Do you believe this?"

Sadira could not speak. She pulled on her pendant's cord.

"Answer me! Do you believe this?"

Sadira gasped. She felt the chill and then heat of Cedar's essence flowing through her pendant and under her skin. "Stop!"

"Do you believe your essence will be stronger than Amur's?"

Sadira's anger heightened as she struggled against Cedar, attempting to pry Cedar's hand from her pendant. "Let go!"

"No! *You* let go! Do you believe your essence will be stronger than Amur's?"

And finally Sadira understood. She could not win against Cedar physically — not in a match of Magistrate against Novillian — but she could win if she fought essence to essence. She remained perfectly still, surrendering her own essence to the effects of the Sephrim. Its warmth suffused her. She could win. *She could win.*

"Do you believe your essence will be stronger than Amur's?"

"I *know* my essence will be stronger than Amur's."

Cedar released Sadira's pendant, allowing it to fall back among the folds of her robes. She leaned forward, kissed Sadira gently on the forehead, and then moved resolutely to the door. She had stepped into the corridor before she turned to speak to Sadira.

"Good night," said Cedar. "Long live the Quintessence."

"Long live the Alchemists' Council," Sadira replied by rote.

Cedar knew that Ruis, who was passing by Sadira's chambers just as Cedar entered the corridor, assumed the recitation of the Council pledge was a show of allegiance staged for his benefit. But she also knew that he wrongly assumed the purpose of her time with Sadira. He thought only of his own sexual past and hopeful future with Cedar. And this jealousy by an otherwise judicious Azoth, whose emotions might blind his reasoning, could well work to Cedar's advantage if she ever needed an Azoth to take her side.

"Kalina," Jaden enunciated carefully, whispering the name to Arjan. Though the act was forbidden as a Council protocol against manuscript damage, she ran her fingertips alternately over the summer and winter images in *Sapientiae Aeternae 1818*. The shade of green used for the leaves of summer appeared particularly radiant. Perhaps the ink had been laced with essences of jade and silver.

"Kalina," replied Arjan. He pushed his black hair away from his forehead, as was his habit. His pendant brushed across the open manuscript as he leaned forward. "Knowing her name will help us find her," he said. "And if you are able to find one of those erased, you may well find others."

Jaden nodded. She had known this woman, Kalina. Of this, she was certain. She remembered nothing, yet she had found a piece of Kalina and thus a piece of her own past — something forbidden and something visibly hidden within its own notable absence. She sank back into her chair suddenly frightened of forgetting even this fragment.

"What if our memory of the name is linked to the manuscript? What if Kalina is erased from our memory once we leave the presence of the manuscript?" she asked Arjan. "What if we have been here before — once, twice, numerous times — but have forgotten repeatedly?"

"No. These depictions are not of the Kalina you have forgotten. She is elsewhere. *This* Kalina," he tapped on one of the images, "is only the name of a tree — a mere word like any other word, a sign that points to something beyond itself. If Cedar were erased from Council dimension, we could still read of cedar trees. Regardless of Lapidarian proximity, we will remember the word."

"So we have her name. But we have no idea where she is or how to reach her."

"Someone does," replied Arjan.

"Yes, the entire Elder Council. But the Elders chose to erase her. And everyone else forgets. No one can help us."

"Yes, someone can help us. Someone has led you here. Someone inscribed the reference to *Serpens Chymicum 1414*. Someone inscribed the word *cruentus* for you to find. In a dimension where manuscript inscription determines destiny, a marginal gloss is not a mere coincidence — nor is the absent name of Kalina in *Sapientiae Aeternae 1818*. The inscription in *Serpens Chymicum* and the erasures of *Sapientiae Aeternae* are connected. One led you to the other. Someone led you to Kalina."

"But who led me here? I don't know — or I don't remember — why I have this," Jaden said as she pulled from amidst her papers the sheet of parchment inscribed with the reference to *Sapientiae Aeternae 1818*.

"Perhaps, then, this parchment was given to you by Kalina herself."

"If so, then she knew she was in danger before she was erased. And she knew that I would help her."

"She also knew that you *could* help her. She knew someone would help you to do it. Perhaps one of the rebels remains undetected on Council."

"Do you think?"

"You must consider every possibility. And you must recognize the dangers. You do not know whom you can trust."

"I can trust you. You understand."

"Yes. I understand."

Jaden set the parchment on the table and reached again for the *Sapientiae Aeternae 1818*. As she pulled the manuscript forward, her right hand briefly brushed against Arjan's left hand. Just as briefly, she wondered if he had noticed.

"You need to respond," he said.

"What?"

"You must respond to the person who left this evidence — these signs — for you to find."

"But if the person was Kalina herself, she won't be able to see the response."

"On the other hand, if the person is someone else, he or she most certainly will."

"Do you have a parchment pen and ink?" asked Jaden.

"I would advise against leaving a note. It could be intercepted by the wrong person."

"I don't want parchment. I want a parchment pen and ink. Do you have these or not?"

Arjan opened his satchel, rustled through the papers and books therein, and retrieved two parchment pens and a small vial of ink from a carved wooden case. Jaden detached the caps from the pens and examined their nibs.

"This one will do," she said. "Stand over there, between the table and the railing."

"Why?"

"So no one, including the Keeper of the Book, will see me."

She pulled *Sapientiae Aeternae 1818* to the edge of the table, drew the requisite ink from the vial, and pressed the pen against the blank space on the manuscript page below the summer image of the *Viburnum opulus*. Thus Jaden made her first inscription into a Council manuscript, forming each letter in the style of the script beneath the other trees: *Crassula argentea*. With two Latin words, placed amidst a myriad of others dispersed throughout the folios of *Sapientiae Aeternae 1818*, Jaden had inscribed her own name into the space left in Kalina's absence.

Sadira was five minutes late for the scheduled joint Initiate session on alembic infusion. The intensity of her conversation with Cedar the previous night had led to her inability to focus effectively this morning. Yes, she had told Cedar she believed the Sephrim would give her victory over Amur, but now she questioned the ethical implications of sacrificing Amur. Her students would already be gathered in the Elixir Chamber. She certainly hoped they were sitting patiently at the tables and not wandering about the chamber examining the fragile equipment and volatile ingredients, as had occurred a few years ago to the detriment of one Senior Initiate's robes.

Obeche had caused her delay, of course. Pompous and demanding in his role as head of security, he had insisted upon an early morning meeting at which all Magistrates were required to review the new war measures protocols at length. Now she moved through the corridors towards the Elixir Chamber as swiftly as she could without losing her breath. Though the Junior Initiates did not yet know that Cedar had successfully commissioned them for duty in the outside world, the Elders had already finalized their plan and protocols for each member of the Council. The Elder Council's strategies for rebel suppression necessarily superseded Magistrates' lesson plans. Thus Sadira had been directed to inform the Initiates that lessons would cease temporarily and exams would be delayed until the Elders were satisfied that the potential for rebellion had been quelled. Of course, the Elders knew nothing of what Cedar intended. They knew nothing of the Sephrim, nothing of its current effects on Sadira, nothing of its future effects on Amur. But most importantly, they knew nothing of Sadira's complicity — a complicity borne from her love for Cedar and, ultimately, from her love for Saule.

As she neared the chamber, she could hear the murmur of Initiates filling time with chatter until her arrival. She recoiled at their naïveté. She stood just outside the doorway, momentarily tempted to remove herself permanently from the battleground being mapped around and, literally, within her thanks to the Sephrim. She need only walk from here to a portal chamber, transport herself to a location of her choice in the outside world, dispose of her pendant, and resume her mortal life. But such temptation was fleeting, her resolution re-established as quickly as it had faltered. She had no lasting desire to resume her mortality in the outside world. Her death, if she were to die, must be both worthy and worthwhile, regardless of the guilt she might always carry for the sacrifices a few others would inevitably make on her behalf. In war, casualties are expected. Death is a necessity of life. If only she could predict who would die.

Sadira adjusted her robes and walked as casually as she could manage into the classroom. She stood on the raised platform near the alembic furnace and addressed the Initiates, who eagerly awaited the relatively rare opportunity to work with Lapidarian Elixir. But instead of reviewing Elixir properties, she recited Elder Council directives.

"The Elders have invoked Council Law 675 as war measures against rebel insurgency."

Audible concern and disbelief filled the classroom.

"War measures! Are we in danger?" asked Laurel.

Ignoring Laurel's panic, Sadira continued her recitation with methodical precision. "Suspension of classes will commence immediately. Each Initiate will be designated as assistant to a Scribe. Scribal endeavours are paramount to ensure dimensional stability. Upon hearing the name of your Scribe, you will report to him or her to be assigned specific duties."

Sadira produced a sheet of parchment from which she announced the Initiate/Scribe pairings. As the names were read, Jaden sat in dread of the possibility that she would be assigned to Obeche. She silently sighed in relief when Ritha was given that honour. One by one, the Senior Initiates left the classroom as their names were read. Finally, only the Junior Initiates remained. Sadira paused. She looked up from the parchment.

"As Cedar originally proposed prior to the rebel threat, she has requested and attained permission for the four of you to accompany the first coalition outside Council dimension. Thus your interim pendants will be infused with Lapidarian essence tonight."

"Tonight!" Laurel exclaimed. "Then we could leave for the protectorates by tomorrow!"

"Theoretically, yes, but practical details — such as departure dates — have yet to be determined. Given evolving circumstances, such determinations will most likely be delayed by a few days, if not a few weeks. As such and for now, you will work within Council dimension on whatever task your Scribe requires of you. So . . . Cercis, you have been paired with Ela, Laurel with Katsura, Jaden with Cedar, and Arjan with Tera."

"Are we in danger?" Laurel asked again.

"The entire Council is in jeopardy, Laurel. Of course you are in danger!"

Laurel appeared startled. Sadira closed her eyes briefly and shook her head. She surveyed the Initiates once again, perceived their fear, and attempted to soften her approach. "The Elders have paired each Initiate with a Scribe as a means to mitigate the danger we face. All Scribes are powerful alchemists. Their veins course with Elixir. They will protect you."

"As we will protect them," said Arjan.

Sadira nodded, appreciating once again Arjan's dissimilarity to the other Initiates.

"You must report for duty now," said Sadira.

Sadira waited as the four Junior Initiates gathered their books and left the classroom. She then retrieved a small gold flask from a pocket of her robes and poured its liquid contents into the Primary Alembic — the vessel that filters all the channel waters. Like blood dripping into a pool, the momentarily vivid intruder dispersed promptly into invisibility. Thus had Sadira completed her assigned task with apparent though discomforting ease.

"Long live the Quintessence," she muttered.

The Night of Albedo arrived years earlier than anyone could have anticipated. Jaden had learned both in texts and from her fellow alchemists that pendant status was not granted until graduation from the Junior Initiate. But tonight, she and the other Juniors would enter the sacred Waters of Albedo — waters infused with ancient salts that lined the walls of the chamber, waters laced with Lapidarian powders gleaned by Novillian Scribes from the Lapis itself — and be ritually purified to receive a pendant infused with Lapidarian essence. Though the pendants were interim, Jaden nonetheless felt both honoured and anxious, eager and fearful. She had imagined taking part in this ritual since she first learned of it, during one of Sadira's classes a month or so after arriving in Council dimension. Of course, as the evening and ritual unfolded, she understood that many of the details were not at all as she had read or imagined. The water was luminescent, as if the Albedo's contents flowed directly from the Lapis itself rather than from the wells of the Council's subterranean caverns.

She stood in ceremonial blue cotton robes behind Cercis and Laurel, beside Arjan, waiting for Azoth Ravenea to recite the Blessing of Dissolution and for Azoth Ruis to open the Albedian Gates. When Ravenea raised her pendant to the beam of light that filtered through the blue crystalline floor from the Scriptorium above, Jaden moved her hands in sacred gesture over her pendant. The other Initiates did the same, heads bowed and eyes closed for the recitation.

The gates were then opened, and one by one the Initiates were led down the stone steps into the Waters of Albedo. Later Jaden would recall the cool sensation of the smooth stone against the soles of her feet, the warm pressure of the water's current against the palms of her hands. Arjan's thick black hair glistened in the light that reflected from the water. Jaden longed to touch him. Perhaps the waters affected her desires. Finally, yet seemingly beyond time, she sensed no separation of herself and the others — she was nothing beyond the moment, nothing beyond the Albedo. In her mind, in her sensation, all was one for the duration of the ritual.

Azoth Ravenea and Azoth Ruis then entered the Waters of Albedo themselves. Azoth Ruis carried with him an emerald-inlaid tray on which stood a small metal tripod supporting an intricately carved silver bowl over a green and blue Phoenician flame. The flame kept the Lapidarian essence within the bowl at the temperature required for pendant infusion. One by one, Azoth Ravenea removed each Initiate's pendant and dipped it into the Lapidarian essence. A brilliant flash of light signified the completion of the conjunctive infusion, after which each infused pendant was returned to its respective Initiate. When Jaden's pendant was returned to her, she held it briefly against her lips and then for an extended period against her forehead, as she had seen so many alchemists do during her time with the Council. She willingly surrendered to the poignant sensation of Lapidarian essence against her skin. Finally she understood the purpose of these gestures. Holding the pendant to her lips, she felt a pleasant, almost sensual, tingling as if she herself were being infused by essence; holding the pendant to her forehead, she noticed a sudden clarity of thought, as if the essence were coursing through her brain, enhancing interaction of its neurons.

Upon withdrawing from the Waters of Albedo, Jaden felt both mourning for the end of the ritual and bliss at the attainment of the essence. Later, alongside her bliss, she also felt remorse when reminded that both pendant and essence were merely temporary possessions. How could she be asked to return to her pre-Lapidarian state? She had been transformed forever on this Night of Albedo.

The morning after the ritual, Cedar stood on the dais platform in Azothian Chambers seething inwardly. Yet again, Obeche had managed to inject his venom into too many unwary victims on the Council. Now he stood on the dais as if he were the Azoth Magen himself — his role as head of security clearly having gone to his head — advising caution before proceeding and effectively silencing her along with any other dissenting voices. Just one year ago, he had sat across from her at an Elder Council meeting nodding in agreement for modifications to Initiate protocols. Now he addressed the Elders, claiming he was uncomfortable with having protocol discussions behind Elder Council doors. Instead, he advised inviting all Council members into the discussion, implying in the process that Cedar had not followed proper procedures in calling a closed consultation. Was it not the duty of the Elder Council to make procedural changes? Had he actually forgotten his former agreement to change Initiate protocols or had he made a conscious decision to be difficult as proof of his newfound supremacy? She could not fathom to what end, beyond discrediting her and the others at what may well become a critical point in Council history. Did he think such a move would increase his power or position in regard to decisions made under the war measures protocols? Did he continue to aspire to Azoth despite his seemingly infinite Novillian status? Or perhaps he merely intended to delay Initiate excursions to the outside world with endless requests for additional protocol meetings.

Whatever his aspirations, Obeche objected and countered and postured to such an extent that he did indeed manage to waylay Cedar's plans for the Initiates. Rather than bemoan his interference, Cedar adjusted her priorities, proceeding after the consultation from Azothian Chambers through the back corridors to the kitchen, through the kitchen to the door to the side alley, and out onto the shaded stone pathways that led to the outbuildings.

Repeatedly, she glanced back towards the main Council building until she veered off the path into the forest, thus becoming safely hidden from the vantage point of all the buildings. She moved swiftly through the forest until she emerged in the clearing at the cliff face.

Sadira and Tesu, as scheduled by the security rotation, were monitoring the area. Cedar would have preferred to have met Sadira on her own, but this could not be. When Cedar emerged from the forest, the Senior Magistrates were chatting quietly, seated side by side on a boulder, their backs against a section of the cliff face.

"Cedar!" Tesu was visibly surprised at her arrival. He moved too quickly away from Sadira. Within seconds, he had his feet placed firmly on the ground, and he stood with hands in the second position of Ab Uno as a sign of respect for his Elder.

"Tesu, you are temporarily relieved of security duty until your next scheduled rotation. I will monitor the cliff face with Sadira for the remainder of this rotation."

Momentarily, Tesu appeared as if he were going to protest. But he must have realized that in doing so he would neither garner praise from Sadira nor anything but censure from Cedar. He thus nodded and walked into the forest along the path towards Council grounds.

"I need to leave Council dimension immediately," Cedar told Sadira.

"From here?"

"Yes. How much time remains on your security rotation?"

Sadira held her pendant towards the sun. "Two hours and forty-three minutes."

"If I am not back in time, you will have to invent a plausible excuse for my absence."

"No! Cedar! Wait!"

"Sadira, stop asking me to explain everything!"

Cedar clasped her pendant in one hand, pressed the palm of her other hand against the cliff face, and recited the portal key. Instantaneously, only her footprints remained in the dust.

Sadira had no idea where Cedar had gone. How was she to continue to trust Cedar when Cedar clearly did not trust her? How could Cedar ask for her help and then keep her in the dark on matters of such apparent importance? She leaned against the cliff face contemplating these and other questions for over half an hour before she decided that she had better things to do than merely wait for Cedar's return. She had her *own* research to conduct, her own quest to pursue in her efforts to help herself and to alleviate her misgivings about the Sephrim and about sacrificing Amur. She needed to learn about the possibility of mutual conjunction. Where better to begin than with the only two alchemists to have achieved mutual conjunction: Ilex and Melia. Thus she did something she never imagined herself doing, something that would undoubtedly be considered treachery. Standing on the bank of the pool beside the cliff face, using ingredients collected from the forest and words recently gleaned from her research, Sadira performed an alchemical transmutation on the waters, one that would affect passersby for the next three hours.

Of course, her alchemy had no effect whatsoever on one particular arrival at the cliff face, whose sudden appearance startled her. Had he read her mind? Did he know of her misgivings? She did not have to wait long for answers.

"Regarding the conjunction—" he began.

"Not here," she said. "Come with me."

Together they made their way through the forest paths.

When Senior Magistrates Nunnera and Zatthu arrived at the cliff face for their security shift, they found no one. They wondered what had happened, and they planned to report the absence as soon as possible. But within moments of their arrival, having breathed in the transmuted mists of the pool just beyond the cliff face, they forgot what they had neglected to see in the first place. And they most certainly did not suspect the truth of the matter.

Three weeks after their pendants had been infused on the Night of Albedo, the Initiates were finally scheduled to depart from Council dimension. Jaden anxiously arrived in the portal anteroom before the others. Cercis and Laurel had left for Santa Fe earlier that day. Now it was her turn. Within the hour, Jaden, Arjan, Cedar, and Tera would leave for Vienna on official Council business — manuscript research, the complexities of which would be explained once they were safely ensconced in the Council protectorate. Other than a reiteration of Linden's initial Viennese manuscript observation and the possibility of Rebel Branch activity both within and outside Council dimension, information had been limited to advice on requisite clothing for the journey. Jaden had asked several questions at both preparatory meetings, but Sadira's responses were negligible at worst and Cedar's cryptic at best. So Jaden replaced her desire to understand her role in the outside mission with her illicit plans to abandon both her pendant and the Council protectorate in pursuit of Kalina. To do so, she would require time alone or time with only Arjan and a means of absconding the protectorate for the streets of Vienna. She imagined various scenarios in which Cedar and Tera would remain with their Initiate wards only long enough to delegate a task before departing on their own mission as assigned by the Elder Council. Perhaps, for example, Cedar and Tera would be summoned on urgent business back to Council dimension, leaving Jaden and Arjan in the depths of the otherwise abandoned foreign protectorate archives to scrutinize myriad manuscripts for bees. Trusting him with her life, Jaden would place her pendant in Arjan's hands for safekeeping. She would then abandon the manuscripts, the bees, and Arjan (with difficulty, given her growing affection for him) and roam the winding streets of the city waiting for memories of Kalina to emerge. If she had paid more attention during Linden's lectures on Council protectorates, her imagined progress in Vienna would be replete with more accurate and vivid details. Jaden shook her head, dismayed at her ability to be swayed so easily by only a spark of possibility with both Arjan and Kalina. Obeche arrived in the portal anteroom where Jaden waited, effectively quenching all sparks.

"Scribe Obeche. What are you doing here?"

Obeche responded with a casual glance — not quite a scowl.

"I was expecting Cedar," Jaden offered, consciously shifting her tone to apologetic deference.

"Cedar has been summoned to Azothian Chambers. She will be delayed. Upon arrival of Tera and Arjan, I will accompany the delegation. Have you ever been to Vienna, Jaden?"

"No."

"Do you know of anyone who has been to Vienna?"

Jaden paused. Was it Laurel who had been to Vienna?

"Perhaps Laurel."

"Perhaps Laurel?" He then paused, took a step

towards her, and reached for her pendant. Jaden recoiled. Obeche's cold hand gripped the turquoise, pulling the silver chain taut against the back of her neck. Jaden struggled against an enveloping frost. She could not breathe. The lunch with the other Initiates in Santa Fe returned unbidden to her thoughts. Laurel was laughing. She was happy about the prospect of attaining a pendant. But in Jaden's forced reconstruction of the moment, the brightly painted decor became a grating kaleidoscope, and Laurel uttered the same words repeatedly: *This is the best thing that has happened to me since that spa day in Vienna.*

The door of the antechamber opened once again, and Obeche dropped Jaden's pendant as Tera and Arjan entered.

"Long live the Quintessence," said Tera in greeting.

"Long live the Alchemists' Council," responded Obeche.

Jaden, shaken and silent, moved a step closer to Arjan, head and eyes down. If only Arjan could read her pendant. Then he would understand Obeche's intrusion without articulated explanation, and she would understand the pleasure of pendant exchange when free of violation.

Moments later, inside the portal chamber, Tera and Arjan assumed positions on either side of a sculpted jade serpent. Before today, Jaden had neither experienced nor witnessed transport through the Quercus portal. Its intricacies unnerved yet fascinated her. With one hand on the sculpture and one on their respective pendants, Tera and Arjan recited the key. The serpent, instantaneously animated, wrapped itself around both men, who gradually slid as liquid silver into the serpent's mouth and out of Council dimension. Obeche and Jaden waited until the serpent had regained solidity. Then they stepped onto the platform beside the serpent and recited their keys. Jaden did not enjoy portal transport at the best of times, let alone in the stifling aftermath of Obeche's assault on her pendant and mind. The visual effects of the Quercus portal — a constant flickering light alternating between cobalt blue and crimson red — combined with the deep vibration, which she could both hear and feel through her body, made her nauseous. After three minutes of agony, having arrived at their destination, Jaden worked to regain her balance enough to observe her surroundings.

In the light and heat of midday sun, she stood with Arjan beside a large imitation Coke bottle attached to a red metal shelter, which she mistook, initially, for a bus stop. However, she soon realized that the broad street was free of vehicles, including buses. Obeche and Tera sat on a bench of the shelter consulting a map. The writing on adjacent storefront signs and in shop windows was primarily Chinese, with an occasional word or two of English. Asian people — presumably Chinese — moved about the streets, apparently uninterested in or oblivious to the new and foreign arrivals. One young man on a mobile phone bumped into Jaden and apologized with an air of both civility and apathy. For as far as she could see down the street, the buildings, virtually from base to roof, were replete with brightly painted murals of seemingly random motifs: birds and plants and people and abstract designs. Jaden was uncertain whether they had indeed been transported to the outside world or whether they had mistakenly entered an alternative dimension altogether. Wherever they were, they most certainly were not in Vienna.

Standing up and gesturing broadly for the others to follow him, Obeche moved quickly down the mural-lined street. To a keen observer, the pace would be judged unusually swift for a tourist group, which Jaden assumed they appeared to be.

"Where are we?" she whispered to Arjan.

"Qingdao," he responded enthusiastically. "I have been here before — many years ago with my grandparents. I do not remember much beyond brief images and blurred impressions. I was too young."

"Cedar told me we were going Vienna."

"On the way to the portal chamber, Tera informed me that the plans had changed and we were headed to Qingdao."

In that moment, Jaden again questioned Cedar's authority. How had Obeche managed to change the plan without Cedar's permission? Was this a strategic move by the head of security in response to the war measures protocols? Were Cedar and Sadira in Vienna with Laurel and Cercis? Was the Council attempting to mislead the Rebel Branch? Jaden thus occupied herself with innumerable questions and possible scenarios, barely noticing the surroundings as she raced to keep up with the others. By the time she realized that she should have paid attention to the route in order to find her way back to the temporary portal ground, they had made too many turns down too many unfamiliar streets. If she lost sight of the others now, she would be irrevocably lost.

After what seemed an hour's journey, Obeche stopped outside a building that looked like an unremarkable small residence. Unlike the elaborately decorated buildings in the immediate vicinity of the temporary portal ground, these exterior walls were yellowish-white and the door was faded green, with chipped and peeling paint. Four Chinese characters were carved into a wooden plaque hanging above the door. A tangle of electrical wires was strewn overhead, and several sheets of paper had blown up against the wall under a small shuttered window.

Obeche knocked at the door, and an elderly Chinese woman opened it. She was dressed plainly in a cotton print shirt and black pants, head bowed in apparent respect to Obeche and Tera as she ushered the Scribes and Initiates through the main room and beyond a heavy curtain into a narrow hallway. The hallway led to a staircase that ascended to a second floor. Once she had reached its landing, Jaden realized that the floor housed an alchemical library in one large room. Against three walls — one of which included the doorway and another two windows — were old, lacquered wood cabinets overflowing with scrolls and small manuscripts. The fourth wall comprised open shelves stacked with large manuscripts of varying shapes and colours. The floor featured a Persian carpet, atop of which were a large wooden table and two well-worn wooden benches. Perhaps this library existed within the Council protectorate of Qingdao. Certainly such an unassuming building had the potential to exist in virtual anonymity, thus shielded from the Rebel Branch. The woman gestured for Jaden and Arjan to be seated. In a language that Jaden did not understand, the woman spoke briefly with Obeche and Tera before departing down the staircase.

"You are to begin here," said Obeche. "For the remainder of the day, you will thoroughly examine the scrolls and manuscripts of the cabinets on the east wall. You are seeking representations of bees or visible lacunae potentially left in their place. These volumes," he gestured towards a case holding several large books bound in blue leather, "contain itemized lists of alchemical images in the Qingdao collection. You will find them useful for cross-referencing. Jinjing — Keeper of the Book of the Qingdao protectorate — will bring you tea and food shortly. Tera and I will return by nightfall."

"Of course, you are not to leave the premises," added Tera.

"Of course," responded Jaden and Arjan simultaneously.

Upon Obeche and Tera's departure, Jaden said nothing to Arjan. Instead, she crossed the room to one of the windows, which provided a view of the street in front of the house. She watched until the Scribes had disappeared beyond her sight. Even then she carefully chose her words, anxious that Jinjing or a hitherto unmet resident of the building might be listening, with or without instruction to do so.

"Do you think these cabinets offer safe storage?" she asked, holding her pendant in her right hand, slightly aloft.

"Presumably," responded Arjan. "However, I would advise against taking unnecessary risks. We have only just arrived. And, as Obeche said, Jinjing will soon bring tea."

"Yes," said Jaden. Though she wanted to stow her pendant in a manuscript cabinet and leave the room until dusk, she knew that Arjan's precaution was prudent. Indeed, she felt reluctant to say anything more to Arjan, including the details of Obeche's pendant reading, until they had regained their relative privacy back in Council dimension. She resigned herself to the assigned task and retrieved a scroll from the uppermost corner of the first cabinet to the left of the window. She then positioned herself on a bench at the table, unfurled the scroll, placed a weight at each end, and began examining its imagery, which appeared typical — a peacock, a green lion, stars, the sun, the moon, circles of red, black, and white. Not a single insect of any variety was depicted therein. Arjan sat on the opposite side of the table, slowly turning the pages of a fragile but exquisite manuscript illuminated almost entirely with gold and cinnabar.

"What are the chances that we will find a single bee or lack thereof?" asked Jaden.

"A Herculean task to be certain."

"This must be a test of patience and endurance."

"Or faith," Arjan suggested. "Perhaps we are in the midst of an Initiate test or rite of passage. I have read of some exquisitely elaborate ones — extending for months or even years to allow the Elders to assess both the competency and allegiance of an Initiate. Perhaps the task has nothing whatsoever to do with bee imagery but with the trust we place in the Elders."

Jaden considered divulging to Arjan her lack of trust in Obeche.

"Yet," he continued, "we must nonetheless begin by pursuing the task as outlined. Later, with knowledge gained from the task, we may choose to veer from the original path — or not."

"Have you ever veered from a path?"

"Of course, when warranted."

Jaden returned her first scroll to the cabinet and attained a second.

"Are you not going to consult the cross-referencing volumes first?"

"I just want to get a sense of the collection first. What good will cross-referencing do without a basic understanding of how the scrolls and manuscripts are organized?"

"True enough. To be honest, I would be content to start the cross-referencing later and simply indulge in the beauty of these illuminations for a few hours. The Chinese collection of the North Library is limited."

"You know too much," said Jaden.

"I know too little," replied Arjan. "And I have forgotten too much."

Thus the next hour progressed in virtual silence. Jaden scanned several scrolls, paying particular attention to those with borders decorated with flora and fauna. She set aside a small scroll that featured a tiny insect of indiscriminate nature. Arjan smiled and nodded at her find — this could indeed be their one and only bee of the day.

Jinjing returned, as promised, bearing a tray of tea, noodles, fried gai lan, and steamed buns. Jaden stood to assist, reaching for the tray, but Jinjing shook her head and proceeded to set the tray on the table. Jaden wondered vaguely if other Keepers of the Book in other protectorates were burdened with similar domestic tasks. Breathing in the aroma of the steam, Jaden realized that she, like Arjan, would be content to find neither bees nor knowledge on this particular day. After all, she was about to share a meal alone with Arjan. Jinjing gestured towards the food and nodded to Jaden. Arjan reached to move the bowl of noodles from the tray onto the table. As Arjan lifted the bowl, Jinjing took a step away from the table and stumbled. Jaden reached out instinctively to steady her. Jaden's left hand caught Jinjing's right hand, thus averting a fall. But something else occurred in that instant — something of which Arjan was seemingly unaware. When their hands met, Jinjing pressed into Jaden's palm something that felt like a pebble. Moments later, the pebble still grasped in her hand, when Arjan closed his eyes as an emphatic response of pleasure or gratitude for the food, Jaden quickly glanced at the object before transferring it to her pocket. She could not fathom why Jinjing would offer her what, by all appearances, was a blood-red gemstone.

## V

### current day

Jaden said nothing to Arjan about Jinjing's gift. At first, she had no reason to think she was hiding anything particularly significant. She merely reasoned that if Jinjing had meant for Arjan to know of the gemstone, she would have offered it openly. Perhaps Jinjing's secrecy was a necessity that Jaden should honour. Yet, a moment later, watching Arjan a bit too closely as he ate a piece of gai lan, Jaden felt an affection for him that made her question why she hesitated to share the gift with him. Certainly he had done nothing to warrant her distrust. But the moment after that, she decided again to keep the gem to herself — something private, something with which she alone had been entrusted. She could not comprehend this fluctuating response.

But then something shifted. Later she would

remember the precise details of this moment. Her left hand rested on the smooth wood of the table; her right held a steamed bun as she waited for it to cool. The warm breeze from an open window moved against her face. The tinkling of a small bell downstairs caused her to turn her head towards the door. Arjan dropped a chopstick and apologized for his carelessness. And she remembered Dracaen.

All the memories of Dracaen and Kalina returned to her at once. She understood then that Jinjing had bestowed upon her not a mere gemstone but a fragment of the Dragonblood Stone. In this deceptively simple act, someone from the Rebel Branch had not only contacted Jaden but also implicated her in their plans for rebellion. Had Kalina herself brought the fragment to Jinjing? If so, someone must have informed Kalina that Jaden would be in the Qingdao protectorate. Who knew of this beyond Tera and Obeche? Astonished by the possibility that Obeche himself was aligned with the rebels, Jaden shook her head as if to rid herself of the thought.

"What is it?" asked Arjan.

Jaden could not respond. She merely stared at him as if pleading for a means of escape.

"What do you remember?" he asked her.

Again, Jaden did not respond.

"You have remembered something about Kalina. I can see it in your face."

He knew. Why had she doubted him? She could

not hide something from him even when she chose to do so.

"Yes. I remember."

"The Lapidarian essence of your interim pendant must not be strong enough to maintain the erasure within your memory."

She did not correct his erroneous assumption.

"Who is she? Who is Kalina?" he asked.

"A rebel."

"Yes, we had assumed as much."

"She works with Dracaen, the rebel leader. Last year just before her erasure, Kalina brought me to Dracaen. He told me certain alchemists support annihilating the free will of the people of the outside world in order to maintain elemental balance."

"How?"

"By releasing all the Lapidarian bees — apparently wing vibration affects free will.

"And you believed him?"

"Yes."

"Why?"

Jaden wanted to answer. She wanted to present to Arjan irrefutable evidence to support Dracaen's claims. But she had nothing to offer Arjan beyond Dracaen's word. Yet she had no reason to doubt Dracaen beyond Arjan's questioning. Here she recognized her dilemma. For now, she existed in conjunctive space — as an Initiate of both the Council and the Rebel Branch, shaped by both the Lapis and the Dragonblood, drawn to both Arjan and Dracaen. For now, she existed in this duality. But she feared the future inevitability of making a choice.

"The Elders have formally agreed on the day and time — your conjunction with Amur will occur under the full moon of the Feast of Vitriol, thus finally bringing an end to the Splendor Solis cycle of the 18th Council."

"Vitriol," repeated Sadira. "*Visita Interiora Terrae Rectificando Invenies Occultum Lapidem: Visit the Interior of the Earth and, Rectifying, Find the Hidden Stone.* Ironic — a feast celebrating the Lapis bears a name gesturing towards the Flaw."

"Ironic only for those who strive to eradicate the Flaw," mused Cedar. "Poor Ruis — he is unlikely ever to achieve what he has undertaken as his primary purpose."

Sadira preferred not to venture further into this discussion. She did not want to risk witnessing even the slightest glimpse of nostalgia from Cedar over what she had shared with Ruis *once upon a time*.

"You need not worry about Ruis" said Cedar, intuiting Sadira's concerns. "Time progresses — no love is eternal, even if some of us continue to hope for such a fiction."

"Ilex and Melia," offered Sadira.

"Eternity is not over," responded Cedar. Then,

immediately recognizing the edge of condescension in her voice, she added, "Though I agree that Ilex and Melia may represent the exception." She did not want to upset Sadira more than necessary at this critical juncture.

"I had been reviewing their history again — as preparation for the next rotation of Initiate lessons — but then lessons were suspended, of course," said Sadira. "Now I may not get the chance to introduce the exception to the Initiates."

"Lessons will resume soon enough, Sadira. And thanks to the Sephrim, you will have an eternity to teach the Initiates whatever you choose."

Sadira closed her eyes. She needed unflinching faith, but she had never possessed such a trait.

"Why did you choose me to help you?" asked Sadira.

"I love you. And I trust you."

*Perhaps you shouldn't*, Sadira thought, turning away to hide her tears.

Jaden longed to leave the Qingdao manuscript room and find Dracaen. She continued to fluctuate in her desire to include Arjan. One moment, she wanted to take Arjan with her. Together they could listen to Dracaen's account of the rebel position and make their choice regarding their Council allegiance. The next moment, she wanted to abandon both Arjan and the manuscripts to seek Dracaen on her own. But though she now remembered both Dracaen and Kalina, she did not know how to find them or to access the Flaw in the Stone. She would have to wait until one of them contacted her. She assumed the transfer of the Dragonblood fragment was risk enough for one day.

Jinjing did not return. Jaden contemplated whether she should go downstairs to find her and learn more from her about the Dragonblood fragment. Again Jaden wondered who other than Obeche and Tera had known that she would be here in Qingdao and not in Vienna. All of the Elders came to mind. She stood at the window for several minutes thinking about this. She watched a young boy in the street kicking a ball against a wall. The boy had a red scarf around his neck; he reminded her of Arjan. She turned back to Arjan, who sat sipping tea at the main table. He waited for her to speak.

"We should work," said Jaden.

Arjan had cleared away the dishes, leaving them and the tray on a small stand by the door. He sat at the large, central table with his hands resting on a closed manuscript. His eyes were closed.

"Yes," he said, opening his eyes. "We should. Obeche and Tera will expect us to have accomplished more than speculation about the Rebel Branch."

"I want to find them — Kalina and Dracaen," she admitted aloud. "But I don't know where to start."

"Perhaps another memory will occur to you

as the time passes," said Arjan. "Perhaps the best approach is, indeed, to focus on work."

For the remainder of the afternoon, they retrieved manuscripts and scrolls from the cabinets, painstakingly searching. The volumes of indexed images were not as helpful as Jaden had hoped, given that they were written in an ancient alchemical script that she had only begun to study. At first she did not even recognize the dialect.

"We need a trained Reader," said Jaden in frustration. "What help can two Junior Initiates possibly be in this process? If something of value could be found in the Qingdao protectorate, the Elders would send experienced Readers."

"Perhaps the Elders merely want us out of harm's way at this time of crisis. Perhaps Qingdao is a safe haven, so they have brought us to this place to hide us from the rebels."

*Or to expose us to them*, Jaden thought to herself, incessantly aware of the Dragonblood fragment in her pocket.

"We're not in danger — at least not from the rebels," insisted Jaden.

"You cannot be certain."

Jaden walked to the window again. The boy in the red scarf was there again, bouncing the ball against the wall.

"Come and see this boy," she said to Arjan.

Arjan came to the window.

"He looks like me."

"That's what I thought! If only we could see his face."

Just then, as if on cue, the boy turned around and looked up to the window. Jaden smiled and waved. The boy raised a hand, but instead of waving, he beckoned.

Jaden laughed. "He wants us to play with him. Let's go."

Arjan stood silent. He stared at the boy, neither moving nor responding to Jaden.

"What's wrong?" Jaden asked him.

"That boy does not look like me. He *is* me."

"What?"

"That boy is *me*, as a child. Look at him — he is *me*. I remember this now."

"Remember what?"

"Being here. Playing ball. Looking up at the window. My grandparents brought me here. Years ago. We stayed for a summer. I missed my friends. The children here would not play with me. I wanted the people in the window to play with me. I remember now. Everything is the same. Only the angle of perception has changed."

"I don't understand."

"I came to Qingdao as a child, but many years have passed since then. I had forgotten almost all of it — the details of it — until moments ago standing here with you. I did not even recognize this street — not until I recognized myself."

They looked again at the child. He stood holding the ball looking up at them.

Jaden turned towards the stairs. "We need to go to him."

"No — not me. You must go. The woman in the window came to play with me."

"What did I say to you?"

"I do not remember. But I do recall she mistook me for someone else."

"Someone else?"

"She called me by someone else's name. Wait . . . I remember now. This is the place I first heard the name *Arjan*."

Arjan then looked at Jaden in a way she had never experienced before. He seemed as if he were about to cry. He reached out, without warning or permission, and touched her hair.

"I liked her hair," he said. "I also remember her hair."

Jaden could not move.

"You must go to him. I will wait here. I will watch you."

Jaden hesitated but then made her way quickly down the stairs and out into the street. She walked more slowly towards the young Arjan, afraid to frighten him away by moving too quickly.

"Hello, Arjan," she said.

He did not respond.

"Is your name Arjan?" she asked.

He spoke to her in a language she did not recognize. Something was wrong, she realized in that moment: the *Musurgia Universalis* of the alchemists that generally allowed for communication between languages — and that had been working perfectly well in Qingdao with the older Arjan — was ineffective with this child. Certainly he was too young to have learned English. And, of course, he did not yet know himself as "Arjan."

"Jaden," she said, pointing to herself. "Jaden."

"Payam," he said.

"Hello, Payam."

He laughed. He kicked the ball towards her. She kicked it back. He laughed again. They kicked the ball back and forth for several minutes. Jaden occasionally glanced up at the window across the street. At first, she could see Arjan watching. But then the sun emerged from behind a cloud, and its light reflected off the glass. Jaden blinked and then squinted, but she could no longer tell whether Arjan remained at the window. Payam called out to her. She did not understand his words, but she soon realized his meaning. She had missed the ball — it had rolled past her and was heading down a slight incline. She ran to retrieve it.

When she turned back towards Payam, he was gone.

"Payam!" she called. She ran back to the spot where she had first seen him playing with the ball. "Payam!"

Jaden looked up towards the window, but she could not see Arjan. After peering around a few corners in an attempt to find Payam, she finally walked back to the door of the manuscript building. She would find Arjan and discuss the matter. But the door was locked, and no one responded when she knocked. She waited several minutes, knocking at repeated intervals. No one answered. She walked far enough away from the building to get a clear view of the row of windows on the upper floor. She could see no one. She walked from one end of the street to the other — back and forth twice — and she saw no one. She then stood in front of the manuscript building with one hand on the door and the other clenching her interim pendant in hopes of attracting Jinjing or Arjan or any Council member in the vicinity. But she could sense no one. She then walked the length of the street again, knocking on each door she found, hoping if not to find Payam himself then at least to find someone. Even a complete stranger would be a comfort to her. But no one answered. For the first time in her life, she was utterly alone.

After her conversation with Cedar, Sadira had made her way to the Amber Garden to sit in her cherished spot — on the ancient and moss-covered stone bench under the tree where she had first shed tears for Saule. Though no one watching her would notice, she could feel herself trembling as she reached out to touch the amber along the tree's glistening trunk. She understood as she sat looking up through the branches of the tree, as the late afternoon light filtered through the leaves and translucent amber, that she herself might be mourned here after her conjunction. What would Saule think if she were still here? What would Cedar think of her? She could not determine whether love meant nothing to her or if, as she decided in the moments when she was fully able to justify her intended actions to herself, true salvation must be granted more value than even the greatest of loves. And surely her love for Cedar was not even close to the greatest of loves throughout the centuries and dimensions. They were not, no matter their history and no matter what Cedar said, a match for Ilex and Melia.

In her Initiate years, Sadira had revered Ilex and Melia; for her, they had epitomized the possibility of eternal love, of making possible the impossible. They had both been Magistrates at the time of their physical consummation. By the time of their conjunction, over a century later, they were both Scribes. Between them, they had mature essence and the means for reading, transcribing, and inscribing Lapidarian manuscripts with exquisite accuracy. They were the envy of all Scribes, not only for their alchemical skills but for what appeared to be everlasting love. Most alchemists, between joining the Initiate and ascending to Azoth, fall in love or lust dozens of times — age and gender being of little concern to those who live for hundreds of years. But Ilex and Melia remained monogamous and committed to each other from the moment of their first kiss; thus, being chosen as conjunctive partners seemed only natural to them, regardless of prohibitions against alliances of love.

Yet despite their inherent intellectual and sexual congruencies, no one could have predicted the outcome of their conjunction. On the final day of the Aurora Consurgens of the 17th Council, Ilex and Melia became known as the only alchemists to have achieved mutual conjunction — both essences reaching equivalency in one body. Physically they appeared as one body, not as the conjoined twins or alchemical hermaphrodite so often depicted in the alchemical manuscripts of the outside world. Within that one body, both essences existed simultaneously with specific physical features shifting between those of Ilex and those of Melia. Sometimes Melia's essence and features would dominate for weeks or even months on end before shifting to those of Ilex. Other times the shifting would occur hourly or even, in certain lights, minute to minute. Their fellow Council members gradually adjusted to the phenomenon, but the new Initiates who arrived within Ilex and Melia's tenure could not help but stare at them, fascinated in particular on the days when the appearance was in constant flux. As an

Initiate, Sadira had read and listened to so many accounts of the pair that she came to know more about them than those alchemists who had actually known Ilex and Melia.

For certain Council members, their mutual conjunction was yet another one of their enviable qualities; for others, the pairing was problematic, a cause for suspicion and mistrust. Eventually, thanks to the persistent efforts of one particular Council member, the suspicion turned to an outright accusation of allegiance with the Rebel Branch, which in turn led to an official investigation. Though Ilex and Melia were acquitted of all charges by a unanimous vote at Elder Council, the "upstart Magistrate" (as he was described in one archival account) who had initiated the accusations, along with a handful of his colleagues, never accepted the Elder Council decision and continued to reproach the conjunctive pair whenever possible.

For reasons that have never been conclusively proven, Ilex and Melia disappeared, presumably having left Council dimension to reside independently in the outside world. Their disappearance and its aftermath had been a subject of debate ever since. Some contended, as they had all along, that the pair was aligned with the rebels. Others argued they had joined the rebels only after their disappearance. Some surmised they had nothing whatsoever to do with the rebels and merely wanted to live in peace, free of accusatory remarks. Perhaps they had merely wanted to live the remainder of their days in the outside world free from alchemical manipulation. Alternate theories proposed they had chosen to live independently of Council or rebels, sustaining themselves with alchemical knowledge and usurped or fabricated Elixir. Despite an inability to locate the pair and notwithstanding all evidence to the contrary, the Council nonetheless officially maintained that Ilex and Melia still possessed their conjunctive pendant and thus their alchemical abilities.

This particular theory, combined with allegations of rebel activity, led to suspicion of their involvement in the Third Rebellion. However, as with all other accusations levelled at them, nothing conclusive had ever been found to link Ilex and Melia to any rebel activity whatsoever. Thus, as time passed, as no evidence surfaced, as they were nowhere to be found, and as they had never been seen again within Council dimension, Ilex and Melia became relegated to the archives and to the occasional late-night conversation among certain alchemists who had known them. For others, Ilex and Melia gradually became a mere curiosity, little more than an intriguing myth to be recounted to Initiates during Council history lessons.

Such had been the case for Sadira — until lately. Years ago she would speak at length about the pair with Saule who, in both intonation and gesture during the conversations, seemed to both idolize and envy them. Sadira adopted a similar attitude.

Like most Initiates who have witnessed a typical conjunction and lived in fear of one day being consumed by another, she was elated to know of the potential for mutual conjunction. However, as time moved forward, as her first century within Council dimension passed, Sadira gradually let go of what seemed to her more and more a mere youthful fantasy. For decades, she had given little thought to the pair. Renewed interest was much more recent.

A few years ago, shortly after she had lost Saule, she began thinking of the possibility that she herself would one day be conjoined. If she were granted that honour, with whom would she be paired? She had, of course, once hoped to conjoin with Saule. But this hope had been thwarted by Cedar. She had grieved for Saule, as sadness for her loss mixed with anger directed at Cedar. However, she knew rationally that Cedar's dominance over Saule's essence was an inherent and unavoidable part of the conjunctive process, and that she should not be angry with Cedar. Eventually she saw Cedar as someone who still possessed all that remained of Saule, even if only a trace. Thus her attitude towards Cedar softened; they became friends and, gradually, lovers. One day, within the first few months of their budding relationship, Reader Wu Tong approached them both with the news that he had read of Sadira's conjunction; he claimed it would certainly occur within the tenure of 18th Council. Sadira had wept that night in Cedar's arms. *I don't want to conjoin*, she had told Cedar. *I want to stay here with you and Saule.*

Cedar did not reveal her secret immediately. She waited. She waited several weeks, until enough time had passed that Sadira was exhibiting physical signs of anxiety over the potential conjunction. *I have a solution*, said Cedar one night. She told Sadira about the power of Sephrim. *It will strengthen your essence; you will dominate, no matter who is chosen as your partner*. Of course, the use of Sephrim was prohibited. Procuring it was dangerous, a crime punishable by erasure. *I have contacts*, Cedar assured her. *No one will know*. And thus was Sadira trapped. She realized in that moment that Cedar herself must have ingested Sephrim in the years leading up to her own conjunction, that her potential for dominance over Saule had been unlawfully enhanced, that the one who had wilfully consumed her beloved Saule was now the one offering her the potential for eternal life.

Sadira had a choice: she could inform the Elder Council of Cedar's illicit acts or she could accept Cedar's offer. She chose the latter. A few nights later — over a year ago now — when Sadira agreed to accept the Sephrim, Cedar could not have been more content. *We will be together for eternity*, Sadira had said, *like Ilex and Melia*. But now she knew that her relationship with Cedar was nothing like the relationship between Ilex and Melia. She and Cedar would remain inexorably entwined not through love alone but through guilt and complicity.

Not long thereafter, both to distract herself from the impending conjunction and to enliven the students in her Initiate classes, Sadira began once again to research Ilex and Melia. She approached the manuscripts and records with what she believed to be an open mind. She found several accounts of their lives in the archives and several within the Lapidarian manuscripts that had escaped her notice all those years earlier. The more she read of them, the more she wanted to know. They swiftly became for Sadira much more than just a romantic story revered in her youth, more than a myth, more than a lesson in class. They began to embody for Sadira a means to an end.

Now, in all likelihood, Sadira would have remained in the Amber Garden until the afternoon light transformed into evening, if not for the event that literally shook her and everyone in Council dimension into a change of plans and perspective. At first, Sadira thought her own body was betraying her, that her trembling had grown more severe as she mourned for Saule and contemplated Ilex and Melia. But then the trembling grew more intense; the amber pieces hanging amidst the leaves on the branches above her began to make a tinkling sound, the sort occasionally caused by an alchemically induced springtime wind. Then, mere seconds later, the entire Amber Garden became visibly agitated, with amber pieces clinking harshly against one another. Finally, Sadira had to steady herself on the bench as the ground itself began to shake beneath her.

A recent arrival to Council dimension from the outside world would have mistaken the event for an earthquake. But as Sadira and all trained alchemists knew, Council dimension was not prone to the geographical or meteorological events of the outside world; all apparently natural events within Council dimension were controlled by the Lapis itself through alchemical manipulation of the elements — and the Council had maintained a virtual paradise for thousands of years. This event, one that within moments had the entire Council dimension shaking at its foundations and every alchemist fearing death, despite the Lapidarian promise of eternal life, had only one explanation: a colossal disturbance in the elemental balance, a balance upon which the Council depended for its very existence.

While Sadira gripped the stone bench in the Amber Garden, Cedar braced herself against the Lapis itself in the Scriptorium. Ruis, with whom Cedar had been meeting to discuss the manuscript lacunae and potential rebel activity, steadied himself against one of the acacia wood pillars — four of which graced the Scriptorium in tribute to the four elements surrounding the Quintessence of the

Lapis. During the height of the tremors, both Ruis and Cedar kept instinctive postures, heads down and eyes closed. And when the shaking ceased, they remained momentarily in position, opening their eyes only to exchange stunned looks.

Though Cedar immediately understood the quake as an elemental disturbance, and though she knew that everything within Council dimension would regain its elemental balance within hours — that even broken glass or cracked stone or spilled waters would be returned to their original state through alchemical transformation — she nonetheless continued to tremble after the dimensional movement ceased. Ruis, perhaps out of honest concern or perhaps merely seizing an unexpected opportunity, moved towards Cedar, proffering comfort with open arms. To the surprise of both Ruis and herself, Cedar accepted the gesture, and the two embraced. Again to the surprise of both, Ruis was the one who broke away, moving from Cedar with a sudden gasp of despair.

"The Flaw in the Stone!" he exclaimed, pointing behind Cedar at the Lapis.

Cedar turned. She held a hand to her mouth to silence what might otherwise have manifested as an astonished cry as she stared at the Lapis. In the place where the Flaw used to be, where its absence had been visible even to the most observant Council member only in a certain slant of light, now lodged what could only be described as a significantly sized fissure. It measured at least a finger's width and an arm's length, scarring the Lapis beyond anything Cedar could ever have imagined.

Ruis heaved himself against the Lapis, pounding his fists against its surface in an act of sacrilege that, fortunately for him, no one but Cedar witnessed.

"Stop!" Cedar cried, making futile attempts to restrain his physical outrage.

"Everything is ruined! Everything is ruined!"

"Perhaps the Lapis will repair itself, along with everything in Council dimension. We need only wait a few hours — a few days at most."

"This is not a mere crack in the floor of Azothian Chambers, Cedar. This is the Flaw in the Stone! I have worked my entire Council life as an Elder to eradicate the Flaw, to re-establish the perfection of the Lapis, to recreate the achievement of the Azoths during the Vulknut Eclipse of the 17th Council. And for what? *For what?* All for nothing. Now, even if I am chosen as Azoth Magen after Ailanthus, I will reach Final Ascension only to die like all who have ascended before me. Perfect union of *all* will never occur. I will have changed nothing. *Nothing.*"

"No, Ruis. No. Like all those before you, at Final Ascension you will achieve eternal life through conjunction with the One."

"No, Cedar, I will die. I will be subsumed by the One. You know this as well as I."

He was right, of course. Cedar did know, as well as any Elder, that Final Ascension meant physical death, despite what the Azoths themselves preached as the official interpretation of the Law Codes. She knew as well what Ruis had wanted, what he had been working towards, and what he may well have been able to achieve if not for all those working against him, including her.

After the tremor had ceased and she had recovered enough to walk, Sadira made her way to Council Chambers. Though such an event had never before happened during her tenure, she knew enough about emergency protocols to assume Council Chambers would be the meeting point in the aftermath of today's cataclysm. Along the path to the main Council building she stopped twice, just long enough to observe the alchemical healing process along the high eastern wall of the main courtyard — small fractures closed seamlessly as she watched. She ran her fingertips over the newly repaired surface and marvelled at the restoration's rapid progression and resulting perfection. She watched as a dozen or so Lapidarian bees moved from blossom to blossom, working to restore the elemental balance of the trees and gardens. Regardless of the disturbance or its cause, Council dimension Quintessence remained alive and well. A Ritual of Restoration, which she assumed would be the first order of business, would ensure a full recovery of

Council dimension grounds and buildings — from the highest tower to the deepest channel waters. Though she had performed portions of the ritual over the years, she had never recited it in its entirety. Chanting the entire text would take several hours of careful concentration, with each alchemist not only chanting the words but also visualizing the Quintessence moving through Council dimension, restoring the elemental balance. She wondered if the outside world had likewise suffered damage, whether people had died in the alchemical equivalent to an elemental aftershock. A disruption within the elemental balance of earth, fire, air, and water in Council dimension could well manifest as an earthquake or volcanic eruption or tornado or tsunami in the outside world. If such a disaster had occurred, the Readers would certainly know within the hour, and the Scribal restoration would begin by nightfall. But manifesting restoration in the outside world would be slow at best. At least, that is what Sadira understood from her readings on the matter; she had never herself taken part in such an extensive restoration.

Sadira could hear the clamour within Council Chambers even before she reached the anteroom. Council members were gathered in clusters recounting events. "I was in the North Library," she overheard someone exclaim, "and was nearly struck on the head by a 14th-century illuminated *Feasts of the Azoths.*" Meanwhile, the Azoths stood in their respective places at the front of Council Chambers, talking among themselves. Shortly thereafter, Azoth Ravenea called upon Readers Olivia, Terek, Wu Tong, and Tilia. Standing together on the Azothian platform, the three Readers and the three Azoths consulted each other animatedly for several minutes. Finally, and with some difficulty given the noise level within Chambers, Azoth Ruis called the session to order.

"As I am sure you have determined, the dimensional disturbance we experienced less than an hour ago was the result of a severe disruption in the elements. Though the Readers have not yet reached a conclusion on the precise cause — whether rebel intention or Council mistake — they have nonetheless managed to pinpoint the geographical location of the disturbance. Having consulted with Olivia, Terek, and Wu Tong, I can confirm that the epicentre of imbalance lay in the Qingdao protectorate."

Sadira, though she gave no outward sign of reaction to this news, felt a chill run through her body. Scanning the benches and chairs of Council Chambers, she observed four notable absentees: Obeche, Tera, Arjan, and Jaden. Were they together in Qingdao? Her earlier concerns over the potential of an outside world aftershock gripped her. Had all four perished? Were they alive but unable to return to Council dimension? Was the disturbance — as malevolent as it appeared to be — part of Cedar's plan? Had Cedar purposely not revealed her full plan? Had she betrayed Sadira through omission of truth? Or, worse, had Sadira's own secrets — those she had most recently kept from Cedar — somehow contributed to the disaster? Or, had someone slain the person she so recently had come to believe would be their saviour?

Cedar was stunned when Ruis announced that the elemental imbalance had originated in the Qingdao protectorate. Though she perhaps should have expected the unexpected, especially given the possibility of interference by Obeche, Cedar had not anticipated such drastic news. *Why, time and again, was Obeche involved when something went amiss?*

The seats directly behind her, normally occupied by Obeche and Tera, were empty. Even if Obeche never returned from Qingdao, and regardless of his hundreds of years with the Council, she would not count his absence as much of a loss. Indeed, she may even revel in the unexpected turn of events. But she could not bear the thought that Tera may not return. She had always found Tera an ally against Obeche in decisions over Scribal matters. And her thoughts darkened even further when she confirmed, with a quick glance towards the Initiate benches at the back of Council Chambers, that both Jaden and Arjan were also missing. With the possible exception of the newly incised increase to the Flaw in the Stone, Council dimension would be repaired. But if Tera, Arjan, and Jaden had been hurt in the outside world, whether or not within protectorate space, the damage to the future of the Council could prove irreparable.

Thus through the entire Ritual of Restoration, through the ceremonial words and vocal intonations and physical gestures, and even during the Procession of the Orders as she moved from her seat towards the Azoth Magen to receive the Sacrament of Elixir, Cedar's thoughts returned continually to Tera and the young Initiates. Were they safe? Had they themselves accidentally caused the disturbance? Would the Elders blame her for insisting that the Initiates be taken to the outside world? Would Sadira blame her for the loss of Jaden and Arjan?

As the ritual progressed, Cedar could feel the balance of elements within Council Chambers — and, indeed, within herself — gradually return to normalcy. Yet she could still sense a disturbance within her pendant, as if the Lapidarian essence itself had been affected by the disruption within Council dimension. Perhaps this effect was the result of the increase to the Flaw. She assumed Ruis would have told Ailanthus and Ravenea of this dramatic change to the Lapis. Perhaps Ailanthus's offering of the Sacrament of Elixir was a means to circumvent any disturbance within the Lapidarian essence of the pendants.

Just as Cedar had returned to her seat and placed her pendant against her lips as a means of determining its reaction to the Elixir, the southern doors to Council Chambers were thrown open. Obeche and Tera, with Arjan in tow, made their way through the group of Magistrates about to receive Elixir, Obeche announcing loudly to the Azoths, "Junior Initiate Jaden has been abducted by the rebels!"

"Abducted?" replied Ruis. "Did you witness the abduction?"

"No, your Eminence. But from his position in a window of the Qingdao protectorate library, Arjan witnessed her disappear from the street below. Despite our efforts, we have not been able to locate her or find any clue that could lead us to her. What explanation could there be beyond rebel abduction? We seek Azothian intervention."

The commotion immediately following Obeche's announcement was enough to astonish even the most stalwart Council member. After several minutes of indecipherable debate among the Azoths, Obeche, and Tera, Ailanthus announced the plan: Azoth Ravenea would stay in Council Chambers to administer Elixir to the remaining Magistrates and eligible Initiates. After the distribution of Elixir, Magistrates and Initiates were to return directly to residence chambers. Readers were to convene in the Scriptorium to seek further explanation of today's events. All other Elders were to report to the portal chamber, where the Ritual of Return would be enacted at the Quercus portal in an attempt to return Jaden to Council dimension.

Thus Cedar, having no say in the matter, proceeded as directed with her Elder cohorts to the portal chamber, relieved at the return of both Tera and Arjan, but distraught over Jaden's disappearance. She knew perfectly well that if Jaden had been abducted, she was not in the hands of the rebels. Her well-laid plans had been dashed beyond recognition.

After pacing the narrow street of Qingdao for more than two hours, Jaden's annoyance turned to apprehension. She wondered how far the Qingdao protectorate extended beyond the manuscript building. Regardless, she considered abandoning the protectorate vicinity in search of someone — anyone — who could direct her back to the street with the murals. She could then wait at the temporary portal ground. But she also worried that in wandering the streets she might find herself irreparably lost or, worse, in danger — unable to communicate her need to find a specific street with a specific portal. She decided the safest option was to remain here. So she sat down on the ground outside the manuscript building and waited. She repeatedly reminded herself that Obeche and Tera would return eventually. But after an hour of waiting, her imagination began to lead her unwillingly to a variety of worst-case scenarios — one of which involved an elaborate plot in which the rebels had captured and imprisoned both Obeche and Tera. In this particular fantasy, Kalina and Dracaen had lied to Jaden all along, luring her outside the relative safety of the protectorate library with the help of Jinjing and her fragment of the Dragonblood Stone. She would be trapped forever in the streets of Qingdao.

She also thought through the actual chain of events. She regretted not having revealed to Arjan the gift Jinjing had bestowed her. She took the fragment from her pocket and examined it closely. Perhaps she could use it to contact Kalina or Dracaen. She held the fragment tightly in one hand and called to Kalina in her mind. She held it to her forehead and called for Dracaen. She held it up towards the evening sky and thought of the Flaw in the Stone. Nothing happened. Finally, in an act she worried might be sacrilege but which she was nonetheless willing to attempt as a last resort, she touched the Dragonblood fragment lightly against her interim pendant. The sudden spark caused by this action startled her.

Jaden stood up. She positioned herself immediately in front of the manuscript building door and firmly pressed the Dragonblood fragment against her pendant. The force threw Jaden off her feet. She could feel herself moving through alternating light and darkness as if she were being transported through a portal. She gripped the fragment and pendant, holding her hand still against the force propelling her body. Flashes of bright colours filled her vision. Suddenly, all movement ceased. Her body wrenched forward, and she instinctually reached out to steady herself, inadvertently letting go of both the fragment and the pendant. Nausea overwhelmed her. She could not make out the features of the figure standing before her in the dimly lit room.

"Welcome back."

Jaden blinked repeatedly to regain her focus.

"The disorientation is an unfortunate side effect of ritual transport. You will be fine within a few hours."

"Cedar? Where am I?"

"You are in the portal chamber. You have been ritually transported back to Council dimension by the Elders."

"I don't understand."

"The transport disorientation prevents us from investigating the matter or explaining our methods now. Please return to your chambers to rest. We will talk in the morning."

"Where is Arjan?"

Obeche stepped forward. Jaden noticed then that several Elders stood silently in the shadows along the edge of the room.

"He is safe. We returned together several hours ago through the temporary portal in the Qingdao main street."

"You returned without me?"

"You were nowhere to be found. Hence our need for ritual retrieval."

"It is late," said Cedar. "We are all tired, and I assume you are nauseated. You will be escorted to your chambers, Jaden. War measures are still in effect. Report to my office tomorrow immediately after breakfast for debriefing. You will feel physically better by then."

Jaden bowed her head slightly to Cedar, to Obeche, and to the other Elders. She understood by Cedar's tone that she was not to attempt to find Arjan. Accompanied by Rowans Kai and Esche, she walked slowly and silently, still quite off balance, through the main building and across the courtyard towards residence chambers. Just as she reached the willow tree near the courtyard fountain, she remembered the Dragonblood fragment. She stopped. In desperation, she checked all her pockets. She remembered holding it tightly before and during the transport. She must have dropped it in the portal chamber — or worse, during the journey within the distorted space between dimensions before even reaching the Quercus portal. How could she have been so careless with such a precious item *again*?

"What is wrong?" asked Kai. "Have you lost something?"

"No. I . . . I thought I felt something. Crawling. Under my clothes. It's nothing."

"You are most likely still experiencing the unsettling effects of ritual retrieval."

As they progressed towards residence chambers, Jaden fought the nausea and tested her memory. She thought of Kalina and of Dracaen. She thought of classes with Kalina. She thought of Dracaen offering her the cup of Dragon's Blood. She thought of standing at the wrought-iron railing watching the mists of the Dragonblood Stone. She thought of Kalina as they stood together under the willow tree near the Amber Garden. Though she feared that the memories would soon vanish along with the Dragonblood fragment, Jaden made every effort to retain them for as long as possible.

After reaching her chambers, after Kai and Esche had bid her good night, she repeatedly brought to mind all she could remember of both Kalina and Dracaen. She thought of them as she moved about her room. She thought of them as she lay down on her bed. She thought of them even as she drifted, overwhelmed with fatigue, to sleep. But most surprisingly and most importantly, she thought of them when she woke again several hours later. *I will remember. I will remember*, Jaden continued to chant silently to herself as she washed and dressed and walked to the dining hall. She had not eaten since the meal in Qingdao.

She hoped to find Arjan awaiting her, but to her dismay, the only Initiate in the dining hall was

Laurel. Jaden contemplated skipping breakfast to avoid having to speak with her, but she was too late. Laurel had already spotted her and, to Jaden's amazement, had suddenly jumped up, run over, and embraced her.

"You're back! Obeche said you'd been abducted by rebels."

"What? No. I wasn't abducted. I'm fine. I just — I was delayed in Qingdao. I'm supposed to meet Cedar after breakfast. But I wanted to find Arjan first. Have you seen him?"

"No — not since Council Chambers yesterday. So what happened to you?"

"I was separated from Arjan, and I didn't know how to return to Council dimension."

Jaden worried that Laurel would continue to interrogate her about the events of Qingdao, necessitating the fabrication of a plausible story. But instead, as she reached in front of Jaden for a biscuit, Laurel asked the most unexpected question.

"What happened to your pendant?"

Jaden grasped for her pendant, afraid for an instant that she had lost it along with the Dragonblood fragment. But thankfully the pendant remained on its chain around her neck.

"What do you mean?"

"Let me see it," said Laurel.

Jaden removed her hand and noticed for the first time what had captured Laurel's attention. The pendant had been damaged. It contained a sizable chip, to all appearances a blood-red scar, just left of its centre.

"A flaw in your stone," Laurel laughed. "I guess you made the wrong choice in Santa Fe. Mine is still perfectly solid." She held her pendant aloft for Jaden to see.

But Jaden sat transfixed. She understood in that instant the reason she could still remember Kalina and Dracaen. The Dragonblood fragment had merged with her pendant. Jaden did indeed have in her possession her very own flaw in the stone.

"I need to find Arjan," she insisted to Laurel.

"Then stay here. He's unlikely to skip breakfast."

"Did you speak with him yesterday after he returned from Qingdao?"

"After he returned from Qingdao? Seriously? As if the war measures weren't enough of an obstacle already, do you honestly think that in the aftermath of an earthquake and potential abduction that the Initiates would be allowed to mingle?"

"Earthquake? What earthquake?"

"When you were in Qingdao, there was a disturbance in Council dimension, and it caused something like an earthquake. They said it originated in Qingdao. Cercis and I were terrified."

"It couldn't have been that bad. Everything looks fine. Nothing was damaged."

"Alchemical transformation," replied Laurel in a slightly patronizing tone. "The entire Council dimension repaired itself in the aftermath — except, if the murmured rumours are to be believed, for the Flaw in the Stone."

Jaden's startled expression communicated her lack of comprehension.

"The Flaw has apparently grown. No one knows yet what the implications will be."

Jaden glanced around the dining hall. Most of the tables on the main floor were now occupied. Only the Elders remained conspicuously absent. They were, she assumed, discussing the rebels, the change in the Flaw, the earthquake, the events of Qingdao, and, most likely, *her*.

"Where is Arjan? He should be here by now."

"Maybe a Scribe already has him working."

"I can't wait any longer. I need to find Arjan before I meet with Cedar."

"I'll come with you."

"To meet Cedar?"

"No — to find Cercis. He and Arjan may be together."

Jaden saw no point in taking the time to argue the illogic of Laurel's theory or to convince her to stay behind. They walked together through the corridors of the main building, across the courtyard, and through residence chambers first to Arjan's door and then to Cercis's. They checked the North Library and then the reading room where Laurel had last seen Cercis. Other than a few of the groundskeepers and a cook, they did not cross paths with anyone in their hour of searching. Finally, just as they turned the corner near the entranceway to the Amber Garden on their way to the South Library, Cedar called out to them.

"Jaden, come with me. Laurel, report to Katsura — you have been paired with her, not with Jaden!"

Jaden did not speak en route to Cedar's office. She remained disgruntled about not finding Arjan; from Jaden's perspective, Cedar had intruded. She had little desire to describe the events of Qingdao to Cedar or any Elder.

But everything changed once Cedar opened her office door to reveal Arjan seated at a small table perusing a manuscript.

"Take a seat at the table," said Cedar to Jaden. "We don't have much time."

Jaden sat beside Arjan. Out of necessity and protocol, she remained calm, eyes on Cedar. But she rested her arms on the table, longing for Arjan to do the same. Arjan sat back in his chair, arms folded across his chest, hands hidden by the fabric of his robes. Did Arjan not understand how desperately she needed to hear his voice, to learn from his perspective what had happened after she had left the manuscript room in Qingdao?

"Later today, we will join the Elders in Azothian Chambers," Cedar began. She stood in the centre of the room, in front of her desk, gesturing emphatically as she spoke. "In the meantime, you are to remain under my supervision. I suggest you spend these next several hours wisely. If I were you, I would spend the time contemplating how to respond most effectively to the Azoths. You will each be asked to recount what happened yesterday. Some Elders believe the Rebel Branch may be targeting the Council through their most vulnerable members — you, the Junior Initiates — outside Council dimension. Therefore, when recounting the course of events, you must include not only your actions and their consequences but also the smallest particulars of your experience: sounds, scents, tastes. The most seemingly insignificant detail could have been the trigger point — the epicentre, if you will — for the collapse of elemental balance that originated in Qingdao and rippled through Council dimension and protectorates yesterday. Do you understand?"

"Yes," replied Arjan and Jaden simultaneously.

Jaden's swift response masked her uncertainty. Could she, *should* she recount every detail? She raced through a flood of conflicting possibilities — truths, half-truths, utter deceit. The hours of waiting were spent in agonizing silence. Cedar refused to allow Arjan and Jaden to rehearse their stories aloud to one another; after the first hour, Jaden had given up even looking to her friend for any sign of reassurance. The agony was punctuated only by the occasional supervised break. Finally, when the time to proceed to Azothian Chambers arrived, Jaden was almost relieved. She just wanted the day to end.

As she followed Cedar and Arjan through the

corridors, Jaden adjusted her robes to conceal her pendant. What if the Elder Council determined that she had been contacted *again* by the Rebel Branch, that she was the one who had possessed *again* a fragment of the Dragonblood Stone, that she was potentially the one responsible for the earthquake in Council dimension? Jaden could feel her knees shaking as she crossed the threshold into Azothian Chambers.

Arjan, for the first time since Jaden had met him, seemed disconcerted. He sat on a bench against the far wall of Azothian Chambers, his back straight, his head resting against the tapestry behind him, his eyes closed. Jaden waited on another bench, directly across the room from Arjan. She breathed steadily, silently willing the fires of the Azothian kiln to emit more light than its current amber glow. Her efforts had no effect. She watched the shadows dart across Arjan's face. She listened to the quiet rustling of robes as the Elders positioned themselves for the proceedings.

"Approach," said Azoth Ruis. He gestured towards Jaden.

As she moved towards the middle of the room, she noticed Arjan open his eyes. She took a seat in the large wooden chair placed in front of the long table, where not only Azoths Ravenea and Ruis sat alongside Obeche and Cedar, but the Azoth Magen himself presided.

"Describe in precise detail your experiences and the sequence of events at the Qingdao protectorate," said Ravenea, an underlying urgency in her tone.

What details could Jaden fabricate to replace those associated with Jinjing and the Dragonblood fragment — with memories of Kalina and Dracaen and the secrets she had been keeping? Would the Elders be able to tell if she lied? What if they forcibly read her pendant? What if they noticed and understood its flaw? She looked first towards Cedar, with whom she felt at least a modicum of comfort. But when she finally spoke, she addressed herself directly to Ailanthus.

"We were working."

"You and Arjan?"

"Yes. We were working with the manuscripts. We had been told to search for images of bees. But we found only one possibility — an insect of some sort, perhaps a bee. Then, shortly after that, Jinjing brought us a meal. We ate—"

"Which manuscript?" asked Ailanthus.

"What?"

"In which manuscript did you find the indecipherable insect?"

"I don't know, your Eminence. We set it aside to show Obeche and Tera when they returned — but, of course, they didn't. I mean — I did not see them return. I had gone outside."

"You ate the meal outside?"

"No. Not then. Jinjing, the Keeper of the Book, brought a tray of tea and food to us."

"You ate in the same room, at the same table, as the manuscripts resided? Did you damage yet another manuscript through your carelessness?"

"No. We had set the manuscripts aside. We were careful."

Various Elders gestured their disapproval.

"Describe the food — taste, smell, whatever you recall," requested Ruis.

"The tea was steaming and fragrant — earthy and dark, like no tea I had tried before. There were noodles in a light broth, fried gai lan, and steamed buns. The buns were filled with spiced meat — pork, I think. Everything was delicious, and I wanted to take more time to relax and talk, instead of returning to work."

"You wanted to continue to relax and talk with Arjan?" asked Obeche.

Jaden felt a rush of blood to her face. "Yes," she stated emphatically, unwilling to be cowed by Obeche. "The work you assigned us seemed pointless — to me, not to Arjan."

"Whether or not you understand the point of the work is irrelevant," retorted Obeche. "The tasks I assign you are to be completed without question, as are all tasks assigned by Elders to Initiates."

"I agree," said Jaden. "But today I have been

asked by the Elders to recount my experience in precise detail."

Obeche's nostrils flared.

"We appreciate your honesty," said Cedar. "Continue."

"When we had finished the meal, we started to work again. But after a while I couldn't bear it any longer. I stood up and walked across the room to look out the window. I wanted to see the city beyond the protectorate library. I watched a boy — maybe seven or eight years old — playing outside. I had noticed him earlier, and he was still there, hours later, playing alone with a ball. I watched him for a while. He reminded me of Arjan. And then, a while later, when Arjan saw him, he said . . . Arjan said the boy *was* him, years ago."

Whispers filled the room.

"Silence!" ordered Ravenea. "Did you believe Arjan? Or did you understand him to be joking?"

"He wasn't joking. But I thought he might be wrong. *How could the boy actually be Arjan?* So I went outside to talk to him."

"And upon meeting the boy, did you believe him to be Arjan?" asked Ruis.

"I don't know. He looked like Arjan, but how could he *be* Arjan? He told me his name was Payam. We played ball for a while, but I turned away at one point — I ran after the ball — and when I turned back, he was gone. I couldn't find him, and I couldn't get back into the protectorate building. So I sat outside and waited. And finally it occurred to me — I held my pendant to my forehead, hoping someone in Council dimension would sense my fear."

"You are fortunate, Jaden, that you are an Initiate of Cedar. Her powers are strong even among others of her Order. During the Ritual of Return, through her pendant, she was able to sense your distress in Qingdao and, more importantly, your location thanks to the Lapidarian essence of your interim pendant," explained Ailanthus.

"What do you recall of your return journey?" asked Ravenea.

"Jarring movements, flashes of light — as if I was being yanked harshly through a portal. I think I may have passed out because suddenly I was aware of the stone floor beneath me and of being with Cedar. We were in the portal chamber."

"Have you anything further to add?" asked Ravenea.

"No, Azoth."

"Very good. Please take a seat on the far bench," instructed Ruis. "You will be recalled later if necessary."

With relief, Jaden made her way towards the back of the chambers. She purposely avoided eye contact with Arjan. She did not want to witness his judgment of her lies. Seated once again on the bench, Jaden lowered her head and visually traced the mosaic patterns on the floor. Flecks of gold and copper glistened in the light of the kiln.

"Arjan," said Ruis. "Approach."

Arjan adjusted his robes and, with both hands, pulled back his long dark hair so that it fell behind his shoulders. Jaden admired the way it cascaded down his back. She wondered if he could sense her feelings for him through his pendant. When the Junior Initiates were preparing for the Night of Albedo, Cedar had explained that alchemists occasionally shared an empathic connection through their pendants with other members of their Order or branch. Perhaps Jaden should be more careful to suppress her emotions.

"Do you concur with Jaden's version of events?" asked Ruis.

Jaden's body reacted with visceral dread. She feared Arjan would admit to the Elders her knowledge of Kalina and Dracaen. Why did her trust in him continually waver?

"During the meal, we spoke of the Rebel Branch," Arjan began.

Jaden glanced towards the chamber door, calculating her chances of successful escape.

"Of course," interjected Cedar, "you would be concerned about the rebel threat. Speaking your concerns aloud to a friend is more than reasonable. Tell us what happened after the meal and conversation — when you saw the boy."

Jaden was both surprised and thankful. Cedar's words had unintentionally saved Arjan from having to discuss the details of their conversation about the rebels.

"I was shocked," replied Arjan.

"Because the boy resembled you?" asked Ravenea.

"No — I was shocked because the boy *was* me. He *was* me. I am certain. Time had . . ." Arjan paused before clearly enunciating, ". . . shifted, converged. And memories came back to me."

"Temporal shifts are impossible within protectorate space," said Obeche.

Arjan did not respond immediately, but when none of the Elders spoke, he stated calmly, "With all due respect, Scribe Obeche, you are wrong. I have borne witness to such a shift."

Ailanthus slammed his jade serpent gavel against its base. Jaden jumped, startled by Ailanthus's force.

"Temporal transmutation is not the concern of Initiates," insisted Ailanthus.

"No, it is not, Azoth Magen," said Ravenea. "However, if these Initiates have fallen victim to temporal manipulation by the rebels, we must forego standard protocols. Arjan, tell us, how can you be certain the boy was indeed you?"

"I remember the event."

"I do not understand," said Ravenea.

"I remember the day — long ago — as a boy — playing ball and looking up at the window. I remember beckoning to the woman — Jaden — to come outside. I remember her walking towards me and then playing ball with me and then disappearing. And I was alone again. Of course, I did not know as a boy that she was Jaden or an alchemist or a member of the Alchemists' Council. And, over the years, I had forgotten her face. But in that moment in Qingdao when I saw myself, I understood the reason I have felt connected to Jaden since the day I met her — for the second time — in Council dimension."

Once again, Jaden felt a rush of blood to her face. She was thankful she was seated in the shadows at the back of the room.

The Azoths and other Elders silently scrutinized Arjan, as if attempting to determine his trustworthiness.

"What were you doing in the Qingdao protectorate as a child?" asked Obeche.

"I did not know of the protectorate. I knew only of my family life. I was spending the summer with my grandparents in China. But we were foreigners, and I was unable to make friends there. I remember that particular day because it was one of the few I was happy to be in Qingdao."

"You were happy to play with someone?"

"Yes. I was happy to play, but I was also happy because my grandparents had finally succeeded. They were joyous. We celebrated. They bought me sweets from the little shop up the street. And they said we could soon leave China for home — so I was happy in the knowledge that I would see my friends again."

"At what did your grandparents succeed?" asked Obeche.

"Transmutation."

"Transmutation?" asked both Ruis and Ravenea.

"Alchemical transmutation?" asked Ailanthus. "Are you saying that your grandparents were charlatans seeking to turn base metal into gold?"

"No. My grandparents were trained alchemists who became adept at various forms of transmutation. On that day, they succeeded at the transmutation of time. And I see now that Jaden was meant to be there — that she needed to be there in temporal convergence or conjunction — for the transmutation to work."

No one spoke. Ailanthus stood and held his Lapidarian sceptre aloft. Jaden expected he would transmute Arjan into stone right then and there if such a feat were possible. *He knows too much.* Jaden had always thought this of Arjan. And now she feared he had revealed more than prudent. Had he done this — revealed his own family secrets — to protect her and her knowledge of the rebels, to attract the attention to him and him alone? She briefly considered standing up and accusing Jinjing of treason as a means of deflecting attention from Arjan. But what proof could she offer beyond the Dragonblood fragment, which Jaden now possessed only in its absence and blood-red stain. What good would her self-sacrifice do for Arjan in the end? And why, she finally wondered, had he not trusted her enough to tell her of his family history before this moment of public revelation?

Arjan sat still and silent, awaiting judgment.

Ailanthus pointed his sceptre directly at Arjan and bellowed in a voice that reverberated through Azothian chambers, "Who were your grandparents?"

Arjan glanced towards the ceiling and shook his head. Jaden watched his black hair shine in the amber light as it moved across his robes. She gripped the edge of the bench.

"Answer the question!" demanded Ailanthus. "Who were your grandparents?"

"Ilex and Melia," said Arjan.

And the fires of the Azothian kiln flared up in response.

In that split second after the names *Ilex and Melia* were uttered, Cedar wanted to laugh. Here, seated before the Azoths, having roamed the halls and grounds of Council dimension for months, was a descendant — perhaps the one remaining descendant — of the only alchemists in history to have succeeded not only at mutual conjunction but at another act that has eluded all other alchemists ever granted Elixir: procreation. But before Cedar could voice her response, Obeche was on his feet, headed towards Arjan, infused with anger more fierce than she had imagined him capable. For years, ever since his Magistrate days, Obeche had despised Ilex and Melia, continually accusing them of being aligned with the rebels. Given the rage evident on Obeche's face, Cedar suddenly feared for Arjan's safety.

"Obeche! Be seated!" demanded Ravenea.

Obeche reached Arjan, grasped his pendant, and held it with both hands to his forehead. Arjan cried out. Jaden gasped and fell from the bench to her knees, remembering the pain of Obeche's assault through her own pendant. Cedar moved swiftly towards Jaden, reaching her just as Ruis and Ravenea reached Arjan. They could not stop Obeche from draining Arjan's essence now that he had Arjan's pendant in hand, but they could prevent Arjan's body from dropping painfully to the floor. Ailanthus remained poised on the Azothian dais, sceptre ready to direct at anyone the full strength of his Lapidarian power. Cedar helped Jaden to her feet and escorted her, despite her cries of resistance, out of Azothian Chambers and into the hallway.

"You must return to your residence chambers," said Cedar.

"No! I need to help Arjan!"

"Jaden! Jaden, listen to me! You cannot help Arjan from here. Do you understand me? You must leave now. Return to your chambers. Trust me. We will help Arjan. Go now."

Cedar watched Jaden move slowly down the

hall. She seemed drained from the proceedings and her empathic connection with Arjan through their Initiate pendants. Cedar longed to accompany her, to offer the support that she owed her Initiate. But for now she had to convince the Azoths and, thereafter, all the Elders to approve their only option of ensuring renewed Lapidarian strength at this time of crisis and breach — a breach, she would emphasize to Ailanthus, of both space and time.

Cedar grasped her own pendant momentarily and then walked with an air of steady confidence back into Azothian Chambers. Arjan lay on the floor, apparently unconscious. Ruis and Ravenea knelt beside him. Obeche stood beside the Azothian kiln, his hands held out over the flames as if for warmth.

Azoth Magen Ailanthus approached Arjan. With one hand, he placed the Azothian sceptre against Arjan's head; with the other, Ailanthus held his pendant to his own forehead. Eyes closed, droning in a low register, he read Arjan for several minutes. Cedar could both witness and intuit that the reading was arduous; she assumed Ailanthus would read not only Arjan's physical condition but the emotional register of his memories — seeking signs of guilt, betrayal, vengeance, or sabotage — to determine if he had purposely infiltrated Council dimension. If Ilex and Melia were aligned with the rebels, if they were Arjan's grandparents, if they had taught him all that they know about alchemy before he had been sought out as an Initiate, then the possibility existed that he had been groomed to disrupt, if not destroy, the Alchemists' Council.

"The boy is innocent," Ailanthus finally and assertively announced.

"Impossible!" cried Obeche.

"Obeche! You will not question the Azoth Magen!" bellowed Ailanthus.

"My apologies, your Eminence."

"I read nothing of a connection with the Rebel Branch," Ailanthus declared quietly. "I read nothing of a sinister plot directed by Ilex and Melia. I read only Arjan's love for his grandparents and his benevolence towards the Council. He can be questioned for details by the entire Elder Council once he has regained consciousness and strength in the catacombs. We will determine the specific ancestral ties at that point. Clearly, any such ties were obscured in the manuscripts — if they had ever been inscribed — prior to Arjan's initiation. If Ilex and Melia have any animosity towards the Council, if they are aligned with the rebels, they did not make such feelings or allegiances known to the boy. As the outside world parable maintains, we cannot blame the son for the sins of the father."

"Your Eminence," said Cedar, "anger towards Ilex and Melia for their desertion is misguided, especially when directed towards Arjan. As the official Scribal records acknowledge, and thus must we all, Ilex and Melia were not rebels. As a couple, they were the exception to the elemental rules governing Council dimension. That is all."

"Ilex and Melia were never *proven* to be rebels," said Obeche, carefully modifying his tone. "Under the circumstances surrounding their desertion, my actions were justified."

"You were justified to read the boy's pendant. However, draining another alchemist of his essence is *not* justifiable, Obeche," said Ailanthus. He then held out his hand and waited.

"You intend to confirm my assessment of Arjan by reading my pendant?" asked Obeche. "I can assure you—"

"No need for assurances," replied Ailanthus. "I have no intention of reading your pendant. I intend to confiscate it."

Obeche froze.

"Now!" demanded Ailanthus.

Obeche removed his pendant and cord, submitting both to Ailanthus.

"Forgive me, Azoth Magen, but may I ask to what end you have issued this demand?" asked Obeche.

"Your pendant's Quintessence is strong. Too strong for your own good, it appears. Releasing a few hundred years worth of its accumulated power back to the Lapis will help us all in these difficult times. It will be safely returned to you thereafter."

"But such action will render me—"

"Impotent?" suggested Cedar. Obeche glared at her.

"Yes, your powers will be reduced," replied Ailanthus. "But, as I am sure you recall from your previous . . . castration, you will still be able to perform the basic functions of your Order. Indeed, you may set the record for the longest tenure as a Novillian Scribe in Council history."

"How am I to fulfull my duties as head of security?"

"I will consult with Ruis and appoint a replacement."

"A replacement? No one—"

"Silence! Effective immediately, you are relieved of your position as head of security."

Obeche refrained from responding, his jaw and fists clenched.

"And one last request," said Ailanthus. "Until we are able to determine, to our satisfaction, the details of Arjan's family history and his own future with the Council, you, Obeche, will refrain from direct contact with Arjan. Leave us."

Cedar kept her eyes lowered as Obeche made his way to the back of the chambers and out the doors. She then walked towards the dais.

"Take Arjan to the catacombs for alembic healing," ordered Ailanthus, looking himself as if he could use an alembic bath for restoration. Amur and Tera stepped forward to assist, together carrying Arjan out of Azothian Chambers where, Cedar presumed, they would seek further assistance in transporting him to the catacombs.

"Azoth Magen Ailanthus," she said, risking censure for delaying not only Ailanthus but the remaining Elders from much-needed departure. "When you yourself have recovered all necessary energy, which I fully appreciate has been drained during these proceedings, I recommend we call together the Elder Council once again to discuss not only Arjan but what I consider to be our most urgent matter of business."

"And what, Scribe Cedar, would that be?"

"The conjunction of Sadira and Amur."

"Surely," interjected Azoth Ruis, "you are not suggesting we simply progress with business as usual. Regardless of Arjan and his unfortunate connection to potential rebels, we cannot ignore other events of late — the lacunae, the rebel breach, the elemental imbalance, the augmented Flaw in the Stone, Jaden's disappearance."

"My suggestion is made not in disregard to recent events but precisely *because* of those events. What we need more than anything right now is a surge in Quintessence in light of the increase to the Flaw. A conjunction, and in particular a conjunction of Lapidarian essence within the pendants of Sadira and Amur, will ensure such a surge — especially given its scheduled timing to coincide with the Feast of Vitriol. Cancelling the feast and delaying the conjunction may be the very acts that permit a rebel insurgence, whereas celebrating the feast and performing the sacrament could well revive us all."

"Your logic is sound, Cedar," responded Ailanthus. "As planned, we will hold the Sacrament of Conjunction on the Feast of Vitriol. Sadira and Amur will begin ritual preparation tonight." He paused, steadying himself with the Azothian sceptre as if it were a cane supporting an elderly man of the outside world. "But you know as well as I what is required to counteract the excess of the Flaw and restore Lapidarian Quintessence to its full supremacy."

Cedar could not bring herself to respond. Ruis, Ravenea, Kai, and Esche lowered their heads. Though she had not expected such a gesture, she knew well what he was about to announce. No one spoke until Ailanthus broke the silence.

"In the name of the Azoth Magen of the 18th Council of Alchemists, in accordance with the Codes of Law and the tradition of Azothian protocols, I hereby declare the dusk of the reign of Ailanthus and the dawn of the 19th Council. Thus, on this night at this hour, in the presence of my Elders, I declare my intention to prepare for Final Ascension. Long live the Quintessence."

"Long live the Alchemists' Council."

## VI
## cũrrent Day

Jaden, visibly distressed by the Azothian inquisition, angry at Cedar for insisting she leave, and distraught over Arjan, felt ready to collapse by the time she reached her residence chambers. The instant Cedar had forcibly removed her from physical proximity to Arjan, Jaden lost her ability not only to see him but also to sense his condition. Despite the overwhelming bond she had shared with him during Obeche's outbreak, their interim pendants evidently were too weak to maintain Lapidarian connection beyond minimal range. Knowing nothing for certain, Jaden could only trust that Cedar and the other Elders would protect him. Surely even Obeche himself — one quick to anger but impeccably rational and disciplined in Council protocols — would desist from further persecuting a fellow alchemist for unspecified and unproven crimes. What had Arjan done beyond revealing his ancestry?

Her hands were shaking as she unlocked and pushed open the door. She crossed the threshold, turned on the stained-glass lamp by the bed, hung her outer robes behind the door, wrapped herself in her shawl, and sat on the balcony bench looking out over Council grounds. The only perceptible movement came from rustling leaves in the gardens and courtyard below. Thankful, even in this time of distress, for the warmth of her Azadirian shawl, Jaden allowed herself to indulge momentarily in a cherished memory: the day Cedar presented it to her. She had gasped at its exquisite beauty, never having seen the likes of its artistry in the outside world.

Yet now its beauty mattered little in the face of her current circumstances. Over and over again, she replayed in her mind the events of Qingdao, of Azothian Chambers, of Arjan's responses, and in particular of his ancestral revelation. What Jaden knew of Ilex and Melia had come to her solely in fragments, through occasional references in conversations about conjunction. She knew they were alchemists, she knew they had achieved mutual conjunction, she knew they had abandoned the Council, and — most disconcerting of all — she knew that Arjan had purposely chosen to conceal his connection to two of the most revered yet most disputed figures in Council history. If not for being intimidated into submission by the Azoths, he may never have revealed his secret. As much as she detested the possibility, Arjan's ancestry and his concealment thereof did indeed leave him suspect.

She had been seated on the balcony for a few hours when she was startled out of her reverie by a knock at her door. Her hope for a visit from Arjan was swiftly dashed.

"Magistrate! What are you doing here?"

"I need to speak with you," replied Sadira.

Jaden did not know what to make of this unexpected visit. She wrapped her shawl even more tightly around her shoulders and gestured towards the sofa near the window.

Sadira took a seat and repositioned a few cushions behind her back. She held her pendant in her right hand, running her thumb repeatedly over its smooth surface. She appeared to be nervous and uncertain what to say, which made the situation even more awkward.

"Why are you here, Magistrate?" Jaden finally asked. "Can I help you with something?"

"Do you remember that day," she began at last, "a month or so after your arrival, when you witnessed two strangers disappear at the cliff face?"

"Of course."

"Do you know who they were?"

"Rebels?"

"Of a sort, but not the rebels others suspected."

"Who was suspected?"

"The Rebel High Azoth and his consort. Even

Cedar thought as much." Sadira sighed before adding, "She has been wrong about so much."

Jaden remained silent. What was she to say to this revelation? Was she to admit knowledge of Dracaen? How did Sadira know something Cedar didn't?

"The intruders, as I have learned," said Sadira finally, "were Ilex and Melia."

"Arjan's grandparents?"

Sadira smiled as if amused by Jaden's response. "Yes," she said, "Arjan's grandparents."

"But I saw two people. Ilex and Melia are conjoined."

"You *heard* two people. You saw only one body — one body shifting between two essences mutually conjoined."

Jaden tried to recollect the details of the event. Had she only *heard* two people? She remembered her view being obscured by leaves and branches.

"What were they doing here?"

"Laying the groundwork of their plan — setting the stage, casting their players."

"I don't understand," replied Jaden.

"You aren't supposed to understand — *weren't* supposed to understand — not until now anyway. But Arjan's ill-timed revelation of his ancestry in Azothian Chambers today has necessitated a change in schedule. The entire Council is virtually pulsating with conjecture and innuendo, debating whether Arjan is aligned with the rebels."

"Why are you telling me this, Magistrate?"

"I need your help."

Jaden waited, eyebrows raised.

"I need you to take something to Arjan."

"Where is he? Is he all right?"

"He is healing in alembic waters deep within the catacombs."

"You want me to go with you to the catacombs?"

"No. I want you to go *without* me to the catacombs."

"What? No!"

How could Sadira make such a request? Jaden had entered the catacombs only once since her arrival in Council dimension. Linden had escorted a small group of Junior and Senior Initiates through the catacombs' labyrinthine passages as part of a lesson on Council history. Jaden had been terrified the entire time. She could barely imagine navigating the complexity of caverns and pathways on her own.

"I cannot come with you, Jaden. Amur and I have been summoned to meet with Ruis and Ravenea to begin preparations for our conjunction. Despite recent events — *because of recent events* — Cedar has requested the conjunction proceed. The Azoth Magen has granted her request. In four days, I will be conjoined with Amur. As you know, Jaden, conjunction strengthens the Lapis. The Azoths fear, especially in light of the breach and elemental disturbance, that the rebels will attempt to stop the conjunction. So, tonight I am to be sequestered with

Amur under Azothian supervision until the Sealing of Concurrence tomorrow. Already the Azoths will be wondering why I have not immediately heeded their call. I know you care for Arjan. I know you can help him."

Sadira paused to observe Jaden's reaction. Jaden sat perfectly still but radiated fear.

"I realize my request is a lot to ask, Jaden. But the Alchemists' Council is in jeopardy. Arjan has a critical role to play in saving us all. And you can play a critical role in saving Arjan. You need only find him in the catacombs."

"If I succeed in navigating the catacombs, if I am able to find him, how am I to wake him? Is he not suspended within the alembic waters?"

"You are not to wake him. You are to reach into the alembic and place the contents of this pouch under his tongue."

Sadira reached into her pocket and held up a small leather pouch.

Jaden froze. She recognized the pouch immediately. It had contained — or perhaps still contained — a fragment of the Dragonblood Stone, the fragment Dracaen had given to her at the bus stop in Vancouver and requested she keep with her at all times. Over a year had passed since she had lost it in the altercation with Obeche. Of course, in the aftermath of Kalina's erasure, Jaden had forgotten the incident entirely until the restoration of her memories in Qingdao.

"I know you are frightened. I know you would prefer that I elaborate, explain the details of all I have touched upon tonight. But you must trust me, Jaden, I have already told you much more than I was sanctioned to disclose. I promise you will eventually come to understand everything. For now you must trust me. You must trust me just as you trusted Kalina."

"You know of Kalina?"

"Yes, I know of Kalina. And I know that you know of her. You told me yourself when you inscribed your name under the *Viburnum opulus* — the Kalina tree — in *Sapientiae Aeternae 1818*."

"You manipulated the manuscripts?"

"No. Kalina manipulated the manuscripts, years ago as a Senior Initiate when her rebel alliances increased the possibility of her erasure. Do you recall being drawn to the word *cruentus* in *Serpens Chymicum 1414*? Kalina inscribed that single word with Dragonblood-infused ink; thus, it triggered your memory of another Dragonblood fragment: Kalina's parchment inscription citing *Sapientiae Aeternae 1818*. By removing her own name from an image of the tree in *Sapientiae Aeternae* for which she was consecrated, Kalina opened a space for someone to find her, to utter her name, once again. And you, by inscribing your name in her absence, left me a means of securing an ally. Until recently, even I did not remember Kalina, but when I regained my memories of her, finding your name in that manuscript gave me a means of knowing I could trust you."

"The pouch — does it still contain a Dragonblood fragment?"

"Yes. Kalina gave it to me. I now know that it used to be yours, but you did not lose it on the day of Kalina's erasure; she purposely took the Dragonblood fragment from you to protect you. But now I return it to you and request that you give it to Arjan. Will you do this, Jaden?"

Despite her apprehension, despite her fear of the catacombs, Jaden agreed. "On one condition."

"Yes?"

"Let me read your pendant."

Sadira appeared startled. She hesitated before replying. "You have not been trained to read pendants, Jaden. I have carried my pendant for one hundred and eighty-eight years. Its essence is strong. Its power will overwhelm you."

"Let me read your pendant," repeated Jaden. "Let me read your intentions."

Sadira stood up and walked to the bed, sitting on the edge and gesturing for Jaden to follow. She held out the pendant and placed it in Jaden's hand. Jaden shook as she pulled it towards her by its silver cord. She held it first against her chest, and then her lips, and finally her forehead. The intensity of sensation was indeed overwhelming. She struggled against the desire to take Sadira herself into her arms.

"Search for only what you need, Jaden. Distinguish from the panoply of my knowledge and experience and emotions and intentions only the threads that will help you to weave your destiny. Take only what you need to trust me. Take only what you need to help you understand your role in saving both Arjan and the Council."

But Jaden could distinguish nothing in particular. Rather than individual threads, she perceived a chaotic mess — flashes of sight and sound and taste and smell and touch.

"Seek my intentions in regard to Arjan. Think only of Arjan."

"Arjan," Jaden repeated. "Arjan. *Arjan*."

She used his name like a mantra — a means of navigating through the sensations that coursed from the pendant through her mind and body. And when, after several minutes, she finally absorbed a fragment of Sadira's pendant memory, when she understood beyond a doubt that Sadira loved and trusted Arjan, Jaden fell backward, unconscious, onto her bed.

By the time she came to, the entire night had already passed. She lay against the pillows under a cotton quilt, the pouch containing the Dragonblood fragment tied to her wrist with a silk cord. The room no longer glowed from the light of her bedside lamp but from the pink and purple skies of early dawn. Sadira was long gone. And Jaden knew she must make her way to the catacombs to help Arjan before her absence from the daily Council routine could be noticed.

As she moved quietly along the residence corridors listening for signs of Wardens or Elders, Jaden thought about Sadira. Without Sadira's agreement to her request today, Jaden most likely would not have read another alchemist's pendant until well into her Elixir years. Ritha had told her of Senior Initiate lessons in pendant reading — presumably such lessons included advice on maintaining consciousness. Despite Jaden's ineptitude at the practice, and despite having been overcome by the pendant's power, Jaden had awakened from her stupor knowing with certainty that Sadira had only benevolent intentions regarding Arjan.

Of course, to help Arjan, Jaden first had to find him, which required her not only to traverse the grounds without being caught but also to navigate the catacombs. Once outside the residence building, she stayed in the shadows, moving cautiously along the courtyard and garden walls, under trees, and out of the sight of early risers. After twenty minutes of stealthy progression, Jaden reached the staircase that led down to the catacombs. Though reading the pendant had given her confidence to trust Sadira, it had not given her the courage to confront her fear of the catacombs. Her heart was beating so rapidly that she questioned whether she would survive long enough to find Arjan.

The catacombs were dimly lit with small lanterns hanging at intervals along the complex web of pathways. Terrifying carvings, designed to resemble human skulls, lined the stone walls. Linden had expounded upon their symbolic intention — each skull was a figurative memorial to death in the outside world, each carved into stone on the day its respective Council member turned thirty, received Elixir, and thus officially renounced his or her former life for life everlasting. Someday a replica of Jaden's own skull would reside in these walls. She shuddered.

She knew the catacombs housed eight alembics — all of which were used intermittently for healing. She need only find the one emitting light to find Arjan. But the catacombs were extensive, descending deep underground to the ancient wells. These same wells supplied the restorative channel waters that flowed through all of Council dimension, but intensive healing transmutation was best achieved in the natural alembic baths nearest the wells' source. Arjan's placement within a catacomb alembic rather than merely a visit to the Albedo waters for a recuperative bath suggested the damage inflicted by Obeche had been extensive. His healing required the elemental minerals that seep into the water from the walls and base of the natural alembics.

Finding the alembic corridor itself took Jaden almost an hour. Once in the corridor, she found that two of the eight alembics glowed with hues of red and orange. Jaden thought once again she would collapse when she peered through the glass of the first alembic chamber and saw Ailanthus stretched out on its altar. She jolted backward into the corridor, momentarily afraid that the Azoth Magen would awaken and find her. But she understood rationally, based on Linden's catacomb lesson, that once an alchemist had entered an alchemic chamber for healing, he or she was prone to its elemental laws. Thus, although she could not fathom why Ailanthus would be in need of alembic healing, she nonetheless knew he would remain unconscious until the chamber lights shifted from hues of red and orange to blue and green.

Arjan appeared to be peacefully asleep on the altar of the second alembic chamber. Unlike the alembic vessels depicted in various alchemical manuscripts both within and outside Council dimension, these alembics were shaped more like oversized bathtubs than globular bottles. Each alembic was situated within a natural alcove, its opening accessible by steps carved into the stone walls. Heavy drops of water clung to the curved walls of Arjan's alembic. Jaden could barely stand the heat. She moved carefully, slowly climbing the steps, moving through the streams of golden light and hot vapour until she reached a position from which she knew she could readily touch Arjan, whose head rested, exposed, in the hollow of a stone pillow, and whose torso, arms, and legs were completely submersed in the alembic waters.

Retrieving the leather pouch from a pocket within her robes, she carefully extracted the Dragonblood fragment. Momentarily observing it in the palm of her hand, she realized two things that had failed to occur to her during her conversation with Sadira: first, Sadira herself must already possess a Dragonblood fragment and, second, Sadira must know that Jaden possessed one. Jaden wondered if Sadira knew that her fragment now existed as a minuscule replica of the Flaw in the Lapis — a fragment that could not be lost or discovered precisely because of its inherent absence. As Jaden was about to place the Dragonblood fragment under Arjan's tongue, an idea occurred to her. Would it not be wiser, safer, less prone to detection if she were able to provide Arjan with an absent flaw rather than a physical fragment — if she were able to purposely duplicate on his pendant the transformation she had accidently exacted on her own pendant in Qingdao?

Thus, rather than reaching for Arjan's mouth — which, she realized, would have been an exceptionally personal intrusion — she reached for the braided silver chain around his neck, pulling it and its pendant just above the surface of the alembic waters. She hesitated briefly, concerned whether the potent conjunctive effect would throw her off her feet once again, propelling her through dimensions. But she was reasonably certain her interdimensional travel had been the result of the Ritual of Return and not of the Dragonblood and Lapis conjunction — a coincidental timing that would not be replicated here in the catacombs. Weighing potential benefits against possible dangers, Jaden decided to take the risk. She held the Dragonblood fragment against Arjan's pendant. The effect was indeed intense enough to throw Jaden off balance, but she remained grounded within the catacombs of Council dimension. Before departing, she reached into the alembic waters once again for Arjan's pendant, bringing it to her lips momentarily to place one gentle kiss against its nascent, blood-red fissure.

Though a few Elders protested quietly among themselves, Council members of the lower orders readily accepted the Azothian decision to proceed with the conjunction of Sadira and Amur. While Ailanthus continued his regeneration in the catacomb alembic, Azoth Ravenea, in full regalia, presided at the Sealing of Concurrence. Thus, as proclaimed to all within Council Chambers only a day after Ailanthus's proclamation, Sadira and Amur were sealed — bound by Council law — to observe the sacramental Ritual of Conjunction under the full moon on the Feast of Vitriol.

Following the recitation of the sealing section of the Law Codes of Conjunction, Sadira and Amur clasped hands and stood before the Council, heads bowed as Council etiquette dictates. Various Council members alternately nodded and murmured. Ruis stepped forward, held his pendant against his forehead, and bowed first to Sadira and then to Amur. Each of the Elders followed suit. Ravenea then gestured in sequence to the Readers, the Senior Magistrates, the Junior Magistrates, the Senior Initiates, and the Junior Initiates. Each Order, en masse, progressed to the Council Chambers platform, positioned their hands in the second position of Ab Uno, and bowed towards the conjunctive pair as a sign of respect, regardless of any individual member's disapproval. When the Junior Initiates finally approached, Sadira locked eyes with Jaden, silently pleading for a sign that all had gone as planned. Jaden nodded and smiled fleetingly. Arjan himself, markedly absent from the Initiates, was still healing within the alembic. *All will be well; all will be well*, Sadira thought to herself.

As the Sealing of Concurrence neared completion, Sadira clutched her own pendant, holding it to her lips with her free hand, swaying back and forth as if immersed in a prayer of the outside world. She had feared this moment — the truth of it, the instant at which potential became certainty. Despite all the Sephrim she had ingested, despite all the placation and words of comfort offered by Cedar through the months of planning, despite the certainty and necessity of her more recent decision to modify the plan, despite the confidence offered her by the Lapis and by the Dragonblood Stone, despite her affirmation that all would be well, Sadira had hoped the Sealing of Concurrence would never be made. She thought back to the years before Cedar and Saule's conjunction, to her own uncomplicated and duty-bound days as Junior Magistrate. She had once hoped to spend her eternal life with Saule and then, much later, with Cedar. Now she hoped merely to survive long enough to fulfill her chosen destiny.

Amur appeared both proud and at ease. For him, conjunction fulfilled a sacrament for which he was willing to offer his life — for the good of the Council and the good of the world.

"Long live the Quintessence!" he called through Council Chambers.

"Long live the Alchemists' Council," replied his audience.

Sadira understood that Amur thrived on the ceremony and attention, even if he were to be the centre of attention only until the end of the conjunction itself. Standing in the shadow of his radiance, Sadira looked at Amur, and he looked back at her, seemingly confident in the role he would play. She turned then to make eye contact with Cedar, who similarly nodded at her with confidence. They were both so naïve. Neither could see the ways in which she was about to betray them both.

As the golden leaves of the Alchemical Tree glistened and the crystalline channel waters trickled softly beneath the stone footbridges, Jaden stood silently in the Grand Courtyard watching the Procession of the Orders. As with the catacombs, she had stood in this courtyard on only one former occasion as part of a history lesson on the Council buildings and grounds. At that time, she had been utterly astounded by the beauty and glory of the monumental Tree. Now, her body plagued by anxiety for both the Council and the rebels, her mind besieged with concern for both Sadira and Arjan — whose four-day absence became more difficult for her to bear with each passing moment — she almost cried when she caught sight of the primordial Tree resplendent in the evening light.

During the history lesson, Jaden had learned that the Grand Courtyard is used only for sacred processions before ritual meals and that the Feast of Vitriol occurs only once every three years. But Linden had neglected to mention that, as part of the ritual, the Elders recount the affirmations of the *Tabula Smaragdina* and reaffirm the conjunction of opposites throughout the dimensions — a protocol that requires over twenty minutes. *As above, so below*, they chanted, shaking palm branches in each of the four directions as they moved slowly through the courtyard. Jaden stood to the side with Cercis and Laurel, bowing repeatedly as the Elders symbolically cleared the path for their fellow alchemists of the lower orders to traverse the hallowed ground, cross the sacred threshold into the foyer, and enter Madrona Hall.

The foyer walls were hung with 12th Council tapestries, intricately woven by ancient Azadirian artisans of the finest wools, depicting verdant landscapes from Council dimension and the outer world. As Jaden moved slowly forward, waiting in the foyer as each Order was invited into the hall, a tapestry covering the entirety of the northern wall claimed her focus. The forest it depicted seemed so real that Jaden felt certain she could walk from the foyer directly into its emerald terrain. She was intrigued by one particular arbutus tree, whose clay-coloured bark curled back and peeled away to reveal a bright green underlay along the trunk. The detail was exquisite. The tapestry colours were so vivid that Jaden wondered whether, as with her shawl, Lapidarian inks had been used to dye the wools. She was so mesmerized by the images, so lulled into an unanticipated but welcomed calm, that she did not realize the Junior Initiates had been summoned until Laurel pushed her gently forward.

Jaden was awestruck when she caught sight of the majesty within Madrona Hall. One would think the entire accumulated wealth of the alchemists comprised the table settings. Ruby crystal goblets, silver flatware with handles of pearl, fine china plates inlaid with gold and lapis, sapphire silk tablecloths embroidered with copper threads. Even after having lived for over a year in the opulent Council dimension, even after donning her luxurious black velvet dress robes, Jaden felt remarkably out of place as a guest at the Feast of Vitriol. In this moment, Jaden did not debate whether she owed allegiance to the Council or to the Rebel Branch, but whether she had been misread as a potential Initiate. Perhaps, instead of here, she should be attending a university class in Vancouver; perhaps Cedar was never meant to have crossed her path. Yet, with eager pleasure, she took her seat beside her fellow Initiates, anticipating the glorious meal.

Azoth Magen Ailanthus stood at the head table and raised his arms to ask for silence, clearly invigorated by his time in the catacomb alembic. "We are gathered," he announced, "for the Feast of Vitriol. Please stand for the recitation."

The entire Council stood. Instead of facing the Azoth Magen, everyone turned to face the east window, through which the golden leaves of the Alchemical Tree were visible.

"*Visita Interiora Terrae Rectificando Invenies Occultum Lapidem!*" recited Ailanthus.

"*Visita Interiora Terrae Rectificando Invenies Occultum Lapidem!*" replied the Council.

The recitation was made four times, once in each direction — ending in the north, thus facing the dais on which the Azoths stood.

"From its nadir to its zenith, we have traversed the dimensions of Earth," intoned Ruis.

"Through our continual journey, we have sustained the Lapis," responded Ravenea.

"Via Quintessence, we preserve all that was, all

that is, and all that will be," sang the entire Council, including the Azoths. "The death of one prolongs the life of many."

Jaden had read of this ritual, but the description on the page could not reproduce the astonishing intensity generated by the resonance of the voices. In this moment, fortified by her successful journey to and from the catacombs, and moved by the reverberation of words, Jaden believed — truly and utterly *believed* — that the Council mission was to protect the world, that those who sought to deny free will to the populace must be a meagre few voices on the fringe. In this moment, Jaden understood that she must work to secure the Alchemists' Council and, thus, to secure the world. Of course, securing *the* Council did not necessarily mean preserving *this* Council; instead, it would mean continually working to retain or, if necessary, to reclaim the *integrity* of the Council for eternity. From this day forth, by whatever means necessary, Jaden resolved she would work to uphold this truth. And she understood that to do so would require the assistance of the Rebel Branch and their allies — of Dracaen and Kalina, of Sadira and Arjan.

Thus when the meal was served, when dish after dish of delicacies beyond what she could ever have imagined, were brought to the table, Jaden savoured each sight, each aroma, each texture, each taste, and even each sound — Byzantine silver spoons clinking against Imari porcelain bowls, Spanish amontillado flowing into Viennese crystal glasses, Laurel and Cercis laughing, Ritha's knife dropping onto the cool stone floor.

During dessert, musicians arrived. They entertained the Council until late into the night. Jaden watched Sadira masterfully participating in a group dance of the sort Jaden had seen only in outside world films set in the distant past. If not for the Wardens visibly and strategically posted around the perimeter of the hall, Jaden and her fellow Initiates may have forgotten the imposition of war measures. But when the candles in the massive chandeliers finally began to burn out and the musicians began playing their final song, the Junior Initiates were approached by two hefty Wardens and escorted from Madrona Hall across the courtyard, over the grounds, and through the forest to the cliff face, where they waited to witness the Sacrament of Conjunction.

Sadira felt the smooth grain of the cliff face against her fingertips. She had already turned away from Rowan Kai and the others. The full moon's light was too intense. Sadira had realized she could no longer face the half-shadowed expressions of the Elders. In particular, she could not bear, or perhaps did not dare, to watch Cedar. Sadira would want to see in Cedar a sign of longing, of reassurance, of gentleness, or perhaps of preemptive forgiveness for her betrayal. Finding no such sign would not be tolerable. Thus she averted from Cedar not just her eyes but herself. *Herself* — regardless of outcome, the self she had known for so many years — would be irrevocably changed mere minutes from now. She pressed her palms against the cold, damp rock.

Moments later, Sadira understood from the shifting intonation of the Elders' chanting that Amur was approaching. She strained even then for release, but she could not move. The alchemical changes had already begun. Despite all the reassurances she had been given, she was suddenly terrified. *I am Sadira. I am Sadira. I am Sadira*, she repeatedly thought. Though her body was paralyzed, though her voice had been silenced, she could still hear herself repeating her name. Then she felt him — Amur — sudden in his invasion. Then deadened, pinned between Amur and the cliff face, she struggled to maintain her being and to move her*self* outside this dimension.

As Jaden watched the ritual, she was saddened. She could not respond like the others. They appeared content, even joyous, in their participation of the sacrament. But Jaden felt the chill of loss coursing through her. Only one would survive. Of the two, she would mourn the loss of Amur, but she would be distraught over the loss of Sadira.

For the first several seconds, both Sadira and Amur cried out in pain. Jaden understood that conjunction took place at the elemental level. But from her perspective — from the perspective of one who watched the event from the sidelines with human senses alone — all Jaden witnessed was the gradual transition from flesh to fire. The two bodies appeared to burn white hot, separate at first but finally melded together as one, a glowing blue ember against the cliff face within the landscape's natural alembic structure. Though a human form was still vaguely discernible, Jaden could see no distinguishing features of either Sadira or Amur. She half-expected the victorious one to emerge from the process a charred skeleton, one that would have to be healed through alchemical transmutation in a catacomb alembic. If this occurred, she would amend all her textbooks with marginal glosses depicting the reality of conjunction to counteract the Council's official description of the splendour and sacrament.

Feeling the need to brace herself, Jaden pressed her back against the trunk of a tree. If only the tree were a portal. Gone were the beauty and effulgence of Madrona Hall within the harsh, hard shadows of the cliff face. Cercis suddenly stood directly in front of her, the anticipation of the conjunction's near completion having urged him forward. Her hypocrisy abruptly evident, Jaden pushed him gently but firmly out of her line of vision: if she had to remain in Council dimension, she wanted to be a full witness to the event.

Jaden could hear the alchemically induced calls of crows and toads, their calls reverberating through the forest. Azoth Magen Ailanthus drew forth the Sword of the Elixir. He stood, sword aloft, reciting another passage of the sacrament. Finally, he plunged the sword into the blue glow of the ember. A final blast of light burst forth, seconds later revealing not a charred skeleton but a resplendent human form, whole but not yet distinct in its detailed features: the Rebis.

Sadira no longer existed *against* the cliff face. Instead, she existed *within* the cliff face, as if she herself had turned to stone. Here she rested for what felt like several seconds, though she knew that time was being alchemically distorted through the course of the ritual. She felt cool and free of pain. Then the earth moved. The earth moved and moved and moved — not as it had during the elemental disturbance, but with a vibration so intense she feared being torn apart molecule by molecule. Then she stood, shaken free and released from the earth, feet again on solid and unmoving ground, moist air brushing her skin, her eyes straining to focus. A figure in full robes was approaching her.

Seconds later, the man stood directly before Sadira. His eyes were bright green; his robes sapphire blue. In his right hand, he held a cup full of dark red liquid.

"I am Dracaen, High Azoth of the Rebel Branch of the Alchemists' Council. I have carried my Dragonblood pendant four hundred and forty-four years. I restored the Flaw in the Lapis on the third night of the Third Rebellion of the 17th Council."

"I am Sadira, Senior Magistrate of the Alchemists' Council. I have carried my pendant one hundred and eighty-eight years. On this the final day of the Splendor Solis of the 18th Council, I am to conjoin with Amur."

"And what is your current mission?" asked Dracaen.

"The restoration of Kalina."

From her position standing among her fellow Scribes, Cedar had a clear view of both Sadira and Amur throughout the Sacrament of Conjunction. But Sadira had avoided her attempts at eye contact, and Amur was no longer of interest to her. So Cedar retreated into her thoughts, hopefully anticipating the soon-to-be-realized outcome. She had waited years for this moment, for Sadira's assured triumph and thus for the permanency of an ally who would help her maintain the integrity of the Council in its relation to the outside world for hundreds of years to come. For too long, Ruis had held supremacy, disseminating his intention to eliminate the Flaw in the Stone. With the encouragement he had continually received from Obeche, his pride had turned to arrogance. For years, she could do nothing outwardly but to obey his every whim.

Finally, all would transform. With the Flaw fortuitously enhanced and with Sadira about to be victorious, Cedar would be well positioned to discourage Ruis from his incessant pursuit regarding the Flaw. He too would come to appreciate the necessity of maintaining free will within Council dimension. She need harbour no guilt over her actions, over procuring the Sephrim, over covertly plotting against the stated intentions of an Azoth. Her own intention was nothing but admirable, even if self-serving. Yes, she would gain the permanency of a lover she adored. But she would also, with Sadira's assistance, continue to ensure individual intention within Council dimension and thus choose to maintain the balance of the outside world. What right had Ruis to rescind the free will symbolically immortalized through their mythological texts, albeit misunderstood as divinely sanctioned? What right had Ruis to return the figurative apple to the literal Tree?

Sadira knew her mission. She had known it for weeks. She had prepared for this mission — for her entry into the Flaw in the Stone. But now that the moment had arrived, now that she stood before Dracaen, uttering her lines for real rather than as part of yet another elaborate rehearsal, she trembled.

"Your eyes are green like the trunk of an arbutus tree," she said to Dracaen. These were the words that would allow Dracaen to recognize her as Sadira alone, as Sadira just prior to conjunction with Amur, as the knowledgeable and talented Senior Magistrate who had successfully traversed a dimensional breach and invoked a temporal shift at the cliff face during the Sacrament of Conjunction, as the alchemist who had volunteered to sacrifice her*self* to the Rebel Branch to support free will both for the Alchemists' Council and the people of the outside world.

Sadira took the cup of Dragon's Blood from Dracaen and drank with the vigour of somone quenching a desert thirst. She knew such rapid intake of the Dragonblood infusion would prepare her best for her role in the conjunction.

"Where is she?" asked Sadira, wiping a ruby-red drop from her lips.

"I am here."

Sadira turned and bowed.

"Kalina," Sadira said. "An honour to meet you again."

"An honour to meet *you* again, Sadira."

"I have ingested both Sephrim and Dragon's Blood. I have prepared both mind and body. I have opened myself to our union."

"Your sacrifice will be eternally engraved in stone — both Flaw and Lapis."

"Enough," said Dracaen. "The temporal shift is limited. We must begin."

A dozen rebels gathered around, united with one purpose on this night: the conjunction of Kalina and Sadira.

"Thus two will be one, and one will be two," recited Dracaen. He recited the entire Sacrament of Conjunction, aided by fellow rebels when needed, and adapted where necessary to account for the negative space of the Flaw in the Stone.

From Sadira's perspective, unlike the opening minutes of the Sacrament of Conjunction in Council dimension, the conjunctive pain, though intense, was fleeting. Kalina's essence enveloped rather than invaded her. And in what seemed like mere seconds later, Sadira thought nothing beyond herself. Finally, unable to take another breath, Sadira surrendered to the negative space that had opened to receive her. Thus, at the end, in what seemed an infinitesimal fragment of time, her being was transformed into the nothing that is all.

"In death shall be life," said Dracaen.

"In death shall be life," repeated the rebels.

The conjunction with Sadira had succeeded, and Kalina stood triumphant before Dracaen and the rebels. She smiled and bowed to her grateful audience.

"You must go. You must return to Council dimension and conclude the Sacrament of Conjunction with Amur," said Dracaen.

"I am prepared for all that awaits me," responded Kalina.

"You will have three days until the Resurgence."

"Until then," said Kalina, stepping back through the breach in dimensional space and time towards the cliff face.

The Sacrament of Conjunction nearly complete, Azoth Magen Ailanthus retrieved the Sword of the Elixir from the body of the Rebis and plunged it into the nearby pool to quell its residual fire. Beside him, the luminous Rebis remained in its place, the return to a solid, physical body not yet complete. The intensity of its vibrating illumination reached even the outer circle of alchemists, causing Jaden and her fellow Initiates to shield their eyes.

Jaden waited anxiously for the Rebis to complete its transformation. She longed to see Sadira victorious — for the only physical change inherited from Amur to be a slight wave to her already beautiful golden hair. Even before their more recently confirmed alliance, Sadira had always been among the few alchemists Jaden truly admired.

*Please be Sadira. Please be Sadira*, Jaden whispered to herself repeatedly.

As the light from the Rebis began to fade, as every member of the Alchemists' Council watched in anticipation, as a distinct figure began to emerge, and as physical traits became distinguishable, Jaden's sense of dread grew stronger until, finally, she gasped.

"I am Amur, Novillian Scribe of the Alchemists' Council," spoke the victorious one. "I have carried my pendant two hundred and ninety-eight years. On the final day of the Splendor Solis of the 18th Council, I conjoined with Sadira."

She grabbed Cercis's arm. "No! No! She can't be gone! She can't be!"

"Quiet!" admonished Wu Tong, who stood nearby. "The outcome of the Sacrament of Conjunction is not to be contested."

Jaden, her only desire to flee, was blocked from her attempts by Cercis and Laurel, as they insisted on following protocols and remaining until the end of the ritual. In particular, by the protocol of procession, Junior Initiates were always the last to leave a sacramental ritual.

"How can this be?" she whispered to Laurel. "How can she be gone?"

"Sadira is not gone. She has been conjoined."

But Laurel's words only added validity to an already harsh truth. Jaden's tears began to well, both out of sadness for Sadira's loss and out of a sense of her own helplessness. Sadira had trusted her, had allowed Jaden to read her pendant, had trusted her with a fragment of the Dragonblood Stone, had trusted her to reach Arjan in the catacombs. Who would lead her on her path now that Sadira was gone? Who could she and Arjan trust as an ally?

"Save your tears for the Amber Garden," said Laurel, her voice lowered so as not to disturb Wu Tong or the other more senior alchemists nearby.

"What? What do you mean?"

"Your tears are wasted here. But in the Amber Garden they can serve as a permanent tribute to Sadira," responded Laurel.

Jaden shook her head, still not understanding.

"The trees of the Amber Garden collect tears of mourning," explained Cercis. "Whether shed on the ground beneath a tree, or dabbed with a leaf, or wiped into the bark, an alchemist's tears of mourning are alchemically transformed — salt water transformed into mercurial fire — an eternal memorial for the person being mourned."

Jaden had on many occasions walked through or past the Amber Garden. She had been told in her first days with the Council that the glistening spectacle was a memorial garden. But she assumed it to have been constructed by talented artisans, like so many other aspects of Council dimension — the mosaics and the tapestries and the inlaid channels. Until now, no one had informed her of its connection to tears of mourning. Months ago, she had noticed Sadira sitting on a bench under one of the amber-laden trees. She remembered having admired Sadira's beauty and apparent peaceful expression. But Jaden had misunderstood; perhaps Sadira had been mourning someone she had known or loved, a friend lost to a previous conjunction.

"Tomorrow — *today* — at sunset we will attend the Song of Mourning in the Amber Garden," said Cercis. "Save your tears until then."

Their attention was then pulled back to the closing of the sacrament. The Rowans, chanting the concluding words of the ritual, led Amur away from the cliff face and through the forest back towards the main Council buildings. As the Rowans and the other Elders walked by her, Jaden's sadness and growing desperation became infused with anger — the same anger she had felt on the day Cedar had told her the truth about conjunction. But when Cedar herself passed by the Junior Initiates, Jaden understood something that had eluded her until now. Perhaps the Sacrament of Conjunction was difficult even for the Elders, even for those who believed in its principles, even for those who had witnessed many such conjunctions, and even for those who had themselves conjoined. Briefly catching her eyes, Jaden understood that Cedar had loved Sadira. She would have even more reason than Jaden to shed tears that day in the Amber Garden.

No one but her allies was the wiser. She looked back towards the Elders and, beyond them, to all the alchemists of the Council. She looked down at her own body, curious about her physicality beneath the ritual robes. She was, for now, Amur. But she would be, for eternity, Kalina. Could Amur sense her, she wondered. If all had gone as planned, even he should not be able to detect her negative presence.

For three days, she would remain hidden in plain sight — free to roam the Council grounds in the guise of Amur. So much preparation had preceded this day, so many details had been determined, so many years had passed, so many manuscripts had been altered, so many lacunae had been opened, so many vials of Lapidarian ink had been absorbed into vellum and parchment. All the work by so many before her had brought her here today. Now, her sacred duty was to complete the final stage of a mission that had begun centuries ago, long before she had even been born. Too much was at stake for all to be wasted or, much worse, lost forever.

When the Rowans had first led her away from the cliff face towards the forest, Kalina had noticed Jaden amidst the other Initiates and was moved by her apparent sorrow. After the Resurgence, she would explain all to Jaden, but for now she must remain hidden within Amur.

"Long live the Quintessence," intoned the Elders as they reached the main courtyard.

"Long live the Alchemists' Council," replied Amur.

Cedar lay perfectly still, both silenced and stunned. What had happened? What could possibly have gone wrong? The Sephrim should have assured Sadira's victory over Amur. At the very least, it should have assured the dominance of her physical traits. But Cedar herself had witnessed Amur's victory. He had stood — smiling, smug — where Sadira should have reigned supreme. How? Why? These questions had plagued her since the Sacrament of Conjunction. She had gasped when Amur appeared victorious, though only a few others noticed her reaction over the applause and congratulatory remarks. She had hurried, fists clenched, back to her office, collapsing in shock and despair into one of the velvet chairs. Eventually, exhausted, she had fallen into a restless sleep, waking again an hour ago and compulsively questioning the situation. She knew she must stop. She knew she must continue with her duties. Later that day, she would have to officiate at Sadira's Song of Mourning. And in only ten minutes she was due in Azothian Chambers. She stood up, straightened her hair and robes, wiped her eyes, and made her way through the halls as slowly as time permitted.

The Elders had yet another official task to complete: the questioning of Amur. As protocols dictated, the newly conjoined was to be questioned not only on the process and experience of the conjunction but also on its aftermath. The Elders must ensure first that Amur was in good health, suffering no permanent negative side effects either physically or mentally, and, more importantly, must confirm the completed dissolution of Sadira and the victory of Amur.

With Amur seated before the Elder Council, Rowan Kai began the prescribed questions.

"Who are you?" she asked Amur.

"I am Amur of the Alchemists' Council. I have carried my pendant two hundred and ninety-eight years. On the final day of the Splendor Solis of the 18th Council, I conjoined with Sadira."

"Do you sense any remaining essence of Sadira?" asked Rowan Esche.

"No. I sense nothing of Sadira."

"Do you sense any changes to your physical body?" asked Rowan Kai.

"No. I sense no physical changes."

"Are you certain? Not even the most *minute* change?" asked Azoth Ravenea.

"No. I sense not even the slightest change to my physical body. I feel precisely as I did prior to the Sacrament of Conjunction."

"Minor physical changes are typical," responded Ravenea. "Perhaps certain changes will manifest over the next few days. Such dormant or latent effects are also typical."

"Yes, Azoth," replied Amur.

"Surrender your pendant for reading," requested Azoth Magen Ailanthus.

Amur stood, removed the silver cord and pendant, and approached Ailanthus.

Beginning with the Azoth Magen, the pendant was passed from one Elder to the next, each holding it to his or her forehead for reading. As the pendant made its way around the Elder Council circle, Cedar watched Amur carefully. She sensed his nervousness. But if nerves were all that were read in the pendant, he would have nothing whatsoever to fear.

From Ailanthus to Ruis, from Ruis to Ravenea, from Ravenea to Kai, from Kai to Esche, one after the next, each Elder in turn made the identical pronouncement: "I sense nothing of Sadira. She has been dissolved. I declare Amur victorious."

Though relieved that no one had sensed anything out of the ordinary, Cedar herself nonetheless expected to sense something of Sadira, some small trace signature made possible by the residual Sephrim. But when Obeche passed the pendant to Cedar, and though she held it against her forehead for even longer than appropriate, she too felt nothing. Nothing. In that moment of realization, understanding the necessity of resignation, it was all Cedar could do to hide her sense of astonishment — and the wave of despair. Cedar, passing the pendant back to Ailanthus, glanced at Amur, sought out in his expression or demeanour an explanation of this turn of events. But he returned her stare only with a quizzical look, one that implied, above all else, innocence.

"I sense nothing of Sadira. She has been dissolved. I declare Amur victorious," she said in a monotone.

*Was Amur's essence powerful enough to resist the effects of Sephrim? Was he* that *powerful?* Cedar asked herself repeatedly. Had he deceived both her and Sadira and, indeed, the entire Alchemists' Council for the weeks and months leading up to conjunction? Had he himself ingested Sephrim, despite its rarity and near impossibility to procure?

Cedar thought back over her more recent interactions with Sadira, recalling Sadira's hesitance and anger. Had she stopped ingesting the Sephrim without Cedar's knowledge? Had Sadira purposely sabotaged their plan? Was Sadira finally and *irrevocably* gone, no longer willing or able to be a member of the Alchemists' Council? Had Sadira herself helped Amur in his victory? Though Cedar knew she would have to retrace her steps, would have to review each and every aspect of the plan they had enacted to ensure Sadira's dominance over Amur, would have to solve the mystery of what had gone wrong, for now she could barely think at all in the wake of such overwhelming remorse. She had loved Sadira. Inexplicably, she had loved Sadira more than she had loved anyone, more than anyone on the Council, more than anyone in the outer world, more than Ruis, which she would at one time never have believed possible. But it was not the loss of love that crushed her so completely; from a devastating loss of love she had recovered in the past and could again recover with time. What crushed her now was the possibility of something much more severe, something that could have repercussions not just for Cedar but for the entire Alchemists' Council: betrayal.

At sunset, Jaden, Laurel, and Cercis arrived at the Amber Garden. The intense slant of light from the west filtered through the honey- and orange-coloured amber, making the trees appear to be laden with embers of fire. Jaden marvelled at the beauty of the spectacle, tears brimming even before she had reached her destination within the garden: a large tree in the southwest corner. Under its numerous branches, Cedar stood with Azoth Ruis; together they would lead the Song of Mourning. Several other alchemists were seated on the ground facing Cedar and Ruis. Jaden, Laurel, and Cercis sat near the outer edge of the group, as was Council protocol.

"Why *this* tree of all the trees in the garden?" Jaden asked Laurel after they were seated.

"The first mourner chooses the tree," Laurel explained. "Cedar is first mourner here. Cedar loved Sadira, and Sadira had loved Saule. And this is the same tree Sadira had chosen when she was first mourner for Saule."

"How is the first mourner chosen?"

"By acclamation of the Azoths," responded Cercis.

"The Azoths can read the bonds of love that form throughout the Council," said Laurel. "They would have read the connections among Saule, Sadira, and Cedar."

Jaden had not known Saule, but she remembered her name. Saule was the one who had conjoined with Cedar, the one who had sacrificed herself to save Jaden's life. *For whom had Sadira sacrificed herself*, Jaden wondered in that moment. Who would be the next Junior Initiate? Who would arrive next to be, like Jaden herself, alternately wooed and shocked and angered and saddened and awed by the world of the Alchemists' Council?

Joining the others, the four Junior Initiates bowed their heads and began to recite the Song of Mourning. Laurel and Cercis knew the words, but Jaden had to read from parchment that Cercis had provided.

*Sadira.*
*As the lion devours the serpent,*
*So too have you been devoured.*
*Sadira.*
*As base metal transforms into gold,*
*So too will you be transformed.*
*Sadira.*
*As the Great Work protects the world below,*
*So too will you be protected above.*

*Sadira.*
*As the Azoth transcends our dimension,*
*So too will you transcend ever after.*

The Song of Mourning was recited several times — as many times as required for all mourners to ensure their tears had been absorbed for transformation. On the first few recitations of Sadira's Song of Mourning, following the lead of Cedar and Ruis, everyone stood, heads bowed with hands in the second position of Ab Uno. But on subsequent recitations, the mourners assumed various postures, all with the same intention: offering their tears to the garden. Some knelt down and lowered their heads, allowing their tears to fall to the ground; some reached up to pick leaves from the tree, wiped their tears on the leaves, and then tucked the leaves back among the others; some wiped their tears on their hands and then placed their hands on a branch of the tree. Jaden, voice faltering as her weeping continued, wiped her tears away with her right hand and then pressed her hand against the tree's smooth bark. She was surprised to feel the bark respond to her touch, vibrating gently under her fingertips.

When she turned away from the tree, expecting to see the mourners departing the garden, instead she saw them all on their knees gazing up into the branches. She heard what they were looking at before she saw it — gentle snapping, crackling sounds. She knelt among the mourners, her gaze following the sounds, and witnessed for the first time new growth in the Amber Garden. Small bits of amber — the size of spring buds that one might observe in the outside world — formed on branches of the tree that had absorbed the mourners' tears for Sadira.

Jaden gradually turned her attention to the other trees in the garden, many of which still glistened in the final rays of the evening sun. At that moment, Jaden began to cry more intensely. She understood the sobering truth behind the glistening spectacle. All the amber in the Amber Garden, all the beauty she had admired, all the branches and buds that caught the light, had been born from the tears of the Alchemists' Council.

## VII
## cũrrent Day

Cedar looked up from Sadira's notebook and sighed. For the past several hours, she had been searching through Sadira's room — through drawers, books, notes, and even her private journals. But she had found nothing to indicate a premeditated betrayal. By all appearances, Sadira had spent her final weeks researching and writing lesson plans on a diverse range of subject matter, predominated by stories of two historical couples: Aralia and Osmanthus — from the primordial myth of the Crystalline Wars — and Ilex and Melia. Certainly, considering both her anxieties over her conjunction and her trepidations about ingesting the Sephrim, Sadira's interest in these unconventional conjoined pairs was understandable. What continued to defy Cedar's understanding was Amur's victory in the conjunction.

Not until a few minutes before she had to meet with Amur did Cedar notice a brief notation in a section of a manuscript facsimile outlining the history of Ilex and Melia. Among the various manuscript glosses, most of which appeared to be in Sadira's handwriting, were five words in a minute font that confirmed Cedar's suspicion of conspiracy: *Arjan has made his choice.*

Kalina waited and observed. Though the waiting was interminable at times, she consoled herself with the knowledge that, in the grand scheme of the Alchemists' Council, three days was no time at all. And she had to admit that the waiting was occasionally both interesting and entertaining. Such was the case at the moment, as Kalina lay hidden in the guise of Amur, who sat across the table from Cedar waiting for his fellow Novillian Scribe to speak. Kalina knew that Cedar's intentions were good, that they had been good for many years. She knew that Cedar would have done almost anything to keep Ruis from completely eliminating the Flaw in the Stone — *almost* anything. She would not have willingly sacrificed Sadira, and she most certainly would not have approved of Sadira's choice, no matter the repercussions to the Council or to the outside world. Kalina could read in Cedar's eyes that she was both saddened by the loss of Sadira and perplexed by

Amur's apparent victory. She longed to reach out to her, to explain everything, but she had no ability to do so at the moment. She could not emerge as herself out of her human alembic until fully matured — that is, until the end of her third day within Council dimension. So she waited within Amur, witnessing events both from her own perspective and from his.

Above all, what she felt now from Amur was arousal. She had never experienced arousal within a male body before this moment. The sensation was both unnerving and amusing. Even more fascinating to her, Amur's thoughts on the matter were certainly entertaining. From Kalina's perspective within Amur, Amur could think of little other than seducing Cedar. However, she was equally aware that Cedar sat across the table completely oblivious to the intensity radiating from Amur. Under general circumstances, especially given that both Cedar and Amur were Novillian Scribes, the possibility existed that Cedar would be able to sense something of Amur's emotional resonance whenever their pendants were within close proximity. But Amur's pendant, thanks to Sadira and her manipulation of the Sacrament of Conjunction, had been rendered virtually unreadable with the sole purpose of ensuring that Kalina herself would not be detected — not by anyone on the Council, including those few graced with a fragment of the Dragonblood Stone. Of course, Amur was unaware of the change to his pendant and, thus, quite frustrated by the entire situation.

"Amur," Cedar began, then paused to look at him directly. "I realize that what I am about to say may be difficult for you to hear. But if we are to work together for potentially hundreds of years to come, I must be honest with you now."

"Yes. I appreciate that, Cedar."

"And thus I must tell you that I had hoped that Sadira would be the victorious one in your conjunction."

"I understand that her victory would have been your hope. You loved her."

"Yes."

"I am sorry for your loss. However, you know as well as I that victory cannot be predetermined. Conjunction remains one of the few aspects of existence — in this world and outside — over which the Alchemists' Council has no control."

"True. But individual alchemists have been known to attempt to gain the advantage."

Kalina felt Amur flinch.

"If you are suggesting that I am one such alchemist, you are mistaken, Cedar. Above all, above even my own life, I respect the Council and honour its sacraments. I would do anything to ensure the Council's survival, including sacrificing my own life. Though we have never been close, you should certainly know me to be trustworthy and principled."

Cedar lowered and shook her head. Kalina sensed that Cedar strained to keep herself from crying — a torrent of emotion Kalina would not have expected from the Scribe.

"I apologize, Amur. You are correct. Since we met, many, many years ago, I have known you as nothing other than honourable. You do not deserve my suspicion or reprimand."

"I understand, Cedar. You miss her."

Both Kalina and Amur could then see Cedar's tears — a sight neither had ever witnessed.

"Yes."

After a lengthy pause, Amur ventured, "Perhaps you will eventually find something of Sadira within me."

"But I thought you sensed nothing of her?" Cedar asked, sitting up, intrigued.

"No. Not yet. I simply mean that someday you might find something of Sadira in me the way that Sadira found something of Saule in you."

The shift from being intrigued to being incensed was instantaneous. Cedar immediately stood up, thus ending the discussion, and beckoned to Amur.

"Enough. We must go. The sun is rising. We must be with Arjan when he awakens from the catacomb alembic."

"Cedar, I am sorry if I offended you. I was projecting into the distant future."

"Even a hundred years into the future, I could not love you as I loved Sadira."

had passed her by without notice, Obeche emerged into the courtyard from the southern archway. Unlike Olivia and Linden, he did not ignore Jaden; indeed, he walked directly towards her.

"Your assistance is required," he said to her.

She did not respond.

"Whether or not you approve of my tactics or agree with my beliefs is currently irrelevant. Council dimension is in jeopardy, and the assistance of everyone, including you, is required. Follow me, Jaden."

"But I haven't been paired with you. What if Cedar requires my assistance?"

"Cedar is otherwise occupied."

Though Jaden desperately wished to continue to wait on the bench for Arjan, she knew better than to argue with Obeche. Despite her genuine dislike of him, she could not bring herself to disobey him. As she had both experienced for herself and witnessed with Arjan, Obeche's temper and power made a lethal combination against which, as a Junior Initiate, she had little recourse. Angry but sensible, she had decided in the aftermath of his abuse of Arjan in Azothian Chambers that her best strategy against him was also the most practical. For the foreseeable future, she would cooperate with Obeche. But someday — even if many years from now — when her power equalled or surpassed his, she would seek retribution for the pendant violations perpetrated on both herself and Arjan.

She had assumed Obeche would lead her to his office or down into the archives where she would be put to work on manuscript bee hunting, as in Qingdao. Instead, as they walked through the main Council building, Jaden realized they were headed towards the portal chamber. She stopped abruptly. She certainly did not want to be transported to Qingdao and risk, once again, being unable to return to Council dimension. Obeche had taken several steps before he realized Jaden was no longer directly behind him.

"What are you doing?" he called back to her.

"I am not going to Qingdao," she replied. *Or anywhere with you*, she thought to herself. In the only act of defiance she could achieve without risking an official reprimand, she crossed her arms and added, "I believe I would be more useful here."

"No, you are not going to Qingdao. And, no, you would not be more useful here." He moved towards her, and she suddenly feared that she would be physically dragged into the portal chamber against her will. "Do you have any idea what is going on?"

She paused before responding. He now stood directly in front of her.

"The bees are disappearing again."

"Yes. The bees are disappearing. Do you know how many bees have disappeared?"

"No, Scribe Obeche, I do not know how many bees have disappeared."

"More than we can count. I am not being facetious, Jaden. Hundreds — perhaps thousands — of bees have disappeared from Lapidarian manuscripts. So many lacunae have been left in their stead that the number is now immeasurable. And do you know *why* the bees are disappearing from the manuscripts?"

"No, Scribe Obeche, I do not know why the bees are disappearing."

"Hazard a guess, Jaden. By all accounts, you are intelligent enough to do so."

She wondered if Sadira had praised her intelligence to Obeche; she could think of no one else who would have done so.

"Rebel activity," she deduced.

"And what interest do you imagine the rebels would have in depriving us of our Lapidarian bees?"

"Perhaps they intend to disrupt the elemental balance of Council dimension."

"Perhaps. But I have an alternative theory, and I have Arjan to thank for it."

Jaden stood perfectly still, despite the flush of blood that had reached her face.

"I have no doubt that the rebels are interested in breaching Council dimension, in increasing the Flaw in the Stone, in assuring that Final Ascension results in death rather than ultimate union. But for many months, I have been troubled with their apparent interest in our bees. Why *bees*? Why not snakes? Why not dragons or lions? Why not the

Green Lion itself or the Rebis? If all they intended to do was open lacunae which, in turn, would increase negative space within Council dimension, then any alchemical image would suffice. So I asked myself, as I am asking you now, of all the recurring images in all the Lapidarian manuscripts within Council dimension and its protectorates, why *bees*?"

Obeche paused as if prompting Jaden to make another guess. As she thought about bees in comparison with the other figures he had listed, only one possibility occurred to her.

"The outside world needs bees to survive," she said.

Obeche smiled. "Very good, Jaden. You may prove a valuable Initiate after all."

"I don't understand."

"Do you know why Arjan's grandparents returned to the outside world?"

"No."

"Nobody knows for certain, of course. But theories abound. I was one among many who assumed, for years, that they had left Council dimension to join the Rebel Branch. But then, as you witnessed, I read Arjan's pendant. And do you know what I learned, Jaden?"

Jaden wished she could sit down.

"I learned nothing whatsoever of the Rebel Branch. Whether or not Ilex and Melia joined the rebels remains a mystery. Instead, I discovered something much more fascinating in its superb simplicity. I learned that Ilex and Melia taught Arjan to cherish one thing above all else."

"What?" asked Jaden, her interest in Obeche's lecture no longer feigned.

"Free will!" Obeche proclaimed, gesturing dramatically for emphasis.

Jaden's perplexed expression prompted Obeche to continue.

"Free will, Jaden! Free will!"

She shook her head, still not understanding.

"We all want free will — or we think we do. In fact, most of us believe we have free will. After all, we are free to make choices. For example, of your own free will, you chose to stop in this hallway, to refuse to accompany me to the portal chamber. Of course, by invoking my Council seniority or by physical strength, I could easily have persuaded or forced you into the portal chamber if I so desired. How free, within a hierarchy of such abundant power, is your will, Jaden? More to the point, how free is the will of the people of the outside world if their world — the very earth upon which they walk, the air they breathe, the water they drink, the fire that keeps them warm, cooks their food, and destroys their enemies — is controlled by mere strokes of Lapidarian ink in a manuscript? How free is the will of the people of the outside world if, with a few more strokes of that same ink, entire populations — the *entire* population — could be completely eliminated at the whim of the Alchemists' Council?"

"The Alchemists' Council is sworn to maintain the elemental balance of the Earth," said Jaden, as if to mitigate the possibility of Obeche's hypothetical depopulation. Her thoughts raced back to her meeting with Dracaen and his allegations regarding free will.

"Have you taken that vow, Jaden?"

"Not yet. As you know, an Initiate's Law Code vows are taken in exchange for Elixir at the age of thirty."

"*Will* you take that vow when you are thirty?"

She hesitated only because she did not know if she would still exist as a member of the Alchemists' Council by the time she reached Elixir years. She may well have been erased from Council by then and — of her own free will — chosen to join the Rebel Branch.

As if Obeche could read her mind, he reworded his question. "If you remain a member of the Alchemists' Council and are granted Elixir, will you take that vow? Will you vow, as a member of the Alchemists' Council, to maintain the elemental balance of the Earth?"

"Yes," she responded. She saw no reason not to help the people of the outside world. After all, that dimension had been her home until the day Cedar initiated her.

"You will vow — *vow* — to maintain elemental balance, no matter the price?"

"The price?"

"Yes, the price. If you vow to maintain elemental balance of the outside world, then, in effect, you simultaneously vow to affect the free will of the people of the outside world."

She shook her head in confusion.

"Jaden, you have joined the Alchemists' Council at a particularly challenging phase. We are losing control of the balance of the outside world. More precisely, too many people of the outside world have abused their free will — particularly during the Vulknut Eclipse of the 17th Council — and I dare say a few members of the Alchemists' Council have done so as well. The population of the outside world has become so abundant, its industry so widespread, its technology so extensively pervasive, that Lapidarian ink, even in the hands of the most skilled Scribes, has begun over the past century to fail in its efforts to maintain balance. Under these extraordinary circumstances, we have only two options left to us if we are to maintain its elemental balance and thus, to use a blunt cliché, save the world: we must annihilate an extensive portion of the population or we must suppress the free will of the entire population. Tell me, Jaden, which of these options would you choose?"

In its tone, Obeche's question was no more complex than if he were asking her what she would choose for dinner. She stood silently for quite a while, thinking through the implications of both options. Finally, she uttered a response she would eternally regret: "Which portion of the population?"

Cedar stood with Amur beside the catacomb alembic. Arjan was scheduled for awakening within the next half hour. Under different circumstances, Obeche would most likely have been the one to accompany and assist her; however, with the exception of Council meetings or other such public business, Ruis had temporarily barred him from proximity to Arjan. Instead, Cedar found herself standing beside the person who had consumed Sadira, about to help the person whom she now suspected to have contributed to Sadira's demise. She could not help but feel both anxious and angry. She breathed deeply, attempting to calm herself. Her efforts were not for her own well-being but to allay the possibility of Amur sensing her emotions. To detract herself from all such thoughts, she broached a topic of business with Amur. At the very least, she would learn his opinion on the matter.

"Ruis is concerned about the Flaw in the Stone."

"Not surprising, of course. The dramatic increase has set his efforts to eradicate the Flaw back by hundreds of years. If I were in Ruis's position, I would be more than a little concerned."

"Are you? Are you more than a little concerned?"

"I have my concerns, though they are unlikely identical to those of Ruis."

"Do you care to elaborate?"

"Like everyone with whom I have spoken, I am

concerned with the potential negative effects of such a sudden and dramatic increase to the Flaw. An increase in the Flaw inherently allows the possibility for increase in rebel influence over Council — both in Council dimension and in the outside world. An increase in rebel influence inherently allows the possibility for an additional increase to the Flaw. And so on, and so on. If we are unable to minimize the Flaw promptly, we risk falling victim to a rebel victory — a victory impossible to imagine since the end of the Crystalline Wars."

At the mention of the Crystalline Wars, Cedar turned towards him abruptly.

"Do you not agree?" he asked her.

"Yes. I agree. I . . ." she began. But she immediately thought better, opting to refrain from telling him about Sadira's ongoing interest in the story of Aralia and Osmanthus prior to her conjunction. She could not risk offering him even a thread connected to Sadira, especially if doing so meant she would be offering the same thread to herself. He was not Sadira. He would never be Sadira. His reference to the Crystalline Wars was a mere coincidence. She decided instead to risk posing a question she knew to be controversial — one for which she required an answer.

"Do you support Ruis's aspiration to eradicate the Flaw in the Stone?"

He paused and looked upward, presumably composing a careful response.

"Eradicating the Flaw in the Stone — perfecting the Lapis — would offer to the Council all that it has ever sought. Responding otherwise would be blasphemous."

"You may be honest with me, Amur, whether blasphemous or not."

Admittedly, she felt a twinge of guilt for playing on his obvious and ongoing desire to be more intimately connected to her.

"Eradicating the Flaw in the Stone," Amur continued, "would ultimately eradicate both the Alchemists' Council and the Rebel Branch. The ultimate Final Ascension would give each individual of each dimension, including those in the outside world, life everlasting as One. It would return all three dimensions to the originary state before the Crystalline Wars. Each one of us would exist eternally without change — without desire for change, without fear of change — perfectly united as One. For generations, for all Councils, perfecting the Lapis and enacting the ultimate Final Ascension has been the aspiration of the Azoths. As One, perfected, we would exist eternally, infinitely — no exceptions, no erasures, no conjunctions, no deaths, ever again. But we would do so at the expense of individual intention: no one would choose for him or herself. We would exist, but we would fail to live. So, Cedar, my blasphemous answer is *no*. I do not support Ruis's aspiration."

For the first time since the conjunction, Cedar smiled. Perhaps all was not lost after all.

"Neither do I."

"Follow me, Jaden," said Obeche. He turned, and she willingly followed him into the portal chamber.

"Are you taking me to a protectorate?"

"Just follow me. No more questions."

Of course, Jaden had many more questions, but for now she kept quiet, thinking through the consequences of the choices Obeche had offered to her. Though her answer disturbed her, and though she continued to second-guess herself, she had to believe that the eradication of a portion of the population was preferable to abolishing the free will of everyone in the outside world. She assumed the remaining people could remain alive without free will, but what sort of life would they have under such circumstances? What sort of initiative would they have to do anything of their own accord? The irony of her dilemma did not escape her: *she would not have a choice in the matter if she had no free will.* Yet, as she also poignantly realized in this moment, her free will could well be her undoing.

Obeche led her into the Salix portal.

"Fortunately for you, my pendant was not completely drained."

"What?"

"Never mind. Just stand still."

The usual whirlwind carried them through interdimensional space. They emerged in a country she could not identify from the landscape alone: flat fields, as far as the eye could see of a flowering crop — lavender, she assumed, though her botanical knowledge was limited. The sky was clear, the sun shone, the temperature was pleasantly moderate. A slight breeze caused a graceful movement of the crop throughout the fields. She ran a hand over the stalks closest to her and confirmed from the scent that the crop was indeed lavender. As she scanned the landscape, she identified the reason Obeche had brought her here: *bees*.

"Do they seem different to you?" Obeche asked. "Are they different from other bees?"

"I've never studied bees."

"No. Why would you have? But I can assure you that if observed closely by any beekeeper of the outside world, these bees would be found indistinguishable in comparison to any other of their specific species. A trained alchemist, on the other hand, should be able to tell that these are a very particular sort of bee. Look closely, Jaden, and tell me what you see."

She bent down towards one particular bee, poised at the tip of a flowering spear. She had never observed a bee this closely, so she had no idea what she was meant to see. But an instant later, she noticed an intriguing phenomenon. The bee, as it lifted itself from the flower, hovering momentarily as if determining where to proceed next, shifted in colour; its translucent wings flashed a bright bluish-green. The flash was so brief that Jaden first thought it to be an illusion of the light. However, she realized that the effect was no illusion: as she recalled discovering months earlier in the memorable classroom lesson with Arjan and Cercis, the blue-green flash was a characteristic of Lapidarian ink. Just as Jaden was about to question Obeche about the bee's origin, it disappeared — not by flying away, but by vanishing before her eyes.

"Where did it go?"

"To the best of my knowledge, it has gone nowhere — literally. It has been erased."

"Erased?"

"These are Lapidarian bees, Jaden. This is the Lapidarian apiary," he explained, gesturing towards the field. "The apiary was constructed many years ago as a safeguard for the future. Each bee appears in the apiary when it is first inscribed into a manuscript — one bee inscribed in a manuscript eventually results in hundreds of bees within the apiary. Some have been here for hundreds of years, maturing in their power to influence the elements as they age. Others have been here for only a few weeks or even a few days. As demand requires, some are released into the outside world or into Council dimension to assist with recalibrating the elemental balance. But, as we have realized of late, and in particular after the quake, bees are disappearing from the apiary just as they are disappearing from the manuscripts. Thus, we can only assume the manuscript disappearances are a form of erasure — though without the necessity or complication of memory alteration. That is, at any rate, the current hypothesis as reiterated to me this morning by Ravenea. Based on their recent observation that bees are disappearing as rapidly from the apiary as lacunae are forming in place of bees within the Lapidarian manuscripts, the Readers have concluded that the two phenomenon are linked. For each bee erased from a manuscript, hundreds may have vanished from the apiary. If the population of Lapidarian bees deteriorates, the outside world will lose its most promising potential to fix its present ecological imbalance. Devoid of Lapidarian bees to assist alchemically in the reproduction of flora and, through the flora, to re-establish elemental balance, the outside world will be unable to sustain its inhabitants. Without getting into more detail than necessary or wise here, let me simply say that without a substantial influx of Lapidarian bees in the near future, the majority of the population of the outside world will perish within a generation."

"The majority? The *majority* is your idea of a *portion* of the population? You would condone such destruction!"

"No, Jaden. I am not responsible for the bees

disappearing — quite the opposite. I hold sacred the vow I took hundreds of years ago to maintain the elemental balance of the outside world. For me, that balance includes its people. I have been consistently vocal on the issue, encouraging the Elders to release as many Lapidarian bees as possible into the outside world, even if doing so would irrevocably decrease the Council's supply of the most ancient and, thus, most potent bees. I have even encouraged *adding* substantially more bees to the manuscripts as a means of repopulating the apiary over time. Of course, repopulation would take decades of Scribal labour and the bees would take hundreds of years to mature within the apiary. Nonetheless, from my perspective, the release of most, if not all, the Lapidarian bees into the outside world provides the Alchemists' Council with its best — perhaps its only — chance to fulfill the vow to maintain balance of that world. Unfortunately, not everyone agrees with me. You included."

"Me? Before you brought me here, I knew nothing of the apiary beyond the occasional reference during Initiate lessons or at Council meetings. And I've had nothing to do with bees beyond the manuscripts of the Qingdao protectorate."

"I posed a question to you, Jaden. I asked whether, to maintain the elemental balance of the outside, you would choose to annihilate a portion of the population or suppress the free will of the entire population. You chose annihilation."

"No! I didn't. I didn't make a choice. I just asked a question."

"Yes, you asked *which portion*. And I now ask you to consider whether identifying and choosing a specific portion of the population would make your decision more ethical. Would it help you justify your choice of slaughter if the portion I showed you were millions of people from the slums of Asia as opposed to those in the wealthy shoreline cities of America?"

Jaden looked out over the fields, watching the bees. Within the few minutes she watched, she counted eight disappear — presumably many more outside her direct sightline had also disappeared in that time.

"I apologize, Scribe Obeche. I should not have asked *which portion*."

"Years from now, you will undoubtedly attribute your hasty response to the folly of youth. When you are three hundred, you will look back on these days as your infancy."

Jaden smiled, something she never imagined herself doing in front of Obeche.

"I know you distrust me, Jaden, and I know you have good reason to do so. My actions towards you and others — Arjan in particular — appeared, from your perspective, to be unjustified. But I can assure you that everything I have done was in the interest of preserving both the outside world and the Council itself. As you are aware, the erasure of the bees has been done covertly, without the permission of the Elders, most likely through a dimensional breach of some sort — one that I continue to suspect originated in the outside world, especially in light of the events of Qingdao. It is one matter to argue against releasing too many bees; it is another to erase them completely. Breaching Council dimension and, worse, choosing *purposely* to deface Lapidarian manuscripts are heinous crimes. In this particular case, the implications of those crimes are, quite literally, life-threatening to millions of people in the outside world. As I am sure you will agree, its perpetrators must be located and punished."

"I don't understand what you want me to do. I am only a Junior Initiate — a mere infant. I don't have Scribal powers to assist with repopulating the apiary or reinscribing the manuscripts. I have no influence at all over the manuscripts or the apiary or the bees."

"No, but you do have influence over Arjan."

"Arjan?"

"You must convince him to lead you to the perpetrators."

"What! What do you mean? How would Arjan know the perpetrators?"

"He is their direct descendant."

Jaden could not respond. The pieces of the puzzle suddenly fit all too swiftly into place. *Above all else, they had taught Arjan to cherish free will*, Obeche had said. *The more bees, the stronger the vibration, the weaker the will*, Dracaen had explained. By eradicating the Lapidarian bees, Ilex and Melia hoped to eradicate the power of the Alchemists' Council to repress free will in the outside world, thus ensuring that its people would remain free to choose, free to reap the consequences of their choices, free to destroy or save themselves.

Surprisingly gratified by Amur's candid responses to her questions about the Flaw, Cedar momentarily relaxed enough for Amur to sense her contentment. Though she sensed nothing from pendant proximity, she could nonetheless recognize his attraction to her. He may prove useful as a future ally in her plans for the Council, but he would never — *never ever* — be welcomed into her bed. She would have reiterated this fact directly if not for the sudden change in colour within the alembic, indicating that Arjan was ready for extraction.

They climbed the steps and positioned themselves to assist Arjan from the alembic waters. Cedar herself had never been immersed in a catacomb alembic, had never personally experienced its effects: unconsciousness of the mind and suspended animation of the body. However, having often helped others emerge from the waters, she knew what to expect. Arjan was likely to be disoriented and to require the assistance of two people as a safeguard against injury. At least wet robes would not complicate the withdrawal procedure — unlike immersing in regular channel waters or the Albedo, alembic waters evaporate from the body and clothing instantaneously, leaving the person and their garments cleansed and renewed.

Within ten minutes, having been assisted down the steps and onto the coolness of the catacomb floors, Arjan regained his composure enough to walk steadily with Cedar and Amur through the narrow catacomb pathways. Along the rather lengthy route, Cedar and Amur alternately offered details of the events that had occurred in his absence. Most prominent, of course, was the conjunction — the news of which caused Arjan to come to a sudden stop.

"It's already happened?" said Arjan, incredulous. He looked at Amur. "*You* were victorious?"

Amur frowned momentarily before advising calmly, "Do not let the alembic effects cloud the sense of common courtesy expected of a Junior Initiate."

"My apologies, Scribe Amur."

Cedar did not know in that moment whether Arjan's apparent astonishment was genuine or feigned. If genuine, she thought, her suspicions of his involvement in Sadira's demise may be unwarranted.

As they approached the main Council building, Cedar suggested that Amur return to work with the Readers. She offered to debrief Arjan and, if she ascertained that he was fit for work, assign him his duties for the remainder of the day.

"Shall we meet again at noon?" she suggested to Amur. Cedar assumed setting a noon meeting would give her enough time to speak with Arjan about Sadira yet disallow sufficient time for Amur to become overly entranced by his imagined expectations of their future alliances, sexual or otherwise. He nodded and then left.

Not until they had settled comfortably into the lush chairs of her office did Cedar offer anything but small talk and tea to Arjan.

"Tell me the truth, Arjan."

"Which truth, Scribe Cedar?"

"Tell me what happened to Sadira."

"You were witness to the Sacrament of Conjunction, not I."

"In title and Order, I am a Novillian Scribe, but I have always been an extraordinarily powerful Reader. Even without holding your pendant, I can sense your emotional bond to Sadira. I am certain you know something about what happened to her, Arjan, and you are not leaving here until you tell me the truth."

"Conjunction is a sacrament whose outcome must be respected," replied Arjan.

Angered by both his words and misdirected confidence, Cedar stood and stared at him. As an Elder, she was well within her rights to demand a subordinate's pendant for reading. But reading an interim pendant — a pendant infused only with Lapidarian essence rather than a Lapidarian fragment — was an intense procedure that, as illustrated by Obeche with Arjan, could potentially deplete its bearer of life's essence. The Azoths would surely reprimand her if she subjected Arjan to further injury and the necessity of another trip to the catacombs. She thus purposely addressed him as calmly as she could manage under the circumstances.

"Evidence suggests that in the weeks, perhaps months, leading up to her conjunction, Sadira developed a fascination with Ilex and Melia. Given that their fame is due in no small part to conjunction, I had no reason to question her interest in the pair — until now. *Now* the entire Council knows that Ilex and Melia are your grandparents. Perhaps Sadira learned of your lineage much earlier than the rest of us. Surely, it cannot be mere coincidence that Sadira's Initiate — the Council's most recent Initiate — is a direct descendant of the two people with whom she had become so captivated? Of the only two people in Council history to attain mutual conjunction? Did you tell her of your ancestry? Or did she discover it on her own?"

"If Sadira had wanted you to know of her relationship with me — of the information I did or did not provide her — she would have told you herself."

"Has it occurred to you, Arjan, that I am now your protector?"

"My protector?"

"I initiated Sadira and she, in turn, initiated you. When she brought you to Council dimension, you became a member of our branch on the Alchemical

Tree with Sadira as your official protector — your teacher, your mentor. She is now gone. So you are now mine to guide. How am I to guide you if you refuse to be honest with me?"

"Scribe Cedar, I am more than willing to be honest with you with regards to myself. A denial to break Sadira's confidence does not equate a failure to be honest."

Cedar could not remember having felt so angry in the last hundred years. Clearly neither threat nor calm persuasion nor logic would work to convince Arjan to cooperate. In that moment, she could think of only one other approach: an appeal to his sympathy.

"Arjan, I loved Sadira. I trusted her. She is now gone. I am sad, and I am angry. I assumed, with good reason, she would be victorious. She was not. Nothing has gone as planned. You know something. I know you do. Can you offer me no comfort in this matter — anything at all to help me understand what appears incomprehensible?"

"Sadira made an ethical judgment call. Her intention was not to betray you. Like you, she wanted to ensure eternal free will for the Alchemists' Council. She believed in your mission, Cedar, but she came to resent your hypocrisy. So she made a radical choice for radical change. She did not tell you because she knew you would not have condoned her decision."

Mouth agape, Cedar sat back down in the chair

across from Arjan. She had been right. He did know the truth. But knowing only this piece of the truth inevitably made her want to know more. She looked at him, the expression on her face both thankful and beseeching.

"Tell me what she did. I beg you."

Her final words clearly moved him.

"She provided my grandparents access to Lapidarian manuscripts."

Though this statement did not explain why Amur had been victorious in the conjunction, it most certainly shocked Cedar into silence.

After returning from the apiary into Council dimension, Jaden had immediately been assigned to relay messages among the Readers and Scribes working in the archives, in the libraries, and in the Scriptorium. No matter how much she longed to speak with Arjan, Jaden could see no time or means to seek him out. Though she assumed Arjan had long since made his way back from the catacombs, likely accompanied by Cedar, she also assumed that he would have been sent to his chambers. Despite the severity of the manuscript lacunae, she certainly did not expect, did not even contemplate, that he would be sent directly to the archives to assist alongside the other Initiates. So as she was ascending the stairs from the archives with the task of reporting the latest discoveries to the Elders working in the Scriptorium, she would have walked right past Arjan if he had not reached out to her, placing his hand on her shoulder.

"Arjan!"

She spontaneously wrapped her arms around him, only recognizing thereafter that doing so might be a breach of protocols. Nonetheless, she waited until Arjan released the hug, which seemed to Jaden at least a few seconds longer than two friends would generally embrace.

"How are you? What happened? What do you remember?"

He laughed. "I am fine — fully recovered. As to your other questions, I would have far too much to explain to you than I can do here and now. I have been sent by Cedar to help relay updates on the manuscript lacunae. I assume you have been given the same task."

"Yes, but—"

"Go. We will talk later."

She knew enough about Arjan and enough about the urgency of her task to know not to resist his suggestion.

"Yes," she said and turned to continue up the steps. She had already ascended four steps before he called out to her.

"Thank you," he said.

She looked back towards him and saw that he was holding up his pendant. She understood in his gesture, as well as from his tone and expression, that he was thanking her for the Dragonblood fragment. She smiled, nodded, and continued on her way. But as she walked towards the Scriptorium, she could not help but wonder precisely what the Dragonblood fragment had helped him to remember. It must have been something specific, something that had at one time been erased from his memory; otherwise he would not have recognized the change to his pendant — if he noticed it at all — as anything other than accidental damage. He certainly would not have held it up and thanked her. Thus amidst her Council duties, as important as they were during this time of crisis, she thought of Arjan and what he might report to her as soon as the opportunity presented itself.

Not until at least an hour later did she suddenly wonder how it was that he knew *she* was the one who had altered his pendant.

On occasion, as a means of reassuring herself that all was well within Council dimension, Cedar would count the alchemists, naming each of the one hundred and one from the Junior Initiates to the Azoth Magen. Of course, for brief intervals throughout Council history, counting to one hundred and one was not possible. Such was the current state; thus, Cedar felt unnerved. She knew from experience that the waiting period between a space opening on Council and the arrival of a new Initiate could last anywhere from a few days to a few years. Though the Readers had already completed the first stage of the location process over the weeks preceding Amur and Sadira's conjunction — that of consulting the ancient manuscripts for alchemical prophecies, indications, and concurrences — the second stage remained: the Ritual of Location and the inevitable waiting period that accompanied it. The imbalance on Council during the waiting period, though minute, often resulted in minor negative effects on both Council dimension and the outside world. The longer the wait, the more Cedar's anxiety increased; the four years awaiting Jaden were almost unbearable. She had longed each day for the Council to return to its stable one hundred and one members, thereby renewing and maintaining elemental balance. Yet in each case, her anxiety had eventually been relieved. How could she have known that on this day, at the dawn of the 19th Council, on the afternoon before the day of Ailanthus's Final Ascension, the unthinkable would occur?

Given the current state of affairs and extenuating circumstances — the likes of which had not been seen since the Third Rebellion — combined with the lack of lead time for Ailanthus's ascension, the Readers had asked for the assistance of the Scribes in locating the new Initiate as rapidly as possible. In addition to expressing frustration about the manuscript anomalies, most likely a direct or indirect effect of the innumerable lacunae emerging over the past few days, Olivia and Terek specifically requested the presence of Cedar and Amur at the Ritual of Location. Thus it was that Cedar came to be standing with Amur in the shallow waters at the side of the Albedo, while Readers Olivia, Terek, Wu Tong, and Tilia floated within the Albedo itself — all temporarily relieved of their duties with locating or inscribing Lapidarian bees.

Though the waters swirled and bubbled as they generally did during the Ritual of Location, and though both their tepidity and colour changed regularly throughout the ritual, it appeared to Cedar after an hour or so that none of the Readers were coming any closer to determining a specific location for the new Initiate. She was about to suggest that they conclude the ritual for the day, dry off, and meet again after dinner in the North Library to consult the manuscripts again, when Olivia let out a piercing scream. Everyone jolted, causing splashes in the Albedo that under normal circumstances would negatively affect the reading of location, thus causing the ritual temporarily to cease. However, the splashes were the least of their concerns. The waters directly surrounding Olivia had not only darkened but ceased all sound and movement. The still and silent darkness spread like black ink throughout the Albedo. As the darkness expanded, the Readers and Scribes reacted accordingly, leaping or stepping unceremoniously out of or away from the Albedo to stand horrified and helpless at its edge.

"What is happening?" Wu Tong finally asked.

"I have never seen or even read about such an occurrence," responded Cedar.

"Nor I," said Terek.

Olivia, still shaking, turned and ran up the stairs towards the door leading to and from the Ritual Chambers.

"Olivia!" called Cedar.

"The channel waters!" she called back. And everyone understood her panic, quickly following in Olivia's footsteps, up the stairs, along the hallway, and out onto the Council grounds.

Within seconds, their fears were confirmed. Several other alchemists who had by chance been standing within sight of the channel waters were now gaping at them with the same shocked expression as Cedar, Amur, and the Readers. The channel waters throughout the entire Council grounds had turned stagnant and black. As they stood, stunned into a shocked silence, the implications began to resonate. If the channel waters were stagnant, then all the waters throughout the Council would likewise become stagnant within minutes, including those of the catacomb alembics. And the repercussions expanded far beyond mere stagnant water.

The channel waters were one of the four primary elements. Without the water, elemental balance would be impossible to maintain, both within

Council dimension and within the outside world. Without water in the Albedo, new Initiates could not be located. Worse, without water in the alembic chambers, healing and recovery in the catacombs would cease. The possibility that alchemists could die, especially in the advent of an anticipated rebellion, swiftly became a probability. And worst of all, without water, without the fourth element, the alchemically constructed fifth element would inevitably decline — the Quintessence itself was at risk. With this realization, the words they had said repeatedly, day after day, for hundreds of years abruptly gained resonance for this brave new world: *Long live the Quintessence. Long live the Alchemists' Council.*

That night, long after the curfew under war measures, exhausted from a day of playing messenger between the Readers and Scribes, anxious after witnessing for herself the inky darkness of the channel waters, appalled by what she had learned about the bees from Obeche, Jaden swiftly made her way to Arjan's room. She would tell him about her conversation with Obeche and ask for his perspective. Then she would make her own decision on what to do, with which side to align herself. The move was risky, of course. If caught by a Warden, she would, at best, be sent back to her chambers and, at worst, be summoned to Elder Council under suspicion of rebel activity. Tonight of all nights was not the one on which to be caught disobeying the rules — not on the night after hundreds of bees had disappeared from the manuscripts, after Obeche's suspicion of an elemental breach had gained prominence thanks to the evidence before everyone's eyes, and certainly not on the night before the Azoth Magen's Final Ascension.

But she decided she must risk reprimand rather than go another night without speaking privately to Arjan. If caught, Jaden would certainly be suspected of rebel alignment. Though Arjan had been cleared of Obeche's rebel charges due to lack of evidence beyond his familial connection to Ilex and Melia, it was that very connection that made him questionable to several members of the Alchemists' Council, not only to Obeche. Perhaps Arjan's current relative freedom to roam Council grounds was merely a ruse on the part of the Elders — perhaps allowing him freedom would allow him to compromise himself. Or perhaps his freedom to perform his Council duties was mere practicality. After all, the help of all the Initiates was needed at this current time of crisis. She could not know.

Having contemplated the risks and possibilities as she made her way to Arjan's room, Jaden now stood outside his chambers trying to determine how loudly she could knock without anyone in nearby rooms or hallways noticing. Poised with her right hand about to knock as quietly as possible at Arjan's door, grasping her pendant in her left hand with the hope she could silently reach him through its Lapidarian essence or Dragonblood fragment, she was startled by the appearance of Cedar a few steps away. Cedar reached over, grabbed Jaden by her extended arm, and roughly pulled her down the corridor, demanding in a whisper, "Come with me!" Jaden knew better than to yell out in resistance. Who of the Wardens or Elders would dare to question Cedar's right to apprehend and command a Junior Initiate? Jaden had taken a risk, and she was about to pay for doing so. If only she had been caught on her return journey rather than before speaking with Arjan, if only her capturer had not been Cedar, Jaden would not feel as desperate as she did in this moment.

*Arjan!* Jaden cried out to him desperately in her mind, her left hand still wrapped around her pendant. Her efforts proved futile, of course; even if he had sensed her cry — which she assumed he had not, since she could sense nothing of him — what could he possibly have done in this situation to assist her?

"Quiet!" demanded Cedar.

Since Jaden had done nothing to warrant being silenced, she reached the disquieting conclusion that Cedar knew she had cried out to Arjan through her pendant. This sudden realization repulsed Jaden. How extensive was Cedar's ability? How much could Cedar read of her thoughts and emotions through Lapidarian proximity without purposely holding and reading her pendant? Jaden did not even possess a Lapidarian fragment within her pendant, only Lapidarian *essence*. Surely Cedar could not read her thoughts through proximity to mere essence. Even the most gifted readers holding a pendant in hand or to the forehead were not capable of downright mindreading — pendant reading, even by the most experienced, allowed the reader access only to another's most intense or prominent thoughts and emotions. Perhaps Jaden's emotional response to Arjan was greater than she allowed herself to imagine. Or perhaps Cedar was far more skilled at pendant reading than any other member of the Alchemists' Council. She had, after all, managed to find Jaden within Qingdao when others had abandoned the search. Whatever the explanation, Jaden resented the invasion of her privacy.

"This is Council dimension, Jaden. You have no privacy," whispered Cedar.

Jaden balked. How—? She stopped herself, instead attempting to clear her mind. *Don't think! Don't think! Don't think!*

Cedar led Jaden all the way to her office and pushed her towards a chair. Cedar's beautiful chambers seemed more haunting than exquisite tonight. A fire in a large kiln cast flickering shadows onto the lavish fabric curtains and Azadirian tapestries. Jaden sat silently, waiting for Cedar to speak.

"Arjan is not to be trusted," she began.

Jaden remained silent. What could she say to convince Cedar otherwise?

"Jaden! I know my words are difficult for you to hear, but you must trust me."

"Trust you!" Jaden was about to protest further when her anger changed suddenly to despair. Kalina had asked for her trust. Sadira had asked for her trust. And where were they now? Sadira had been consumed in the fires of conjunction, and Kalina was nowhere accessible. She glared at Cedar, willing her to read her mind. *Yes*, she thought, *I know about Kalina*. But she regretted her thought immediately afterward when she realized that, by inference, remembering Kalina meant Jaden possessed a Dragonblood fragment. *Don't think about the Dragonblood fragment*.

"It's no use, Jaden. I know everything about you. Think what you will."

"Fine! You know everything about me! You know of all my thoughts and all my actions. Then why am I here? What else do you want from me beyond everything I know and think?" Jaden paused before derisively adding, "Am I about to be erased? Does my destiny depend on your powers with Lapidarian ink?"

"Yes."

Jaden flinched.

"Yes, your destiny depends on my powers with Lapidarian ink. However, if you were about to be erased, you would not be here. You'd be in a portal chamber on your way back to the outside world. And I would not be the one accompanying you."

"Why am I here then?"

"Because *you* do not know everything about *me*."

"I don't even know what I thought I knew about you!"

"Who do you think are your allies here, Jaden?"

"You already know what I think, so why are you asking?"

"Yes, I do know. I know you trusted Kalina. I know you trusted Sadira. And I know you now trust Arjan, that you believe him to be your only remaining ally. But the truth of the matter is that you did not — *do not* — know much at all about any one of your apparent allies or their true intentions."

"And you do?"

"I certainly know more than you do."

"Certainly."

"I know what it means to be betrayed by an apparent ally. I have recently learned that even after hundreds of years, one can be deceived . . . led astray by someone who appears trustworthy. I have made the mistake of letting emotions overrun logic. I hope to keep you from making the same mistake with Arjan that we both made with Sadira."

Jaden waited, more interested in listening to Cedar than in opposing her.

"Sadira betrayed me, Jaden. She betrayed you as well. She used you to reach Arjan, who is more than capable of betraying not only you but the entire Council."

"Sadira did not betray me. She was consumed in the fires of conjunction."

"Yes. And in allowing herself to be consumed, she betrayed us both."

"I am sorry that you lost a person you loved. But, as you told me months ago, right here in this office, conjunction is a sacrament. In my opinion, it's a cruel sacrament, but it's nonetheless a sacrament whose outcome, however crushing, must be respected."

"Sadira was aligned with the rebels, Jaden."

Jaden watched Cedar carefully, hopeful for additional details yet anxious about her intention behind these revelations.

"So was Kalina. And so, potentially, is Arjan," continued Cedar. "Do you not find it problematic — or, at the very least, *unusual* — that all your allies are associated with the rebels?"

"Perhaps my destiny is with the Rebel Branch," ventured Jaden.

"You risk erasure with that statement."

"Kalina was erased, yet she survived with the rebels."

"Yes, she did. But did she tell you how she found them? Or, more pertinently, did she tell *you* how to find them from the outside world?"

Jaden did not respond. Cedar laughed — one definitive syllable that Jaden mistook for triumph.

"Kalina had a fragment of the Dragonblood Stone and extensive knowledge that allowed her to access the Rebel Branch once she had been returned to the outside world. You will not have such a fragment, Jaden."

Jaden clasped her pendant, realizing with sudden panic that her pendant would be confiscated if she were to be erased. She would have to search for the rebels.

"You cannot find them without a fragment of the Dragonblood Stone, Jaden. Do you think the Rebel Branch would allow its dimension to be found by an outsider? The Council has been searching for years — hundreds upon hundreds of years. The only members of the Alchemists' Council who know how to access the rebel dimension are those whom the rebels themselves contacted and presented with a Dragonblood fragment. For generations, the rebels have sought their own Initiates. They do not wait to be found, nor do they risk discovery. They reach out to those from the Council they believe destined to join them. Are you telling me, Jaden, that you believe yourself destined to join them? Do you believe if you are erased from Council dimension that the rebels will contact you?"

"Yes."

"Then you leave me no choice."

Jaden grasped the arms of the chair and pushed herself up, expecting to accompany Cedar to the nearest portal chamber. She had only two regrets: first, that she had not been able to speak in detail with Arjan prior to her departure and second, that she did not possess a Dragonblood fragment separate from the absence within her Lapidarian pendant, which seemed about to be confiscated.

Cedar walked to Jaden and reached for her pendant.

"No!"

"I am not going to take your pendant, Jaden. I merely want to look at it."

"You are not touching my pendant!"

"Listen to yourself, Jaden. And look at everything that has happened to you since your arrival here. Then look at it again from the other perspective."

"What other perspective?"

"Mine."

Jaden felt Cedar's breath against her neck, her lips against her ear, whispering, "My sweet, dear Jaden, you do not need to seek the Rebel Branch. We have already found you."

## VIII
### cūrrent day

Jaden panicked. She leapt out of the reach of Cedar's touch. Surely Cedar was lying to her — testing her, enticing her to say something she would regret, to reveal what she knew about Dracaen or Kalina, about the Dragonblood fragments, about her visit to the dimension that housed the Flaw in the Stone. She stood by the door clenching her pendant in one hand, the other hand outstretched as if to push Cedar away if she dared to come closer.

"I am not lying to you, Jaden."

"Stop! What are you doing? How are you doing it? How do you know my thoughts?"

"Let go of your pendant."

"No!"

"Let go of your pendant, and I will no longer be able to read your thoughts."

Jaden hesitated. If Cedar was lying and Jaden were to let go of her pendant, Cedar might physically confiscate it from her. But if she were telling the truth, then letting go of her pendant would free her from Cedar's intrusion of her mind.

"Explain!" demanded Jaden, holding up the hand with which she still clenched her pendant. "Explain!"

Instead of speaking, Cedar grabbed her own pendant, gripping it as tightly as Jaden did her own. And within seconds, Jaden understood. She could hear Cedar's voice within her own thoughts as clearly as if Cedar were speaking aloud.

*You hold in your hand a pendant infused with both Lapis and Flaw. As do I. You already know the powers of the Lapidarian pendant — the empathy of proximity, the ability of one alchemist to read another's pendant by holding it in one's hand or to one's forehead. The conjunction of Lapis and Flaw within a single pendant increases such powers exponentially. By merely holding such a pendant in one's own hand, the person opens his or her thoughts to anyone else who also possesses such a pendant within physical proximity. I hold such a pendant now, Jaden. I too possess a pendant conjoining both Lapis and Flaw. If I let go of my pendant, you will no longer hear my thoughts. If you let go, I will no longer hear yours.*

Jaden did not know in that moment whether to keep the connection open or to sever it by letting go of her pendant. With Cedar holding her own pendant, Jaden possessed a power she could never before have imagined. She could, with enough time, know all the truths Cedar had concealed since the day they had met.

*Such knowledge all at once might be too much for you to bear. Power comes with a price, especially for someone so new to it.*

She released her pendant, and Cedar followed suit. Jaden thought back to her experience reading Sadira's pendant — to the overwhelming sensation of being unable to sustain an influx of unmitigated thoughts. Jaden stood still, exhausted. She still wanted — needed — answers.

"If you have been with the rebels all along, why did you not help me? Why did you send Kalina away? Why was she erased? Why did you not just tell me the truth from the beginning? Why did you not bring me as an Initiate to the Rebel Branch? Why have you tortured me in this way?"

Cedar laughed. "You were being *tested*, Jaden. You are an Initiate. You were being *initiated.* You were being *recruited*, not tortured. Dracaen and I needed you to make the choice to align with the Rebel Branch of your own free will. We could not risk that you would reject us and inform the Azoths that one of their Novillian Scribes had rebel sympathies! From your perspective, our apparent lack of assistance may have seemed torturous. But, rest assured, you were being helped every step of the way and, more importantly, practising for your future with both the Council and the Rebel Branch. The lessons you have learned, the skills you have gained, you will rely upon repeatedly in your future."

Jaden moved away from the door and sat in a large, lush velvet chair by a window looking out over the courtyard. Cedar took an adjacent seat and offered Jaden some tea.

"How did you help me?"

"*Let me count the ways*. By creating various manuscript lacunae to obscure passages that otherwise would have led the other Scribes away from choosing you as the new Initiate; by agreeing to Kalina's erasure so that she could work unencumbered among the rebels to increase the Flaw in the Stone; by providing Jinjing with the Dragonblood fragment to give to you in Qingdao so that you would remember Kalina. Shall I go on?"

"I don't understand."

"No, you do not understand. You do not understand because you are a Junior Initiate, and you have much to learn before you can make your choice."

"Then teach me something right now to help me understand, to help me choose. *How* are you a rebel? How long have you been a rebel? How do you even know the rebels?"

"All Elders know the rebels, Jaden. All Elders work with the rebels."

"What? All the Elders are rebels?"

"No. Of course not. Do you seriously believe that Ruis or Obeche would align themselves with the Rebel Branch?"

"I don't know what to believe anymore."

"When I said that the Elders all *work* with the rebels, I was referring to manuscript work. The Elder Council *must* work with the rebels in order to seal an erasure."

Jaden did not respond. But somewhere, somehow, she sensed a glimmer of understanding: erasure, absence, nothing, the Flaw. Of course.

"The absolute nothing of the Flaw ensures the absolute negation of memory. Our Scribes begin the process of erasure in Council dimension — the process of physically erasing ink in relevant sections of Lapidarian manuscripts. However, only within the Flaw, only within the dimension that houses the Flaw, can the *unknowing* of erasure be completed. After the work in Council dimension is completed, one Council Elder meets with one Rebel Branch Elder in the outside world. A Scroll of Erasure changes hands and is taken to the Flaw dimension by the rebel. Once officially sealed, it is returned to the Council Elder who returns it to the archives in Council dimension. Ironically, the rebels themselves must aid in the erasure of rebels. The process is alchemical — a combination of Lapis and Flaw that began with the Prima Materia of the *Calculus Macula.*"

"Then why are we taught that the rebels are the enemy?" asked Jaden.

"In my opinion, they are not the enemy. But in the official opinion of the Council, rebel desire to increase the Flaw is a rebellious act that must be resisted. Though tolerated as a necessary evil, the Council cannot allow the Rebel Branch to attain dominance, which, of course, would have repercussions, both in Council dimension and in the outside world. When I became a Novillian Scribe, when I first worked with the rebels on an erasure, Dracaen convinced me of his position. Even before then, Jinjing had spoken with me about her connection to him. Together they convinced me of the necessity of preserving, and even of increasing, the Flaw in order to maintain the rebels and the Council, the Flaw and the Lapis. Herein lies the alchemical paradox: without one, the other could not exist."

"So I now know the secret of the Elders. Aren't you afraid I will tell others — Arjan, Ritha, perhaps even Laurel? Aren't you afraid your secret will spread well beyond the Elder Council?"

"Given that I am aligned with those who hold the ultimate power of erasure, your memory of what I have told you will last only as long as I permit."

"Then how can I ever trust you?"

"You must trust that I have your best interest at heart."

"Why?"

"I need you."

"Why? Why *me*? Have I been groomed to replace Sadira?"

"Here I must admit something to you that will leave me even more vulnerable: my weakness. I have been so blinded by my desire to attain allies against

Ruis's efforts to perfect the Lapis that I failed to notice that the person I trusted the most had her own desires."

"What do you mean?"

"I trusted Sadira. I loved her. But she has betrayed me, as Arjan has confirmed."

"Arjan?"

"I know of your feelings for him, Jaden."

Jaden blushed.

"But I ask that you think carefully through the consequences of basing your actions on emotional ties — a lesson I learned far too late."

"What has he done?"

"He has colluded with Sadira, who has been allowing Ilex and Melia access to the manuscripts. They are responsible for the bees disappearing."

"I know."

"You know? How? What do you know?"

"Obeche took me to the Lapidarian apiary."

"What?"

Finally Jaden had information that Cedar didn't.

"He wants me to convince Arjan to convince Ilex and Melia to stop erasing the Lapidarian bees."

"Yes! You must do so! Arjan will listen to you!"

"What are you saying, Cedar? You agree with Obeche? You never agree with Obeche! Yet you agree with him now?"

"Yes. *For now* I agree with Scribe Obeche."

"I don't understand. You are aligned with the

rebels. You say you have been helping me in a way that would encourage *me* to align with the rebels. The rebels want to increase the Flaw in the Stone. An increase in the Flaw increases negative space. An increase in negative space increases the possibility of a rebel breach, which in turn allows the possibility of additional manuscript lacunae, which in turn allows for additional erasure of bees. Yet you want me to try to stop the bees from being erased. You want, I presume, to release the Lapidarian bees into the outside world? I don't understand. Which side are you on, Cedar?"

"I am aligned with the rebels, but I am also working to maintain elemental balance of the outside world as I vowed to do as a member of the Alchemists' Council. We — all of us, the entire Council, regardless of varying opinion on the matter — *required* an increase in the Flaw in order to continue our role in maintaining that balance."

"Why? The Council has been doing this for thousands of years! What is the difference now?"

"It is complicated, Jaden."

"Yes! I gather it's complicated! But how can you or Obeche or Arjan or Kalina or *anyone* expect me to make a choice — a choice whether to help the rebels or the Council or both — if you do not explain these complications to me? You claim Sadira has betrayed you, but I feel now as if *you* have betrayed *me*. Tell me the truth, Cedar!"

"Which truth, Jaden? What I tell you may be different from what Obeche or Arjan or Kalina tells you."

"Then tell me *your* truth, and I can decide whether or not to believe you — whether or not to trust you."

"Why did you trust Kalina when she first came to you?"

Jaden hesitated briefly.

"I don't know. She seemed sincere. And I was curious. She showed me another possibility, another perspective. She offered me a choice, where the Council did not. And then the choice was taken from me when she and my memories of her were erased. And all I knew then was that there was something I needed to remember, something I needed to know."

"You needed to know what you *did not know*, what was *unknown*, the knowledge that had been taken from you. You needed to have that knowledge in order to make a choice. You were given that knowledge when you were given a fragment of the Dragonblood Stone."

"The first fragment was taken away."

"Another to be provided when you showed me that, given free will, you would choose to look for that which was absent."

"Stop speaking to me in philosophical riddles!"

"Jaden, the Flaw in the Stone allows alchemists to choose. It allows the Council to fulfill its intention — to, among our other tasks, maintain the elemental balance of the outside world. Without the Flaw, the Lapis would be perfected, and we would be unified as One. Official Council doctrine lauds this act as our ultimate goal: attaining absolute perfection for the Lapis and thus achieving ultimate Final Ascension for all, eternal life as One for everyone from all three dimensions. But if we were to be unified as One, we would lose our individuality. We would no longer be able to choose. We would no longer fulfill our chosen intentions. For years, perfecting the Lapis was no more than a mythical ideal. But then it happened — albeit for only three days — during the Vulknut Eclipse of the Third Rebellion. And the outside world suffered the consequences."

"What consequences? What suffering? You just said all would be One."

"After the ultimate Final Ascension, all would become One. In the meantime, the entire Alchemists' Council worked towards preparing for the Ritual of Ascension, which would have taken place on the fourth day if not for rebel interference. Without intention beyond preparation for the ritual, the Alchemists' Council neglected its duties, preparing en masse for Final — *the absolute final* — Ascension. During those three days, for the first time in centuries upon centuries, the people of the outside world were free from our influence — completely free to make their own choices regarding their world and its people without our influence or assistance or, as some claim, *interference*. Though the rebels ensured the Flaw in the Stone was returned before the Ritual of Ascension, and though Council dimension itself suffered no lasting damage, in those few days certain individuals of the outside world made choices that, over the next few years, resulted in the deaths of millions. And although the Vulknut Eclipse lasted only three days, the results of the choices made during that period — choices over which we had no influence — have rippled throughout the years to the crises we now face. The only viable solution to mitigate damages *that we caused* to the outside world in our pursuit of perfection is a mass influx of Lapidarian bees."

"Without which the majority of the population of the outside world will perish within a generation," said Jaden, echoing Obeche while attempting to find logic within the chaos of Cedar's revelations. She stared at the ceiling momentarily and then suddenly and icily at Cedar as she realized the implications. "Do I understand you correctly, Cedar? Are you saying the only time the people of the outside world had complete control over their choices, the only time their choices extensively and negatively affected the elemental balance of the world, the only time the people of the outside world enjoyed *complete* freedom from influence of the Alchemists' Council, the only time the people of the outside world truly — really and truly — enacted *absolute* free will, occurred when the Council was preparing to eradicate free will for eternity?"

"I am saying that the people of the outside world need us to assist them in the aftermath of the exploitation of their free will, which began during a three-day period a century ago and has wreaked havoc ever since."

"I'm beginning to understand. You used the rebels. You used them to ensure an increase to the Flaw so that you, and all members of the Alchemists' Council, would maintain not only free will for yourselves, but power *over* the free will of others. Having accomplished that feat, you now want the bees released to ensure that power over the outside world remains with the Council, to ensure the choices — the *apparent* free will — of the people of the outside world have no lasting effects whatsoever on elemental balance. You keep for yourself and the Alchemists' Council what you take away from others. You are a hypocrite, Cedar."

"And you are naïve, Jaden. What is it that you thought you were learning in your Initiate classes? You have known all along of the Council's duty to maintain elemental balance of the outside world. How is it that you think we can accomplish this without *power over*, as you say? Or were you too distracted from the truth by the beauty of *this* dimension, by the splendour of this world that you *chose* to inhabit when offered that choice, this world with its blue mist at dawn and verdant grounds and copper channels flowing — until recently — with crystal clear waters. Or perhaps you were distracted by the mysteries it opened to you — by Kalina and Dracaen and the possibilities offered by potential rebellion. Or perhaps you were distracted by your own desire — for Arjan or Sadira or any number of physical temptations available to you for a virtual eternity. How is it that you have enjoyed the pleasures accessible to you through the Alchemists' Council without thinking through the repercussions of that very enjoyment?"

"You have tricked me."

"No, Jaden, I have taught you. I have taught you as I taught Sadira. She learned well, and she agreed to help me to help the rebels increase the Flaw. She even agreed to poison the well, so to speak. She poured a solution of Dragonblood essence into the Primary Alembic in order to begin the process that increased the Flaw. But, in the end, she chose to betray me by helping Ilex and Melia erase the only chance we have to maintain elemental balance. And now you have to make a choice, Jaden. You can choose to betray me or you can choose to betray yourself — the self that you only *think* that you know. Either way, your destiny is inextricably linked to mine — a destiny if not carved in stone, certainly inscribed in Lapidarian ink by Scribes and rebels generations ago. What I am about to say you will not fully understand for years to come, but this is your destiny, Jaden: you will be my saviour, and in saving me, you will save the Alchemists' Council."

Though a Final Ascension had not occurred during her years in Council dimension, Kalina knew that the movement towards the event could be interminably slow. She had learned of its stages in a Senior Initiate class. The Azoth Magen makes his announcement of intention, and over the next year, in consultation with the Elders, he or she works towards the transition. Of course, Ailanthus had made his announcement under circumstances radically different from the norm — in a moment he surely understood as necessary self-sacrifice. To Ailanthus, both ancient and erudite, his proposal to Ascend and thus return his fully matured Quintessence to the Lapis was the only means he knew of assuring the Council's survival at this critical juncture. Kalina recalled from her classes that such selfless gestures had worked in the past: during the 16th Council the Final Ascension served to significantly increase Lapidarian Quintessence and decrease the Flaw in the Stone. Yet to her knowledge no Azoth Magen had ever experienced the Flaw at its current augmented size. Not since the Crystalline Era had the Flaw permeated so much of the Lapis. Thus, as she stood watching the Azoth Magen move to the dais in Council Chambers to begin the Ritual of Succession, Kalina smiled within Amur. Still veiled to those who surrounded her, she waited in eager anticipation both for Ailanthus's announcement of his successor and for the residual effects of the increased Flaw to permeate not only the Council grounds but the Alchemists' Council itself. If all went according to plan, she would be both witness to and participant in the most radical breach and transformation of Council in thousands of years. She must remain patient for only a few more hours.

As a witness to the Ritual of Succession, Jaden sat among her fellow Initiates, including Arjan. Having been escorted directly to her room after her meeting with Cedar and arriving at dawn to Council Chambers to attend the ritual, Jaden still had not had the chance to speak privately with him. Obeche had caught her eye when she first entered Council Chambers, his expression demanding a sign to indicate if she had convinced Arjan to dissuade Ilex and Melia from their pursuits. She merely shrugged, hoping he would understand that she had not yet been provided the opportunity. He frowned in return. Now she sat, anxiously, alongside Cercis, Laurel, and Arjan, clasping her pendant, hoping for time alone with Arjan after Ailanthus had announced his successor.

*We don't need time alone.*

Jaden started slightly, surprised by the intrusion of Arjan's voice into her thoughts. Cercis and Laurel both glanced at her as if to question her sudden movement. Jaden noticed that Arjan too was clasping his pendant.

*I have so much to tell you!* thought Jaden. *Too much! And too many questions to ask you!*

*The Ritual of Succession is relatively short. We do not have much time.*

*Why did you not tell me of Ilex and Melia? Why did you not tell me of their plan — and yours — to erase the bees?*

*I did not know of their plan.*

Jaden hesitated, not knowing if she should believe him. Yes, she could hear his thoughts, but only those most prominent in his mind. Having such limited experience, she did not know how — if it were even possible — to read his truth, the way one trained to read a pendant might be able to do.

*My knowledge of my grandparents' work was limited, and my memories both of them and of their work became muted once I arrived in Council dimension. I believe now that my memories were somehow manipulated, perhaps partially erased. As it has become clear, they are experts at erasure. Council manipulated both of us.*

*Both of us?*

*When you left me in the Qingdao manuscript room to talk to the younger me — to Payam in the street — two timelines crossed. The alchemical power of that temporal conjunction created a surge in elemental energy that allowed my grandparents enough Prima Materia to succeed at a transmutation of time. It allowed them, years ago, to create a breach — an aperture of negative space — that opened in current time in Council dimension. The residual effects of that breach allowed the rebels to assert temporal influence over Sadira's conjunction — a complicated matter that would take more time than we have now to explain. But the breach created in Qingdao has also contributed to the dramatic changes in dimensional equilibrium — the quake, the increase in the Flaw, the darkening of the channel waters. I have to believe that even my grandparents did not anticipate or desire the extent of the repercussions.*

*What about the bees? They began to disappear long before our trip to Qingdao.*

*Yes, for the past few years, my grandparents have sought to decrease the Lapidarian bee population and thereby return responsibility for the outside world to the people of the outside world. Initially, Kalina had helped them gain access to Council dimension manuscripts. After Kalina's erasure, they still managed to manipulate the most vulnerable of manuscripts: those in outside world libraries and those in the protectorates, which are much easier to breach than Council dimension itself. More recently, Sadira learned of and came to believe in their cause. With her help, my grandparents ensured that the manuscript lacunae began to multiply exponentially.*

"Kalina!" said Laurel.

"What?" both Arjan and Jaden asked, astounded.

"I remember Kalina. She was erased."

"*How* do you remember?" Jaden asked, wondering suddenly if she too had a fragment of the Dragonblood Stone and could read their minds.

"I don't know."

"It's the Flaw in the Stone," suggested Cercis. "The increase in the Flaw must be decreasing Lapidarian power to maintain memory erasure. I remember her too now — Kalina."

Though Jaden would gladly have continued this conversation, everyone's attention was diverted in that moment towards the dais for the climax of the ritual. With Azoth Ruis to his right and Azoth Ravenea to his left, the Azoth Magen called for silence. Rowans Kai and Esche together carried the Lapidarian sceptre from its ornamental case in the Scriptorium, along the main aisle in Council Chambers, to Ailanthus, first raising it above his head and then placing it into his hands. Ailanthus, sceptre held with both hands, bowed in each of the four directions, reciting the requisite passage from the *Ars Transmutatoria*. He then faced the Council and made the announcement that would officially end his reign as Azoth Magen.

"Tonight I enter Final Ascension. My Quintessence will return to the Lapis, and I will return to the One. With the choice of my successor, I hereby enact the inauguration of the 19th Council. Long live the Quintessence!"

"Long live the Alchemists' Council!"

Ailanthus turned towards Ruis and Ravenea, who were now standing side by side, each anticipating anointment by the Azoth Magen. Ailanthus bowed his head in an honorific gesture to each of the

Azoths. He then raised the Lapidarian sceptre and lowered it onto the shoulder of his chosen successor.

"Long live Azoth Magen Ravenea!"

At dawn on the day of Ailanthus's Final Ascension, before the preparations for the event had begun, Cedar made her way to Council Chambers intending to contemplate the icons, as was her custom on the night before primary decisions. Thus she would silently and privately honour the Azoth Magen on his final day in Council dimension. She should have known — indeed, perhaps she *had* known and was only feigning surprise even to herself — that she would find Ruis standing beside the Lapis in the Scriptorium. He stood, hunched over the segment containing the now highly visible Flaw, peering into its crevice as if seeking its point of origin. If only their lives had moved along the same ideological pathway, he could have accompanied her into the rebel dimension. She, Ruis, and Dracaen all could have worked together to increase the Flaw. Perhaps he would not have betrayed her in the way Sadira had done. Certainly, he would not have believed her to be hypocritical. He would have understood the difference in priorities between the Council dimension and the outside world. At least, these are the fantasies onto which she now so desperately clung in the aftermath of recent events — in the figurative shadows cast by the darkened waters, by Arjan's revelations, by her doubts about the efficacy of her own choices. She should be revelling in the increase to the Flaw, but instead she felt as disappointed as Ruis clearly did. For Ruis, the increase in the Flaw represented a crushing defeat to his work. Cedar could sense the intensity of his sadness, even without reading his pendant. She saw the depth of his emotion just by looking at his face, a subtlety of expression that perhaps only someone who once loved him would notice. If only Ruis had not come to care so deeply for the possibility of perfection — for perfect, flawless union with both her and the One.

He sensed her in that moment, perhaps through pendant proximity, and turned to her.

"Have you come to mock me, Cedar?"

"Of course not."

He shook his head, as if apologizing for his unfounded accusation.

"You have come to contemplate the icons before the Ascension. You did not expect to find me here. I had assumed my failure to conjoin with you had been my lowest point. Yet here I am — utterly defeated in my ultimate goal. I could not have predicted such an end to my efforts. I was so certain — *too* certain — of an alternate outcome."

"As was I," said Cedar. "It would appear that pride still goeth before the fall."

He smiled despite his obvious despair.

"Amidst the confluence of unprecedented events

of late, I have forgotten to offer you my condolences. I truly am sorry for your loss, Cedar. Sadira was exquisite."

"Yes," replied Cedar, not wanting as yet to reveal what she knew of Sadira's betrayal. She could not show herself to be as vulnerable as she felt — as vulnerable as she knew him to be. "Thank you for your sincerity. And may I offer my condolences regarding Ailanthus's choice of successor. I too was certain you would be our next Azoth Magen."

"Look no further than the Flaw in the Stone, Cedar. My work for so many years has so manifestly met with failure. I do not deserve to be Azoth Magen. If I were to live for another three hundred years, I could not erase the Flaw. Ailanthus's Final Ascension will certainly help the Council take its first indispensable step towards repair, but we have far too great a distance to travel now to reach my objective." He paused and laughed under his breath before continuing, "That must bring you some comfort, Cedar. You always spoke against perfecting the Stone. The possibility of ultimate union as One never appealed to you, whereas for me it was the glorious end to the Great Work for eternity: for me, it was the Holy Grail. I choose my analogy purposely, Cedar — I see now that it was as unattainable, as mythical as the Grail. Perhaps I should wear a green sash to Council Chambers today."

"You are mixing your Arthurian metaphors, Ruis."

"Only you would notice." He paused and laughed again, nostalgic now rather than sarcastic. "I miss our literary gaming. Remember, Cedar? We used to play for hours on end as Initiates. When not playing, we were reading literature of the outside world, practising for the next round."

"I remember." She smiled.

"I always liked the early mornings in particular — under the trees in the Amber Garden, before anyone else was awake. It was just a game, but I have never felt as close to you as I did back then — back when I fell in love with you through your words." He sighed. "If only you had been able to love me in the way I have loved you."

"'Let me be that I am and seek not to alter me,'" quoted Cedar.

"'There's a double meaning in that,'" replied Ruis.

Cedar did not know whether to laugh or to cry.

Nearing the end of the third day, Kalina trembled within Amur. The Resurgence was imminent, and the timing was ideal. Especially since learning of his opinion on the Flaw, she had begun to empathize with his current plight more than was advisable under the circumstances. Amur was seated among his fellow Novillian Scribes — Cedar, Obeche, and Tera — entranced by the Ritual of Final Ascension.

Azoth Magen Ailanthus, Azoth Ravenea, and Azoth Ruis stood silently beside the altar, Ravenea holding aloft the Sword of Elixir. Rowans Esche and Kai recited the solemn, ancient words from the *Ghayat Hakim*, as everyone watched Ailanthus — or more specifically, the mature Quintessence within Ailanthus — gradually succumb to the alchemical power of the intoned verses. As the Quintessence emerged from Ailanthus, visible to all as it swirled upward like thick golden steam, instinctually moving, above the heads of everyone assembled, towards the Lapis in the Scriptorium, Ailanthus's body gave way to the ravages of age.

"Long live the Quintessence," said Ailanthus, thus uttering his final words as Azoth Magen.

Within seconds, hundreds of years manifested within his physical being, transforming him swiftly from a vibrant, healthy mature man to a barely cohesive skeletal frame. Ravenea then plunged the Sword of Elixir into what remained of his corporeal form, and Ailanthus collapsed into dust at her feet.

"Long live the Alchemists' Council," responded everyone, including Amur.

A bright flash filled Council Chambers as Ailanthus's Quintessence returned itself to the Lapis. Ravenea knelt beside Ailanthus's remains, took some of the dust into her hands, then rubbed the collected dust onto her face and hands and, finally, into her pendant. Ruis, Esche, and Kai followed suit. All four then stood and faced the Council.

"Having been chosen by Ailanthus as his successor," spoke Ravenea, "I hereby accept my role and pledge my duty to the Council as Azoth Magen."

"And I, as Azoth," said Ruis, "pledge my allegiance to Azoth Magen Ravenea."

Applause rang through Council Chambers.

Ravenea then invited members of each Order, beginning with the Novillian Scribes, to partake in the tradition of transferring dust to pendant. When Amur rubbed Ailanthus's dust into his pendant, Kalina felt a slight surge of energy, as if minute traces of Quintessence remained in the dust and reacted to that within Amur's pendant.

When everyone, including Jaden and the other Initiates, had taken a turn, Azoth Ruis stepped forward to report on the state of the Lapis.

"You will be pleased to know," he announced, "the Flaw in the Stone has begun to decrease thanks to Ailanthus's sacrifice."

Though unheard amidst the joyous responses to the news, Kalina laughed. She laughed so much that she worried Amur would sense her presence. Her concern was short-lived, however, since immediately thereafter she felt the first birthing pain of the Resurgence. The sensation, imagined Kalina as she surrendered to its power, was similar to that of an earthquake or severe disturbance in the elemental balance. Within seconds, the tremors became even more severe, and Amur, as he took a step forward to congratulate Ravenea on her Ascension to Azoth

Magen, collapsed as if succumbing to a seizure. Kalina looked up from within Amur, watching as others gathered around and tried to assist him. She assumed the Council members had never seen an alchemist in this sort of distress. Amur's vision was blurred, so Kalina could not make out faces, but she could hear the dread in their voices — someone whose voice she did not recognize suggested transporting Amur to the catacombs, a plan to which others quickly agreed until Obeche pointed out the futility of such a move given the darkened and inert state of the channel waters.

Then Kalina could see or hear nothing — only darkness and silence. She thought perhaps the plan had failed, that she had been enveloped permanently by the negative space in which she had hidden in relative comfort for three days. But such was not the case. Within seconds, the intense light of the flames consuming Amur's body overwhelmed the darkness. She watched Council members, shadow figures beyond the bright light, backing away — a cacophony of voices and concern and movement. She could only assume they were horrified. The blazing consumption of Amur reached its completion so quickly, however, that they had no time to react beyond initial horror.

Before the entire Council, Kalina stood victorious where Amur had turned to ash.

Along with everyone else who witnessed the spectacle, Cedar gasped. Her reaction was a response not only to the appearance of Kalina but to the immolation of Amur. She rushed forward, spurred on by knowledge she did not quite recognize, by an awareness etching in slow motion from the depths of her mind that somehow, somewhere, by some means that would someday become clear to her: Sadira had been involved in the restoration of Kalina. Perhaps she had not betrayed her after all. Perhaps she had provided a port of access for the rebels — a means to ensure the Flaw would never again decrease. And with that mere but hopeful fragment of knowledge, Cedar could think of only one action to take. She wrenched the Sword of Elixir from the hands of Azoth Magen Ravenea and plunged it into Kalina.

Initially, nothing happened — absolutely nothing. Kalina stood perfectly still and upright, the Sword of Elixir partially buried beneath her flowing robes. From its position, one could only presume the sword had pierced her flesh mid-torso. Yet unlike Ailanthus and Amur, she did not turn to dust. She merely stood surveying all the Council members before her.

Since only mere seconds had passed, many of those who observed Kalina could barely comprehend the sight — once known to them, remembered again recently by only a few, Kalina had been erased from their memories; thus, her sudden presence, sensed perfectly well with their eyes, could not be processed by their brains. Observing her fellow Council members of the lower orders, Cedar understood that Kalina existed for certain observers as negative space and, as such, could be comprehended only once they had adjusted their ways of seeing. The adjustment would take only a few moments, but within those moments it would seem as if Kalina had brought the Flaw in the Stone itself with her into Council dimension.

Ravenea screamed, "No! Cedar! What have you done?"

The space around Kalina had begun to glow, golden at first but quickly progressing to bright orange, like an ember in the pit of a fire. In using the Sword of Elixir, a sacred relic of Council dimension, to wound a manifestation from the negative space of the Flaw, Cedar had initiated the conjunction of opposites necessary to open a chink in the wall between dimensions — a fissure that, once expanded, would allow the rebels immediate access to the Alchemists' Council.

"Rebels!" cried Ravenea.

As Cedar glanced from Ravenea back to the glowing fissure, she thought for an instant that she saw Sadira rather than Kalina vanish within the expansion of bright orange light. But the illusion disappeared as quickly as it had appeared, as rebels began to emerge one by one through the breach. As the rebels adjusted to the light of Council dimension, as Obeche bellowed for all Initiates to return to residence chambers immediately, as the Wardens rushed towards the rebels, Ravenea and Ruis moved behind the rebel line and extracted, with difficultly, the Sword of Elixir from its stronghold in the fissure, thus closing the breach. Though only moments had passed since Cedar had pierced Kalina with the sword, at least fifty rebels had crossed through the breach into Council dimension. The Fourth Rebellion was underway.

Alchemists are not warriors. Though some have argued over the centuries that they were "soldiers for the world," the expression was merely a gesture built on a conjunction of metaphor, philosophy, and science. Alchemists are not blood and bone warriors. They can manipulate the elements into an iron-forged arsenal, yet most cannot physically wield the weapons of their own creation. Thus while the Wardens fought the rebels, many Council members fled — some to the relative safety of their chambers, some to classroom laboratories to render alchemical assistance, some to the portal chambers to stand guard within the various protectorates, some to the Scriptorium with an eye to defending the Lapis. Only a few dozen remained to engage in the fight. Among those few, those who stood alongside Cedar were Ravenea, Ruis, Obeche, and Linden. Only Cedar witnessed both Jaden and Arjan running from Council Chambers, and she realized they were not running away from the battle to protect themselves.

They were chasing — or perhaps eagerly following — Kalina and Dracaen.

As she raced beside Arjan across the dark, damp grounds towards the forest with Dracaen and Kalina, Jaden glanced back towards the main Council building. A few figures — presumably rebels — had already emerged and were hurrying towards them.

"Don't worry," said Arjan. "We have been chosen."

*Who*, she wondered in that moment, *is "we"?* Had she been chosen? If so, by whom had she been chosen — by the Alchemists' Council or by the rebels — and for what purpose? She swiftly placed one foot in front of the other as if she was running for her life, and her thoughts raced in step with her body. As she reached the edge of the forest, her thoughts culminated from myriad fears into one most prominent: Whether chosen by the one or the other, she realized that today would be the day she would have to make her choice — not between the Council and the rebels, but between one ally and another.

**one month ago**

"Sadira," we have brought you here because we require your assistance."

An hour ago, she had been in Council dimension transmuting the mists after Cedar's disappearance through the cliff face. Now she stood in the muted crimson light letting the sound of wooden wind chimes wash over her. She could barely hear Dracaen, though he stood close enough to touch her. She did not want to hear him, so she was not listening. She listened instead to the music of this other dimension — to the hollowness of the chimes, to the silence within the sound, to the nothingness of the Flaw. For so long, she had wondered what this other dimension would be like. For many years, she had imagined something so different from what she now understood being present within the absence. For too long, Cedar had refused to provide her with details beyond what she believed Sadira needed to know.

"Sadira," said Dracaen. "Please focus. You must listen to what I have to say."

He handed her a cup of dark red liquid. Curious yet unafraid, she drank from the cup without questioning its contents. She knew that the liquid would help her remember all that she had forgotten of those erased.

"We need your help." Dracaen was firm without pleading.

"Who are *we*?" Sadira asked.

"The Rebel Branch."

"Why me?"

"You suspect the truth. We know that you do.

Since Arjan arrived in Council dimension, you have known he is different."

"Everyone knows he is different."

"Everyone knows he is *special*. But everyone else is blinded to the truth of that specialness, whereas you remain curious. You notice. You question. You research."

"Yes," she responded, retracing the details of her memory. "I did notice. I noticed little things. The month he arrived, I felt off-balance. Something was different. And then Jaden spilled the ink, and I remember thinking that it may have been Arjan instead of Jaden, that she was merely covering for him. But why would he spill the ink? Nothing made sense. But I knew that I had to help him, to protect him. I *knew* without knowing."

"Yes. And he too was off-balance — adjusting both body and mind to the elemental effects of Council dimension. His presence re-established for us the means needed to accomplish our goals."

"You have goals other than to increase the Flaw?"

"To increase the Flaw in the Stone and to decrease the bees in the manuscripts."

"*You* are responsible for the disappearing bees?"

"Not *me* specifically. Not even the rebels specifically. We have sent our emissaries, those who were able to access Council dimension through the space that was opened for them. They have accessed and, with your assistance, will continue to access the manuscripts that depict the Lapidarian bees

— the bees that, when first inscribed, manifested in the apiary."

"To what end?"

"We believe the bees are doing more harm than good. We have determined that we must erase them — one by one. Once erased from the manuscripts, the original bee and all progeny remaining in the apiary will disappear. They have exerted too much power in the outside world — ensuring its survival based on the agenda of the Alchemists' Council rather than the free will of its people."

"But the Council has vowed to maintain the elemental balance of the outside world. They will not be able to do so effectively without Lapidarian bees."

"Precisely. The time has come for the Alchemists' Council to rescind control over the outside world. It is our turn."

Sadira laughed. "Your turn? If only dimensional politics were as simply as taking turns."

"You know of the myth, Sadira. You have taught it — the Prima Materia, the *Calculus Macula*. The Flaw will spread — with the help of our allies — and it will then be our turn to take responsibility for the outside world. We believe it is our responsibility to give the people of the outside world autonomy. It is now your turn to choose which side you will take."

"I have already chosen a side. I have sided with Cedar. At her request, I have chosen to take Sephrim and, thereby, to remain in Council dimension after conjunction in order to help her *to help you* increase the Flaw."

"To what end?" Dracaen echoed Sadira's own words.

"To prevent perfect union and, thereby, to ensure the continuation of free will."

"Increasing the Flaw will ensure free will within Council dimension. However, it will not ensure free will for the outside world; in fact, one could argue precisely the opposite. The greater the will of the Council, the greater the potential for the Council to abuse their control over the outside world. We want to ensure free will for all — for both the Alchemists' Council and for the outside world. Thus the bees must be erased."

"Without the bees, people will die."

"Of their own accord, of their own choices, rather than due to the actions of the Alchemists' Council."

"Of *your* actions," replied Sadira.

"Initially, yes. But our ultimate goal is equivalency among dimensions: free will for all, including at conjunction."

"At conjunction?"

"How do you feel, Sadira, about killing Amur?"

She felt stung.

"No need to answer, Sadira. We know how you feel: guilty. You feel guilty because you are cheating him. You have *chosen* to cheat with the Sephrim, *of your own free will.* You have chosen to exert your will over his, just as Cedar has instructed."

"Cedar is on your side."

"Cedar is on our side regarding the Flaw. She is not on our side regarding the bees. She is not on our side regarding mutual conjunction. You, however, *are* — both by choice and necessity. Thus you, not Cedar, are the one we have brought here today."

"What choice? What necessity?"

"You chose to ensure free will when you agreed to help Cedar to increase the Flaw. You chose to pursue mutual conjunction when you researched Ilex and Melia."

"I chose to research Ilex and Melia out of curiousity. I have not *pursued* mutual conjunction. I would not know how to do so."

"Not yet. But we — *they* — can offer you the opportunity to do so." He stared intently at her face. "You would be lying if you were to tell me that such an opportunity does not entice you."

She was indeed enticed. Mutual conjunction with Amur would alleviate her guilt.

"How? I have already taken the Sephrim."

"Yes. Thus Amur's demise is already certain — no matter what choice you make today. But the sacrifice of one will help to ensure the eventual good of all. Even if you had not taken the Sephrim, you would not be able to mutually conjoin with him. He is not of the bloodline."

"What bloodline?"

"Ilex and Melia were the first to succeed at mutual conjunction. The ability to do so is contained within their blood, and thus within their bloodline."

"What bloodline?" she repeated.

"They had a mutal ancestor whose elemental make-up was unique — a mutation, so to speak. I share this mutual ancestor." He paused, stepped towards her, and placed a hand on her shoulder. "As do you. And as do their descendents."

"As do I? What ancestor? What descendants?"

"The ancestor matters little now. The descendants, on the other hand, are the alchemical gold of our future. They are the ones with whom you and I are meant to conjoin. Together we will move the dimensions towards complete equivalency — two bodies as one, mutually present and mutually absent. We will be the living exemplum of perfected duality — the physical embodiment of the *Calculus Macula*."

"What descendants?" Sadira asked again. She was shaking, afraid of hearing the answer she already subconsciously knew.

"Kalina and Arjan."

She nodded then as if the truth she had understood but never known had finally revealed itself. "Earlier you implied that Arjan opened the space, that his presence in Council dimension opened the space for your emissaries to enter and adjust the manuscripts."

"Yes. As did Kalina before her erasure."

"Who are they, your emissaries?"

"Ilex and Melia, of course."

"And what do you want of me?"

"We need you to assist Ilex and Melia in accessing Council manuscripts. We know you are familiar — more familiar than most — with the tunnels that run under Council dimension. You could bring them manuscripts through the tunnels, meeting with them where no one would think to look. And," he paused here, as if anticipating her protest, "we want you to agree to sacrifice Amur in order to mutually conjoin with Kalina."

"How? How am I to accomplish the impossible?"

"Years ago, Ilex and Melia set into motion events that will allow the seemingly impossible to become a reality. They are prepared to provide both the means and knowledge for you and Kalina to succeed at mutual conjunction."

"I do not understand. What will happen to Amur?"

"His body will be alchemically manipulated temporarily to survive the conjunction, to act as a human alembic for three days — an incubator of sorts that will ensure the success of your conjunction with Kalina."

"I do not understand. If Amur survives the conjunction, where will we be — Kalina and I — for the three days?"

"You will both be incubating within Amur. Kalina will be conscious within him, and you will be dormant within her. Rooted in his physical consciousness, Amur will sense nothing of the incubating pair. Mutual conjunction across dimensions requires an alliance of three — one body to be the sacrificial vessel within Council dimension from which the other two — alchemist and rebel — will be born. Until birth within Council dimension, one of the two must remain conscious and one unconscious within the physical vessel: the presence and the absence, the blue and the red, the Stone and the Flaw."

"And then, after the birth?"

"For eternity, you will mutually share both body and consciousness with Kalina."

Sadira realized in that moment the error of her ways. She would no longer regret her failure in attaining with Cedar the depth of love shared between Ilex and Melia. Instead, she would become, alongside Kalina, a living incarnation of the primoridal myth.

### current day

Having moved quickly over Council grounds and through the forest, Kalina stood beside the cliff face and laughed.

"We have succeeded," she said.

"Thus far," responded Sadira.

"Yes, thus far."

Dracaen nodded, watching the mutually conjoined pair with admiration. Depending on the angle of the light, he could see one and then the other.

"You are next, Dracaen," said Sadira. "Thanks to our breach, you will not require a vessel. You need only the ritual."

She then turned away, leaving Kalina to face the others: first Jaden and Arjan, then the rebels who had assembled to form a defensive barricade for the duration of the ritual.

"What is your mission?" asked Kalina, facing Dracaen.

"To preserve the Flaw in the Stone," responded Dracaen.

"What is your mission?" Kalina asked Arjan.

"To save the Alchemists' Council," replied Arjan.

"And what is your mission?" Kalina asked Jaden.

"I don't know," responded Jaden, lowering her head in embarrassment.

"Think, Jaden."

"I no longer know what to think."

"Then think nothing, Jaden. Move yourself beyond thought. Do not attempt to resolve the paradox. *Be* the point of nothing between the one and the other. *Be* an alchemist in the way alchemists were meant to be."

"I don't understand," said Jaden.

"You will when you stop thinking of yourself."

Jaden was not thinking of herself; she was thinking of them — of Dracaen and Arjan — and what they were about to do to each other in order to fulfill their respective missions. In other circumstances, the setting would be hauntingly beautiful, but at this moment, the dark trees reflected in the tranquil pool served only to heighten her sense of confinement. She and the others were trapped here now — nowhere to run. Though she did not yet understand her mission, she understood the truth behind the image she had gleaned from reading Sadira's pendant: Arjan poised, pendant in hand, calling out his intention to save the Alchemists' Council. Is this the reason Sadira had required Jaden's assistance? To ensure that Arjan, Dragonblood fragment at the ready, would be prepared to meet with Dracaen in battle? Perhaps her mission was to stop the battle, to ensure that both Dracaen and Arjan survived.

With that thought, Jaden held up her arms in a futile gesture of opposition, an attempt to keep the two men apart. Kalina pulled her back and away, causing her to fall onto the moss-laden ground. She expected a battle to erupt then between Dracaen and Arjan. She expected swords forged in ancient alchemical fires to be drawn from their hiding places in the darkness of the forest. She expected a victor waving a flag triumphantly. Yet even still, in these final moments before the impending fray, she could not decide for whom to cheer. She wanted both to win: her allegiances remained divided to the end.

But the men did not move. The battle she expected did not occur. Instead, Jaden suddenly faced what she should have anticipated but had not dared to fathom. The chanting was barely audible at first. She thought the break in the silence came from the wind, from the rustling and whispering trees of the surrounding forest. Not until the clouds parted and the moon illuminated the scene fully did Jaden understand. She rose to her knees, clasping her pendant as if in prayer to an unknown god, pleading for the ritual to stop. But her words came too late. The chanting heightened, and the rebels filled the space between the water and the trees. Jaden closed her eyes, refusing to witness the manifestation of the very thing she had secretly fantasized: to have both Dracaen and Arjan.

Several minutes later when the ritual ended, when she opened her eyes, when she stood and faced the person in front of her, Jaden shuddered.

"Long live the Quintessence," cried a few Council members who had gathered alongside the rebels.

"Long live the Alchemists' Council," responded the one conjoined — a man with the face of Dracaen and the dark flowing hair of Arjan.

"Your eyes are green like the trunk of an arbutus tree," said Kalina.

Cedar arrived at the cliff face just as Dracaen cried "Victory!" His hands clenched into fists, he crossed his wrists in front of his chest, and the rebels responded in kind, imitating the traditional gesture of rebel alliance and cheering with pride.

Cedar did not share equally in their enthusiasm. She had wanted a permanent increase in the Flaw, not an outright takeover by the rebels. But as Dracaen and Kalina turned towards her, as the moonlight illumined their faces, Cedar stood awed and confused. In that instant, in that strange muted light caused by the brightness of the moon and the smoky mists now rising from the pool, Cedar no longer saw Dracaen and Kalina but, instead and inexplicably, Arjan and Sadira. She shook her head, questioning her vision, but the effect continued unabated — a continual fluctuation between Dracaen and Arjan, between Kalina and Sadira — an optical illusion, surely.

"Arjan!" cried Jaden.

She stood beside Cedar, clearly experiencing the same visual phenomenon. Cedar grabbed Jaden's arm, assuming Jaden was about to rush forward to embrace Arjan.

"He is gone," said a rebel with whom Cedar was unfamiliar. He then added condescendingly, "If Council dimension survives the elemental changes, you can mourn him in your precious Amber Garden."

"Arjan is not gone," said Jaden to the rebel. "You are blinded by your allegiance."

"And you by yours," he said, gesturing towards Cedar.

"Arjan!" Jaden called, ignoring the rebel and pulling against Cedar's grip.

Everyone around her assumed Jaden was calling Arjan's name in mourning, in the wake of her loss of a friend or lover.

"Sadira!" Jaden gasped.

Knowing then that Jaden could also see both Arjan and Sadira, Cedar understood an improbable truth.

In an attempt to communicate that truth to Jaden, Cedar held her pendant and thought, *They have conjoined. Somehow, beyond what I can fathom right now, they have managed to enact mutual conjunction. Presumably, they received guidance from Ilex and Melia. But unlike Arjan's grandparents, who were both Council members at the time of their conjunction, Dracaen and Kalina are rebels who have purposely conjoined with alchemists. In doing so, they have conjoined — in human form — the Dragonblood Stone with the Lapis.*

Jaden relaxed in her struggle to free herself from Cedar's grip.

*Why?* thought Jaden, holding her pendant. *What do they hope to accomplish?*

*They have already accomplished it. They have proven that the rules that have governed the Alchemists' Council for millennia can be changed.*

Cedar had no time to explore her hypothesis further. Just then, Dracaen stepped forward and addressed the rebels, looking directly at Jaden for the first few seconds. Perhaps he had overheard their conversation.

"Our mission is accomplished. We have conjoined — rebel and alchemist, Rebel Branch and Alchemists' Council. Though the Final Ascension of Azoth Magen Ailanthus has decreased the Flaw in the Stone within Council dimension, our conjunctions," he nodded to Kalina, "will ensure its continued prominence. I will return to the Flaw dimension victorious. Kalina will remain here. Thus a conduit between our dimensions will remain permanently accessible."

"The Council will never accept Kalina. She will be removed upon discovery. The conduit will be closed once again," argued one of the rebels.

"No one on the Alchemists' Council will know she is Kalina," responded Dracaen. "They will see only Sadira. Only a chosen few will recognize the one and the other."

The rebels laughed and applauded, seemingly understanding the illusion despite their inability to see the physical truth, to see Sadira for themselves.

Cedar looked towards Sadira, now prominent and seemingly permanent in her vision. She longed to move towards her, knowing that Sadira, in her collusion with Kalina, had done only what she thought best for the Council. She knew, in time, she would be able to forgive her, but Cedar likewise knew she would not be given the chance within Council dimension. Thus Cedar, eyes locked with Sadira's, realized she may not for much longer be able to keep the vow she had taken, so long ago, when she had first received Elixir, to maintain the balance of the earth.

"Come with me, Jaden," she said aloud, grabbing her arm once again.

And they ran.

As they made their way through the forest, as they hurried across the field, past the Amber Garden, through the main courtyard, and down the halls of the main Council building, Jaden kept looking back to see if they were being pursued. They were not. Perhaps the rebels were too focused on their victory to pay attention to a few wayward rebel sympathizers.

When they reached the portal chamber, breathless, Jaden assumed Cedar was going to transport them outside Council dimension, that Cedar would take her to the equivalent of a safe house — somewhere in the outside world beyond both rebel and Council influence.

"Why were we the only ones who could see the truth?" Jaden asked her.

"We were the only ones there to possess a pendant conjoining both Dragonblood and Lapis."

Cedar directed her into the chamber, held her hand, and recited the key. In the minute or so of the journey, as the familiar sensation of portal transport began to overwhelm her, Jaden found herself hoping that they would arrive back where they began — at the café in the Vancouver Art Gallery where they had met. To her dismay, they arrived at one of the only places Jaden had been to which she hoped never to return: the lavender field of the Lapidarian apiary.

"Many but not all have been erased," said Cedar, gesturing towards the bees buzzing about the lavender stalks. "We must release those that remain into the outside world."

"Yes," said Jaden, despite her earlier objections to both Cedar and Obeche. She walked with Cedar through the field towards a large tree in the distance.

Not wanting to broach more difficult topics — such as what would happen to them when the Council discovered they had released the bees without consensus in Elder Council or permission of the Azoths — Jaden asked something more immediately relevant. "Why do the bees not sting us?"

"They are Lapidarian bees, and we are wearing Lapidarian pendants. They will not harm us as long as we bear our pendants."

Jaden did not respond. Instead she clasped her pendant tightly, realizing that she would be relieved of her pendant by the Elders after they learned of her divided allegiances and questionable actions. She may never see Cedar again.

"You will see me again, Jaden. As I told you, you will be my saviour. If I did not know that for a fact, I would never have initiated you into the Rebel Branch."

"I don't understand, Cedar. What do I have to do? And when do I have to do it?"

"There is no point in me even attempting to answer those questions right now."

Jaden raised her hands in frustrated despair. But she could press Cedar no further now. They had reached the tree, and work took precedence. The tree's trunk was marred by a large fissure. *A flaw in the tree*, Jaden thought to herself.

"Place your pendant here," Cedar instructed, pointing to one side of the fissure.

Nodding at Jaden's placement, Cedar placed her own pendant on the other side of the fissure. Cedar then recited words that Jaden recognized, without understanding their meaning, as belonging to an alchemical dialect of the 12th Council. Shortly thereafter, the fissure in the tree emitted a soft white light, the effect of which was to draw the bees from the field into the tree's crevice. Jaden watched the bees, hundreds if not thousands, disappear into the light of the tree, presumably to re-emerge in the outside world.

She heard them before she saw them — footsteps approaching from the distance. She could not tell whether they were from the Rebel Branch or the Alchemists' Council. Either way, she understood that her time in Council dimension was drawing to its end.

"Thank you, Cedar. Thank you for giving me the opportunity to make an ethical choice."

"As you have taught me," Cedar replied.

"What do you mean?"

"Jaden, what I am about to do is for your own good."

Cedar ripped away Jaden's pendant.

"No!"

But that was the last word she was able to say to Cedar. Void of her connection to the Lapis, Jaden became vulnerable to the Lapidarian bees. She cried out in pain as her body, repeatedly stung, collapsed at the base of the tree.

# EPILOGUE
## several weeks later

"Good afternoon, Magistrate," said Jaden to Sadira as she crossed her path, walking through the main courtyard on her way to Council Chambers. Jaden had stopped to admire the beauty of the crystal-clear channel waters. All appeared well once again.

"Good afternoon, Jaden. The catacomb alembic has done its job, I see."

"Yes. The swelling and wounds have vanished. I still feel quite weak though — *bone-weary*, as Rowan Kai called it when she helped me out of the alembic."

"To be expected, under the circumstances," Sadira said with an intonation that implied more than her words revealed.

"*The circumstances*? Just what are the current

circumstances, Sadira? How many were lost in the battle?"

"None of the Council died, Jaden. Yet many were hurt. And much has changed. Later I will explain the details; for now you need only understand that, as a combined result of Ailanthus's Final Ascension, my conjunction, Arjan's conjunction, and an unanticipated, complicated erasure of an Elder, a significant shift in Order has occurred while you were in the catacombs. You will be pleased to know that you have ascended to the Senior Initiate and I have ascended to Reader. You must now address me as such."

Though the news of her own ascension was a pleasant surprise and though she was not completely sure who had conjoined with either Sadira or Arjan, only one aspect of Sadira's revelation concerned her in that moment. "An erasure?"

"Did you not hear my last sentence?"

"An erasure, Reader Sadira?"

"Yes, an erasure — one that will not be without complex repercussions. Do not be concerned if your memories seem slightly askew for the next several weeks, perhaps months."

"What do you mean?"

"I cannot say for certain what you will remember and what you will not. Current circumstances are unprecedented. For the first time since the dawn of time in the dimensions, conjunction between the Alchemists' Council and the Rebel Branch has occurred. You must wait along with the rest of us to observe the outcome."

"I do not have the patience to wait, Reader Sadira. I want to understand everything now."

"To be a proficient alchemist, Jaden, you must learn to appreciate *unknowing*. You must strive to live with paradox, with flaws amidst perfection, with the Flaw in the Stone — simultaneously to know and to not know; to be both yourself and your other; to make choices and to be denied choice; to seek that which you may never find; to do that which you never thought you would do. Without such paradox, you would be nothing beyond yourself."

Jaden nodded in silent response, appreciating but not fully understanding Sadira's impromptu lesson. They walked slowly together down the main aisle of Council Chambers until they stood beside the Senior Initiate section, where Jaden would momentarily take a seat beside Cercis and Laurel.

"Your time as a Junior Initiate was unusually brief yet extraordinarily illuminating," said Sadira. "As a Senior, you must impart the lessons you have learned to the new Junior Initiates when they arrive."

"Have they been located?" Jaden asked.

"The Readers have located several potential Initiates. One looks particularly promising: a young woman studying alchemical manuscripts at the University of Edinburgh. But, in our new world — in the conjunctive aftermath of the Fourth

Rebellion — the Initiate must make the choice to search for us before we can make direct contact. The Scribes have left the requisite signs to be found, points along a path that will lead the Initiate to us if one chooses to follow, if one learns to recognize the alchemical secrets hidden between the lines of the forbidden text."

"Forbidden text?"

"We have sent a book to the outside world — a book inscribed with both Lapidarian ink and Dragonsblood, a book whose pages are imbued with the wax of ancient honeycomb, thus inoculating its readers against the debilitating frequency of the vibration of the wings of Lapidarian bees. And we have forbidden the world to read it."

"So we'll be waiting for years," responded Jaden cynically.

"Or mere days from now, having read between the lines of text on the page, having deciphered both letters and icons, having located the imperfections within its intricate designs, having recognized that one must first interpret and then abandon all interpretation, a potential Initiate will know without knowing, read without reading the Flaw in the Text. Such a potential Initiate will then intuit precisely where to find honey infused with Lapidarian essence. Having ingested several teaspoons of this liquid gold over the requisite eighteen days, donning a turquoise and silver pendant transmuted in the smoke of a Lapidarian beeswax candle, standing in the mist at sunset under the right tree at the right time, such a person could choose to call to us. The Elders will be listening for the knock upon our gate — or portal, as the case may be."

"Lapidarian honey and wax? In the outside world?"

"Ilex and Melia were not merely erasing the bees, Jaden. They were alchemically transforming those that remained. You must learn not to trust initial appearances."

"Where are they now? Where are these insect alchemists transmuting their liquid gold?"

"Dispersed in colonies throughout the world — though the most potent are housed in a small apiary established by a literature professor in Vermont."

"What do you hope to accomplish by telling me this?"

"You are not the only one I am telling."

She turned away and walked towards her seat among the Readers. Jaden, too tired to ponder the implications of the bees and the honey and the outside world, watched the Novillian Scribes take their seats among the Elders. How long would it take before Jaden herself became an Elder? Hundreds of years, she supposed. She longed, in particular, to be a Scribe like — she searched her mind, inexplicably but fleetingly forgetting her name — Tera. She watched the Scribes talking among themselves. Then, resigned to the fact that she would remain a

Senior Initiate for at least a decade, she made her way to her seat beside Cercis and Laurel.

Jaden thought fondly of Arjan and wished he were still here, that the Junior Initiate quarto was still intact. She could not quite remember the circumstances of his conjunction. Perhaps such fuzzy-mindedness was what Sadira had meant by "slightly askew."

"I wonder who they will be," said Laurel, gesturing towards the four empty seats of the Junior Initiate section.

"And how long it will take before contact," added Cercis.

"I doubt I would *ever* have found my way here without Obeche making initial contact with me. Do you remember the day I arrived — how nervous I was?"

Laurel and Cercis began to quietly reminisce, leaving Jaden to her own thoughts about Initiate contact. She was certainly thankful Obeche had not been the one to bring her to Council. If the choice had been hers, she would have chosen Sadira. Indeed, if Sadira had been the one to make initial contact with her at the café in Vancouver, Jaden knew she would have accompanied her back to Council dimension without a single question. She smiled, imagining the scenario. But then she paused in her reverie, suddenly frightened. Jaden could remember the day and the table and the latte; she could remember the scar on her hand and the healing offered her by the first touch of a Lapidarian pendant to her skin; she could picture the long silver cord and the layers of fabric from which the pendant and its cord had been pulled. But she could not — she simply *could not* — remember *who* had been wearing the layers and the cord and the pendant. She clenched her hands together under her robes. Recognizing the implications of this imposed absence, she shuddered.

"Long live the Quintessence!" called Azoth Magen Ravenea.

"Long live the Alchemists' Council!" replied all but one.

## Acknowledgements

Thank you to Marni Stanley and Kathryn Barnwell for your insights, friendship, and the pen I used to inscribe the first words of this book. Thank you to my friends and colleagues at Vancouver Island University, who have supported both my academic and creative work for over fifteen years. In particular, thank you to colleagues Susan Juby and Joy Gugeler for graciously sharing publishing wisdom with me; and to VIU support staff Sheila Davidson, Ros Davies, Faye Landels, and Annette Woolf for patiently responding to my coffee-break queries on everything from bee images to alchemical hand gestures. Thank you to my students, especially those in the alchemical literature classes of ENGL 340, for reacting enthusiastically when I asked, "Would you read a novel based on medieval alchemy?"; and thanks, specifically, to former VIU students Jessica

Legacy, Jayde Bazinet, and Sarah Corsie for your manuscript work. Thank you to my friends from the Whedon Studies Association, especially those who were with me in the Albuquerque parking lot on the day I first mentioned the book (and who have cheered me on ever since). Thank you to my friends at Cedar Grove for years of dog-park talks, many of which included discussions of my ongoing book project. Thank you to Ann Saddlemyer and Joan Coldwell for various inspirational retreats on Saltspring and, in particular, for the Veuve Clicquot celebration. Thank you to Tami Joseph for providing feedback on design elements during one of our chats at Tim Hortons. Thank you to Jacqueline Jenkins, Melanie Williams, Sandra Hagan, and Anita Young for decades of friendship and support. Thank you to my family for ongoing encouragement no matter the circumstance. Thank you to everyone at ECW Press for providing the best editing and publication experiences I have ever had, especially to Crissy Calhoun, Erin Creasey, and David Caron. And, most of all, thank you to Jennifer Hale, not only for the brilliant editing and brainstorming sessions but also for the laughter we repeatedly shared during the edits of Book One.

CYNTHEA MASSON is a professor in the English department at Vancouver Island University. After completing a Ph.D. in English with a focus on medieval mysticism, she undertook a postdoctoral fellowship involving work with medieval alchemical manuscripts at the British Library. In addition to articles on mysticism and alchemy, many of her publications over the past decade have been in the area of television studies. She is the co-editor of the academic book *Reading Joss Whedon* (Syracuse University Press, 2014); her fiction includes *The Elijah Tree* (Rebel Satori, 2009). She lives in British Columbia.